A *USA TODAY* a
Robin Covington h
around and falling
American author of
romance where eve
She is an unapologetic comic book geek and hoards
red nail polish and stalks Chris Evans. She is thoroughly
obsessed with her Corgi, Dixie Joan Wilder (yes—the
Joan Wilder).

Drop her a line at robin@robincovingtonromance.com—
she always writes back.

Find out everything about Robin at her website
(robincovingtonromance.com), follow her on Instagram
(robincovington), Twitter (@robincovington) and like
(really, it's love) her Facebook page.

Silver James likes walks on the wild side and coffee.
Okay. She loves coffee. Warning: her muse, Iffy, runs
with scissors. A cowgirl at heart, she's also been an army
officer's wife, a mum and a grandmother, and has worked
in the legal field, fire service and law enforcement. Now
retired from the real world, she lives in Oklahoma and
spends her days writing with the assistance of her two
Newfoundland rescue dogs, the cat who rules them all
and the myriad characters living in her imagination. She
loves interacting with readers on her blog and Facebook.
Find her at silverjames.com

Discover more at millsandboon.co.uk

SEDUCING HIS SECRET WIFE

ROBIN COVINGTON

TWICE THE TEMPTATION

SILVER JAMES

MILLS & BOON

First Published in Great Britain 2021
by Mills & Boon, an imprint of HarperCollinsPublishers,
1 London Bridge Street, London, SE1 9GF

Seducing His Secret Wife © 2021 Robin Ray Coli
Twice the Temptation © 2021 Silver James

ISBN: 978-0-263-28282-5

0121

MIX
Paper from
responsible sources
FSC™ C007454

This book is produced from independently certified FSC™
paper to ensure responsible forest management.

For more information visit: www.harpercollins.co.uk/green

Printed and bound in Spain
by CPI, Barcelona

SEDUCING HIS SECRET WIFE

ROBIN COVINGTON

To Melissa Dark.
You were there at the beginning.
Ten years ago we started this dream together
and I know that I wouldn't be here without you.
Thank you so much. Xoxo

One

Las Vegas, Nevada

There wasn't much in the world that could lure Justin Ling away from a poker table.

He loved the game. The strategy and the psychology and the emotion evoked with every hand that was dealt. It didn't hurt that he'd won far more than he'd ever lost. But he didn't need the money; he was a billionaire from the success of his company, Redhawk/Ling, so winning was a lucrative but empty victory. The upside was that he'd won enough to score invites to some of the largest private games and several of the popular public tournaments. Justin loved the game and when he earmarked weekends to devote to it there was almost nothing that was going to distract him from the cards in his hand.

That's why he couldn't explain why he was sitting down next to the sexy raven-haired beauty at the bar.

She was tall, slim and the kind of sexy that came from a confidence that ran deeper than the superficial trappings of a pair of high heels and makeup. This woman was the kind who made you work for it.

On a break from his current game, he'd seen her walk past the private rooms and head toward the lobby of the casino. And she'd seen him, too. It was a lightning strike of a moment when their eyes locked for several seconds, and the recognition of a reciprocal spark of sexual hunger was enough to find him cashing out and following her into this sad little bar.

"Can I buy you a drink?" He wasted no time getting to the point. Justin always went for what he wanted and this woman had captivated him.

She glanced over at him, giving him a thorough perusal from his toes to his four-hundred-dollar haircut. Her gaze lingered on his face and he thought he saw another flicker of interest in her espresso-colored eyes, but her expression gave nothing away before she turned to watch the football game on the TV at the back of the bar.

"I can buy my own drink." She picked up one of the three shots in front of her and downed it in one quick swallow.

"I'm sure you can," he answered, mirroring her position on his bar stool with his eyes mostly on the game. He eyed her in his peripheral vision, noting the way she tensed but also noting that she didn't make a move to leave or to tell him to get lost. It gave him encouragement. "In fact, I think *you* should buy *me* a drink."

A few beats of time passed, ratcheting his heart rate up a notch or two when the silence stretched out a little longer than comfortable. He wondered if he'd miscalculated the edge of challenge he'd glimpsed in the way she walked, the strength he'd seen flash in her eyes. If he'd been a betting man, and he was, he'd have all his money on her taking the bait.

And then she laughed.

It wasn't a giggle or a belly laugh. Her lips curved in a sexy twist and the low, husky rumble in her chest made him immediately think of Kathleen Turner, the finest aged whiskey, and secrets whispered in the dark and lost in the folds of tumbled sheets. He turned to face her, unable to resist the need to see her, to witness how the light played across her features and the glossy strands of her hair.

"Are you laughing at me?" he asked, feigning offense as he joined her in chuckling. "I could be offering to use my last twenty to buy you a beverage."

She snorted then and threw in an eye roll for good measure before reaching out and tapping his watch. "This is a Rolex Cosmograph Daytona 40mm. You can afford to buy this bar, so I'm not worried about cleaning out your bank account with an on-tap special."

Damn. His mystery lady had taken the bait, but the only one on the hook was him.

"How do you know so much about watches? Are you a jeweler?" Justin leaned on the bar to move in a little close and didn't even try to keep the impressed tone out of his voice.

She waved a hand in dismissal. "Paul Newman had one just like that and he wore it when he raced cars. I don't know jack about watches but I know cars."

Okay. This woman just got better and better and he had no choice but to keep wading into the deep end even though it looked like she wasn't going to throw him a life raft.

"I'm Justin—"

She shook her head. "I don't do last names."

Fine. If that was how she wanted it. It was how he usually liked it, too. He stuck his hand out.

"Okay, then. I'm just Justin."

She eyed his hand for a minute, an eyebrow raised with a mocking skepticism that took him back to high school and his ill-fated attempts to get the attention of Brandilynn Post, the head cheerleader. Obviously a crash and burn he'd not forgotten, but there'd been a million head cheerleaders in his bed since then and he wasn't scared off by a woman making him earn her attention. With all the women who normally threw themselves at him, this was an exciting change and one that had him hot and intrigued. He knew that if this night ended with her under him, she'd be magnificent.

"I'm Harley." She grasped his hand but instead of lingering on the handshake her long fingers traced along his palm to blatantly examine his ring finger. Now it was his turn to raise his eyebrow in question. She released his hand and shrugged. "Just checking. I'm not into married guys."

"You're assuming that I'm *into* you."

"We both know you are…" she said, taking a sip from her beer before giving him a lingering, hot look that had him shifting even closer. Close enough to feel the silk of her ink-black hair as it brushed against his face. Close enough to see a tiny scar that cut through the outer part of her perfectly arched left eyebrow. He took it as a good sign when she didn't move away and knew it for a fact when she continued, "…and for the moment, *you interest me*."

Bingo. Justin barely repressed the grin that plucked

at the corners of his mouth. He shifted on his bar stool with a pool of fire settling in his groin and making him hard. But while she was currently into him, everything about Harley screamed that she was an untamed filly, ready to bolt at the whisper of anything she didn't like. He wanted to lean over and kiss her but he glanced down at the bar in between them to resist the urge, deciding to circle back to the beginning of this adventure.

"Okay then, can I buy you a drink *now*?"

She picked up the second shot and drank it down. "I'll buy. You need to catch up."

She signaled to the bartender for three shots and motioned for them to be placed in front of him.

Justin picked up the first one, pausing before he put it to his lips. "Are we celebrating something?"

Harley cocked her head to the side, considering the question for a long moment before picking up her remaining shot and tapping it lightly against his own. "Freedom. New beginnings."

"Whoever he is, he's an idiot." Because the man who'd let this woman slip through his fingers had to be the dumbest man on the planet. Well, the second dumbest... Justin wasn't going to keep her, either. He wasn't deluding himself that what was happening here was a love match or anything.

The vodka burned as it went down; it wasn't as smooth as the brand he normally bought but any criticism disappeared with the chaser of the second shot. He shook his head a little, eyes watering as the alcohol took the first hit at his system and created a slow burn under his skin.

When his vision cleared, Harley was staring at him, her own gaze filled with a different kind of heat, a spark of something. She licked her lips, the universal symbol that she liked what she saw. He found himself back on familiar ground but he braced himself for the moment when she'd knock him off his feet. It wasn't a position he was used to being in with women, but he enjoyed the push and pull with Harley. It was different…more alive and more real than the usual games he played before taking a woman to bed.

"So, who's the guy?" Justin surprised himself with the question. What did he care about the dumb guy who'd let her go? He wasn't interested in the past or the future, just the right now. And unless the loser who'd lost Harley was walking into the bar at this minute to get her back, he didn't care.

But he didn't take back the question, either. Justin wanted to know everything.

Harley cut him a sly look, clearly amused by his curiosity. "His name was Sam. He wanted a commitment that I wasn't ready to make."

Well, that sounded familiar.

"Not ready to commit to him? Or anyone?"

"I think that settling down with someone for the long term is extremely overrated." Justin didn't hide his surprise at her words and so she continued with a tease and tug at the lapel of his jacket. "Whoa. Did I just morph into your dream girl?" She slid her fingertips over his jacket, tugging him closer as she ticked off her list. "No commitments. Can hold her liquor. Likes cars."

Justin grasped her hand and got even closer, murmuring against her ear. She shivered a little and he smiled at the reaction. "If you tell me that sex is your favorite indoor activity, I might just have to marry you."

Harley froze for a moment and he felt the jump and

stutter of her pulse under his lips. But in a flash she pushed him away and picked up her beer, taking a drink before leveling him with a glare that had more sizzle in it than censure.

"And you had to go and ruin it with the *M* word." She gestured toward his last glass. "Take your penalty shot."

He did as he was told, hooking his foot under the rung of her bar stool and easing her closer as he swallowed the liquid fire. "Is Harley your real name?"

She rested her right elbow on the bar, angling her body into the curve of his own. It was intimate, a mirror of his own posture, and he wondered if she knew she was doing it.

"It's a nickname. I like to restore old cars and bikes. I ride a 1975 Harley."

That was an answer he wasn't expecting. "You're a mechanic?"

"I'm between jobs right now. Taking some time to see this part of the world before I make any plans." Her vague nonanswer was delivered with enough finality that he knew it was nonstarter. But she intrigued him and he wanted to know more about her, so he decided to change tack.

"What's the last song you listened to on your phone?"

The change in topic threw her for a minute but she recovered quickly. "'Jolene' by Ray LaMontagne."

"Nice. Moody and soulful but also very sexy. It suits you," he commented, signaling for another round from the bartender after Harley gave a nod of agreement.

"Okay, now you. Last song," she prompted, as they both tipped back a shot.

Justin hesitated, remembering what he'd been listening to when he'd pulled into valet parking. Oh hell. This is what he got for letting his nephew program playlists into his account. "'Cool' by the Jonas Brothers."

"I don't even want to know what that song says about you." She grimaced and eased a shot glass closer to him. "I think you need to drink to make up for that terrible musical choice."

He paid his penalty, wiping his mouth with comic exaggeration that made her laugh. Damn, but he loved that sound and it made him wonder how her husky tone would wrap around a moan of pleasure. Justin reached down and tangled his fingers with hers, giving them a squeeze of encouragement. "Your turn."

Harley pondered a moment and then said, "Okay, beach or the mountains?"

"That's easy. I'm a California boy. Beaches." He held up his hand to stop her from answering and then reached out to skim the hair off her face and let the silky strands cool his skin, savoring the slow burn this woman stoked in him. "Let me guess for you."

"Take your best shot."

Justin's fingertips lightly stroked the smooth golden line of her cheekbone and down along her jawline until his hand curled behind her neck and pulled her closer. Harley eased into him, one leg sliding in between his own and her hand resting on his thigh. She was close enough for him to count her long lashes and to feel the fluttering beat of her pulse point. To hear the catch of her breath and the stifled moan of her desire.

Or was that his own?

He leaned in close, his lips brushing against her ear and body pressed against the length of her. Somehow they had ended up in alignment, mirrors of each other except for the brushes of knees, hands and feet. He was hard, every part of him yearning, aching to strip her down and discover all of her secrets. Not just the curve of her body, not just the places that made her want and need—he wanted to know it all.

But he'd start with her in his bed. Under him. Around him.

"Mountains."

"Lucky guess."

Harley shifted, moving just enough to look him in the eye, her mouth only a moment of bravery away from his own. Her eyes were dark, pupils blown with her desire and burning into his with focus flecked with flickers of doubt. Justin wondered what side would win, knowing with every fiber of his being that this had to be her choice. It was her move to make and he was helpless to do anything but wait and see if she would fold or bet it all on one night.

"Ask me what you really want to know," she whispered, biting her lower lip and then running her tongue over the plumpness left behind.

"Will you let me kiss you?"

Her answer was unexpected and exactly what he wanted. Her mouth on his own, soft but not tentative. It told him what he needed to know—that she wanted this, too. That she wanted him. Justin wove his fingers into her hair, anchoring her in place when he increased the pressure, his tongue against the seam of her lips, begging permission to enter and taste her secrets.

Harley's fingers curled around his lapel as she took over the kiss, slanting her mouth over his and opening to entice him inside. They both groaned and he took what he wanted, took what he needed, but it wasn't enough to quench the craving she'd ignited in him.

He pulled her into his lap, balancing both their weights as she straddled him on the stool. Justin's hands shifted, lifting her under her ass cheeks and pressing her against his achingly hard shaft through his pants. She wrapped her arms around his neck, her own desperate need to be closer evidenced by the scrape of her nails against his skin. The pain was good, just enough to ignite his lust to where it was flash point along his veins.

Harley broke away for air and he took the moment to get the answer he needed before they went any further.

Justin couldn't bear to break the connection, so he murmured his question against her mouth, their eyes locked and focused on each other. "Tell me what you want."

"I want you."

It wasn't the first time Justin had woken up in a strange hotel room.

He loved to travel, for business or pleasure, so it wasn't uncommon for him to awaken in a room and have to take a moment to recall the facts, the details of what VIP suite he was in in what VIP city. It also wasn't uncommon for him to wake up with a woman in his bed whom he desperately wanted to leave as soon as possible. But he couldn't remember a time when he'd woken up alone and regretted that a woman left in the middle of night.

Well, there was a first time for everything.

Harley was gone. Like a figment of his imagination or the silky remnant of a dream that he desperately tried to hold on to but couldn't solidify into a memory. Justin knew she had been real. The ache of his body and the scent of her, of them, of sex, lingered on his skin and on the tangle of sheets bunched around his waist.

He eased out of bed, grabbing his discarded pants and slipping them on as he navigated the detritus of their amazing night together flung all over the space of the penthouse suite: empty glasses and bottles on the floor alongside the remnants of an early-morning room service order of celebratory steak and lobster.

And…her wedding veil.

Justin leaned over, his throbbing head immediately signaling to him that it was the worst idea he'd ever had, and his stomach rumbled in ominous, queasy agreement. The veil was one of those cheap ones sold by every wedding chapel on the Strip. Harley had taken her time choosing it, laughing as she attempted to find one that matched her black leather pants and gray T-shirt. When she'd slipped it on, the combination of sex-on-wheels and virginal sacrifice had decimated what had been left of his very iffy mind and he'd marched down the aisle and said two words he'd never planned on saying in his life: "I do."

What had he been thinking? Nothing. That much was clear. He wasn't reckless but he was a risk-taker, never one to shy away from something just because the payoff wasn't guaranteed. It had served him well in business; he could run numbers better than anyone and he'd made himself and a lot of other people a metric ton of money. But nothing was a sure thing and he made people nervous, people who only liked to play it safe, people who hesitated to work with Redhawk/Ling because they couldn't pin him down.

People like the investor group currently considering

partnering with the company and giving them the ability to branch out even bigger than they thought possible.

The people who would have a coronary if they heard what he'd done here last night.

He'd gone to Vegas for a poker game and married a complete stranger.

A stranger who had left in the middle of the night.

Justin knew what he had to do. He needed to find this woman and get this marriage dissolved before the press found out and filled every news outlet with another story about his wild and reckless ways. Adam, his best friend and partner in Redhawk/Ling, was going to be pissed. Just last week he'd pleaded with Justin to lie low, to keep his profile more on the respectable side until they'd secured this investment deal and solidified their financial status in the eyes of potential partners. Justin had agreed and he'd kept his end of the bargain.

Until Harley.

And now he had to do damage control, find his wife and keep it out of the press.

He was a gambling man, and he didn't like his odds.

Two

One week later

This had been a mistake.

Sarina Redhawk stood on the deck of her older brother's house counting down the seconds until she could leave and head back to her hotel. In front of her, a crowd of people she didn't know ate barbecue and kept the bartenders occupied pouring fruity drinks while the guests placed their vote in either the blue box with a big bow on top or the pink box with a big bow on top. She'd dropped her ticket in the blue box under the incredibly insistent watch and instruction of someone called Nana Orla.

Adam's house was nice, not Kardashian massive but large enough to ensure that everyone knew that he was one of the top tech billionaires in Silicon Valley.

It had been professionally decorated, that was obvious, in bachelor-chic style but personal photographs, quirky artwork and splashes of color against the neutral sofas and such testified to the entrance of the fiery redhead into her brother's life. Tess wasn't timid, she stood tall next to her brother, and Sarina liked her for it. Adam had chosen well, that much was clear.

Just behind her the canyon spread out beneath the deck and dipped into deep purple shadows that reminded her of faraway places she'd served in the army, places that gave her memories that would always follow her no matter how many oceans and miles she put between them. But those memories had taken a back seat lately to the ones she'd been too young to remember, the ones re-created for her and contained in the package her brother Adam had given her and her twin, Roan, when he'd found them again.

Twenty-five years, seven crappy foster homes, one shitty adoptive home, one GED, one enlistment and two tours in the Middle East later and she was here: at the gender reveal party for her older brother Adam and his fiancée, Tess.

And completely out of her comfort zone.

She'd agreed to come to the party tonight because she felt bad about storming out of here the last time, repaying Adam and Tess's hospitality with hostility and painful words. She hadn't meant to hurt him but playing "happy family" with two brothers who were essentially strangers had been beyond her ability at the time.

She'd left that night, hopped on her Harley-Davidson and headed straight out of California, needing to put as much distance as she could between her guilty conscience and Adam and Roan's pleas for her to give them all a chance. She'd ignored Adam's voice mails and dodged Roan's FaceTime requests for a couple of months, taking her bike to every small-town, forgotten, one-stoplight spot on the map, enjoying the freedom of choosing her own path for the first time in her life.

She'd been a military policeman in the army and had liked her job but she'd hit the time when she'd had to get out or stay in until retirement. And she'd opted to get out, explore and figure out who the hell Sarina Redhawk was supposed to be when she grew up. She'd thought it would be scary but it had been amazing. Freedom. Time to think. Space to figure some crap out.

Sarina had camped in Tonopah, hung out with Area 51 enthusiasts in Rachel and explored caves in the Great Basin National Park. In the pretty town of Austin, Nevada, she'd found a stray dog outside her hotel and adopted the little Chihuahua, naming her Wilma, and then headed for Las Vegas. She wasn't much of a gambler but she'd picked up some work from an old army buddy for some extra cash while she figured out if she was ever going to answer her brother's phone calls and what she was going to do with the rest of her life.

Las. Fucking. Vegas.

Bright lights. The Blue Man Group. Five ninety-nine steak buffets. The scene of the best night and worst morning after in her life. Sarina had met a man so sexy in the casino bar that she'd violated her newly established rules to not hook up with guys she met in bars. But his smile had been intriguing, his focus unrelenting and their chemistry so explosive that she'd woken up the next morning naked, hungover and very much married. She'd taken one look at the sleeping man in the bed and the simple gold band on her finger and thrown on her clothes faster than tourists snapped up tickets to see the Britney Spears show.

Then she'd done what she did best: she ran. Right back to California to figure how to track down her husband and fix that colossal mistake. And to make amends with Adam and Roan.

And that was why she was at this party. Saying she was sorry for walking out on them before. Trying. It wasn't easy for her to open up to new people, and despite their shared DNA, they were strangers to each other.

Sarina watched Adam and Roan from across the room as they laughed together with Tess. Both men were slender and tall, but Adam was broader in the shoulders and Roan wore his hair long and halfway down his back. If you watched them closely, they had some of the same mannerisms and expressions, the proof that DNA did not lie.

Roan was a successful artist, his star on the rise. He was often in the tabloids, either due to his breakout talent or his revolving bedroom door that admitted both women and men. He was charismatic and outgoing, and drew everyone to him like he invented gravity. Adam was as successful but leaned into the strong, broody and silent vibe to command a room. It didn't surprise anyone that he'd been on the most eligible billionaire tech wiz list for the last decade.

And here Sarina was. Strong and capable—give her a firearm or a mountain to climb and she was the girl. But she was always an outsider; her superpower was knowing when to leave. The hard part was figuring out how to stay.

And figuring out how to ask for help.

Now that the panic had worn off, she had no idea how to find the husband she'd left behind in Vegas. So, she was going to toast her brother's new family tonight and tomorrow she was going to take him up on his offer to help her get her new life started. How surprised was he going to be to find that the first thing she needed was to locate a husband she had no intention on keeping?

Fun times.

"Everybody make sure to cast your vote for the gender of the baby," Nana Orla admonished the crowd in her delightful Irish accent. She was small and smiling but clearly a force of nature because nobody ignored her. Sarina smiled in spite of herself; the army had master sergeants who wished they had the command that she had. "Come in closer, everyone! Move in closer for the big moment!"

Sarina moved with the swell of the crowd, keeping to the outer edge of the mass of bodies but close enough to see the secret smiles and laughter Adam and Tess shared as they moved into place. Always touching in some way, there was no doubt about how much they loved each other. Sarina had been excited to hear about their engagement. She'd liked Tess from the first time they'd met when her future sister-in-law had tracked her down for Adam. She was a straight shooter, strong and smart. The perfect partner for Adam.

And now they were going to be parents and she was going to be an aunt.

Things were changing, and she had no idea where she belonged.

But it was time to figure it out.

Nana Orla summoned everyone closer for the long-awaited moment. People jostled against one another to get in closer to the happy couple and Sarina was suddenly thrust forward into the middle of the group, mumbling her apologies for the elbows jabbed into people's sides and drinks sloshed to the point of spilling. No one seemed to mind—it was a party and they were ready to forgive. She tried to squeeze in between a laughing couple and had to sidestep into a hard, tall body to avoid an elbow to the face. Another shuffle to keep her balance and she stepped onto the foot that belonged to the hard, tall body as did the hands that grasped her hips to keep her upright.

"I'm sorry."

"I've got you," the man said, his voice deep and smooth and interwoven with a thread of humor that had her lips curving into an involuntary smile.

She chuckled, memories of a night full of laughter and passion coming back with the impact of muscle memory. Her reaction was visceral, immediately sending warmth and heat along her skin. How many times had she shivered from the sizzle of just the memory of that night, craved the touch of the stranger she'd left in that bed?

It wasn't new.

Wait.

The voice wasn't new.

The man wasn't a stranger.

Sarina twisted away from the man, braced herself for what she knew was coming and looked up into the face of her husband.

The ground beneath her feet shifted, the room suddenly becoming too hot and the crowd unbearably close. She braced herself for impact, her body knowing full well what was coming even if her brain wasn't there yet.

"What the hell are you doing here?" she demanded, noticing the curious looks of the people immediately around them.

"Me? What about you?" the man replied in a hushed tone, his eyes scouring her face with eager curiosity and hunger that she knew all too well. It had been like this from the first, some unexplainable heat that sparked between them like electricity trying to complete the arc.

Justin. He'd said his name was Justin.

"Justin, right? What the hell? This doesn't make sense," she sputtered, chasing her erratic thoughts around like a dropped bag of marbles. "What are you doing in my brother's house?"

"Your what…brother?" Justin said, shaking his head as if to dislodge whatever was stuck in there. "The name on the marriage license is Sarah Moore…"

"It's my adopted name," she answered, holding her hand up to stop him from asking new questions before she got answers to her own. "Are you going to tell me why you're in Adam's house?"

"He's my best friend, my business partner. I'm Justin Ling." He gestured with his hands between himself and Adam standing a few feet away. "I'm the Ling part of Redhawk/Ling." He scrubbed a hand over his face, gazing up at the ceiling in disbelief with what looked a lot like disgust. "Not only did I marry a stranger, she turns out to be my best friend's little sister."

Sarina opened her mouth to tell him to keep his voice down but she was interrupted by a loud countdown from the crowd, and both she and Justin turned to watch as Adam and Tess pulled the string on the box in front of them. A huge bouquet of blue balloons sprang out of the box and shot to the ceiling.

"It's a boy!"

"Congrats!"

Applause rang out around them, loud and disorienting, as everyone around her toasted the new parents, completely oblivious to the shitstorm she had created with the man standing by her side. Life had a way of messing with you and right now she knew she was solidly in its crosshairs.

"It's a boy!" rose up again from somewhere behind her as she raised her eyes to the handsome face of the stranger she'd married.

She almost laughed at the ridiculousness of this moment, but it wasn't that funny. While Adam and Tess were celebrating the imminent arrival of their bouncing baby boy, she'd just been handed a sexy-as-hell, six-foot-something bundle of holy-shit-I-married-a-stranger-in-Vegas.

It was a boy all right.

What was she going to do with him?

Three

Adam was going to kill him.

Justin glanced over to where his best friend and business partner was kissing his fiancée and accepting the congratulations from the crowd assembled here to celebrate the biggest event of his life.

Well, the biggest event if you didn't count the recent discovery of Adam's long-lost siblings.

So, the fact that Justin had gone to Vegas, gotten ridiculously drunk with an incredibly captivating stranger and married her was bad enough. But the fact that the mesmerizing, mind-blowing, amazing woman turned out to be Adam's baby sister?

Justin. Was. A. Dead. Man.

He raked his eyes around the space for somewhere he could grab a minute of privacy with his newly surfaced wife. They had a lot to talk about.

Like why the hell she'd left that morning and where the hell she'd been.

"Come with me." Justin took Sarina's hand and guided her through the crowd, headed straight for Adam's office. He knew this house as well as he knew his own, and that room would be safe from curious partygoers.

"Where are we going?" Sarina asked behind him, her voice steely with warning that she was going to give him a little bit of rope and then she'd string him up with it if he didn't get to the point.

In spite of the absolute insanity of this moment, he caught himself smiling. It was her backbone, her direct promise to call him on his bullshit that had intrigued Justin back in that Vegas bar. People didn't call him on much—either because of his money or his family's position in society—and he liked that she didn't care.

The Lings were big money, and had even bigger social prominence in this part of California, his father a self-made man in real estate and his mother the queen of the fundraising committees. Justin, even with a billion-dollar company with his name on the door, was the runt of the over-achieving Ling litter. His siblings were upstanding members of the community while Justin gambled and had a revolving bedroom door and refused to even play Putt-Putt at the country club.

He bet that Sarina played a mean game of miniature golf.

"Hello? Where are we going?" she insisted, balking at being dragged across the room with no explanation.

"To Adam's office. We can get some privacy in there," he answered, feeling the acquiescence in her grip on his hand as they navigated the bodies in the crowd.

Once he reached the large double doors, he opened them and drew her inside. The immediate impact of blocking out the swell of voices was enough to disorient him for a few seconds.

Or maybe it was the woman standing before him.

She was tall, only a few inches shorter than his six feet two inches, muscular, slim, with straight hair the color of black licorice down to her shoulders. Her eyes were the deepest brown with flecks of bronze and her face was cut glass, angles etched in amber.

Sarina was stunning.

And he was staring and holding her hand like a kid who'd just figured out that girls were hot.

The only consolation was that she was staring right back at him, heat answering heat. The pull from that night was back, leaving no question about how they'd ended up in this mess.

Hormones. Chemistry. It was as simple and hard and confusing and amazing as that.

Justin let go of her hand, his body singing in protest at the break in the connection. He stalked around the room, needing the activity to think this through. There were so many moving parts to this catastrophe but he could figure it out. He'd bashed through other barriers, done stuff that nobody thought he could accomplish. He was the kid that nobody thought would make it and he'd figured out how to fight to make sense of stuff that came so easy to other people. He'd become an expert at solving problems. This was just another puzzle to solve, right?

"So, you're Adam's business partner?" Sarina asked, her expression dark with a healthy dose of confused thrown into the mix. She wasn't any happier about this than he was. "Does he know about…"

"About our getting hitched? Nope. I just got back to town a couple of days ago and I was trying to figure out how to deal with it without getting him involved." Justin paused, recollecting one pertinent fact that might be the solution to their problem. "Wait. You married me under a fake name. That must mean that our marriage is invalid."

She shook her head, her hand slashing across the air between them. "Not fake. *Adopted.* I'm in the middle of getting my name officially changed back to Sarina Redhawk but Sarah Moore is my name…for now."

"They didn't let you keep any part of your given name? Adam's adoptive parents let him keep his name," he said, realizing too late that he was probably not telling her anything she didn't know.

"Well, that was mighty nice of them, wasn't it? I guess it made them feel better about taking a kid from a perfectly happy family and erasing every piece of his heritage from his life. I'll make sure they get a prize."

Sarina did nothing to cloak the bitterness in her words and it was so potent that even he tasted the acrid taste of the betrayal. Justin had sat through many long talks with Adam over the years, wishing he could do something to help him, and this moment with Sarina was no different. He didn't know the details of her life—they weren't Adam's to tell—but Justin knew that Adam's younger siblings hadn't had easy lives.

Unfairly taken from their family by the state when Adam was six years old and the twins, Sarina and Roan, were three, they'd been shipped off to families in separate parts of the country. Adam had hired Tess to find them as soon as he had the means, a search that had resulted in their reunion several months earlier. It wasn't the happy event that Adam had envisioned, and Justin had ached for his friend. A quintessential first-born, Adam wanted to take care of everyone and it killed him that the pain of his siblings' lives wasn't something he could just fix with a wave of his hand.

Adam and Roan were making progress in their relationship but Adam had relayed that his sister had been angry, unwilling to even give it a try. She'd been through too much… They'd all been through too much.

"Yeah, Adam's family isn't great," Justin said, knowing that it was the worst of understatements but it also wasn't the point right this minute. Any minute now they could be interrupted, and they needed to figure some stuff out first. "But right now we have more pressing matters to worry about. No matter what your name is legally, we've got to figure out a way to end this marriage as quickly and as quietly as possible."

"Agreed. How do we do that?" Sarina asked, one hand on her hip, the other making the speed-it-up motion in the air.

Justin bit back a laugh. She was snarky and prickly but he thought it was sexy as hell. He was pretty sure that telling her that right now would end in his death, so he kept his mouth shut.

"What the hell is going on? What marriage?"

Justin and Sarina both jumped at the sound of Adam's voice, pivoting to take in the figures of Adam and Tess standing in the open office doorway. Sounds from the party drifted into the space, disguising Justin's muttered "oh, shit" as he motioned them inside the room.

So much for breaking it to Adam at the right time and place, and forget not telling him at all.

He looked at Sarina, knowing her irritated but resigned expression was echoed by his own. Finally, she lifted a shoulder in a shrug that said it all: it was what it was. It wasn't going to get any better. They needed to just get it over with.

Justin took a deep breath and faced his best friend, unconsciously moving closer to his wife as he broke the news. Maybe they weren't destined for a ruby wedding, but they were in this together for now.

"This isn't how we wanted to tell you…"

"I didn't want to tell you at all," murmured Sarina.

"That, too." Justin's lips twitched in a smile in spite of the seriousness of the situation. Sarina was a badass with a really twisted, dark sense of humor. He liked her. A lot. "When I went to Vegas last week I met Sarina at the casino…"

"You were at that high-roller poker game last week," Adam interrupted, his brow creased in confusion. "How…?"

"They don't tie us to the tables, man," Justin said, rushing into the next part. "I met Sarina and we hung out and got married."

It was overly simplistic and left out a shit ton of details, but did it really matter?

Apparently it did.

"How the hell do you go to Vegas and end up married to my sister?" Adam asked, not quite yelling but pretty damn close.

Justin really didn't want to go into the how and why of the entire night. Not when he couldn't remember all of it. But Sarina had no qualms about it. The brutal honesty he'd admired a few moments earlier was less appealing at the moment.

"Adam, it's not that hard to figure out," she said, her expression daring him to call her on any of this. "We met in a bar, got drunk, and woke up the next morning covered in glitter and in possession of a marriage license. I had no idea who he was."

"I've only ever seen pictures of her as a child, Adam. I had no idea she had a different name." Justin filled in his part of the story, hurrying to explain the insanity.

Adam's mouth fell open and Tess grabbed on to his arm in an attempt to calm him down. Justin wasn't worried—Adam wasn't the kind of guy who punched first and asked questions later. But Justin had never married his sister before, so there was always room for error.

"Justin, did you *sleep* with my sister?"

"Adam." Tess groaned at the question, flashing Sarina an apologetic look and Justin a lift of the eyebrows as if to say *really*.

Sarina wasn't having any part of it, either. "Nope. We're not going there. I wasn't some innocent virgin lured over to the dark side. I was a fully participating *adult* in all activities including the marriage part and the *sex* part…which was great, by the way."

"Agreed," Justin couldn't resist adding at the look of horror on Adam's face. It really wasn't funny but the alternative was facing up to the fact that he'd fucked up again and was living up to his reckless reputation. Adam was too shocked to be pissed right now but his anger when it came would be well deserved. Justin had one job and he'd messed up big time.

"No. No," Adam spat out, his hands shooting up in

a gesture meant to ward off all mention of his sister's sex life.

Tess jumped in, stifling a laugh as she steered the conversation back to the heart of the matter. "So what are you two going to do about the marriage? Are you going to stay together or what?"

"No," they both replied in unison, their gazes pulled together in a search for confirmation. The impact of the moment shook Justin again, as he felt the same connection, the same spark, the same flood of memories of smooth naked skin and hot, sweet kisses traded in the midst of tangled sheets.

His mind knew that he needed to end this marriage. His body said that he needed to get her back in his bed and indulge until he was ready to move on like he always did. His gut said that he'd be hard-pressed to find someone it was so easy to laugh with and talk to. Sarina had gotten him from the first moment.

Damn.

Sarina's cheeks pinkened and she blinked hard, breaking the connection with a sharp turn of her body away from him and several steps in the opposite direction. Justin fought the urge to go over to her but they didn't need to complicate this, especially since she'd still be in his life after this marriage was over because she was Adam's sister. Damn, this was tricky.

"Justin, I don't need to tell you how bad this would be if it got out in the press," Adam continued, oblivious to the undercurrent pulsing between the two of them. "We have the chance to partner with Aerospace Link. This is huge."

Sarina turned to face them with a confused expression, and Justin filled her in. "Aerospace Link is the largest satellite company in the world and it's still a family business. They are pretty old-school and have expressed hesitation at some of my lifestyle choices."

Sarina shook her head in confusion. "Your private life isn't part of the deal. One is business and one isn't."

"When you're asking people who've invested billions in a joint venture to trust a company that's a relative infant in the tech industry to deliver what we promise, the behavior of the guy who runs the financial end of the business is part of the deal," Justin explained. "If they can't trust me, they can't trust Redhawk/Ling."

"They act like he's the poster child for *Billionaires Gone Wild* and aren't thrilled that the CFO of our company spends a lot of time on the front page of tabloids," Adam added, his tone protective of Justin. It was a familiar theme of their friendship; Justin had been the black sheep of his family and Adam was his biggest cheerleader.

Justin appreciated it but he couldn't let Adam downplay the truth of the headlines. "I like women and parties and high-stakes poker games," he explained with unapologetic honesty. "But I don't gamble with company money and I'm a damn good CFO. Numbers are the easiest thing in the world to me and I can sniff out a turn in the market faster than anyone else. I'm not interested in letting them dictate my personal life, but I have to agree that getting married while drunk in Vegas isn't a great thing to put on my résumé and is a legitimate reason for them to question the stability of Redhawk/Ling."

"So dissolving this marriage needs to stay off the front page," Sarina stated, her expression reading more exasperated than confused.

"It needs to stay off *any* page, or Aerospace Link will back out and other partners and investors will wonder why. Big business leaders talk to each other and we'll be loath to find anyone who'll want to do business with Redhawk/Ling. This could be a long-term disaster for us," Justin said, flashing a look of regret at Adam. Once again he was a disappointment to the people in his life. "I'm sorry, Adam."

His best friend waved off his apology, his expression kind as usual. They'd been through a lot together, supported each other through the worst and celebrated each other through the best. It would take more than this to make Adam Redhawk turn his back on him, but sometimes Justin wondered where the line was and when he would cross it.

"Justin, you didn't do this by yourself." Sarina's voice was firm and clear across the room. She walked over, stopping to stand shoulder to shoulder with him to face her brother. "And I don't want to be part of the reason Redhawk/Ling suffers."

She didn't reach out to touch him but there was no doubt that she was in this with him, that she was here for the long haul. Justin recalled that she had been in the army and her body language was the definition of loyalty born from a shared experience in the trenches. This situation wasn't ideal but it would be easier if they weren't at each other's throats.

Justin smiled at her, hoping she read the high level of thanks in the expression before turning back to Adam and Tess. "I'll contact our attorneys to get this wrapped up as quickly and quietly as we can."

Sarina nodded at each of them as she backed away and headed for the door. "So let's recap—we get divorced but keep it off TMZ. Adam and Tess, congratulations on the baby boy. I'm tapped out on family time for now, so I'm going to go."

And just like that morning in Vegas, she was gone.

Justin watched the door shut behind her, admiring her style. It was why they hooked up in the first place and why he couldn't take his eyes off her. Sarina was direct, no-holds-barred and a challenge. Hell, he never could resist a challenge. And Sarina Redhawk was a walking, talking invitation for him to keep making bad choices.

Adam stepped into his field of vision, arms crossed as he glared at him. "Don't think I forgot that you *slept* with my sister."

Justin grinned. What else could he do? "But I married her first. That should be a consolation."

Four

The Valley Hotel was a shithole.

Okay, maybe that was a little bit harsh, but Justin felt like it was one double murder in the parking lot away from being in the category of hotel that was featured prominently on cable television shows with titles that included "unsolved" and "most wanted" and played in constant cycles of syndication. The faux-Spanish, single-story hacienda-style building was old and decaying and had given up a long time ago.

A Silicon Valley landmark it wasn't. He wasn't even sure it passed the fire code. He shuddered when he thought about what a black light would reveal if it was aimed at any surface in this place.

Justin navigated a discarded bag of fast food on the asphalt, narrowly missing stepping in a puddle of spilled milkshake and half a joint. He pulled his phone out of his pocket and tapped the screen to call Adam.

"Adam, do you know where Sarina is staying?" he asked, disgust coating every one of his words. "Why isn't she staying with you?"

A big sigh wafted over the connection and he could picture Adam sitting at his desk, hands reaching for the ever-present drumsticks to tap out his frustration. His buddy was secretly in a band that played at a local dive bar once a month. The members were a group of engineers from Stanford so it wasn't going to hit MTV anytime soon but they were pretty decent and had a rabid following. "Yeah, I do. It's a shithole. She won't stay with me and insists on paying her own bill. I'm not arguing with her about it anymore. It's exhausting."

"You can't let her stay here, Adam. This place is disgusting and very likely dangerous," Justin said as he scanned the room numbers for the correct one. He spied it across the lot and headed over, determined to find Sarina and get her out of here.

"Well, she's *your* wife, Justin. So good luck with that." Adam drawled, his tone more you're-an-idiot and less I'm-going-to-kill-you than it had been since they'd revealed the Vegas wedding to him. It was an improvement. Justin expected him to hang up so the chuckle over the line surprised him. "She was in the military, Justin. Trained in firearms. Be careful that she doesn't shoot you."

The call ended and Justin jammed the phone into his pocket and cursed out his best friend/brother-in-law. Sarina's staying at this place wasn't funny at all. It wasn't safe and she *was* his wife. He wouldn't sleep at night knowing that she was here. He had enough money to buy this hotel about thirty times over and he could pay for her to stay anywhere else. This was unacceptable.

He headed across the lot, growing more determined with each step to get to Sarina's room and get her out of here. Justin stopped at the door to room 18 and knocked, listening for any sign that she was inside. He glanced around the lot, looking for her motorcycle, but it was no-where in sight. Sarina loved that bike—that was something she'd made clear that first night in Vegas—so its absence didn't bode well.

He heard someone approach the door and he knew that he was being observed through the peephole. He smiled and pointed at the doorknob.

"Let me in. I need to talk to you," he said, relieved when he heard the lock slide inside. The door opened enough for him to see Sarina scowling at him. Her hair was pulled back into a ponytail and she wore no makeup, but he'd never seen a more beautiful woman.

She didn't need any of that stuff his mom and sisters spent hours applying and hundreds of dollars stocking in their larger-than-life bathrooms. Her skin was flawless, a honey-caramel color, black lashes thick and heavy as they lined her deep, expressive brown eyes. Her lips were full even when they pulled tight in a frown, even when her smile only hinted at the plump, sexy pout.

Justin swallowed hard; his first instinct was to lean in, kiss her and claim that mouth just like he had that night in Vegas. He knew how to get that mouth to soften, knew how to coax her into opening to him and letting him take deep, drugging kisses that left them both shaking. Damn, he'd wanted her so much and they'd been combustible in bed. She'd been responsive and demanding and insatiable and completely into him. He'd had a lot of women under him over the years but none of them had left him aching and wanting more like her. It was the best time he'd ever had inside and out of the bedroom.

Sarina had been his match but he'd been too caught up in the maelstrom of passion that night and he'd had no time to overthink it. And the next morning when he'd woken up to her gone he'd experienced a level of disappointment he wasn't accustomed to. There wasn't much in life that Justin wanted that he didn't get. He'd grown up in a wealthy family and now he had his own money, a fortune that put his family's bank account to shame.

"Why are you here, Justin?" Sarina asked, noticeably not inviting him inside. He wasn't surprised; there was nothing easy about her.

"Can I come in? I need to talk to you about the divorce proceedings," he said as he cast a disgusted glance around the hotel. "And we need to talk about your current accommodations."

Her eyebrows shot up at the last part, and then her eyes narrowed into be-careful-what-you-say slits. "Did Adam send you?"

"Nope. In fact, he told me not to waste my time."

"So my brother is smarter than you are. Good to know who the brains and the beauty are in your relationship," she observed, stepping back to let him in the room.

It was as bad as he thought it would be. Shabby carpet and curtains in colors that were muted from sun exposure and many washings. The bed was unmade and there was an overwhelming smell of bleach wafting up from the linens, which made him feel better about the cleanliness of the place. None of it changed his mind about her staying here.

"At least you still think I'm pretty," he joked, scrambling for something to say now that they were alone and face-to-face in this odd place.

Sarina paused in her hurried effort to pick up a jacket thrown over the arm of the only chair in the room. She looked him over, nice and slow, not hiding the heated approval that slid across her expression. "Justin, my thinking you're pretty is how we got in this mess."

And there it was. He moved in closer, so they were standing chest-to-chest, close enough for him to see the flash of humor that battled with the attraction in her eyes.

Close enough to hear her growl.

"Did you just growl at me?" he asked, taking a step back just in case it really was her.

The bedcovers next to him moved and he jumped back, not sure what the hell was going on. The growling got louder as the thing under the covers crept closer and closer to the edge of the bedspread. Then, after much wiggling and growling, a small white fur-covered face appeared in the opening. With teeth bared and long pointy ears projected from each side of its head, it looked like something from a science fiction movie.

"Did you pick up Baby Yoda in Vegas?"

Sarina scoffed, lifting the creature in her arms and cradling it against her chest. It was a little white dog, a Chihuahua with big buggy eyes and wearing a tiny black T-shirt with Lady Gaga on it.

"This is Wilma Mankiller," she said, pressing a kiss to the little head and snuggling her closer. "I found her in a little town in Nevada. She bites."

Justin pulled back his hand, taking Sarina at her word. "That's quite a name. Has she actually killed a man?"

"Not yet," Sarina said, setting her down on the floor and watching as she headed over to a bowl of water. "But she's named after the first woman chief of the Cherokee nation. My Wilma is a badass. She was fighting off a really fat feral cat behind a dumpster at a diner. I had to take her."

"Does this place allow pets?" Justin asked, cringing at the worst segue in history. But he needed to get back to the subject of why she was staying in a dump like this.

Sarina plopped down in the chair. "It does and I can afford it. If you're here to tell me it's not the Ritz-Carlton, I know."

"Sarina, you can't stay here. I can afford to put you up in a much nicer place."

"I don't want your money, Justin. If I won't take Adam's money, why do you think I would take it from you?" Sarina crossed her arms across her chest, signaling that this was going to be a lot harder than he'd predicted. "This place is fine. I shouldn't be here that long. Once we put the marriage in the rearview mirror, I'll be back on the road."

"I heard back from the lawyers this morning and it's going to take six weeks for us to get the marriage dissolved. They think they can get it annulled."

"Six weeks?" Sarina scrunched up her nose in distaste. "I didn't think it took that long."

"Apparently, a quickie wedding doesn't equate to a quickie divorce." He sat down on the edge of the dresser, doling out the less-than-exciting news he'd received this morning. "The lawyers are drawing up the papers and they are contacting the Las Vegas officials to do what they can to keep it quiet. The six-week time frame should coincide perfectly with closing of the Aerospace Link deal so if we can keep it on the down low, it won't impact Redhawk/Ling."

"Well, damn." Sarina shook her head in frustration. "My money is going to run out before that happens." She glanced at Justin. "My bike needs work I can't do myself and I'm bleeding cash on that bill. I'm going to need to find a job to fund the repair and my next road trip. I still haven't made it to the Grand Canyon."

"I can give you the money," Justin said. "It's the least I can do." He knew the minute he said it and her arms crossed her chest that the answer to that offer had not changed. Time to try another option. "Okay, okay. I've got a job for you."

"Sure you do." Sarina scoffed, motioning toward him in a give-it-to-me waggle of her fingers. "Do I look like I was born yesterday?"

"It's a real job, Sarina. I swear." Justin lifted his hand in the Boy Scout pledge, chuckling when Sarina laughed and shook her head in disbelief. "Adam and I started a foundation called Rise Up to offer outreach to kids in the foster system. We provide sports, crafts, music, language lessons, all kinds of things for them. We're still looking for a new full-time director but we need someone to coordinate stuff in the meantime. I figure with your army background, you could do this in your sleep. I know you perfected organization and dealing with people in the service. All I need you to do is organize some activities for the older kids, be a presence at the center, show up for them. This will be a walk in the park."

"Foster kids? Still in the system?" Sarina was interested and he knew enough from her background that she had a lot in common with them. "Private home placement or group home?"

"Both. And these kids are getting ready to age out so we're helping them prepare for it. We offer them some support after they age out, but we can't do it forever."

"It's a hard thing for a kid to face." Sarina considered the offer, reaching down to pick up Wilma and put her on her lap. Her tone remained skeptical but he took it as a good sign that she was still asking questions. "It pays?"

"Enough to get your bike fixed and for you to put some money away for your road trip."

"And this is a real job? Not something made up to just give me a handout?" Sarina was suspicious and direct. "I don't take handouts, Justin. I'm not afraid of hard work but I want to earn what I have."

"Look, while I have enough money to fill your hands and about a million other people's, I respect your need to carry your own weight. *Believe me*, I get it. I wouldn't insult you by making up a job that didn't exist." And he really did get it. Being the black sheep in a family of overachievers wasn't the worst position in the world but it had made him determined to make it on his own. It also made him incredibly stubborn. Justin stood, not ready to take no for an answer. "But I have one condition on the job."

"And what is that?"

He looked around the room and shuddered. "You can't stay at the No-Tell Motel."

"It's fine."

"It's cheap," Justin countered, refusing to leave her here for one more minute. He cast another glance around the room and shuddered. "And terrifying."

Sarina rolled her eyes. "Well, I'm not staying with you."

Justin shook his head. He'd anticipated this. If she wouldn't stay with Adam, she wasn't going to shack up with him. "No. You're going to stay with Nana Orla."

Five

Sarina didn't like to owe anyone.

Justin had helped her pack her few belongings, then bundled her and Wilma into his Porsche 911 Turbo and peeled out of the parking lot so fast she expected to see a zombie horde chasing them in the rearview mirror. She'd debated fighting him on the move but the bottom line was that she couldn't afford to stay at that hotel for six weeks and pay for the repairs on her bike. She had some savings after leaving the army but she'd spent a lot of money on her road trip, and the truth of the matter was that it was flowing out faster than it was flowing in.

She'd spent the morning scouring the want ads for jobs she could walk to or get to by bus. It didn't matter what the job was; she'd done every kind of work there was to put money in her pocket and food on her table. Honest work was honest work. She wasn't too proud to clean a toilet but she was independent.

And while she was currently married to one billionaire and was the younger sister of another, she wasn't ready to lean on them for her livelihood. She'd spent most of her life trying not to owe people anything.

Owing people gave them power over you and while it was a given that everybody had to work for somebody, she wanted to choose who had any control over her life. But she also knew when she had to take what was on offer in order to get back to where she was in control of her life again.

So this job was a lucky break and she'd earn her keep and some cash. She didn't like the condition of accepting a free room but she really didn't have a choice. Justin had been 100 percent correct when he'd said that she'd never get her bike fixed if she had to pay for a room for that long.

This was practical and smart, but she didn't have to like it.

But there was something she needed to clear up first.

"Who is Nana Orla and why is she going to let me stay at her house?"

Justin chuckled, giving her a side-eye glance as he changed lanes. "She's my grandmother on my mother's side. She came over from Ireland when I was five or six years old to live with us. You couldn't have missed her at the party. She's loud and bossy and takes no shit from anyone." He winked at her. "Sound like anyone else I know?"

Sarina ignored him, refusing to be drawn in by his amusing sex appeal. "And why would she let me live with her?"

"Because I'm her favorite."

"Uh-huh."

"True story."

Sarina sneaked a peek at the man she'd married as they drove toward Nana Orla's house. He focused on the road, tapping the steering wheel to the beat of the Red Hot Chili Peppers song pouring out of the speakers, so she took the opportunity to take a longer look.

Justin was still ridiculously hot. Tall and slim, with dark hair and tanned skin, he moved like a man who was in complete control of his life. She'd known he was rich the first minute she'd laid eyes on him. He walked like someone who owned the world around him and could buy several others. Charming and charismatic, his sparkling eyes and contagious smile were the things that drew her to him from jump. Justin was like the pied piper—his sex appeal the only flute he'd needed to entice her to follow him into that wedding chapel.

Yeah, they'd been drunk but she'd married him because he'd made her feel like she was all he needed. And that was something she hadn't felt in her life. Ever.

And that night in the hotel room had been like nothing she'd ever experienced before. Sarina had never felt so wanted or needed or desired. Sex had always been good. She liked it a lot and never felt ashamed of taking what she wanted. But sex with Justin had been…earth-shattering. So gravity-shifting that she'd felt compelled to run as fast as she could the next morning. And now that she'd found him again it was terrifying that the last thing she wanted to do was run. She wanted to stay. To get to know him better. To satisfy her curiosity and figure out why this man intrigued her.

Which was why she was going to keep as much distance between them as she could until they were no longer bound for better or for worse…richer and poorer wasn't an issue. His bank account testified that money was never a problem for him.

Justin glanced over, catching her in mid-ogle. He lifted his lips in a smirk, his eyes dancing with mischief. "To be honest, I thought you'd fight me more on this."

She chuckled, turning to face the window and watching the scenery change from the Amanda Jones side of the tracks to the Cher Horowitz suburbs. "I'm self-sufficient, not stupid. I need to get my bike fixed."

"And that place was disgusting. Zero stars."

She rolled her eyes. "Justin, I was in the army. Two tours in Afghanistan. I can stay anywhere. I've stayed in places with no heat or running water. My biggest worry was wondering what would have crawled into my clothes during the night."

"Yeah, well," he said, shifting in his seat and clearing his throat. "You don't have to do that anymore."

"Why? Because my brother is rich?" She snorted out a laugh. "Because I married you?"

"Well...yeah." He sounded perplexed, like he didn't understand why she didn't just rush out and buy a Rolex or apply for an American Express Centurion card.

Not gonna happen.

She leaned back in the seat, turning to look at Justin as they navigated the road up into the hills. "Justin, that's not my money. Never has been and never will be. I'm not trying to be mean but that's just the only way this is ever going to be."

"I know you didn't have it easy growing up. I know Adam would like to help you," Justin said.

"What did he tell you about my life?" Sarina asked, her voice harsh with the anger that suddenly erupted in her gut. She sat up, the seat belt pressing against her chest with the sudden movement and slapping her back against the leather seats. "What do you *think* you know?"

Justin jumped in. "Whoa. Adam told me nothing, but I'm his best friend. It didn't take much for me to figure out that wherever you ended up after you guys were taken wasn't great. It upset him. In case you hadn't figured it out, your brother has a huge white knight complex going on. He takes that shit on like it's all his fault. I put two and two together." He cast a meaningful glance in her direction, a mix of confusion and disapproval. He didn't like her thinking poorly of her brother—and his best friend. That was clear. It made her feel good knowing that her brother had this guy in his corner. "Adam would *never* betray you like that. He's the best man I know."

Sarina let that sink in, recalling a similar observation from Adam. "That's funny. He said the same thing about you."

Justin huffed out a laugh. "Was that before or after he found out about Vegas?"

"Both." Sarina shifted the sleeping Wilma on her lap, smiling at the snuffling snores that racked her little body. "Back at the hotel you said you got that I needed to carry my own weight."

"Is there a question in there?" Justin asked, his voice guarded and his body shifting away from her. It was a subtle move but she was hyper-focused on him and didn't miss it. It was a touchy subject for him, so she'd tread carefully.

"Just the obvious one. You grew up rich—"

"And that means I've never had to work for anything? I was handed everything on a silver platter?"

She sighed, realizing that she'd stepped in it. "I'm sorry, that's not what I meant. I'm genuinely curious. I want to know what you meant."

A long silence stretched out between them. Anthony Kiedis sang about a bridge and she settled back in her seat, totally okay with passing the rest of the ride without talking. She'd learned to live in the quiet spaces and the army had exposed her to every kind of person. She didn't take everything personally; just because someone didn't want to share the intimate details of their life with her, it wasn't the end of the world. Justin didn't owe her anything. Especially not an explanation of his life.

If they kept this arm's length, that would be better anyway. Neither of them needed to form an attachment.

"Let's just say that my path to success wasn't the one my parents expected me to take. Compared to my brothers and sisters, I was the intellectual runt of the litter," Justin said, his voice flat with the effort to try not to sound like it mattered. But it was obvious that it mattered...a lot.

"You did okay, *more* than okay," Sarina said, stating the obvious when they were sitting in a car that cost over one hundred thousand dollars.

"I proved what I needed to prove," Justin answered, turning into a driveway framed by a pair of elaborate metal gates. He rolled down the window, keying in a code that opened the gates and let them onto the property. "I never had to prove anything to Nana Orla. She accepted me just the way I was." He flashed her a grin, but Sarina didn't miss the genuine affection in his eyes when he talked about his grandmother. "I *told* you I'm her favorite."

Sarina sat up straighter, the large estate spreading

out as far as she could see. Landscaped grounds spilled into water features and orchards that opened up to a majestic Spanish-style manor house that sat nestled into the shelter of the rising hills. She leaned forward, jaw dropping at the sheer mass of the mansion. It looked like something featured on one of the reality TV shows that had nothing to do with actual reality. Instead of pulling up into the circular driveway, Justin followed the road around the mansion, heading past an elaborate garden and pool area straight toward a smaller home set in the middle of a grove of orange trees.

The house was built in the same style of the mansion, but it was much smaller. Large enough to hold a few bedrooms, it was bigger than any house she'd ever lived in. With pots of flowers on each side of the front walk and a hand-painted welcome sign on the door, it was inviting. Staying here would be…nice.

A smaller pool and patio with a firepit and barbecue were nestled next to the house, just beyond the two-car garage. Justin pulled to a stop in front of it, turning off the car and waking up a grumbling Wilma, who growled at the disruption to her nineteen-hour-per-day nap routine. Sarina shushed her, stroking the silky soft fur between her ears and getting a doggy kiss reward.

The interior of the car was quiet but not uncomfortable as they both stared forward. For her part, Sarina was processing all that had happened in the last few days to get her in this spot with this man. She didn't know Justin well enough to know what he was thinking but she could probably guess.

He shifted in his seat to face her and she mirrored his movements. Sarina held her breath, trying to still the flutter of butterflies in her stomach and the race of heat-induced goose bumps on her skin. He smiled, the slow, I-know-how-to-flip-your-world-on-its-head grin that had kept her glued to that bar stool in Vegas and then following him down the path to the altar. It was hard to believe that this man ever had to prove anything to anyone and harder to believe that he might not have measured up.

She wasn't the only one feeling something. Justin swallowed hard, his gaze hot and heavy on her. His focus drifted from her mouth, down to where her breasts pushed against her tank top with the ridiculously fast beat of her heart, and then lifted again to her eyes. Everything from the taut lines of his muscles under his shirt, to the fierce grip of his fingers on his thighs, to his heavy breathing that mirrored her own proved he was right here in this craziness with her. And it scared her to death.

"Sarina…" Justin reached out, his hand sliding over her own, the rough brush of his fingers sparking all of her nerve endings. He leaned in closer, his breath drifting across her cheek, his gaze drifting down to her mouth and back up to her eyes. He wanted to kiss her. She *wanted* him to kiss her. It was a bad idea and she didn't care. "You are trouble."

"I think you *like* a little trouble."

His grin turned sultry and he nodded, leaning in even closer. All she had to do was move forward an inch and she'd be able to taste him again.

A knock on the passenger-side window made them both jump and Wilma barked in warning as she scrambled to lunge at the window. Justin peered over her shoulder, rolling his eyes as he recognized the woman gesturing at them through the glass.

Justin reached over to hit the button to lower the window. "Brace yourself. Nana Orla is one-of-a-kind and we are all thankful for that."

The older woman quickly assessed the situation, the eyebrows raised in disapproval and the hands on her hips testifying that she wasn't going to put up with any nonsense. She spoke in a flurry of words that left Sarina blinking in astonishment.

"Justin, what are you doing sitting in my driveway with a girl? Weren't you raised to bring her inside the house? Where are your manners? It's like that boy that used to pull up and honk for your sister on dates. Disgusting." Nana Orla turned her attention to Sarina, her grin a matching twin to Justin's. "I apologize, love. Raised by wolves, I swear."

Her accent was amazing, full Irish and the kind that made getting chewed out a pure pleasure.

"Here, give me the wee dog." Before Sarina could warn her, Nana Orla reached in and picked up Wilma, tucking the dog close to her chest as she opened the door to the car.

"Be careful, Nana. Wilma bites," Justin warned, alarm wiping the smile from his face.

"I doubt that," Nana Orla responded, waving off the warning and placing a kiss on Wilma's little head. "Get out of the car and explain why you're the one bringing Adam's baby sister over instead of him? He's not been here for weeks and we have baby plans to make. And wedding plans, too. I don't want him to think he's getting away with not having a wedding."

Sarina got out of the car, squinting against the sunlight as she watched Justin fold the tiny woman into a hug, cutting it short when Wilma growled from her place tucked against Nana Orla's generous chest. Justin's grandmother was miniature, no more than five feet tall, her silver hair cut in a short angular bob that framed her face. Her eyes were a gray-blue and she wore little makeup except for the bright pink lipstick that matched the linen tunic and flowy pants she wore.

There was only a little physical resemblance between Justin and his Nana, but they had the same energy and his grin was definitely due to her genetic contribution. In fact, the more Sarina observed them both together, the more she saw the similarity in their smiles and the mischievous gleam in their eyes.

There might be two of her but Justin was the heir apparent of her brand of trouble. Sarina smiled in spite of herself, their obvious love and happiness at seeing each other was infectious.

"Nana Orla, Adam asked me to bring Sarina over here. I'm just helping out my best friend," Justin explained, sticking to the joint decision to let as few people as possible know about the marriage.

Nana Orla's gaze ping-ponged between them like she was at Wimbledon, her expression skeptical. "Don't give me the shite, Justin Ling. I saw the two of you having some sort of altercation at the baby gender reveal party and then the two of you skittered off to Adam's office and you were in there an awfully long time with Tess and Adam for me to buy that crackpot explanation." She narrowed her gaze, her eyes lighting up as she looked Sarina up and down. "Are you pregnant, Sarina? Am I finally going to get a great-grandchild?"

Sarina scooted backward, putting as much distance between her body and that insane idea as she could. "Uh, no. I'm not pregnant."

"That's a shame," Nana Orla said.

"You already have five great-grandchildren, Nana Orla. You can drop the Princess Leia impression because I am not your only hope," Justin said, acting like there was nothing weird about this conversation. "I'm just helping out a friend. *We* are just helping out a friend."

Nana Orla considered him for a moment and then she swiveled, turning all of her intense focus on Sarina. "Are you going to live under my roof and tell me that pack of lies, too? Justin is used to sweet-talking everybody and getting away with it but I'm not so easily fooled. I watched him fine-tune those skills from the crib." She cocked her head to the side. "Spill it, Sarina. I know something's going on. What mess has my grandson dragged you into?"

Sarina glanced at Justin and he let out a long sigh. It was more resigned than frustrated so she took that as permission to come clean with Nana Orla…her new roomie.

"I'm his wife." Sarina rushed in to cut off the woman when she looked far too happy at this news. She didn't want to see the fallout of raising her hopes and then being the one to let her down but it couldn't be avoided. "Only temporarily. We're getting it annulled."

Nana Orla eyeballed Justin, her expression disapproving. "I'm guessing one of your trips to Vegas was involved." She shifted over and poked him in the chest. Her voice was chastising but her words were coated in the love and affection they clearly had flowing between them. Sarina looked away, pushing down the pang of longing that threatened to rise up in her chest. She turned back just in time to see Nana Orla flick him upside the head and then pat him on the cheek. "I've got you, Justin. I want to throttle you but I've got you."

"Geez. Warn a guy next time," Justin grumbled, rubbing the spot on the back of his head with exaggerated care.

The older lady shifted to include Sarina in her appraisal. Nana Orla scanned her up and down, her gaze assessing and thoroughly unnerving. It was like she could see right through her. "You look like a smart girl. How did you end up in this mess?"

Sarina ran through the events of that night, discarding all the things she was never going to tell someone's grandmother. She settled for the truth, minus a few details. "Justin is charming."

"He is," she said, nodding. "I just can't believe it worked on you."

"Hey!" Justin protested. "I'm right here."

Nana Orla waved him off. "I still love you anyway."

"Thank you, Nana Orla. One more thing. Don't tell my folks about the marriage."

She rolled her eyes, poking him one last time and wagging a finger of warning in his face. "Now you need me to lie for you, too? Jesus, Mary and Joseph. I'm not doing this in the driveway, let's go inside and get Sarina settled."

Justin leaned in to kiss Nana Orla's cheek and Wilma bared her teeth, growls rumbling up from the little body cradled in his grandmother's arms.

"Well, at least Wilma's got sense to stay away from you and your 'charm.'"

Six

"How was the pajama party?" Justin asked.

He grinned over at Sarina in the passenger seat of his car, trying to gauge how she'd fared her first night with Nana Orla. His wife was a blank slate, her expression neutral as she gazed out the window as they cruised down the highway toward the Rise Up Center. She looked over at him, one eyebrow raised and a smirk tugging at her lips.

"Nana Orla stole my dog," she said, her tone telling him that she wasn't upset about this theft. "She bribed Wilma with lunch meat and tummy rubs so I slept alone."

Justin bit back the first thing that came to his lips: the offer to personally make sure she wasn't alone in the king-size bed in the guest suite of his nana's house. He had his own place, a sterile professionally decorated penthouse in the nicest retail/living town center in Silicon Valley. It was a place to sleep and grab a shower but he didn't consider it a home. He'd taken women there and ushered them out the next morning with a cup of coffee and an apology that he didn't have any food in the fridge. No, it wasn't a home and he didn't want to take Sarina there.

If he had a home, it was at Nana Orla's house. He'd crashed there before, usually when he just couldn't stomach so much family time with his parents in the main house. It was why he'd immediately thought of moving Sarina there; that house was a safe place, a place where a person could weather storms with support and love. Tough love—Nana Orla was always going to call you on your crap—but you never doubted you were loved.

"Don't worry, I'll make sure you get her back before you leave," he said, turning off the scenic highway, navigating busy streets and the typical glut of morning traffic. He glanced over at Sarina, surprised to find her still examining him. He maintained eye contact as long as he safely could, regretting that he hadn't ordered a driver today. Sarina intrigued him and he couldn't take his eyes off of her. "Although I'm not surprised Wilma gets along with Nana Orla."

"Me either," Sarina mused, her voice resigned but amused. "It kept her from asking too many questions so I'm not complaining." She laughed. "But I'm pretty sure that it was a reprieve, not a cease-fire, from the interrogation that is coming."

"You're probably right," he said, pausing before he asked a question he knew Sarina wasn't going to answer. "So, what don't you want to tell her?"

Sarina turned, her gaze locked on his face, and he

could just feel the mind-your-own-business death ray aimed at him.

He shrugged. "What? I want to know more about my wife."

"You know what you need to know."

Justin knew he shouldn't poke at her but he couldn't stop himself. He wanted to know more about Sarina. If he was honest, he wanted to know everything. She fascinated him, and his desire for her had been immediate and visceral. He was a risk-taker, but that didn't include making foolish, drunken mistakes. His risks were calculated and thoughtful and while they looked reckless, they weren't stupid. Sarina had been…undeniable.

He pushed. Because he was Justin Ling. "Why'd you leave the army?"

She pushed back. Because she was Sarina Redhawk. "Why are you avoiding your parents?"

Okay, score a point for Team Redhawk. He hadn't said he was avoiding his parents but he'd shared the fact that he didn't fit into his family and he hadn't taken her to the mansion, he'd hidden her away at Nana Orla's with strict instructions not to tell his folks.

She was right. But that didn't mean he was talking.

"You first," he said, winking at her.

The pause was longer than usual, no doubt giving him time to retract the question. She had read him wrong. He was fine with awkward silences. He could do this all day long.

"I had been in the army almost ten years and it was time for me to either sign up for the long haul toward retirement or to get out. The people I served with were all making the same decision, moving on with their families…it was time for me figure out my own path."

"And have you? Figured out your own path?"

She shook her head. "I answered. Your turn."

That was the deal. "My parents don't approve of my life choices. They think I could be better, could have done better. They think I don't act like a Ling."

Sarina turned fully in her seat, the expression on her face incredulous. "Wait. A billion-dollar company isn't good enough?"

Justin turned into the entrance to the center, pulling his car into one of the reserved spots at the front. He unfastened his seat belt and turned to face Sarina. "Look, I don't want to sound like a poor little rich kid, so don't take it that way." He paused, waiting until she nodded before he continued. Sarina's expression was placid, no indication of where she was falling on this. "I wasn't the high achiever like my brothers and sisters in the things that counted—school, grades, tests, appropriate behavior. I dropped out of Stanford after squeaking in because of my math ability, the one thing that made sense to me. I was dyslexic and a smart-ass and not the obedient son. They think my success is a fluke and that it will be gone in a minute." He mimicked his father's severe tone. *"It's not a stable undertaking."*

Sarina scoffed at that. "That's nuts. You're a mega success. Most parents would kill to have a son who's done as well as you have."

Justin shrugged it off. It wasn't what he hadn't thought a million times before. "My dad grew up in mainland China and broke all ties with his family, refusing an arranged marriage to be with my mom. They met when he was studying in England and she was there working at the university. They fell in love but his very traditional Chinese family disowned him when he ran off to the United States with her and got married. The marriage they were pushing on him had been a business arrangement and his refusal embarrassed them in the eyes of their friends and colleagues. Luckily my father had other family, also exiled, living here in California, and they took them in, helped him to build his business."

"So your parents were badass rebels who chose love. Sounds like they would totally embrace your way of life." She patted the dashboard of the expensive car they were sitting in. "And it looks like it worked out okay, at least from the monetary point of view."

"Yeah, yeah. But my parents went old-school when it came to raising their kids. They went super-traditional and conservative, in a way, to make up for their rebellion. They loved us, I never doubted that, but their expectations didn't leave room for a kid with a learning disability who had a gift for numbers and finance but who also likes to gamble and have no-string affairs with women." He shook his head, still stumped by his folks. "We were expected to do the private school to college to good job in a respected field of work that pays well and marriage with a suitable woman. My parents are the poster children for social status. If it involves doing the 'right' thing and supporting the 'right' charities and all that rot, they are on it. It would be funny if it wasn't so exhausting. It has put a strain on our relationship, to put it mildly."

Sarina considered this, nodding her head in understanding. "And your brothers and sisters went along with it?"

"Two doctors, a lawyer, and one taking over my dad's real estate business. I'm the black sheep."

Silence settled between them. Sarina looked at him, shrugging in answer. "I don't know what to say about that. Family is weird."

"It is." Justin didn't know what else to say about that, either. He'd just shared more with Sarina than he did with anyone and he needed to let it sit for a while. He needed to think about why it had been so easy to tell Sarina, why he'd *wanted* to tell Sarina. Time to change the subject. "This is the Rise Up Center."

He gestured at the building in front of them, opening his car door and motioning for Sarina to get out. He squinted against the bright sun. The sky was clear and the rising heat promised that today was going to be a scorcher. He clicked the lock on his key fob, joining his wife on the sidewalk. She was soaking it all in and he would be a liar to say that he wasn't a little bit proud of the admiration on her face.

"So, Nana Orla picked the name for the center. She's a *Hamilton* fan, so…we went with it."

"Like you were going to tell Nana Orla no."

"Yeah, that's never going to happen," he agreed with a grin. "This center is something that Adam and I thought up on one of our many all-nighters in college. We made a pledge that when we made a shit ton of money, we'd create a center for kids who were in the foster system, specifically targeting the older kids who have a smaller chance for adoption or who are close to aging out. This place is for those kids."

Sarina smiled, her face lit up with approval and interest. "This is amazing. You have *got* to show me around."

Justin grinned, opening the door and waving her inside. "That is exactly what I was hoping you'd say."

* * *

The center was incredible.

Sarina was completely blown away with what her brother and her husband had created. Taking over a large, abandoned community center and athletic facility in a poorer neighborhood, they'd gutted the building and created an indoor gymnasium, studios for dance and yoga classes, tutoring and group therapy rooms, and space for arts, crafts and music lessons. Outside they'd added all-new soccer fields, baseball diamond, tracks and a swimming pool. Kids from all over the Valley came here, using transportation provided by the center, and when they aged out, Rise Up provided a year of post-support and classes geared toward helping them start their new life.

It was ridiculously amazing.

"Justin, this is incredible," Sarina said, grabbing his arm in her excitement. "I cannot believe what you're doing here. This is life-changing."

"That means a lot, coming from you." Justin shifted their bodies, grabbing her hand and weaving their fingers together. She wanted to touch him, needed to feel that connection, and she just went with it. It didn't make sense but nothing with Justin did. "We knew we wanted to do something good with the millions we'd make." He waggled his eyebrows, completely owning his cockiness. Considering that they'd made billions, it was well-deserved. She'd give him a pass. "We knew that we wanted to give back to the community. Adam always wondered about where you and Roan had ended up. He didn't know if it was in care or with a family. He worked with kids when we were in college, foster kids…this was his idea, really."

"And you just went along for the ride?" She knew that Justin's role was bigger than he let on. Everyone in the center, staff and kids alike, knew him by name and he knew personal details about them. It was clear that he spent a lot of time here. Not just writing checks or giving tours to big donors; nope, he was here all the time.

"Something like that," he said with a wink, leading her by the hand to the gymnasium where a dozen or so kids were playing basketball. She should have dropped his hand, broken the connection, but it felt good. It felt kind of right.

The group stopped the game and all turned when the doors clanged shut behind them. Within seconds their skeptical expressions morphed into wide grins and excited chatter erupted and bounced off the high ceilings.

"Justin!"

"Hey, man!"

The kids were ecstatic to see him, most of them swooping in to give him a hug or a back slap. He had a connection with these kids. He loved them and they loved him right back. She was starting to think that resisting the charisma of Justin Ling was easier said than done.

Justin turned and led her over, still holding her hand as he introduced his fan club. "That's Mike, Sarah, Ruben, Marcus, Big Pete, Little Pete, Katie, Teresa and Jose."

Each kid saluted her in turn, their smiles genuine even if a little shy. All of their gazes drifted down to where her hand joined with Justin's. She didn't miss the looks they gave each other. Sarina let go of Justin before anyone got the wrong idea, extending it to shake each of their hands.

"I'm Sarina Redhawk. Nice to meet you."

The impact of her name was immediate. Their grins got even wider, their excitement almost palpable.

"What? You're Adam's sister?"

"That is so cool."

"Does Adam know you're hitting on his sister, man?" The last question came from Little Pete, a tall kid who reached to at least six and half feet. Big Pete was closer to seven feet, so the name was appropriate. "He's gonna kill you."

"Adam knows, you goofball." Justin lightly punched the boy in the arm. "And he doesn't scare me."

"Uh-huh," Little Pete mused, his expression saying that he didn't believe any of it. He tossed the basketball at Justin, who caught it easily. "You got time for a game?"

Justin tossed the ball back, shaking his head. "No man, I've got to get back to the office. We're working a big deal but I'll come back in a couple of days, I promise."

"I can stay." Sarina didn't realize she'd said it until everyone turned to face her. She twisted to look at Justin. "I've got nowhere to be and this is where I'm going to be working for the next few weeks. Why not start now?" She reached over and popped the ball out of Little Pete's hand, dribbling past him to make the shot. The ball swooshed through the net and all the kids whooped and hollered. "I'm a little rusty but I think I can remember how to play."

"All right," Katie said, throwing an exaggerated wave at Justin, motioning for him to exit the gym. "You can go. We've got Sarina."

Justin grabbed his chest in mock dismay, stumbling back from the group. "Whoa, you guys suck."

The kids erupted in laughter, piling on Justin to offer him hugs of apology.

"Okay, okay." Justin held his hands up in surrender. "I'd love to leave Sarina here but I'm her ride, guys. She's got to go."

"I can get a ride back to the house," Sarina said. It couldn't be that hard to order an Uber or to get Adam to come get her. "I'm a grown person. If I could figure out how to get around Afghanistan, I can get home."

"You were over there?" Katie asked, her voice a little awestruck.

Sarina grinned at her. "Yeah. Two tours." She looked around at the group of kids. They would be spending a lot of time together the next few weeks. If they were going to trust her, she needed to let them know she trusted them. "I joined the army when I aged out of care."

"So, you weren't adopted like Adam?" This time the question came from Marcus. He was shy, speaking out from behind Mike's back, but his smile was genuine if tentative.

"I was…" She faltered at this part. Her past was complicated and hadn't been pleasant to live through, and talking about it wasn't easy, either. Justin was watching her, his eyes inquisitive but his expression kind. He inclined his head, letting her know that it was up to her. She took a breath and dived in. "I was adopted but it didn't work out."

"They gave you back?" Teresa was disgusted, her hand on her hip in indication.

"No. CPS came in, took me out and put me back in the system." She debated about how to tell the next part, going for a middle-of-the-road answer. "My adoptive parents weren't great people and they didn't treat me so well. Care wasn't great but was better than what I had."

Silence fell on the group and she watched as each of the kids processed her story.

"That really sucks, Sarina," Marcus said, nodding along with the other kids. "It's a good thing that you're here. You've been in the system so that makes you a center kid. You belong here with us."

And just like that, she was one of them. It felt good. Right. As easy as it was with Justin.

Sarina nodded at each of them in thanks, letting a grin take over her face. It was time to lift the mood in this joint. "Well, then it won't hurt so much when I kick all of your butts."

Catcalls and trash talk filled the room as the kids moved into their positions on the court. Justin came up beside her, one arm looping around her waist as he drew her in closer. He was warm, body as firm and taut as she remembered, and he still smelled so damn good. Sarina leaned into him involuntarily, giving in to the pull of attraction that always pulsed between them.

"You're pretty amazing, Sarina Redhawk Ling," he murmured low so that only she could hear. She ignored the little flip her heart did when she heard her name joined with his. "It took me months to get these kids to accept me like that."

"Well, I'm a center kid. You heard Marcus." Sarina was more pleased with the approval in Justin's eyes and voice than she wanted to admit. Knowing that he didn't pity her or pepper her with a million questions meant a lot. He was giving her the time and space she needed to share, or not. It was seductive.

And she didn't mind the use of her married name. Not at all.

That was...interesting.

Justin gauged her mood accurately and let it drop. Instead he pulled out his key fob and dangled it in front of her. "I'll call a car to come get me and take me to the office. I'll leave the Porsche for you."

"What? You're going to leave me your one-hundred-thousand-dollar sports car? Are you high?"

"California is a community property state so techni-cally, the car is half yours," Justin answered, jangling the key fob so that it made a metallic clinking sound. His grin slid into seductive, a little dirty. "Come on, you know you want to drive it. If I recall, you prefer a wild ride."

Sarina flushed, her skin hot and goose bumps racing down her arms. She remembered this Justin.

This Justin had kept her up all night.

She let her gaze drift down to his mouth, her heart racing when his lips curved into a smile that told her he knew exactly where her thoughts had gone. He leaned in, so close she almost tasted his kiss.

"Are we going to play ball or are you two going to kiss it out?"

Sarina had no idea which kid said it but it broke the tension immediately. Justin's grin got wider and he rolled his eyes, releasing her from his hold.

Sarina snatched the key fob out of Justin's hand, her grin wide and her heart light for the first time in a long time. "Get out of here. I'm going to play some ball."

Seven

"Your car handles like a dream, Justin."

Sarina stretched out her hand, dangling the key fob over the open palm of the car's owner. Justin was kicked back on a lounge chair by the pool at Nana Orla's house, his grin as warm as the lingering sunshine. The beer in his other hand looked as cool as the water spilling out of the fountain water feature. At the last minute she yanked back her hand.

"Nope." She smiled at his shocked expression. "No beer, no expensive car keys."

"Are you holding my car hostage until I get you a beer?"

Sarina glanced over at Nana Orla, winking at the older woman. "He's cute *and* smart. If *only* he was rich."

Nana Orla cracked up, a belly laugh that had her doubled over on her lounger. "Justin, if you let this girl go I will disown you."

"*Really*, Nana? I thought I was your favorite!" Justin said, fishing an ice-cold bottle out of the outdoor fridge, popping it open and heading back over to Sarina.

"I don't have any favorites, Justin. I love all of my grandkids equally," Nana Orla assured him. "But if you don't keep this girl, you won't be my favorite anymore."

"You wound me, Nana. I'm gutted." Justin handed the beer to Sarina.

She took it and slid into his vacant lounger with a grin on her face, effectively stealing his seat. "Sorry. You're too slow."

Justin paused, his head cocked at her, his smile big but confused. "What's gotten into you?" He held his hands up in the universal gesture for surrender. "Don't get me wrong. This is the Sarina I met in Vegas and I like her a lot. I'm just wondering where the grumpy, prickly one went and is she coming back?"

Nana Orla snorted. "If that's your best pickup line it's no wonder you're single."

"Ignore him." Sarina waved him off. She was riding high and nothing was going to knock her off this mountain. "I had a great day with the kids at the center. They're so smart and brave and the center is extraordinary. I think I can do some good with them in the next few weeks. You and Adam have created something really special there."

Justin sat down, straddling the lounger to face her. He reached out to take her hand and she let him, leaning into the moment. His smile was bright and contagious and only for her.

"You had a good day, yeah?" Justin asked, his thumb rubbing softly against her wrist. It was mesmerizing, sucking her into his orbit once again. She knew it was a bad idea but she couldn't bring herself to stop it.

"Yeah, I did." She leaned forward; it was impossible to wipe the smile off her face. "Those kids are so great. Thank you for taking me there."

"I knew you'd love it."

"Oh, Ma, I didn't know you had company."

Sarina jumped at the female, Irish-tinged voice, shifting quickly to look over her shoulder at the couple standing on the patio. Justin stilled beside her, his fingers tightening on her own, his body tense. The couple were in their early 60s, tan and fit and dressed for a cocktail event in clothes that reeked of money and status. They were both tall, the man broad-shouldered with dark hair sprinkled heavily with silver. The woman was also willowy, but athletic and fit, with dark hair pulled up into a sleek updo. But what stood out to Sarina most was the fact that the woman had Justin's smile and the man moved like him, quick but controlled and smooth.

It didn't take a genius to figure out that they were Justin's parents, Mr. and Mrs. Ling.

It also didn't take a Mensa member to realize that they were not thrilled that she was sitting here holding their son's hand.

Nana Orla put her drink down on the little side table before rising from her lounger and greeting the newcomers with open arms.

"Come here, you two. Give someone a heart attack sneaking up on somebody like that." She pulled them both in, fussing over them as she kept talking. "Where are you going all dressed up? It's Wednesday. What could possibly be happening on a Wednesday?"

"It's a cocktail party to meet the new director of the

arts coalition, Mother. I thought I told you," Saoirse Ling responded, her gaze settled intently on Sarina, so focused it was almost like a physical touch. "Who is your guest, Ma?"

Her accent wasn't as intense as Nana Orla's, softened by either years spent in the United States or purposefully polished down to the point where it hinted at time spent abroad in places more glamorous than California. But her gaze was 100 percent her mother's, inquisitive and not missing a thing.

Justin's father was just as intense but more quiet and removed. Sarina got the impression that he didn't have much to say but that he missed nothing, especially where his children were concerned.

Either way Sarina had met them before; they were echoes of the countless parents of potential friends she'd met through the years who'd been thrilled that little Molly/Susie/Amanda had a new buddy until they'd realized it was a kid in foster care. Especially a kid in foster care who had a folder of failures and problems as she moved from home to home. She couldn't blame them for protecting their kids, but she couldn't forgive them, either.

Mr. and Mrs. Ling weren't thrilled at the stray Justin had brought home this time if their reactions were any indicator. She allowed herself a small huff of laughter when she thought about how they'd react if they knew she was their daughter-in-law.

"My new friend is Sarina Redhawk," Nana Orla answered, turning to grin down at her, letting everyone know that she was very welcome here. It was a kind gesture, protective, and it set Sarina on alert. "She's staying with me for a few weeks while she assists Justin at the Rise Up Center." Nana Orla gestured to the newcomers. "You've probably guessed that these are Justin's parents, Allan and Saoirse."

"Redhawk?" Allan Ling, looking at her more closely. Man, his razor-sharp, dark-eyed gaze reminded her so much of Justin. "Adam's sister? The one who recently left the army?"

Sarina stood, noting that Justin rose with her and let go of her hand but kept a protective hand at her back. She held out her hand, falling back on her military training to handle this awkward situation. "Yes, sir. It's nice to meet you."

He took her hand, shaking it and nodding in greeting. "Thank you for your service, Sarina. Adam speaks highly of you."

"I think Adam is a good brother, sir." She shot a glance at Nana Orla. "I'm grateful to Nana Orla for letting me stay here while I have my motorcycle fixed. She's a wonderful lady."

"Yes, well, Ma can't resist a stray in need." Saoirse interjected, her smile an attempt to dull the edges of her blade. She didn't want to kill, only wound and warn. Sarina appreciated the transparency in the rules of engagement. "Justin gets that from her."

"Well, if that's true, then they've found the right project in the Rise Up Center," Sarina replied, taking pains to keep her words and tone respectful, but making sure her position was clear. She didn't want to make trouble for Justin or Nana Orla but she wasn't going to let anyone put down their incredible hearts. "They are doing incredible things with those kids… I guess you'd call them 'strays.'"

Justin's hand on her back slid around her waist, drawing her ever so slightly closer to him. It wasn't a big move but it made his point and both of his parents noticed. Both tensed, standing taller and straighter in their fancy clothes.

"Mom and Dad, Sarina has agreed to fill in at the center for the next few weeks while we look for a new director." He looked at her, his gaze full of admiration and his smile only for her. "We are lucky to have her. She's already bonded with some of the kids."

There was a long pause but nobody rushed to fill it. *Awkward* was the appropriate word but it didn't even come close to describing the width and breadth of all the things unsaid. Mrs. Ling finally broke the impasse and it was like someone had let the air out of an explosive-filled balloon.

"Well, that's nice, although it will be a shame when you have to go. But we all understand, and appreciate your work for these few weeks." She reached out to give a half hug to her mother as they prepared to leave. Then she let the other shoe drop so casually that it almost didn't make an impact. "Justin, Heather Scarborough will be at this party. I'll make sure to tell her you said hello."

Justin cleared his throat. "Sure, Mom. Tell her I said hello."

Sarina didn't have to be a genius to read between the lines here. Saoirse didn't like whatever she sensed was going on between her and Justin and she made sure that Sarina knew that her presence in his life had a shelf life. *Check.* She was also reminded that Justin had other options, more suitable options who attended Wednesday-night charity parties and got along with his mother. *Check.* Message received.

They watched as the Lings made their exit, heading toward their Mercedes and leaving behind a lingering scent of expensive perfume, aftershave and money. They had killed the mood for the evening, ushering in a chill that mimicked the one brought on by the setting of the sun.

Justin let out a heavy sigh, his hand tightening on her waist as he looked into her eyes. "Well, you met your in-laws."

It wasn't funny but it let loose the tension in her shoulders, stress from the last few moments expelled in a laugh that sounded off to her ears. Holy hell, why was a short-term marriage suddenly so complicated? It didn't take a rocket scientist to figure that out. It was complicated because she cared for Justin and so it mattered that his parents thought she was trash.

And if she was honest, they were just the latest in the long line of parents who didn't think she was good enough for their kids, their lives. Some things never changed.

She couldn't stop how she felt. But she could stop her feelings for Justin from growing any bigger.

Sarina moved to go inside. She'd take a shower, grab something to eat and hide in her room watching Netflix. She needed time to process, to construct stronger barriers around her feelings when it came to Justin Ling. She needed to remember that they did have a shelf life, that there was a pending divorce looming between them.

"Sarina, come with me. I want to show you something."

It was his voice. Soft, intimate, a tone and cadence she knew was one he only used with her. All he had to do was say her name and all her reservations vanished.

She'd waited her whole life to have someone look at her the way he did, speak to her the way he did.

Even if it was just for now, she couldn't walk away from it.

Justin took her hand and scooped up two beers, saying a quick goodbye to Nana Orla. He led her across the lawn toward the grove of trees filling the space between the house and rising hills. It was quiet and serene here, a million miles away from the bustle of the Silicon Valley just beyond the perimeter of the property. Here, it was just the two of them; no parents, no long-lost brothers, no lawyers or investors.

They entered the copse of trees, the waning sunlight now just dapples of light on the ground all around them. It was like nature's version of those fairy lights people draped all over the place at the holidays. The temperature dropped in the shade of the trees, causing goosebumps to erupt on her skin. Or it could have just been anticipation that had her alert and aware of every breath and brush of skin as they walked side by side.

It took her a moment to adjust to the shadows and then she saw it. A small house, nestled in the crook of the limbs of a huge old tree. It was made of wood, so expertly interwoven with the trees around it that it looked like it had been there forever. A staircase curved along the tree trunk, and led to the structure now rising up directly over their heads.

Justin flashed her a smile that took over his face, lighting his eyes up with childish delight. She smiled back, unable to resist his undiluted joy or the tug of his hand as he led her up the stairs.

If she thought the approach was amazing, the inside of the structure took her breath away. Exposed hardwood, maybe oak or pecan, formed the one-room tree house, the ceiling tall enough for them to stand easily, glass skylights and a wall of windows giving them a full view of their surroundings and the sky. From this vantage point, everything disappeared except for the treetops and the stars filling up the darkening sky.

"Oh my God," Sarina breathed out, her eyes darting from one detail to the next. Shelves built into the walls held books, candles, a fallen bird's nest, the mementos of exploration and indulgence. Colorful quilts were piled on an oversize daybed stationed in the middle of the room, an inviting place to take a nap, read a book or gaze at the stars.

Justin let go of her hand, placing the bottles on the small table next to the daybed before walking over to the windows and unlatching them in several places before he pushed them to the side, effectively joining this space with the great outdoors.

"Justin, I have never seen anything like this in my life."

"It's awesome, isn't it?" His smile was now full of pride; he was clearly pleased that she liked his show-and-tell surprise. It made her blood warm, knowing that her opinion mattered so much to him. "Nana Orla didn't want us to forget what it was like to just be kids, so she had this built for us when I was little. It was just a simple tree fort back then but I had it renovated a couple of years ago, had an architect shore up the structure, add the windows and electricity that can run a small fridge and add a powder room at the back. It's one of my favorite places in the world."

"This is incredible. I cannot believe it. It's like something in a fairy tale."

Justin's grin got wider as he opened the two bottles, settling down on the daybed and stretching his long legs out in front of him. He nodded toward the spot next to him. "Sit down. Check out the stars."

She knew that this was dangerous territory. This man, the stars, a tree house. Everything was tailor-made for her to do something foolish. She did it anyway.

The bed was comfortable, perfectly situated to give them the best view of the stars that were taking over the darkening sky. The birds were settling down for the night, adding their own muted sounds to the show.

Justin's arm stretched out on the daybed behind her, his movement shifting the cushions between them and easing their bodies together so that they touched from shoulder to knee, their body warmth mingling and causing Sarina to shiver with the contrast of the cooler night air.

"You know what was the worst thing about waking up in Vegas and realizing you were gone?" Justin asked, his voice low, as if he thought he'd spook her.

She shook her head. She had her suspicions, but really she didn't know. She only knew how she'd felt when she'd realized that she had to leave.

"It wasn't that I was horrified or embarrassed about waking up married. It was the thought that I'd made up the way we connected, the way I felt when I was with you." He swallowed hard, taking a sip from his beer before continuing. "I wanted that to be as real as I thought it was. I still do, even if I know we can't stay together."

She could go two ways with this: she could lie and tell him that it was just the shots at the bar, or she could tell him the truth and assure him that she'd felt it, too. But she knew she couldn't lie because she understood completely what he was saying, because it was the reason she'd left.

"It was real, Justin," she whispered, taking a deep breath to steady the frantic beat of her heart. "It was why I had to leave."

Justin placed his beer bottle on the table and turned to her, his free hand sliding over her jaw, fingers winding into her hair. She lifted her face to his, shutting her eyes to the intensity of his gaze at the same time his mouth pressed against her own. Soft lips, quick breaths, and then groans and mouths opening to each other, tongues tangling and the kiss deepening to the point where she didn't know where she ended and he began.

Sarina wrapped her arms around his neck, hungry to be as close to him as she could get, her body craving what it remembered was so good. Justin's hands roamed over her body, coasting over her back, her hip, back into her hair. Everywhere he touched her was liquid heat, nerve endings responding to him and sending messages to her brain that defied logic and drove out any rational thought.

It was need and connection and pheromones and hunger.

Justin groaned, lifting her onto his lap. She straddled him, the tender, aroused center of her body pressed against his hard dick under his jeans. Sarina gasped, releasing his mouth as she threw her head back, eyes open, with nothing but the stars above and Justin's hard, sexy body beneath.

"Damn, Sarina," Justin moaned out beneath her as his body bucked up to meet every one of her downward thrusts. His fingers went to the neckline of her V-neck T-shirt, tugging it and the soft cup of her bra down to expose a nipple. She looked down just in time to see his mouth close over the tight peak and then she felt the tug of his wet, hot mouth on her nipple. She was close, so close.

It was so primal, something she hadn't indulged in since a teenager, the not-so-innocent humping of two bodies together as they pursued one of life's best gifts. But she couldn't get naked with Justin, not now. It was too much. Her body wanted him but she couldn't be that vulnerable. Not when she knew she had to leave.

But she would be selfish and take what she could. Because she needed him.

She bore down on his hard length, pleased when he released her breast on a moan that was half pain and half pleasure. Their eyes locked, mouths swollen and lips wet as they ground their bodies together, both needing the same thing.

One minute she was on the edge and the next she was arching into him, crying out loudly as her orgasm hit her like a bolt of lightning. Hot, intense, sharp-edged with pleasure that tightened every muscle in her body, it was drawn out by the sound of Justin moaning underneath her, his hips and cock pulsing against her body as he came.

Sarina collapsed against him, trying to catch her breath and glad for his arms around her as she tried to wrap her brain around what had just happened.

It had been real in Vegas. It was real in the here and now.

But it didn't change anything.

Eight

Sarina was avoiding him.

The mind-blowing orgasm in the tree house had been unbelievably hot. They'd needed to talk about it but in true Justin and Sarina avoidance protocol, they'd cleaned themselves up, headed back to the house and then retreated to their corners to process what had just happened.

And two days had gone by with no contact and it was driving him nuts.

He'd gone to the office, burying himself in the financials he was working up to accompany the deal they were executing with the investors at Aerospace Link. This wasn't a typical deal for Redhawk/Ling but it was exciting. In the past, they'd been the ones seeking people to assist them, doing the work to prove that they were a good investment. Now they were one of the frontrunners in app and cloud-based technology and

Aerospace Link was a leader in satellites. And this new venture would put them both in the position of leading the next wave of technological innovation.

This was a collaboration that would lead to opportunities that Redhawk/Ling wanted and needed to be a part of in order to solidify their lead in the market, so nothing could jeopardize it. They had made the money and the money had gotten them a spot at the table but Justin and Adam wanted to be at the head of the table and this deal would put them there. Which was why it was so important to keep the marriage to Sarina a secret.

Adam wasn't wrong when he said that Justin's reputation wasn't always an asset to the company. People admired his ability to crunch numbers and project trends in finance, to think outside of the box and make people a shit ton of money. There was a reason why the upstart companies who had nothing to lose were the ones that shook things up and pushed the boundaries. Once people got rich they got scared and they played it safe.

So they didn't like that he loved poker, high-stakes poker with players who could match his skill. Outsiders saw his participation as an indication that he lacked control and that he had a problem. But he wasn't an addict, he was a puzzle solver, a human calculator. It wasn't risky, it was statistics and probabilities. Poker was numbers and numbers always made sense to Justin; it wasn't risky for him because it was just math.

But the only thing that they mistrusted more than the poker was the women. No matter how trend-setting the men and women of Silicon Valley were supposed to be they were pure 1950s when it came to sex. Stability was going home to the same partner every night for dinner, and investors preferred to trust people who were *stable* with their bank accounts.

Justin was never going to apologize for enjoying sex with a variety of partners. His parents would love for him to settle down but the women he picked weren't there for *him*. They showed up for his money and they stayed for the orgasms and the good times. Everybody was an adult and everybody knew the rules. Nobody got attached and nobody got hurt.

But Sarina was different. He wasn't in love with her but they had *something*. A connection. She made him feel good, like he was doing it right by doing it his way.

Which is why he was walking into the Rise Up Center in the middle of the day to see her when he should have been at the office. Estelle, the assistant extraordinaire he shared with Adam, had given him a sly smile and amused side-eye when he'd told her that he'd be taking the rest of the day. He didn't even stop to wonder how she knew what he was up to; Estelle knew everything.

After a quick exchange with Kori at the center's front desk, he headed to the rock climbing room, following the excited voices.

He entered the space, familiar to him since he'd designed it. He'd wanted it to be a place for the kids to push themselves, to try something new and different. The result was a room surrounded by climbing walls from floor to ceiling with every level from beginner to advanced. The kids loved it.

The sight of it made him a little queasy.

Teresa spotted him first, hanging from a rope halfway up the wall. "Hey, Justin! You here to join us? Get your climb on?"

"Holy crap, Teresa, pay attention to what you're doing!" Justin shouted, his unease impossible to hide. Didn't she see how far up she was? And with nothing beneath her but air. He shuddered a little.

"Green ain't your color, man!" Big Pete joked, inspecting his equipment on one of the benches that ran along the center of the room.

Justin waved them off, eyes searching for the person he came here to see. He scanned the room, heart jumping in his chest when he spotted a familiar figure, wearing black form-fitting clothes and hovering forty feet above the ground. Sarina was stunning, her body strong and in perfect control as she strained to climb higher, muscles tense with the effort.

His fingers flexed, memories of touching her body, gliding along her smooth skin as she responded so sweetly to the passion that flared between the two of them. The other evening in the tree house it had been combustible, something he'd known was coming and he'd done nothing to stop. The next few weeks were going to be agony if he stayed around her and couldn't touch her.

But he knew that staying away was going to be impossible.

His current location was proof of that.

He held his breath as she reached the top, grinning down at the kids who yelled out their congratulations to her. Their eyes locked and it was a moment of recognition, a spark, and he saw delight in her gaze. It made his stomach flip and he grinned up at her unabashedly, not caring who saw. His excitement didn't even dim when she checked her equipment, glanced behind her and then descended at a rate of speed that made the floor move under his feet.

Damn it. Why had he built this rock climbing gym?

Sarina landed with sure-footed confidence, turning to high-five the kids who swarmed around her to offer their congratulations. She laughed, her usual placid expression replaced with the enthusiastic affection she already had for the kids. He gave himself an inner high five for taking the chance that she would be the right fit for this group. They were older kids, pasts full of disappointment and with few adults to look up to, but he'd known that they'd find what they needed in Sarina.

"Don't you have a job?" Sarina's question broke into his thoughts. She walked over to him, hand on her hip and head cocked to the side. "Don't you have a bunch of tech billionaire things to do?"

He laughed, moving in closer just to catch a little bit of the citrus scent that clung to her hair and skin. His first impulse was to lean in and kiss her but he knew they had an audience. A young, impressionable audience.

An audience that would rat them out to Adam.

"I do, but I wanted to invite myself over tonight. I've got a present."

"For me?" she asked, her nose scrunched up in confusion. "For what?"

He shook his head, knowing she'd never accept a gift from him. "No way. It's for Wilma."

"Ah," she replied, giving him a dubious side-eye. "You know that she can't be bribed."

"A man has to try."

"Good luck with that." Sarina unhooked the equipment from around her waist, offering it up to him. "You want to climb?"

He couldn't back up fast enough. "Oh no."

"He's afraid of heights, Sarina," Katie offered. "We can't get him up there for love or money."

"Really?" Sarina looked really confused now. "What about the tree house? You know it's up in the air, right? Off the ground?"

"Yeah, but it has a floor. I'm okay with things that have floors. I just can't have the vast expanse of nothing below me."

Sarina moved into him, her fingers brushing against his midriff. She meant it to be teasing, comforting, but it made him ache for her. "So I guess you wouldn't walk the Grand Canyon Skywalk with me?"

He reached down and took her hand, his thumb rubbing over her knuckles. "Not if it doesn't have a floor."

"Oh no. It's a glass bridge that extends seventy feet out beyond the rim of the Grand Canyon and four thousand feet above the bottom of the canyon. My old master sergeant said that if you stand on it you can look down and see your future."

"Is that before or after you puke?" he asked, horrified by the image that popped into his mind.

"Ha! Before, I would guess." Sarina winked at him, turning and pointing at Marcus. "You ready?"

The boy nodded, his expression tentative as he shifted his big eyes between Sarina and the wall.

"Don't worry. We'll do this together," she assured him, giving his arm a squeeze of encouragement.

Justin moved back, keeping his eye focused on his wife and the young man she gently guided through the steps of preparing to climb. Marcus was nervous but Sarina was calm, telling him that he could do it and running him the through the steps until he could repeat it back to her verbatim.

They positioned themselves along the wall, both making the final preparation to ascend. Sarina looked around at the kids standing around. "Come on, join us. Marcus needs the support and he's *sidanelv*—that's Cherokee for *family*. We don't let our family do it alone, right?"

Big Pete, Katie and Teresa all stepped up and prepared to climb with their friend. And they did it—together. Marcus stumbled at times and he was scared, but the other kids and Sarina kept him going, cheering him on and giving him helpful pointers when necessary. Forty-five minutes later Marcus was standing on the ground again, smiling proudly as his buddies all piled on with hugs and high fives.

Hair mussed and cheeks pink with her efforts, her grin contagious, Sarina moved over to Justin. "So, when am I going to get you up on that wall?"

"I think you need to reconcile yourself to disappointment," Justin said, helping her as she divested herself of her equipment again. He sneaked a peek at her, turning over in his head something he'd wondered about since meeting Sarina. "You were really good with him. I could see your military training working so well and it makes me wonder why you left the army when you were obviously made for it."

Sarina messed with the stuff in her hands, taking so long that he wasn't sure she was going to answer him. When she did, it was in a quiet tone, edged with regret and little wistfulness. "The army works because we all have the same purpose but also because we become a family for one another. My people had moved on to the next duty station, left the service, gotten married and had babies. It was time for me to find my own life, my own future."

Justin debated asking her the question on his mind. The obvious question. He did it anyway. He wasn't good with waiting. "How is that working out for you?"

She flashed him a half smile, shaking her hair out of her eyes. "I'm working on it."

And while he knew he shouldn't, he wanted her plans to include him.

Nine

"**P**ermission to come aboard?"

Sarina popped her head out the window of the tree house and looked down at the man standing at the bottom of the steps. Justin was so sexy, wearing a black T-shirt and shorts, a pair of flip-flops on his long feet. He had his sunglasses pushed up on top of his head and he was holding a bag with a local sandwich shop name on the side in one hand and a six-pack of beer in the other.

It had only been a couple of hours since she'd seen him at the center and he was still hot. Still making her stomach flip with the jolt of heated sensual recognition.

"Justin, that's for boats, not tree houses," she chastised him with a laugh. "And this is *your* tree house."

"Nope. I think I've lost ownership of the tree house while you and Wilma are in residence. That's what Nana

Orla says," he answered, nodding toward his uplifted hands. "I come bearing food and drink."

"Well, in that case, come on up."

Sarina retreated into the tree house, pulling the scrunchie off her hair and fluffing it up. She caught her reflection in the small mirror over the bookcase on the wall; her cheeks were flushed even without a stitch of makeup. She'd seen the photos online of Justin with women and they were all beauty queens with perfect hair, clothes and makeup. Sarina had never worried about it before and now was too late with her messy hair and old cotton sundress.

She couldn't do anything about it in the next five seconds She was who she was.

And why was she thinking about this at all? This was never going to be anything. Her husband wouldn't be her husband in a few short weeks. She needed to stop acting like every encounter with him was a first date. It wasn't anything like that.

So why did it feel like that's exactly what it was?

"You look gorgeous."

Sarina spun, surprised to see Justin standing behind her so soon. He must have raced up the steps and here he was, his expression telling her that he liked what he saw. She blushed, heat spreading over her skin like the breeze whispering through the windows of the tree house.

Wilma growled from her little nest of blankets on the daybed. She was buried underneath the covers; the only visible part of her little body was her nose and two big dark eyes.

"Oh wait, I forgot to offer my tribute to the lady of the manor," Justin said, dumping the food and the beer on the side table. He fished a little gift bag covered in a design of various cartoon dogs out of his pocket, the paper crumpled from being shoved in there. "I noticed that our grumpy Wilma needed a new collar and tag. I took the liberty of getting her one that's fit for the badass she is."

Sarina took the bag from him, opened it and pulled out the little collar. It was black leather with three rows of shiny silver studs and a metal piece that had "Wilma" engraved on it. From it dangled a motorcycle-shaped silver tag with Sarina's name and cell phone number. It was perfect.

"I figured she'd love the motorcycle babe theme. You know, for when you get your bike back and you two start your road trip up all over again." Justin dipped his head, his demeanor unsure and shy.

"I love it. She'll love it." Sarina wavered, not sure of what she should do and finally sitting down next to Wilma, drawing the little dog onto her lap. She removed the old collar, easing the new one around her neck and fastening it securely. It looked great on her. "She looks like a little badass."

"She does."

"Thank you, Justin," Sarina said, nodding her head when Justin reached out to pet the dog's head. Wilma growled at first, dipping her head in submission when Justin stroked the silky spot between her ears. She hid her face in the crook of Sarina's arm, peeking out to look up at Justin with sweet, sad eyes. "Wilma says thank you, too."

"She didn't bite me. I'll take that as a win."

Sarina put down the little dog and they both watched as she crossed the room, curling up in a ball on a floor cushion. Wilma burrowed into the fabric, huffing out a long sigh before she closed her eyes and ignored the humans.

"Here, I'll thank you properly," Sarina said, rising to her feet and pulling Justin to her in a soft, sweet kiss. Just barely a brush of the lips; she meant it to be brief, a throwaway, but she felt it down to her toes.

His arms slid around her waist and she gripped them, drawing him closer to her body. They didn't deepen the kiss; it was enough to be wrapped around each other, sinking into the sweetness of the moment.

"Sarina," Justin breathed, his fingertips ghosting over her face, tracing her lips and cheekbones. "I want you all the time."

"I want you, too," she sighed, kissing his palm, her breath catching in her chest. "This is such a bad idea."

"The worst," he agreed, tightening his hold when she tried to pull away. "The best." He groaned, kissing her mouth, his tongue dipping inside, teasing her. Driving her crazy. "I think we should keep doing it."

"Of course you do." Sarina smiled against his lips. She should be putting an end to this but she just couldn't. It was beyond her power. "You *are* a gambler, right?"

"Hear me out," Justin said, pulling back enough to look her in the eye. "We have this connection, attraction, that has been there from the first. But neither of us is looking for anything serious or permanent, right?"

"If we were, we'd stay married."

"Exactly." Justin ran his thumb across her bottom lip, visibly holding back a moan when she licked it. "But I'm here and you're here for the next few weeks. We want each other. We know we're good together. So why not indulge? All we're going to do is give in over and over and then beat ourselves up for it." He pulled her closer and she could feel the heat of him, the hardness of his cock pressed against her body. "I want to be inside you again. I want to make you fall apart all over me. That's what I want, Sarina."

Sarina considered him; there were a million reasons why she should say no to this and push him away. She wasn't classy enough to fit in his life. She didn't know how to be with someone in a relationship. They weren't headed for a happily ever after. Their divorce papers were in the works.

But the bottom line was that she didn't want to. She was lonely, or at least tired of being alone in her bed, and she knew that Justin wouldn't try to stop her when it was time for her to leave.

And she wanted him. She liked the way he looked at her, as if she was important to him, as if she had a power over him that she'd never had with anyone else. The power to linger, to be remembered, to be yearned for.

But she'd never tell him that. It wasn't necessary for their current arrangement.

"Yes. I want you inside me again. Please, Justin."

"Thank God," he breathed and she was suddenly surrounded by him. His hard, muscled arms wrapped around her and his mouth possessed hers. The kiss was intense, hungry, and so was his touch as it roamed all over her body, tracing heat over her bare skin.

She clutched at him, finding it frustrating to be unable to get close enough. To feel enough. Sarina tugged him back, sitting down on the mattress of the daybed and pulling him down on top of her. She needed to feel his weight on her, to have something to strain against, something to hold on to when he drove her out of her mind.

"Justin, please." She reached down, snagging the hem of his T-shirt and dragging it over his head. Sarina sighed, some of the tension in her gut easing when she touched him, skimmed her fingertips over the warm expanse of his skin. It was as if her body had been waiting for this moment, the moment when she could feel him again, connect with him again. "I remember this."

Sarina traced a finger down his chest, over the tensing muscles of his abdomen to the edge of his waistband. She watched his face, the way he bit his lip in pleasure, the soft flutter of his eyelashes as he fought the urge to close his eyes and just sink into the anticipation of her touch.

"Do you remember this?" she asked as she unfastened the button on his shorts and eased down the zipper. His cock was hard, straining upward behind his boxer briefs, and she wasted no time in easing down the fabric and holding him, hot and heavy in her hand.

"Damn, Sarina. Touch me, please." Justin panted above her, his words deep and guttural.

She was never going to tell him no, never going to deny him. Not this. Not when she wanted to taste him again so very badly.

Sarina shoved him over onto his back, using the movement to push down his shorts and boxer briefs to his thighs and then slide them down his legs. Justin sprawled out beneath her, his long, hard body so gorgeous in the sunlight that filtered through the windows of the tree house.

"You don't have to," he whispered, his fingers tangled in her hair.

"But I want to. I need to taste you."

Sarina leaned over and took him in her mouth, tentatively at first as she got used to the width and length of him. He smelled of heat and salt and sweat and the sand-and-sun fragrance that was Justin to her. He reached down and wrapped his long fingers around his dick as he offered it to her like a present.

Sarina moaned at the invitation, taking more of him in her mouth as his hips rocked forward in an invitation too good to pass up. She opened her mouth wider and slid him in, indulging in the weight of him on her tongue. His taste was intoxicating, seductive and familiar as she sucked and teased him in turn.

Justin moved beneath her; with each stroke of her tongue he grunted and gasped, his fingers digging into her hair, pulling and leaving a shock of tingling pleasure on her scalp. He grew harder, skin tighter, his moans of pleasure louder in the silence of the treetops and Sarina reveled in her power to make him feel all these things. Giving him pleasure made her wet, the ache in her breasts, her belly, her sex building with each thrust and suck. If this was only temporary, she was going to make sure she had amazing memories to take with her.

"Sarina, stop, baby." Justin pulled away from her, his expression half pain and half feral as he reversed their positions and flipped her underneath him.

He dipped his head, taking her mouth in a kiss that was meant to calm him—or her, she wasn't sure. She wove her fingers in his hair, opening her mouth to him, spreading her legs in a sexual invitation. Justin ground against her, the friction delicious but not enough with her clothing still between them. She whimpered in frustration and he broke off the kiss, pulling back enough to be able to look down at her.

"Sarina, I'm going to take this dress off you and then

I'm not going to stop until you come." He swallowed hard, his eyes intent on her face. "If you don't want it, tell me to stop."

Sarina pushed against his chest, urging him to sit back on his knees. He complied immediately, trying hard to mask the disappointment that slid back into heated desire when she lifted the hem of her sundress and slipped it over her head.

"Does that answer your question?"

Sarina was the answer to all of his questions.

Justin knew this as sure as he knew that he would die if he didn't get inside her soon. But first he needed to explore her, taste her, make her feel a tenth of what he was experiencing right now. Sarina was usually an island unto herself, insulated from the world, and he understood why. But she let him in and now he wouldn't be satisfied until he had it all.

He inched backward off the daybed, reaching down to slip off her panties on the way down her body. He paused over her abdomen, placing soft, searching kisses along her flesh, loving the heavy inhales and exhales. Justin peered up at her, finding her eyes locked on his, intense and dark with her desire.

Sarina licked her lips and reached out to touch him but pulled back at the last moment, her swollen lips curved into a hint of a smile. He watched, riveted, as she let her fingers coast across her collarbone and in between her full breasts. She took her time, killing him slowly but he had no power to look away when she lifted a finger to her mouth, sucked on it and then used it to slowly caress a dark, hard nipple.

"Oh, you asked for this," he groaned, dragging her

to the edge of the couch and spreading her wide with the breadth of his shoulders.

Justin locked his eyes on her face, soaking in every flutter of her lashes, every bite of her teeth into her lower lip, every moan that escaped her mouth. The first glancing touch of his fingertips against her clit had her moaning and biting her lip.

"No way," he murmured. "Don't hold back. I want to hear you, Sarina. You've been haunting my dreams for weeks and now I want the real thing."

The next pass of his fingertip against her clit had her throwing her head back, exposing her throat to him as her moan washed over his skin and carried across the treetops.

"Look at me, baby. Watch." Justin was patient, waiting until Sarina returned her gaze to his before he lowered his head and licked her, letting her taste explode across his tongue. His mouth watered and her hips thrust upward in an invitation he fully intended to accept. Justin was going to dive in and take his fill, try to satisfy his cravings for this woman.

There was no rush. He'd cleared his calendar for the evening and he had nowhere to be, so he took his time, in spite of the voice in his head urging him to take her now, to bury himself inside her and come. Sarina hadn't been taken care of enough in her life; she hadn't been made a priority enough. He couldn't give her forever but he could give her this now.

Sarina writhed against his mouth, pressed into the deep thrusts of his tongue, moaned and clutched his hair in a painful twist when he lavished her with sucking strokes of his tongue that ended circling her clit. She was wet and he was hard as a rock. Her legs shook with pleasure and her body shifted under him, her muscles taut and straining as she came against his mouth and shouted out her pleasure.

"Justin, fuck me," she panted out between attempts to catch her breath. "Do you have protection?"

"Yes." Justin had never been a Boy Scout but he was glad that he'd slipped a strip of condoms in his pocket before he'd come over. He hadn't been sure that anything would happen but he'd known he was at his limit of restraint with Sarina, and he'd come prepared.

He fished them out of his pocket and ripped one off, opening the wrapper with shaking fingers. He slid the condom over his length, took himself in hand and stroked the tip of his penis against the slick flesh of her sex. Sarina gasped, arching against him and trying to press down on his cock. He let her push down and watched as he entered her body; her sweet, searing heat made his eyes cross. Then he retreated, gathering up his strength to make this last.

Justin pressed in deeper, bearing down and into her, letting gravity and desire take him to the place he'd dreamed about since that night in Vegas. Sarina wrapped her arms around his neck and pulled him tighter against her body, her nails scraping the flesh of his back in long, nerve-tingling strokes. He claimed her mouth in a kiss, opening her lips with his tongue and greedily taking what he wanted, what he needed. Sarina gave as good as she got, nipping his bottom lip with her teeth as she thrust up against him, driving him deeper and deeper.

Sarina clung to him, a strangled sound of protest erupting from her when he pulled back as he started a slow, deep glide in and out of her body.

"Look at us, baby." Justin adjusted the angle to give them the perfect view of the way they moved together. He was hard and she was soft and it was agony and heaven to watch him enter and retreat, empty and fill. He needed to slow down; he needed to look away because the combination of her body and scent and the sounds of their lovemaking was driving him toward his orgasm too fast. And he wanted this to last.

But looking at her didn't work any better. Their gazes locked. Her face flushed with her passion, lips swollen with kisses, was a whole new kind of hell, the good kind. Justin leaned down, covering her body with his as she wrapped her legs around his waist, hooking her ankles together behind his back. The movement tensed her body and her sex clenched around him as he entered her again and again.

Justin slammed over and over into her heat. Deep, primal, possessive groans he could not stop erupted with each thrust as his entire world narrowed to the woman in his arms. He wanted her to come, needed her to come. He needed to be the man who brought her to the point where she let down all of the walls that kept her heart safe, that kept everyone at arm's length. Justin needed to be the only man she let in.

Her orgasm hit and he reveled in the way that she screamed his name, dug her nails into his skin, wrapped herself tighter around him. Justin sped up his thrusts, holding her even tighter as he gave in to his own orgasm, coming with a roar buried in her hair and against her sweat-damp skin.

He held her close, shifting their bodies into a tangled mess of arms and legs and tousled blankets as they both settled back into their retreat in the trees. Sarina was quiet, her eyes shut as her fingers traced sweet circles on the skin of his chest. He could feel her withdrawing from him, her brain reconstructing the walls that she'd needed to survive.

Justin didn't want her to shut him out. He knew that eventually it would happen when they both went their separate ways but he couldn't face it today. Not after what had just happened.

"Don't run, Sarina," he whispered.

"I'm right here."

"You're running away, in here." He lightly tapped a finger against her temple. "Just don't. Not tonight."

The silence dragged out between them and he waited for her to sit up and get dressed, to hurry back to her room at the house. But she didn't do any of those things. She stayed, wrapped in his arms as the stars popped up in the sky above them.

But when she did speak, it wasn't what he wanted to hear.

"I won't run tonight but it's what I do, Justin. It's what I do."

And he accepted it—for now.

Ten

"And this deal is done."

Justin pushed back from his desk, setting down his pen as his eyes scanned the three huge monitors sitting on the large surface. The screens were filled with spreadsheets, charts and computations. A few feet behind them on the wall, large TV screens featured the major news stations on mute, covering the domestic and foreign markets. The screen to the far right had a running Twitch feed of one of his favorite gamers taking down alternative civilizations in a CGI environment.

But the stuff that mattered, the stuff that he and Adam had busted their asses to make happen, was going to work. The deal with Aerospace Link was going to solidify their leadership in the future of cloud-based technology.

And it was going to make them even more ridiculously rich than they already were.

More importantly, it was going to allow them to fund and mentor other scrappy kids who dropped out of school with nothing but Red Bull-fueled dreams and a couple of laptop computers.

"Are you sure?" Adam paced across the floor in front of Justin's desk, his brows scrunched together in an intense expression. Adam was the worrier and he wasn't great with numbers, so Justin walked him through it one more time.

Numbers were as basic as breathing for Justin. When words twisted up on him and made things that came so easily to everyone else so hard for him, so hurtful, numbers had been his solace. So he gladly walked Adam through all of it and showed him exactly how their dreams were still coming true.

"And this is solid. A sure thing?" Adam asked, gesturing toward the multicolored pie chart on one screen.

"Well, nothing is guaranteed but our part is solid. Worst case—we make millions. Best case—we make levels of fuck-you money that will enable our great-great-great-great-great-great-great-grandkids to tell people to fuck off." Justin went over to his fridge and pulled out two bottles of beer, popping the tops and handing one off to his best friend. They clinked bottles and both took a long drink. "Now, normally we don't drink on the job but this is a celebration and we are done for the day."

Employees walked by just outside the glass walls of Justin's office. His space was on the same floor as Adam's but at the opposite corner. They both had windows that looked out over the lush green campus of

Redhawk/Ling and he loved to watch their employees come and go from the building, enjoying lunch or coffee in the sunshine on the patios, or exercising on the trails. Standing here, shoulder to shoulder with his best friend, it was a little…incredible.

"I can't believe we're doing this," Justin said, nudging Adam with his elbow.

"I can't believe we *did* this," Adam replied, his smile huge as he waved his hand around like a sovereign viewing his subjects from the balcony of the palace. "I wouldn't have wanted to do it with anyone else."

"Me either," Justin said, his voice tight with emotion. He wasn't going to start bawling or anything but he loved the man standing next to him. He was more of a brother to him than his own blood and one day he'd tell him. Just not here in the middle of their business. He had a professional reputation to try to uphold. "Hey, Nana Orla and I want you, Tess and Roan to come over for a cookout tonight. You don't need to bring anything, we've got it covered."

"What's the occasion? Other than the obvious?" Adam asked.

Justin shrugged. "Nana Orla and I thought that Sarina would love to see you. Get a little family time." He walked over to his desk, moving aside piles of papers to find the documents he'd pulled about the center for Sarina. "She's doing so great with the kids at Rise Up, Adam. Your sister is an incredible woman. What she has done with those kids is insane. I don't know how we are ever going to find anyone to replace her." He found the folder, placing it in his briefcase so that he wouldn't forget it. When he straightened up, Adam was staring at him, a strange expression on his face. "What?"

"Are you sleeping with my sister?" Adam's voice was even, raising Justin's hackles. He couldn't tell if Adam was going to hit him or welcome him to the family. They'd never really talked about his quickie-Vegas-temporary marriage to Sarina.

It looked like it was happening now.

"Yes. I am." Justin wasn't going to lie about it. Hell, Adam would see the two of them together tonight and with one look know that they were involved. "She's my wife."

Justin closed his eyes the minute the words had left his mouth. They were true but not the ones to say.

"Not for long." Adam leveled his gaze at him, placing his beer bottle down on the table by the window. "Unless the plan to get a divorce has changed?"

"No, that plan hasn't changed."

"Then what the fuck are you doing, Justin? Sarina isn't one of the many women you cycle through your life like food that's about to expire. She's been disposable her whole life, Justin. So I'm going to ask you again—what the hell are you doing with Sarina?"

I'm falling for her.

Shit. Where did that come from? Justin rolled it around in his head, over his tongue, let it settle in the vicinity of his heart.

Nope. It wasn't romance. It wasn't feelings that lead to forever and golden wedding anniversaries. It was just a sex-induced crush on a woman he admired and respected.

Justin didn't do love and he didn't do permanent. All the women in his life prior to Sarina had known this and Sarina knew it now. This was just a longer-term hookup and he had no business confusing it with anything more than that.

But that wasn't what you told the brother of the woman you were hooking up with. Not if you wanted to live. "I care for her. She cares for me. We're friends," Justin replied, not encouraged by the tightening of Adam's jaw. "We're working it out, Adam. There's been something there since the night we met. We have…a connection. I don't know where it's going to end up but I swear to you that I'm not going to hurt her."

"You can't promise that, Justin. The only way to do that is to not get involved with her."

Justin sighed, holding his hands up in surrender. "I don't think anybody is going to get hurt. We're two adults and we both know the score."

The silence that followed was awkward. Not only because it stretched out but because Justin couldn't breathe. His chest hurt like he'd taken a stray kick in the ring at the gym.

Finally, Adam huffed out his answer, his voice equal parts pity and warning. "I don't know which one of you is the bigger fool."

Eleven

"Did you tell Adam we're sleeping together?"

Sarina pulled Justin aside, hissing the question into his ear as everyone filed down the buffet line and piled their plates with food. She'd arrived home from a day at the center and found her brothers, Nana Orla and Tess all on the patio with cold beverages and the boys fighting over who got to control the grill.

Tess had won the argument, and now she was Sarina's vote to always run the barbecue. The food was delicious.

"Adam is giving me these weird sad eyes and Roan and Tess are giving him the cut-that-out eyes and then looking at me so I can only assume that you spilled the beans with my brother-slash-your best friend," she whispered, looking over her shoulder to find Adam staring at them both, only to be nudged out of stalking mode by a poke from Tess. "What did you tell him?"

"The truth, when he asked me point-blank. I didn't think it would do anybody any good to lie about it." Justin moved over to the buffet table, grabbing a plate and adding a piece of steak and some shrimp to it. He stopped, sneaking a look over his shoulder toward her brothers and then back to her face.

Justin paused to consider something and then put down his plate, reaching for her and pulling her into a kiss. It wasn't porn-level but it was deep, intense, wet, and left no doubt that they were more than friends. Spouses with benefits?

And everyone was staring. Not that she had eyes in the back of her head but everything had gone silent around them. Even the birds had stopped chirping.

They parted and Justin rubbed his thumb against her bottom lip, pressing another quick kiss to it before picking up an empty plate and placing it in her hands.

"Eat up, baby." Justin grinned, then continued to load his plate up with grilled veggies and potatoes.

Sarina glanced over to where her family was seated, shaking her head at their reactions. Roan and Tess had their thumbs up, Adam acted like he hadn't seen anything, and Nana Orla was fanning herself with her napkin and pretending to faint on the lounger.

Sarina shook her head. "Family is weird."

When they finished filling their plates and took seats nearby, everyone decided to act like nothing had happened. She was okay with that. One hundred percent.

They ate their food, trading small talk while the sun set behind the hills and the solar lights cast a warm glow over the patio. This house was beautiful, the setting stunning, and tonight the company was perfect. Sarina soaked it in, pushing aside the somber thoughts about what they could have had if she and her brothers had grown up together instead of being separated. Would they have spent summer evenings eating hamburgers off the grill and trading inside family jokes? Would Adam and Roan have given her boyfriends the stink eye when they came to pick her up?

Would she have been braver? More willing to take a chance on what was happening between her and Justin?

Woulda. Coulda. Shoulda.

"So, Sarina, how do you like working at the center?" Tess asked, her plate balanced on her belly like a pregnancy party trick. "Adam says you're doing great."

"I love it. The kids are wonderful and so supportive of one another." She flashed appreciative glances at Adam and Justin. "You guys did an amazing thing by giving those kids that place. Giving them each other. It's something to be proud of. I hope you know that."

"I knew you'd get it," Justin answered, reaching over to cover her hand with his own. "And the kids. I knew you'd get them." He turned and winked at Adam. "We don't even rate anymore, buddy. I stopped by the other day and the first thing out of Little Pete's mouth was, 'Where's Sarina?'"

"All I got was, 'You're so lucky to have Sarina as a sister.'" Adam mimicked the big guy's booming, puberty-cracking voice. He turned his gaze toward Sarina, his smile tender and sweet enough to bring tears to her eyes. "But I have to agree with him. I'm really lucky to have you as a sister, Sarina."

She cleared her throat, trying to pull herself together. There were things she needed to say, but this wasn't the time. But she could set one thing straight. "I think I'm the lucky one." She looked between her two brothers. "I'm lucky to have both of you."

And she was lucky. Their family had been broken, torn apart by people in the system who decided that the three kids would be better off with families who could give them "a better life." They weren't the only Native kids who were taken from their parents and adopted by non-Native families, but having company didn't make the pain it had caused any easier.

But Adam had found her and Roan and now they had a chance to be a family again.

Adam and Roan exchanged a look and she wondered what was going on. Roan got up and walked over to where he'd placed his messenger bag next to the back door. He opened the flap and pulled out a small package, handing it to her when he came back to the group.

"Adam and I had some things from our folks, things we managed to keep when they split us up. I don't know how I got any of it when I was so young but it followed me around and I just stashed it away." Roan pushed a long chunk of hair behind his ear, giving her a shy smile as he handed it over. "We wanted you to have it."

She took the package, placing it on the table in front of her, squeezing her hands to stop the shaking. Justin scooted closer to her, his hand at her back, soothing and supporting. Sarina looked at him and he smiled, nodding in encouragement.

"Baby, go ahead," he whispered, nudging the package closer.

"Okay. Okay," she replied, voice shaky and thready to her own ears. With a deep breath she opened the package, sliding back the zipper and upending the bag to let all the contents slide out.

Photographs. Two of her parents. They looked happy, her mother sitting in her father's lap. One of Adam, holding a football in a Pop Warner uniform. One of two fat babies—clearly her and Roan.

Sarina covered her mouth with her hand, choking back emotion. Tears slid over her cheeks but she didn't wipe them away as she sorted through the remainder of the items.

A Christmas card signed by people whose names she didn't recognize. A beaded woven bracelet with red and black beads on a leather strap.

And a CD. Linda Ronstadt's *Living in the USA*.

"This was my mother's." She glanced up at Adam and Roan, surprised to see the tears on their faces. "This was our mother's CD. The only thing I have from our home is a copy of Linda Ronstadt's *Heart Like a Wheel*. I know it was hers because she put her name on it. I listen to it all the time." She wiped away the tears and let Justin take her hand. "My only memory is her singing to me."

"'Different Drum,'" Adam said, nodding his head in agreement. "She used to sing 'Different Drum' to us when she was trying to get us to sleep."

Sarina laughed. Really it was more of a snort joined with a weepy half sob but it was as good as it was going to get tonight. This was…a lot. Good *a lot* but…a lot.

Roan started humming the tune and Adam joined in. They were awful, tone-deaf, and any minute now Wilma was going to start barking.

Her brothers were awful but they were hers and now that she had them back, she was never going to let them go.

But she might temporarily lose them if they kept making the terrible noises they thought was music.

"If either of you start singing, I'll punch you in the face."

Justin buried deep inside her was the best part of her day.

"Deeper. Harder. Please." Sarina pulled him closer, her arms and legs wrapped around his sweat-slick body as he drove into her. It wasn't enough. She could never get enough.

It had been a long, incredible day. First, the kids at the center and the way they'd pulled together at the rock climbing wall and then the amazing dinner with her brothers, Tess and Nana Orla. The package of items from her parents had been overwhelming; she still hadn't processed all the memories that it had dredged up.

It really had been one of the best days of her life.

They'd wrapped up dinner and all she could think of was getting Justin in her room, stripping off all their clothes and making each other feel good all night long.

But it wasn't enough. Sarina strained, moaned, clutched him closer, and she needed more. Wanted more.

"Hold on, baby." Justin flipped them both over, lifting his arms and resting them over his head as he stared up at her.

It was dark in the room but his body was illuminated by a swath of moonlight pouring through the window. He was smiling at her, his eyes roaming over her face and body, his fingers flexing with his obvious desire to reach out and touch her. Take control. But he knew what she needed.

She didn't want to think about how that made her feel or what that meant.

"Baby, you take what you need."

"Justin."

"Sarina, take what you need. Use me." He reached a hand up and touched her lower lip with his fingertips. "Whatever you need, baby. I'm here for it."

She nodded, placing her hands on his chest as she began a slow glide up and down his cock. He was deep, hitting all the spots where she needed him the most. And she was in control of this, in control of her pleasure and his, when she wasn't in control of anything in her life right now.

So she took control. Riding him, taking him inside her body, clenching around him until he writhed beneath her. He kept his hands above his head, his moans and upward thrusts adding to her pleasure, the fire growing in her belly and racing along her skin. This was what she needed.

Justin. Sex. Power. Control.

The way he looked at her like she was the only person in his world.

Sarina leaned over him, joining their fingers at the same time she joined their mouths in a kiss. His tongue tangled with hers as they moved together, faster and harder and deeper. She came, crying out her pleasure against his neck, inhaling his scent and ignoring the tears that stung her eyes.

Justin froze underneath her, his cock stiffening inside her as he shattered, crying out her name.

A million heartbeats later he shifted them over on their sides, facing the moon. She was the little spoon to his big spoon and there was nowhere she wanted to be other than wrapped up in his arms.

"Big night. The stuff Roan and Adam gave you was pretty amazing." Justin whispered against her hair, his lips brushing against her temple. "You okay?"

"I don't know." Sarina reached back to stroke his hair, laughing when he pressed a kiss against her palm. "I think I will be."

"What was the word you used with the kids at the rock climbing wall? It started with an *S*."

She thought back to that day, finally realizing what he was referring to. *"Sidanelv?"*

"Yep. *Sidanelv.*" He hugged her tight. "You've got a good *sidanelv.*"

She giggled at his butchering of the word but loved that he tried. "I do. Adam and Roan are great."

The house settled around them, the evening slipping into deeper night as they held each other. Sarina closed her eyes, drifting in that place between sleep and wakefulness, the place where she had it all figured out.

But she didn't have anything figured out. Not even close. And the more time she spent with Justin the easier it was to forget that this was temporary. They had a committee of lawyers making sure they never got to their first anniversary and while she and Justin were having fun with the "honeymoon" part of the marriage, the rules had not changed. Justin liked her and he liked sex with her even more but that wasn't a love match and it never would be.

Justin interrupted her thoughts, his voice scratchy with sleep. "I want to take you somewhere. As a surprise."

Sarina shook her head. "I don't like surprises."

"You'll like this one."

Twelve

"How long have you been able to fly a helicopter?"

Justin glanced over to where Sarina sat in the passenger seat of the Redhawk/Ling helicopter. Her cheeks were flushed, her eyes lit up from within with excitement. She hadn't balked at all, jumping into the passenger seat immediately and soaking in every bit of the scenery outside the front window during the flight. They weren't even at their destination and his plan was already a success, worth all the hassle he'd had to navigate to get a couple of days off.

"I learned to fly when I was twenty-three and we bought the bird last year. It's easier to get to meetings when we have our own helicopter."

"And you love it," Sarina said, her grin wide and knowing.

"I love it," he agreed. He pointed out a few dolphins

swimming in the ocean below them as they headed up the coast. "You really can't beat the view."

"I have to say I'm surprised that you enjoy flying with your fear of heights. Doesn't this freak you out?" Sarina asked, watching him closely.

"Shockingly, no. I think it's because I'm in control of the machine. I'm so focused on flying that I just don't worry about it." Justin scanned the gauges, expanding on a topic he'd thought about often. "I'm dyslexic— reading is so tough for me but I can unravel numbers and math problems in my sleep. Brains are so strange, such a mystery, and mine is not the same as other people's. So how much weirder is it that I can't climb a wall but I can fly over the ocean?"

"I think your brain is pretty amazing."

Justin bit back a grin, the warmth in his belly caused by her words threatening to spill over in a laugh. "And I thought you wanted me for my body."

"Well, your ass *is* mighty fine," she teased, her voice coming through the headset as she turned away from him to look out the window. "But I think I'm more interested in your helicopter."

"Keep it up, baby. I'll just turn around and you'll never know where we're going."

She whipped back around, her face full of horror, prompting him to laugh out loud. "You wouldn't."

"Try me," Justin replied, looking over his shoulder and easing the helicopter into a turn back toward Silicon Valley. "It will be no problem to just head on back home. Wilma will be thrilled to see us."

"You don't scare me." Her lips pressed together in a frown but her voice and her side-eye glance were full of mischief.

"Well, that's good because we'll be landing in five minutes."

In spite of his ridiculous level of excitement, Justin carefully went through all of the maneuvers to get them safely on the ground. He settled it all with the staff at the heliport, turning over the keys to the helicopter and making arrangements for it to be ready in two days for their return home. The whole time he watched Sarina out of the corner of his eye, soaking in her excitement and barely contained curiosity.

Finally, he grabbed their bags and headed over to the car he'd ordered. She slid into the passenger seat and he couldn't wait another minute to end the suspense—whether for his own benefit or hers, he wasn't sure. All he knew was that he wanted to give this weekend to Sarina because she deserved it and more.

And he was beginning to realize that he wanted to give her more than a romantic weekend away; he wanted to give her the world. He wanted to give her a part of himself that he was pretty sure she'd already stolen.

It wasn't pity that drove him to want to take care of her, to make her life easier. Sarina was a survivor and had made a great life for herself. And when you got past her walls, she was generous and supportive and totally in your corner. When she told him that she believed in him he believed her. When she looked at him like he was enough and perfect just the way he was? He believed her.

That was something he'd never gotten from anyone else in his life and so Sarina deserved all the best things because she'd given the best thing to him.

But she was skittish, only comfortable in the construct of their having an end date, and she was poised to run.

And he needed more time to figure himself out. Because of one thing he was certain: he never wanted to be part of the long line of people who let Sarina Redhawk down. He just didn't know if he could be the man to break through her defenses.

Their divorce papers would arrive any day now, so the clock was ticking on his time to figure it out.

But today it was all about giving Sarina a weekend she'd never forget and a memory to last a lifetime.

"Are you going to tell me where we are? Where are we going?" Sarina asked, fastening her seat belt. "I don't like surprises."

"Really? I haven't heard that before."

Justin leaned over the middle console, tipping up her face to kiss her. She opened to him, humming into the kiss as he drew it out, relishing the taste of her. Reluctantly, he broke it off, his excitement at getting to their final destination greater than his desire to keep kissing her.

"So, we're in Malibu," Justin revealed as he ended the kiss.

"Malibu? What's in Malibu?"

"The ocean." He started the car and pulled out of the heliport.

"Funny."

"Let me spoil you, baby. You deserve it." Justin dropped his voice lower, shamelessly using all his tools of seduction to get her to let him do this for her. Sarina's cheeks flushed, the bashful shake of her head telling him that she didn't believe she deserved it. But he knew she did; that was enough.

"Fine," she huffed out on a pout that didn't look real. He knew she was enjoying this but she'd never admit it.

They drove down the highway a few miles. Sarina focused on the scenery that whizzed past the windows: gorgeous homes, green hills, and on the one side the Pacific Ocean spreading out as far as the eye could see. He saw his landmark mile marker and pulled his next-to-last surprise out of his pocket and handed it to Sarina. She took it, shaking it out and staring at it and then Justin with a raised eyebrow.

"A blindfold?" Sarina tossed it back in his lap. "I'm not into that stuff, Justin."

"That's an interesting place you went there, Little Miss Kinky, but that's not what the blindfold is for. I want you to be completely surprised. So put it on, please." He tossed it back at her, slowing the car down as if he was going to pull over to the side of the road. "Don't make me stop the car."

"Fine," she sighed heavily and put the blindfold on over her eyes.

"You can't see anything?"

"No, Justin, I can't see anything."

"Okay, grumpy, we'll be there in five minutes." Justin navigated the traffic, turning into the Colony enclave. He rolled down the window and showed the gate guard his ID, mentioning that their final destination was a surprise for his wife. The guard winked at him and pointed to the direction he needed to drive. The directions were perfect and before he knew it they were on the right street and slowing down for the house number.

The houses were similar, many built in the 1920s and then greatly expanded in the successive decades as oceanfront property became the hottest topic in California. These houses were passed down from generation to generation, only rarely hitting the open market. The one he was looking for wasn't usually available for rent but he knew a guy who knew a guy and he asked him to help make a dream come true for his girl.

Being a billionaire absolutely had its perks.

He saw the house he was looking for and turned into the driveway, shutting off the engine and undoing his seat belt with shaking fingers. Justin couldn't believe how nervous he was; he desperately hoped that Sarina would love it. He just wanted to make her happy. It was quickly becoming the most important part of his life: making her smile and living for ways to keep her smiling.

This weekend would be big for the both of them. The divorce papers were on the way and he wasn't so sure he wanted to sign them anymore.

He had no idea how he'd arrived at this point but he knew he had to face up to the feelings he had for Sarina. Justin was scared shitless; he loved his commitment-free life and just a few short weeks ago he'd have bet all his chips that it was never going to change. And now he was more worried about Sarina signing those papers and leaving than he was about giving up his freedom.

He had no idea how Sarina felt about him but this weekend he'd find out. It was the emotional equivalent of walking out on that crazy Grand Canyon glass bridge but he was going to do it.

And he really hoped the glass didn't shatter underneath his feet.

"Stay here. I'll come around and get you," he said, leaving their bags for later. He opened the door, taking her hand and easing her out of the vehicle. She was unsteady, her fingers gripping tightly on his arm as she found her balance. She was scowling, and so cute that he couldn't resist leaning forward and stealing a kiss. He'd meant for it to be quick, light, but he couldn't resist Sarina when she was this close. He deepened the connection, lingering, tasting and exploring. "You are addictive."

She hummed out her reaction, licking her lips and leaning toward him for more. Justin loved this part of the surprise but he missed seeing her look at him like he was the answer to all of her questions. Sarina's approval drowned out a lifetime of missing the mark on his parents' expectations and he wanted to give her everything in return. He'd start with the next couple of days and then see if they could have forever.

"Okay, hold on to me. I'll lead you inside, don't worry. I won't let you fall."

The scents in the air were already different, salty and warmed by the sunshine with a hint of sunscreen and outdoor cooking. Sarina lifted her face to the sun, head cocked to pick up nearby sounds as he guided her toward the front of the house.

He unlocked the front door and she paused, stopping briefly as the first wave of air-conditioning hit their bodies. "Okay, two more steps and then I need you to stand still while I close the door and pull back the blinds. Just wait here."

"Okay," she said. Sarina stood in place, her body adjusting to follow the sounds of his progress around the room.

He watched her closely, the anticipation building inside him like Christmas and his birthday all rolled up into one moment. Justin made his way back to her, placing his hand on her cheek, sighing when she leaned into his touch, her hands reaching out to seek him, her fingers snagging and tangling with the cotton of his T-shirt.

"Are you ready?" When she nodded, he eased around her, stopping when he stood behind her and she leaned back against his chest. Justin reached up, fingers hovering over the ties to the blindfold. "I really hope you like this. I'm going feel like an idiot if you don't."

She laughed. "Justin, you do realize that the longer you drag this out the bigger this gets and then the chances of you looking like an idiot increase?"

"Well, when you put it that way..." he huffed out in mock indignation, pulling the ties loose. "But I really do hope that you love this, baby."

The blindfold slid off and he stepped to the side so that he could watch her as she took it all in. She blinked a few times, letting her eyes adjust to the light, brushing her hair back from her eyes. Her face scrunched up in confusion and he could see the cogs of her brain working as every synapse fired in an attempt to put two and two together. She moved forward, stepping down into the sunken den that led to the wall of windows that framed the patio, the deck, and the Pacific Ocean beyond.

"Justin, this is beautiful," she said, peering at a line of black-and-white photographs on the wall. He watched as she froze, moving closer to get a better look, reaching out to trace a finger over an image. She put her face a little closer, squinting as if she didn't believe what she was looking at, and then she turned to look at him. "This is not..."

"Number thirty-eight Malibu Colony was the home

of Linda Ronstadt from 1975 to 1980. She moved here just after she released *Heart Like a Wheel* and this is where they filmed her in the *Wonderland* documentary." Justin stopped, not sure how to continue. "That's all I know about her but I thought…" He faltered, feeling like an idiot now that they were here and this surprise that had felt like such a big deal in his head sounded really dumb as he was saying it out loud. "…I don't know, Sarina. I know she's one of your favorites and your mom…damn, I just thought you might like it."

Sarina was all big eyes and open mouth and looking at him like he'd lost his damn mind one minute and then she was in his arms, kissing him, and his whole world was right again.

"You *are* an idiot," she said between kisses and laughter. "But you are the sweetest idiot I know and I don't know why you're so good to me."

"Because you deserve to get all the good things, Sarina. I don't know what's more wrong, the fact that you don't think you deserve it or that someone hasn't made it their business to ensure you always have the best of everything." Justin said it without thinking, knowing that he was revealing more than he probably should.

Sarina placed her palm on his cheek, her eyes searching his for something she needed to know. But Sarina was direct, so she just asked him.

"Do you think you're that person?"

He paused for only a minute, feeling like he was at the top of the rock wall, getting ready to take a plunge with no net beneath him. "I think I might be that person."

They stared at each other for several long minutes,

both waiting for the other to say something, to do something. He took the coward's way out.

"I'm going to get the bags while you go explore."

They had a great day in Linda Ronstadt's house.

The four-bedroom beach bungalow sat right on the ocean, with only an expanse of outdoor space and large rocks to buffer it from the waves that lapped right up to the edge of the wooden deck when the tide was at its highest. Right now there was a wide swath of sand, full of people running, children playing and neighbors enjoying the gorgeous California sunshine. A private beach, it wasn't crowded, and Sarina was easy to find once he'd moved the luggage into the gorgeous master bedroom on the second floor.

Swimming. A long walk on the sand. It was a perfect day that led to a perfect dinner. Shrimp and lobster, grilled to perfection with vegetables and the perfect bottle of wine on the deck, under the stars. Now they were full, skin warm from hours in the sun, and just the two of them talking about nothing and everything.

Except the one thing he couldn't get the nerve to ask her because if the answer was that she still wanted to leave, he didn't want to hear it. Not today. They had all the time in the world to mess this up, to walk away from something that was really great.

"Top three things you love to eat," Justin said, refilling her wineglass.

"What? Are we playing some weird version of twenty questions?" Sarina leaned back in her chair, long bare legs extended with her feet in his lap.

"Yes, we are. It is my incredibly transparent attempt to get you to tell me more about yourself," Justin replied, running his hand up her calf, admiring the way her mini sundress fell off her shoulder. She was so damn sexy and didn't even know it. He knew a dozen women in LA who spent the price of a small car to look the way that Sarina did without even trying. "Would you divulge all of your secrets if I just asked you flat out?"

"Probably not."

"So indulge me. I don't think there has ever been a husband in the history of husbands who knew so little about his wife."

She stared at him over the rim of her wineglass, shaking her head at him and trying to hide a smile. "Okay, fine. Top three favorite foods…a rare steak, cotton candy and MRE beef Stroganoff."

He cocked his head at her. "MRE? Like a military meal that you shake and heat up?"

"Yep. Most of them were awful but I really loved that one." Sarina pointed to him. "Your turn."

"So, easy. Nana Orla's corned beef, my father's *youtiao* and shrimp scampi."

"What's *youtiao*?"

"It's like a fried breakfast doughnut except that it's a stick, two sticks connected, not a ring. He made them on our birthday and holidays." He chuckled. "I think it was one of the only times that fried foods were allowed in the house."

"You need to make that for me."

"Only for your birthday. When *is* your birthday?" He sat up, realizing that he had no idea.

"September second." Sarina raised an eyebrow in question. "Yours?"

"March twenty-first." He stood, holding his hand out to her. "Do you want to dance?"

She shook her head, taking his hand and standing, looking him right in the eye. "No."

"No?"

"Let's go to bed," she said, leaning forward to kiss him. Her lips were soft, tasting of the wine and the intoxicating flavor of Sarina. "I think I know everything I need to know."

Justin knew only one thing: that he needed Sarina Redhawk like he needed his next breath. He pulled her close, taking her mouth in a kiss that was full of everything he was feeling, everything she made him want and need. He didn't want it from just anyone, he wanted it from her and only her.

She tasted like secrets and risk and the forbidden, but she felt like home and the future in his arms. She was perfect for him and she was his. Now he just needed to figure out how to keep her.

Justin ran his hand over the bare skin of her shoulder, catching the thin little strap of her sundress and lowering it slowly, only stopping when her breast was bare to him. He leaned down, taking her nipple in his mouth, sucking on it with a moan, circling the puckered tip with his tongue. Sarina's hands wove into his hair, gasping as she kept his mouth exactly where they both wanted it to be.

"Take me upstairs, Justin. I want you naked, now. I need you. Please."

She would never have to ask him twice.

Justin leaned over, picking Sarina up and carrying her over his shoulder. She gasped, laughing out loud as the snagged the bottle of wine on their way to the stairs.

"You're going to drop me," Sarina protested, her fingers squeezing his ass cheeks as he mounted the stairs.

"If you keep playing with my ass I can guarantee that I'm going to drop you on yours," he half joked as he arrived on the second floor, entered the bedroom and placed her on the floor.

Sarina took the wine from his hand and put it on the side table, turning to give him a sexy, lingering once-over. When she straightened, she took one finger and hooked it under a sundress strap and lowered it, then did the same on the other side.

The tiny little sundress slithered down her body and pooled on the floor at her feet. She was naked, skin glowing in the low lights of the room, her body long and lean and mouthwateringly beautiful.

Justin let out a wolf whistle. "You are the most gorgeous woman I've ever seen."

Sarina moved forward, stopping right in front of him, and began unfastening his shorts. Her eyes were dark with her desire, her smile full of challenge. "Prove it."

Thirteen

Issuing Justin Ling a challenge was the best idea she'd ever had.

Her husband was kind, mischievous, challenging, outspoken, dedicated, romantic and sexy. She still couldn't believe that he was still available, that a woman hadn't snatched him up and put a ring on it before now.

But she wasn't any different from any of the women who'd cycled in and out of his bed before. She hadn't put a ring on it—at least she hadn't put one on again after ditching him the morning after their wedding.

And now she needed to decide if she wanted to see that ring back on her finger for good.

She'd worry about that later. After about a dozen orgasms.

Because what crazy woman would get bogged down thinking deep thoughts when Justin was standing in front of her completely naked?

"I love your body," she said, taking her time checking him out. He was so fit, his muscles under skin so smooth and tan from days spent in the California sun that all she wanted to do was taste him all over.

So she did.

Sarina slowly dropped to her knees, tracing a path down his body with her lips, pressing openmouthed kisses across his collarbone, just under his heart, on his stomach, and landing at the top of his dark treasure trail. She looked up at him, placing her hands on his thighs and offering herself to him.

"You're going to kill me," Justin murmured, taking his cock in his hand and offering it to her.

Sarina took him in her mouth, tongue caressing the long length of him, closing her eyes and savoring the pleasure it brought her to draw out his moans of desire and gasps of surrender. She opened her eyes and found him gazing down at her, his eyes dark with his passion but lit with the feelings she knew he had for her. Unspoken but there nonetheless.

She recognized it because she also felt it, knew it to be true in her heart, deeper in her soul.

It was something she'd never had before. It was precious, fragile, but also stronger than she would have thought possible with her brokenness.

He groaned above her, his thighs trembling under her hands as he struggled for control, and suddenly she wanted nothing more than to be under his control, under his body.

She released him, standing on knees liquid with her own desire. Justin took her face in his hands, the calluses on his palms abrasive against her skin, igniting sparks of need in her blood, making her wet and hot and heavy for him. He kissed her slowly, deeply, tenderly—in total contrast to the slide of their bodies, the sweat-slick friction of hard body against soft skin, smooth flesh against coarse hair.

"Lie down on the bed," Justin ordered, his tone fierce with need.

Sarina walked backward, maintaining eye contact as she complied with the gentle command. The sheets were cool on her heated skin, silky against the back of her knees, her thighs.

Justin covered her with his body, kissing her mouth and then traveling lower to press kisses along her jaw, down her neck, into the shallow between her collarbones, lower still to the valley between her aching breasts. He layered them with kisses, the merest whisper of lips along the swell of each, until she writhed beneath him, her fingers clutching his back with long scrapes of her nails.

Justin finally claimed her nipples, licking, sucking, swirling them with his tongue until she was wet and needy between her thighs. He shifted on top of her, his fingertips trailing along the tender, sensitive skin of her thighs upward until he stroked her wet folds, finding her clit and rubbing it in small, firm circles.

"Oh, yes. Please." Sarina opened her legs wider, arm thrown over her eyes, lower lip bitten as she fought the sensation he drew out of her, as she gave in to the sensations he created inside her.

"I can do better than that," Justin murmured, releasing her breast and easing down her body with single-minded determination. "So much better."

She watched as he lowered his head between her legs, his broad shoulders opening her even wider. Justin kissed her wet folds, his tongue swirling around her clit, inside her heat, his attention's sole purpose to bring her pleasure. Justin was on his knees, but he was in control and she was completely subject to his power.

She writhed under him, thrusting herself against his face, riding his tongue, his mouth, straining for the orgasm teasing along the edges of her electrified nerve endings. Every time she got close, Justin changed his angle, pressure, intensity. He kept her on the edge, so close that when it hit, she cried out in surprise and relief. The pleasure hit her with its expected ferocity and she lurched forward, draping herself over the broad expanse of his back as she pulsed and shook with pleasure.

Sarina collapsed against the mattress, gasping for air and clutching at him when he moved over her, his body covering her as he took her mouth in a sex-flavored kiss. He stared down at her, his eyes dark and hot, molten pools of whiskey-colored lava that she could not ignore, could not break away from.

Justin broke contact only long enough to put on a condom, easing it down the length of him with sure strokes.

"Sarina, I want you so much." His chest heaved with each of his labored breaths, body taut with desire. "I'm going to fuck you until you come again because I can't get enough of it. I can't get enough of you."

"Please, Justin. I need you inside me. Please." She knew she was begging and she didn't care. She held so much of herself back from everyone but she couldn't do that here, not in this bed. They might not know what the future held for them but when they were together like this, they were infinite. They were complete; just the two of them were perfection. She didn't want to ruin that, didn't want reality to intrude.

Justin groaned at her words, and his fingers dug painfully into her hips as he dragged her forward and positioned her over his hard cock. He trembled and she thrilled at the power that she had over this man. But his words shook her control.

"Sarina, I want you to come for me. Getting you off, feeling your body grip me so tight, hearing the whimpers and sounds you make for me, just for me, keeps me up at night. I can't stop thinking about you. I want you all the time and I need to know that I'm not alone in this." Justin reached down between them and grabbed his dick, pushing inside her and joining them in the best way possible. She moaned, bucking up with a flare of pleasure when he began a slow, deliberate circle of the pad of his thumb over her clit. "Don't leave me alone in this, Sarina. Show me that you're here with me. Show me that you feel what I feel."

She couldn't have denied him even if she wanted to. Justin was so open, so vulnerable in this moment, so raw and naked. Not just in the physical sense. They were both stripped bare and even if she wanted to deny him, she couldn't. If she tried to hold it in she'd explode with the intensity, come apart in a way she was afraid would leave nothing of her remaining. So she opened herself to him; her body, her heart. She let him have all of her.

Justin drove into her, his cock moving in deep as she pushed back against him, struggling and straining to get even closer. She was playing with fire, she knew, and she wasn't the risk-taker. Nothing was settled between them and the voice telling her to run was getting louder and louder in her head. She knew that if she left, Justin would move on and fill his life and his bed with someone who was better suited for him. She just wanted this for tonight.

"Sarina, I need you," Justin moaned on a deep thrust, his body covering hers as he took her hands and lifted them over her head. Their fingers tangled together, bodies moving in the same rhythm, their heartbeats and the thrust and retreat of their bodies in perfect synchronicity.

Sarina looked up at him, letting him take over as her orgasm built tighter and hotter in her belly. Justin thrust deeper, harder, groaning his desire out between clenched teeth. Their skin was slick with sweat as they pressed against each other and his hardness rubbed against her clit with every stroke.

"Sarina, please."

She tightened her legs around him. The orgasm was building inside her, up from the base of her spine, making her legs shake and grow weak with the effort. It was terrifying, this all-consuming need, and she fought the urge to disengage her body, her heart, to run from this man.

Justin leaned down, his lips brushing her, his tongue exploring her mouth. He ended the kiss, whispering, "Don't run."

Sarina gasped out loud, her arms breaking free from his grip to wrap around his neck and hold him against her as she came. Justin's cock drove inside her one last time and his muscles shook with the impact of his orgasm. His fingers wove into her hair, clutching and releasing as his body came down.

Justin moved to shift off her, complaining quietly that he was hurting her, but she shook her head. She wrapped herself tighter around him, wanting to draw this moment out as long as she possibly could.

Justin wanted more, that message was coming through loud and clear. And she wanted it too. But she was afraid. Terrified.

She'd been wanted by people before and they'd rejected her in the end, sending her back into the system. She'd learned to not need anyone, to reject them before they pushed her to the side. She ran—it was what she did—and now she had to decide if she was willing to stay and see if the risk was worth the reward.

They were spooning again. This was quickly becoming one of her favorite ways to spend the hours of quiet between the busyness of the day and stillness of the night. The stars outside the open French doors of the bedroom were better than anything on TV and Justin was warm, strong and surrounding her as if he wanted to protect her from the world. She wanted to let him.

"Thank you for this, Justin." The words weren't enough but they were all she had.

"I wanted to do something for you." He kissed her shoulder, spanning his hand across her body in a gesture that made her chest tighten and warm with emotion. "It was risky. I wasn't sure if you would like it or not."

She rushed in to reassure him; the vulnerability in his tone wasn't something he allowed to come through very often. "I loved it. This has been the best day." Sarina peeked over her shoulder at him, taking his hand and weaving their fingers together. "You're good with risks. You take them. It's better than not taking any at all."

"Being cautious isn't a character flaw," he said, his breath stirring her hair, warming the back of her neck. "I know people wish I was more careful."

"Sometimes being cautious feels a little like being the walking dead. It's like standing on the edge of the game but never going in."

"You're braver than you realize."

"If I were brave, I'd say that we need to talk about it…about us. My bike is fixed. The divorce papers have arrived."

His fingers tightened on her hand and his heartbeat started a hammer against her back. "Are we going to talk about it?"

She rolled his question over in her mind, letting the sound of the waves as they eased in and out on the sand and the rocks below soothe her fear. They needed to talk, needed to get things settled between them. Now was the time.

But she didn't want to lose this, lose this moment. She'd learned over the years to take each moment as it came. She didn't give the bad ones the power to take more of her than the time she had to endure them, and the good ones were places she could be fully in the moment.

And this moment, this weekend, was the best of her life and she was too scared to end it too soon.

She didn't want anything to spoil it.

She wasn't so brave after all.

"Not tonight," she murmured, drawing him closer. "Not tonight."

Fourteen

The Mountain Winery was the perfect place to hold a celebration gala.

The historic location in the mountains of Saratoga, California, was part of the Paul Masson company. It hosted weddings, corporate events, concerts and wine tastings. Redhawk/Ling had rented the entire place for the party to celebrate signing the deal with Aerospace Link. Tonight, not only Redhawk/Ling employees but also the staffs of their new business partners would mix and mingle to live music and multiple open bars.

It was not a cheap evening but Adam and Justin weren't guys who skimped on the good times when their employees busted their asses.

Sarina walked into the massive space with Nana Orla, Tess and Roan and realized that finding their hosts was going to be the great mission of the evening. Sarina was anxious to see Justin; the week since they had returned from Malibu had been hectic for him as he finalized this deal and he'd slid into bed late every night. She missed him. So much.

But it had given her a lot of time to think about them and tonight was the night she was going to tell him that she was ready to take a chance on them. She didn't want to sign the divorce papers. Sarina was ready to stop running.

She was scared but he was worth the risk.

"This place is huge," Sarina said, hanging on tight to Nana Orla. The crowd was bustling and although she was a tough lady, Sarina didn't want her trampled on her watch. "I'm going to text Justin and see where the hell they are."

"I just sent a text to Adam," Tess replied, waving her phone in the air. "Nothing yet. I'm sure they're both busy wining and dining their new best friends at Aerospace Link. We won't see them until they are dancing on top of some wine barrels or something."

"No way," Roan said, looking the women over and punctuating his appraisal with a definite thumbs-up. "You girls are smokin' and there is no way that Adam and Justin are going to let you just wander around a party with a bunch of drunk idiots hitting on you."

"What about me?" Nana Orla asked, a hand placed on her hip while she made the what-am-I-chopped-liver gesture with her free hand. "I didn't spend three hours at the salon today to get ignored by all the hot guys at this party."

"Since you're my date tonight," Roan replied, looping her arm through his, "all these guys better just back off."

"That's fine but if I give you the signal to go away, do it. I don't want you to ruin my game," Nana Orla teased.

"Your wish is my command."

"Excuse me, Ms. Redhawk? Miss Lynch?" A young guy with glasses and an earpiece carrying a clipboard approached them and gestured toward a waiting golf cart. "I'm Evan. Mr. Redhawk and Mr. Ling arranged for transportation to take all of you to the VIP section on the Vista Deck."

"You don't have to ask me twice," Nana Orla said, making her way to the empty cart. "Take me to the open bar, young man."

"Yes, ma'am." Evan smiled, waiting until they were all settled before starting the machine and slowly navigating the crowds of people wandering around in all kinds of party clothes.

Sarina took in the entire property, comparing the reality with the photos she'd viewed on the internet. It really was a large place and she was glad she didn't have to walk all this way in the ridiculously high heels she'd chosen for the evening. They were sexy as hell but they weren't walking shoes.

They passed several terraces and open-air spaces, strewn with fairy lights and dotted with tables groaning with food and bartenders making every cocktail known to man. People were dancing, laughing, enjoying their success after having worked so hard the previous months. If this didn't make them all loyal employees, Sarina wasn't sure what would do the trick.

They passed the large amphitheater-style concert venue, with its Spanish-inspired decor lit up with colored lights. A local band with a huge following was playing a live show and the seats were packed with bodies swaying back and forth to the tunes. Sarina would have to convince Justin to come back here later and catch some of the show.

The golf cart turned a corner and directly in front of them, the area marked as the Vista Deck, was an area cordoned off by a velvet rope and monitored by a really big guy holding a clipboard.

Evan stopped the cart and they all piled out, offering him smiles and waves as Roan slipped him a business card with his cell phone written on the back.

"Did you just hit on Evan?" Sarina asked, turning her head to catch the guy still checking out her brother.

"He was adorable. Why not?" Roan shrugged, approaching the bouncer with the clipboard and giving their names.

They passed the test with flying colors and were all admitted into the exclusive area of the party. There were lots of people here as well, but they were better dressed and the waiters came to you for your food and drink orders, no waiting in lines.

Sarina checked out the women in the section, noting the sexy, sparkly dresses they were wearing. These women were glamorous, dressed like movie stars, and she was thankful she'd gone with Nana Orla and Tess to the salon and had her hair and makeup done. Even with the best that money could buy in beauty preparation, she was no match for these women.

"There they are." Tess pointed to an area just to the right where Adam and Justin were standing and talking to a number of people whose clothes and jewelry proclaimed that they were definitely rich and maybe famous.

Adam was dressed all in black, his resemblance to

Roan so pronounced at this angle. Sarina's breath caught at the way they both resembled their father, the dark hair and high cheekbones making them ridiculously handsome.

And then she saw Justin, in dark pants and a white button-down shirt with the sleeves rolled up. He was the epitome of everything she thought was sexy. Strong, masculine, confident, charming—he made her smile and her chest tighten with an emotion she'd never really felt before.

In Malibu she'd asked him to wait to talk about their future, fear making her put off accepting what she wanted. But standing here, watching him and feeling the pull of her body and soul toward him, she knew what she wanted.

Justin.

A future together.

She wanted to remain Mrs. Ling.

And then he looked over and did an honest-to-God double take as their eyes met and she knew that he wanted the same thing. No words could have convinced her, but that look, that absolute and immediate connection between the two of them, told her what an entire dictionary full of words would never be able to tell her: Justin wanted her, too.

She started walking, grinning like an idiot with every step she took across the stone pavers to meet Justin halfway. He was smiling, too, giving his lips a sexy curve as he perused her body with eyes full of desire. And just like that, she knew she'd chosen the right thing to wear.

"You're beautiful," he breathed as soon as they were close enough not to be overheard.

They'd decided not to publicize their involvement to-night. The journalists would latch onto any whisper of a new woman in Justin's life and with nothing settled between them, she'd been wary of any attention. It had been the right decision. She was already nervous about this event and didn't need the extra pressure.

But it was damn hard not to kiss him, not to touch him.

"This old thing?" she replied, looking down at the black jumpsuit with its plunging neckline and almost nonexistent back.

"I can't wait to take it off you later," he replied, his fingers lightly brushing against the inside of her wrist, sending lightning up her arm and racing across her skin. She shivered with the impact of his touch. "Are you cold?"

She didn't get to answer, interrupted by the approach of one of the most beautiful women she'd ever seen. This woman was stunning, tall and willowy with her blond hair in loose curls falling around her tan shoul-ders. She wore very little makeup, her skin dewy and fresh, lashes long, and lips stained with a red gloss. This woman was the epitome of a California girl, the kind of woman men dreamed about and boys had on posters in their rooms.

"Justin, your parents want you to meet their friends from the hospital board," the woman said, her hand grasping his so easily that Sarina knew it wasn't the first time. Her eyes got wide when she saw Sarina standing there, her expression immediately apologetic. "I'm so sorry, I interrupted you. Forgive me."

Great. And she was nice, too. Sarina was good at

reading people and nothing about this woman rang false.

Justin gestured between the two women, deftly removing his hand from the other woman's grasp. "Sarina Redhawk, this is Heather Scarborough."

"It's nice to meet you," they replied at the same time, causing them both to stutter and smile awkwardly.

"Oh, good. You found him." Mrs. Ling appeared over Justin's other shoulder as if she'd been conjured out of Sarina's most awkward nightmares, and the older woman's smile faltered when her gaze landed on Sarina. "Hello, Sarina. It's nice to see you here." She turned to Justin and gestured over to the other side of the space. "Justin, I need you to come and meet some people from the hospital board."

"Mom, I was just going to dance with Sarina. I'll meet them later," Justin answered, his tone tired. He held his hand out to her, his smile apologetic. "Come on."

Sarina placed her hand in his, relieved to have a few more moments alone with him, but they were stopped by the arrival of a man at their side. She didn't recognize him and by the look on Justin's face, he didn't know him either.

"Mr. Ling, Tim Gilbert from *Celebrity News*. I'm writing an article and I was hoping to get a quote." The man punctuated his question by shoving a digital recorder in their faces.

The *Celebrity News* was a trashy tabloid specializing in gossip and half-truths that barely kept on the right side of slander. This was not a good thing and the tension in Justin's body told her that he knew it.

"I'm sorry, Mr. Gilbert, but we'll be answering questions about the new deal at the press conference in a couple of days. I'll be happy to talk to you then. If you'll excuse me, we're off to dance." Justin nodded at the man with a smile and moved to go around him but the guy fell back and blocked their path.

"I'm not interested in the new deal, Mr. Ling. I was hoping you could talk to me about your secret marriage to Sarina Redhawk."

Fifteen

"Justin, what is this man talking about?" his mother demanded, her raised voice drawing the attention of nearby VIPs.

Justin closed his eyes, knowing that he should have seen this coming. He'd been congratulating himself that they'd pulled it off, that they would be able to sneak off for a couple more days and plan their future together and then announce it to the world on their terms. And now they were exactly where he didn't want to be at the worst possible time.

So close and yet not even in the damn zip code.

"Mr. Ling, I'd like to give you and Ms. Redhawk… Mrs. Ling—" the reporter turned to smile at Sarina "— the chance to tell your story."

"I'm not going to talk to you about this here," Justin replied, pointing toward the exit and the bouncer. "Call my office and we'll schedule an interview at a better time."

"It's not going to work like that, Mr. Ling. I'm sorry. I'm going to run with this story tomorrow, with or without your comment."

Justin looked around them. They were starting to draw the attention of the crowd in the VIP area and his mother continuing to ask what was going on was not helping. His father approached, closely followed by Adam and three of the investors. He had to do damage control and he had to do it fast.

"Justin, what is he talking about?" his mother repeated, her voice filling in the silence that developed whenever people sensed a scandal looming on the horizon. "Tell him that you are *not* married to Sarina!"

"I can't do that, Ma."

The reporter smiled, the triumphant grin of a man who had a solid story that he'd file by midnight.

"So, can you confirm that you two were married in a Vegas quickie wedding? Witnesses say that you were drunk and that you both stated that you had only met a few hours before. Is that correct, Mr. Ling? Ms. Redhawk? Did you guys get married when you were total strangers and drunk? What do you plan on doing about it? We heard that you've hired divorce lawyers to end the marriage on the down low. Keep it out of the press. Although nobody would be surprised about it with your reputation, right, Mr. Ling?"

If possible, their audience got even quieter as they all processed that information. Justin couldn't blame them; this was good stuff. Better than reality TV. Did they have a popcorn station at this party? They should.

Justin motioned for the bouncer to take care of this problem. "Get this guy out of here, now."

The reporter went quietly if not entirely willingly,

his expression smug. He didn't need their statement and so he wasn't going to make a fuss to stick around until he got it. His removal did little to dissolve the crowd although Roan and Adam tried to get people to give Sarina and Justin some privacy. In the end he still had his parents and several investors standing by and waiting for answers.

This time it was his father's turn to ask the million-dollar question. "Justin, is any of this true?"

The question was echoed by two of Aerospace Link's highest executives, their frowns telling him exactly what they expected his answer to be.

Justin looked at Sarina, unable to gauge where she was with this. Her face was blank, the old Sarina back in place. The one who gave away nothing and had walls that nobody could climb.

He wished that they'd had their talk because he didn't know where she was on all of this. The last time they'd talked about it they were getting divorced and she'd avoided any discussion about a change in status since then. Justin knew she cared about him, and he knew that she enjoyed sex with him, and he knew that she still planned to get on her bike and leave him behind once the ink was dry on the divorce papers.

And he knew that a couple thousand people were here celebrating a deal that would guarantee that employees still had jobs and Redhawk/Ling could survive any downturn in the tech sector. He knew this deal was security for many people and he knew he couldn't kill it at the eleventh hour.

What he didn't know was if his wife loved him enough to stay.

He couldn't make a grand statement that they were

in love and staying married when he didn't know if Sarina was willing to play along with that story. Because that couldn't be a short-term thing. It would have to be a long-haul commitment to convince everyone that it was the truth and as far as he knew, she was still going to sign those divorce papers.

So, he really had no choice. He didn't have a winning hand and it was time to fold.

Sarina would understand. He'd make her understand. It was time for him to do some damage control.

"Look, I'm married…we're married…but it was a mistake and we are in the process of having the marriage dissolved." He reached for Sarina's hand and she let him take it, but it was cold and her body was stiff. "We are committed to staying friends and remaining in each other's lives in the future. We are both part of the Redhawk/Ling family and that is how it will remain even though we will no longer be married."

"Excuse me, I think you've got this. I'm leaving." Sarina ripped her hand away from him and turned, pushing her way through the crowd and heading toward the exit.

Roan and Tess followed in her wake, their withering looks of disappointment unmistakable. Adam stayed behind but he was pissed, anger setting his jaw in a hard line and his eyes almost black with his emotion. Justin looked behind him one more time, watching Sarina's retreat, and suddenly he didn't care—he had to talk to her.

"Sarina, wait!"

His father's grip on his arm, firm and strong, stopped him in his tracks. His tone was brittle, voice deep and loud enough for only Justin to hear, but it sounded like a gunshot going off in his brain. "Justin, where are you going? Let her go. Don't throw this away right now, son. You need to keep your priorities straight and at this moment your priority *has* to be your company."

His father cast a meaningful glance at the investors, who were talking quietly together in a group, throwing the occasional skeptical glance in his direction. Nothing about their demeanor said that they were holding him or Redhawk/Ling in high regard. Everything about them said that he'd fucked up and needed to fix it—now.

His father continued. "Justin, you're always trying to tell me that I don't understand or respect your business and your accomplishments. You're wrong. I do respect your work ethic, but I think your personal life leaves a lot to be desired. You're reckless but I wouldn't care if it just impacted your personal life. You do what you want and then get offended when your poor choices jeopardize your business." His father gestured around, his movement meant to encompass all of the guests enjoying themselves at the party. "You have a lot of people who depend on you to do the right thing, to be the right thing. And I'm presuming that your new partners have insisted on the standard morality clauses?" He didn't wait for Justin to confirm it; a businessman in his own right, he already knew the answer. "So be the man these people can depend on and fix this. You are the only one who can fix this."

Justin looked in the direction where Sarina had disappeared, wishing he could do what he wanted but knowing he had to do the right thing. He'd created this mess and his father was right: he was the only one who could fix it.

He'd make this right and then he'd find Sarina and fix their forever.

Sixteen

Sarina was used to packing light and fast.

Years of moving from foster care situation to foster care situation with nothing but a few things thrown in a plastic trash bag had prepared her for the military. The army had perfected her ability to move quickly and disappear when she wanted to be gone.

She'd left the party after that humiliating fiasco and ordered the car to take her back to Nana Orla's as fast as it could without getting pulled over by the police. She'd barely set foot in the house before Wilma was growling at her. And not fifteen minutes after that, Sarina heard a car pull up outside the house and Nana Orla burst through the door on full alert, wanting to know if everything was okay.

But Sarina couldn't answer her. How could she talk about the moment when she'd been humiliated in front

of the press and all of Justin and Adam's rich friends?
She'd known that going to the party was a bad idea
but she'd been fooled by Justin, blinded by what she
felt for him.

Stupid, stupid girl.

Sarina wiped at her eyes, refusing to let the tears
fall. It had been years since she'd cried over something
as stupid as a guy or having her feelings hurt. She'd
cried over dead men and women in the desert, so far
from home and family. She'd cried as a child, missing
her mom and dad and her brothers, confused by being
surrounded by strangers.

She wasn't going to cry over Justin Ling.

Sarina stripped off her jumpsuit, throwing it over the
chair in the room. She wouldn't need it where she was
going and it would take up space in her backpack. She
was back to being Sarina, finally awakened from the
spell that she belonged in a world of money and power
and privilege. She didn't belong in that world. She didn't
belong with Justin. She'd just forgotten that for a while.

Wilma paced the floor, sensing her agitation and
whining with her own anxiety. Sarina scooped her up,
speaking soothingly to the dog as she showed her that
she was going with her.

"Don't worry, baby." Sarina pressed a kiss to the
dog's head, nuzzling against her when Wilma pressed
into her body. "Look, I'm putting your toys in the bag.
You're going with me. You always go with me."

"I'm going to miss the wee dog. She's mean as a
snake but I love her anyway."

Sarina turned to find Nana Orla standing in the doorway. She'd changed into her nightclothes; her robe was
teal tonight, embroidered with flowers and edged with

multicolored pom-pom trim. It was eye-wateringly bright, but suited her with its loud and cheerful colors and design. Sarina was going to miss Nana Orla's outfits; they were a never-ending source of curiosity for her.

"You two get along because you're both little and you both bite," Sarina said, her smile hopefully conveying how much she cared for this woman. She approached Nana Orla and handed her the little dog, who went with copious wiggles and kisses. Man, leaving this time was going to hurt. Not only leaving Justin but saying goodbye to Nana Orla and Adam and Tess…these people were going to be hard to let go.

But it wasn't letting go. Not really. Her brothers would understand that she had to go and they'd support her. Their bond was new but it was strong and she knew they'd give her time to figure out her future because they were destined to be a part of it.

"Well, that's true enough, I guess." Orla entered the room, eyeing the half-packed bag and the chaos of clothing strewn all over the floor. "You can leave your things here if they don't fit in your bags. I'll keep them for you until you come back home."

Home.

Oh hell. Sarina turned from her, biting the inside of her cheek to stop the tears that threatened to spill over onto her cheeks.

"That's really sweet but I don't think I'll be back." She cut off the words *anytime soon* because they sat on the edge of her tongue, poised to add a caveat and hedge on the decision she knew she had to make. This needed to be the last time she came here, at least until she could get over the ache in her chest that throbbed every time she thought of Justin.

Home. Justin had become that place for her. She couldn't pinpoint the exact moment it had happened, but she couldn't deny it and now she had to figure out her exit plan. Time and distance would help her get over him.

"This is your home, girl." Nana Orla's voice was soft but firm, the Irish brogue wrapping around Sarina like a warm blanket. The older woman moved in close, locking eyes with Sarina before she spoke. "You know better than anyone that family is not just blood and DNA, it's the people you choose. What Justin did, it doesn't change the fact that you and I are family and always will be." The older woman reached out and placed a hand on Sarina's cheek. Her touch was warm but the surge of emotion, of love, that Sarina felt for her was enough to loosen the tears and important enough that she didn't care. "I choose you, Sarina. You and I will always be family."

"She's right, Sarina."

They both turned to find Adam standing in the doorway. He was still dressed in his tux, a tense expression on his face. He smiled apologetically at Nana Orla.

"I used the key you gave me," he explained, his gaze drifting back to Sarina. "How are you doing?"

She could feel the big-brother protectiveness rolling off him in waves and for once it didn't piss her off. It made her feel wanted, included. When he walked over to her and pulled her into a tight hug, she didn't fight him but hugged him back. Tighter. Harder. She was going to be gone for a while and she needed to make this one count, make it one she would remember.

"I'm doing better now," she admitted, surprising the both of them with her honesty. Adam went still for a moment and then he pulled her in tighter, pressing a kiss to her hair. "But I've got to go, Adam. I'm sorry."

He released her, looking down at her, clearly gauging how successful he would be if he tried to change her mind. She shook her head, wishing that this could be different. "Adam, you know I can't stay. This thing with Justin, it got complicated and so real, so fast. I have to go to get my head straight, to figure things out."

"You can't outrun these feelings, Sarina. You love him. That isn't just going to go away just because you have a few states in between the two of you."

"I know, Adam. But I need time to put this behind me. I need to find a place where I can land and stay, build a life." Sarina glanced at Nana Orla, wishing that this could be different. "I thought it might be here but I was wrong. This way I can move on and so can Justin."

"Justin is being an ass," Nana Orla said, setting Wilma on the bed. "I still can't believe what he said to that reporter."

"Look, he told them the truth," Sarina broke in, needing to make sure that they all understood exactly what had gone down between her and Justin. "Justin and I never changed our plans. He didn't betray me with what he said tonight because he was absolutely correct. I just made the mistake of thinking that things were going to be different without saying or hearing the words. The only thing we're guilty of is getting caught up in our feelings, in the emotions of the moment."

"I know what I know, Sarina," Nana Orla insisted. "I know that you love Justin and he loves you."

Sarina didn't deny it. She wouldn't disrespect what

had happened between them. It was real and it was powerful. It just wasn't forever.

"But that doesn't change the truth of the matter. His
parents are right—I'm not the girl for Justin. It's that
simple."

"You can't just give up, Sarina," Adam said, his voice
pleading. "Don't give up on Justin. Don't give up on us."

Oh no. She couldn't let him think that this had anything to do with them. "Adam, no, we're good." She
swallowed hard, realizing that there were things she
needed to say this man, the brother who had loved her
enough to never stop looking for her. "You're my family, my brother. My *agido.* And I have never thanked
you for finding me. I have never thanked you for looking for me and not giving up. All I ever wanted was to
be the person who mattered to someone, a person worth
remembering. A person worth missing. You gave me
that. I'm prickly and stubborn but I love you, Adam.
Nothing will ever change that, not ever again."

"Damn, Sarina, it took you long enough. I love you,
too," Adam said, tears streaming down his face as he
pulled her to him again for a longer and tighter hug.
She was going to miss this. She was going to miss her
brother.

She considered staying and just dodging Justin but
she couldn't face that prospect. It would take longer to
get over him if she stayed, and she *needed* to get over
him. Distance and time would give her the strength to
watch him forget about her and move on to the next
woman. It wasn't brave but it was reality. Running
wasn't always a bad thing. Sometimes the best defense
was an organized retreat.

And this wasn't going to get any easier the longer

she dragged it out. Sarina needed to go and she needed to go now.

But there was one thing she needed to do first. Sarina pushed on Adam's chest, laughing softly when he refused to let her go. After a long moment, he finally did, grumbling in protest. She walked over to the desk in the corner of the room and picked up a manila envelope, sliding out the papers and flipping to the one with the "sign here" sticky note on it. She didn't need to read the document. She'd read it a million times; the words never changed.

Those words put an end to the first time she ever dared to believe she could have the happily-ever-after. The first time in a long time she'd allowed herself to think that she could be someone's everything, the person they couldn't leave behind.

Sarina picked up a pen from the desk and weighed it in her hand. Then she signed her name.

It was that simple. A few strokes of black ink and she broke her own heart.

Sarina gathered the papers and stuffed them back in the envelope, hesitating for one moment before she took a piece of notepaper and scribbled a few words on it and shoved it in with her divorce papers. Knowing she was doing the right thing gave her the strength to turn and hand over the package to Adam.

"Can you give these to Justin for me?"

The tic in his jaw was the only sign that Adam wanted to argue with her. In the end he nodded, taking the papers from her with a grimace. "You matter to Justin. He loves you and he will remember you. He'll miss you. These papers won't change that."

She laughed, wiping the tears away as she reached

for her bag and the keys to her bike. He was right. The stuff in his hand was just paper and ink, words that did nothing to change the pain settled in her chest. "Those papers aren't meant to help Justin get over me, they're what I need to get over him."

Seventeen

Sarina had just vanished.

Justin stood in the doorway to the room she'd made her own the last few weeks. He stared at the bed where they'd made love and he'd given his heart away without even realizing it. They'd been happy together.

And for the first time in his life he'd been good enough just as he was.

And now she was gone with her motorcycle and her dog and all the ways she'd made his life complete.

All because he was a coward.

He'd been stuck at the party until the early-morning hours, making sure Aerospace Link wasn't going to jump ship and bail. Adam had disappeared and it had been impossible for Justin to leave.

The investors hadn't been happy with the news of his quickie Vegas marriage, most of them giving him disapproving looks that rivaled ones he'd received from his father over the years. At first he'd downplayed the whole night in Vegas, omitting the parts about the alcohol that fueled their matrimonial bravado and emphasizing the instant connection with Sarina.

He'd found himself telling them about how amazing his wife was. They'd heard about her separation from Adam and Roan and while he didn't get into the details of her life, he'd relayed how she'd grown up in foster care and then joined the army and served her country with bravery and loyalty.

And then he'd found himself telling them about her work with the kids at the center, how she loved his Nana Orla, and even how she'd found a dog behind a dumpster in some tiny little town in Nevada and now spoiled it rotten with love and cuddles. And he'd told them about how she loved Linda Ronstadt and that the best moment in his life was seeing her smile on the beach in Malibu while an old beat-up CD of *Heart Like a Wheel* played in a constant loop on the stereo system.

And that was when he'd known that he had just made the biggest mistake of his life.

Justin would never forget the shocked looks on their faces when he'd stood up from where they were all seated and announced that he was going to find his wife and tell her that he loved her and beg her not to sign the divorce papers. He'd made it clear that if the deal was off, he understood, but he didn't care.

They'd blown his mind when they'd shoved him towards one of the property golf carts and told him to go get her. The deal was solid. Now was the time to save his marriage.

And so he'd raced home, not surprised when all of his calls to her had gone straight to voicemail. He'd pleaded with her to just wait for him, that he didn't want to finalize the divorce. He'd not told her that he loved her. Justin wanted the first time he said it to be in person, with her in his arms and agreeing to forever with him.

But he'd been too late.

Now, with the sun rising over the hills, Justin walked over to the large bay window and looked over the expanse of landscaped gardens and lawns, seeing Sarina everywhere. On the patio by the pool. Walking in the orchard with Nana Orla or playing with Wilma on the grass. If he focused he could see the tree house just on the edge of the horizon, the place she'd turned into magic. He reached up and rubbed the palm of his hand over his chest, trying to massage out an ache that he knew had nothing to do with the physical. It was marrow-deep. Painful. Permanent.

"Justin."

He turned quickly, almost falling off balance with surprise. Adam was standing in the doorway, his face taut with anger and eyes soaked in disappointment. Everything about his posture, ramrod straight and muscles tense, radiated how much effort it took for him to maintain his control. Adam had never raised a hand to him but Justin braced himself for the blow. He deserved it.

"Adam." Justin motioned around the empty room, everything about Sarina gone except the lingering trace of the citrus-sweet scent from her shampoo. She was on the run. Again. "She's just gone."

His voice cracked on the last word and he didn't even try to cover it up. He'd spent his life hiding how he was really feeling, protecting himself with a quick smile and the pretense that nothing touched him. This was killing him and he had nothing, no joke or defense or mask. His hand was exposed for all to see and he'd gone all in and lost.

Adam cocked his head to one side, his eyes narrowing into laser-focused slits as he examined Justin like he was a specimen at the zoo.

Heartbroken Homo sapiens. Genus Dumbass.

"Jesus, Justin."

He could see the anger leach out of Adam's body, replaced with sympathy and pity. He'd thought Adam being pissed at him was the worst but he'd been wrong—this was worse.

"Adam, if you have any idea where she's gone, please tell me. I have to get her to talk to me. I have to explain and tell her I'm sorry." He approached his best friend, the man who was like a brother to him, raking his hands through his hair in frustration and rising panic. "I know you're pissed at me and I deserve it but you've got to help me find her." His voice wavered again, his emotions spilling over the dam after a lifetime of keeping them bottled up. "I don't know how you did this, man. When Tess walked away, how did you breathe?"

"Justin, I—" Adam broke off, his gaze drifting to the window and then back to his face. "Sarina asked me to bring these to you."

Adam held out a manila envelope to him. Justin's name was scrawled across the front in Sarina's sharp, dark handwriting and he knew immediately that he didn't want whatever was in that envelope. He took a step back and shook his head.

"Justin, take it. I saw her before she left town. I tried to get her to stay with us but she was determined to leave as soon as possible. She made me promise to give this to you."

"Adam, why didn't you keep her here? I know I fucked up and you want to kill me but you should have thought of some excuse to hold her up and called me."

"Yeah, right. Like I had any chance of keeping Sarina here when she was determined to go." Anger was back in his tone as Adam thrust the papers at him. "You did fuck up, Justin. I'm not going to force her to stay so that you can shit on her again. I wasn't thrilled when I heard about your marriage but I've watched you two together the last few weeks and it was good, man. You were good for her and she was good for you. You were amazing together." Adam's voice dropped lower, and he shook his head with obvious disappointment. "I love you like a brother, Justin, but I saw Sarina's face when you denied all of that last night and I don't know if I ever want to give you the chance to make her feel like that again."

"Adam, I'm so sorry." He had some apologizing to do and it needed to start with Adam. "Look, I made the wrong move tonight. I panicked when the reporter showed up and brought my biggest fear to life right in front of the Aerospace Link partners. Sarina and I hadn't talked about our next steps. We both kept putting it off because we didn't want to ruin how good it was, so I defaulted to a conversation we had weeks ago and ignored everything that had happened between us." He ran his hands through his hair, sitting down on the bed to get off legs suddenly too wobbly to hold him up. The adrenaline was wearing off and all that was left behind was bone-deep weariness. "I should have told the reporter 'no comment' and talked to Sarina but I didn't. All I could think about was the deal and the people who depended on us and I didn't want to be the reason we let them down. I couldn't be the fuckup again."

Adam settled beside him with a deep sigh, his voice scratchy and gruff with the fatigue of the last twenty-four hours. "Justin, you're not a fuckup. You're bold and energetic and you do things that nobody else can do because you're willing to take the risks necessary to make it happen." He nudged him with his elbow, pausing until Justin turned to look at him. "It's why we work so well together. I'm cautious but you push me and our company to be innovative and that has made all the difference in our success. You're not reckless, you're brave. If something gets fucked up then we fuck it up together just like we've done since college. I wouldn't do this with anyone but you. We're in this together. That's how it works."

Justin nodded, wondering how he'd lost sight of the way things were between them. He'd let the voices of his parents and all the crap they'd piled on him over the years drown out the fact that Adam believed in him and always had.

"Thanks, Adam. I came clean with the Aerospace Link people, told them that I didn't want to divorce Sarina. They were fine with it, practically drove me here themselves."

"Good. I knew you'd fix it," Adam said, his jaw tense with the frown that returned with the mention of the situation with Sarina. "Business is business. But the bigger issue is, you hurt my sister. Why should I trust you not to do it again?"

Justin deserved that. He struggled with the words to make Adam believe that he was sorry, that he was the guy he could trust with Sarina's heart. There was only the truth. It was the only thing that had any chance to set him free.

"I love her, Adam," Justin said, his words loud in the empty room. "I *love* her. With everything I am."

Adam observed him, letting the revelation settle between them. A new truth between old friends. Finally, he sighed, reaching out to pull Justin into a hug. They stood that way for several long moments before Adam spoke.

"I'm sorry, man."

Justin pulled back, finally taking the envelope from him, turning it over and over in his hands. His gut told him that he knew what was inside. He glanced up at Adam, huffing out a heavy breath as he peeled back the sealed flap of the envelope and pulled the papers out.

Their divorce papers. Sarina's signature stood out, decisive and final in bold strokes of black ink.

Damn.

"She put a note in there, I think," Adam said, gesturing toward the envelope. "She wrote one. I saw her."

Justin riffled through the papers, heart sinking when he didn't find a note. He tipped the envelope over, shaking it. Something that felt like relief coursed through him when a half sheet of paper slid into his hand. He turned it over, eyes skimming over what she'd written.

Justin—I'm going back on the road to find my future. Thank you for the place to land even if it was only temporary. You're good enough. More than enough. Sarina.

"What did she say?" Adam asked, concern etched over his features. "It's good that she wrote a note, yeah?"

Justin turned it over in his mind. Was it a good thing that she wrote a note? All she had to do was sign the papers. The note had to mean something, didn't it?

"I think it has to be a good sign, Adam, but it doesn't matter. I'm going to find her anyway." Justin motioned toward the door. He was going now. He wasn't wasting any more time reading papers that he was never going to file. "I've got to go."

Justin headed toward the door, his mind going over every conversation he'd had with Sarina searching for a clue about where he could find her. He knew her and if he could just focus for a minute he'd figure this out. But time was flying by and with every minute she was on her bike and putting distance between the two of them.

Adam was right on his heels, pulling his phone out of his pocket. "Let me call Tess. She'll know how to search for Sarina. She found her once. She can do it again."

Justin entered the family room, looking for Nana Orla. He would say a quick goodbye and then hit the road. Only she wasn't alone.

"Mom. Dad. I didn't know you were here," he said, walking over to where his nana sat to give her a hug goodbye. "I can't stay. I've got to go and find Sarina."

"That's why we're here, Justin," his father said, tone firm with the conviction that whatever he was going to say was correct. "We need to talk about your marriage to Sarina."

"Dad, I know what you're going to say, so I can save you the time. She's not right for me and I need to just get divorced and marry someone like Heather." He held his hands out in a how-am-I-doing? gesture that he knew would piss off his parents. The only difference was that today he didn't care. Not anymore. "That's never going to happen. I love Sarina and I'm going to go find her, beg her to forgive me, and come back and build a life together."

"Justin, think about this. She's not the wife you need by your side." His mom looked beyond him to where Adam stood, her smile apologetic and expression sincere. "Adam, we mean no offense to your family. Sarina is a wonderful girl, I'm sure. She's just not what Justin needs. He needs someone who is more polished and familiar with the social circles you both have to navigate now. Justin needs a cool head, someone who will protect him from his worst impulses. I'm sure you agree."

Adam scoffed, shaking his head as he walked farther into the room. "No, Mrs. Ling, I don't agree. Sarina and Justin brought out the best in each other. I couldn't have asked for a better man for my sister and I think he's lucky to have her."

"We're not here to disparage your family, Adam. That's not the point," Allan Ling interjected in obvious frustration. His face was flushing red as he stood up from where he sat on the sofa. He focused his stare on Justin. "It is time for you to understand and accept your responsibility to this family, Justin. What you do reflects on all of us and it is time for you to stop putting yourself first and think of others. It is already all over town that you ended up in this drunken sham of a marriage. How am I supposed to do business with these people when they read your exploits in the tabloids? Why should your brothers and sisters have to hope that your behavior doesn't negatively impact their livelihoods? The circles we run in are small and memories are long. Your honor and reputation are all you have in the end, it's what keeps you on top."

Justin was done. The things he needed to say were long overdue. "Mom and Dad, I've spent my whole life worrying about reflecting poorly on the family and

I'm done. I work hard and it's not good enough. I build a successful business with Adam and we land on the front page of *Forbes* and it's not good enough. I help kids who have nobody in their corner and it's not good enough." He held his hand up when his father moved to interrupt him. "No, I'm not finished. I understand that you want the best for me and I know that you sincerely think you know what that is, but you don't. You think the best thing for me is playing it safe, traditional, the road trampled by the million others on the same path, but you're wrong. I'm never going to do it the way everyone else does. I'm different. I've had to find my own path and I'm so damn proud of what I've accomplished, what Adam and I are doing." He took a deep breath, getting to the heart of it, and he could almost hear Sarina whispering in his ear. "I work every day to leave this world a little better than I've found it. I'm a good man, friend, boss, and God willing, I'll be a good husband. I don't know what the future holds for me because I'm open to any possibility but I do know that I can't—won't—do it without Sarina. I love her. She looks at me and I know I'm good enough because I have her love. If that's not good enough for you, then you need to live with the fact that you won't be a part of our lives."

"Justin," his mother sniffled, her cheeks wet with her tears and her voice choked with emotion. "We just don't want you to make a mistake."

He walked over and sat down next to her on the couch, pulling her against him in a hug. "Dad's parents thought you were a mistake and look at how wrong they were. You two came to the United States because you weren't accepted by his family but you loved each other too much to walk away. You proved them all wrong. I would think that you would understand."

"It wasn't always easy, son," his dad said, staring down at the woman he'd defied his family to love. "We want it to be easier for you, Justin."

"I don't need it to be easier. I just need it to be with her," he answered. "A hard day with Sarina is better than easy with anyone else. I think you both know that I'm right. It's what you lived every day right in front of me. I just want a chance to have what you have." He smiled at his parents, hoping that they were really listening to him. "I don't want to do it without you, but I will."

He let that sit in the air between them. He'd said his piece and his parents knew where he stood. He loved them but he also loved Sarina. If he had to choose, it wouldn't be an easy choice but it would be a clear one.

"Allan. Saoirse." Nana Orla spoke out from across the room and they turned to look at her. Her usually cheerful expression was gone, replaced with equal parts censure and compassion. She spoke slowly, her words clearly chosen with care and love. "I don't know if you know how proud I am of you both. I watched you struggle with loving each other and knowing that you'd have to give up so much to be together. You taught your children, you taught me, how important love is and that it's worth fighting for. You've raised a son who knows the value of love, the real kind of love that makes you want to be better. The kind that makes you stronger. I've watched Justin and Sarina together for weeks and they remind me of the two of you. If you don't see that, you're blind. If you don't give them your blessing, then you've been living a lie."

His parents looked at each other, several decades of marriage and love allowing them to communicate without words. He'd seen this a million times over his lifetime, finding it fascinating and terrifying at the same time. Whatever passed between them was settled with a nod from his father and another round of sniffles from his mother.

"Justin, do you have any idea where Sarina could be?" his father asked, his question settling it all between them.

He shook his head, memories of his wife ping-ponging around in his head as he searched for the answer. She had her bike and Wilma; she could be going anywhere. He picked up the note, reading it over again, letting the words sink in.

"She said she was going to find her future…"

And suddenly it was crystal clear.

"I know where she's going." Justin stood, scooping up the papers and calculating how much of a lead she had on him and how fast he could get there. If he hurried he could intercept her and beg her to come home with him. It was worth a shot. Sarina was worth everything. "I need to hurry and I need a helicopter."

Adam grinned from across the room, pulling out his phone to make the call. "Luckily, we have one."

Eighteen

Justin Ling had ruined the Grand Canyon for her.

Sarina stood on the Skywalk, the glass bridge cantilevered seventy feet beyond the west rim, and glanced down at the view beneath her feet. Only air came between her and the valley of the canyon four thousand feet below. This place had been on her bucket list, one of the most anticipated stops on her road trip and she'd headed straight here after leaving California a couple of days ago, but she couldn't get beyond the tumult of thoughts banging around in her mind to register the beauty. A perfect combination of man-made genius and creator-formed nature, this Skywalk should have taken her breath away.

But she couldn't breathe around the pain ripping through her chest.

Dramatic? Yes.

Inaccurate? Damn, she wished.

The sound of a helicopter approaching from behind the visitor center caused the crowd to turn from the natural beauty to gape at the sleek black vehicle coming closer and closer and then lowering itself down to the ground. From where she stood, it looked like the bird had landed in the parking lot. Unmarked by any National Park Service logo, it had to be a private ride bringing someone here to the Grand Canyon for a VIP tour of the area.

Sarina couldn't help but remember the incredible weekend in Malibu with Justin. He'd orchestrated every move to make sure that she'd had the type of weekend only featured in celebrity magazines. The luxuries had been sweet but the way he'd looked at her, touched her, made love to her—those were the things she would never forget.

But she had to forget them. She had to put them behind her and move forward toward a life she could build for herself. For a minute she'd imagined that maybe she'd found a place where she could stop running, stop searching and put down roots. It had been a mistake.

That much Justin had gotten right.

A family walked past her, the young boy noticing Wilma with an excited tug at his mom's hand and a pointing finger. Wilma wagged her tail in excitement, standing on her hind legs and pawing at the air in the direction of her new friend.

"You can pet her if you want. She's friendly with kids," Sarina offered, watching closely as Wilma worked her magic and claimed another willing admirer.

Not for the first time did she wish she knew how Wilma still had this boundless joy for life and trust in people, even after she'd been abandoned and disappointed by an owner who should have done better by her. Once she would have scoffed at such optimism, counted it as the ultimate in stupidity to keep leaving yourself open for more heartbreak. But now Sarina knew that it wasn't foolishness—it was courage.

And even though she'd faced moments that teetered on the edge of life and death, risking heartbreak was scarier.

The little boy leaned over and hugged Wilma, pressing a loud, smacking kiss on her head before being led away by his mom. Wilma wagged her entire body at the kid, tugging at the leash to follow her new friend.

"Good girl." Sarina gave Wilma a scratch behind the ear, making a mental note to give her an extra treat when they got back to the bike. She glanced at her watch and realized that it was time to leave and get back on the road. If she was going to make Kingman, Arizona, before sundown she needed to go. She'd hang out there a couple of days and then she'd figure out where to head next. Anywhere was fair game. As long as she kept moving.

She needed to put miles between her and Justin. At some point she would stop feeling the pull to return to him and the tree house and Nana Orla.

She didn't belong there. No matter how much she wanted it to be the place where she belonged. She'd learned a long time ago that wishing didn't make anything true.

Sarina stood and turned to head back to the visitor center, squinting into the bright Arizona sun as she scanned the growing crowds of tourists. It was time to get back to the bike, grab some water for her and Willa, and hit Route 66.

"Sarina?"

The sound of her name stopped her in her tracks. Wilma tugged on the leash, whining in confusion at the sudden halt in forward momentum.

"Sarina."

She scanned the crowd, finally seeing the face that belonged to the voice when a family of four with "Brecken Family Reunion" T-shirts parted like the Red Sea and Sarina glimpsed the man who'd somehow become her promised land.

"Justin?"

Wilma whined louder and tugged even harder on the leash, the whines erupting into low growls as she fully recognized the man standing a short distance away. Sarina let Wilma pull her closer to Justin and unlocked the retractable leash so the dog could cover the last bit of distance between them. Justin loosened his white-knuckle grip on the Skywalk railing but didn't let go as he leaned over and patted Wilma on her head.

"Hey, girl, did you miss me?" Justin scratched behind her ears, huffing out a chuckle as she growled at him but leaned into the touch at the same time. "Well, that's progress, I guess." He pulled back his hand when Wilma bared her teeth and retreated to hide behind Sarina. "Or maybe not."

Justin straightened and moved closer to Sarina, his right hand wrapped around the railing as he shuffled closer to her one inch at a time. He was pale under the tan of his skin, every part of his body stiff with the fear she knew was coursing through him. For a guy who had a fear of heights, this had to be his worst nightmare on steroids.

"You had to pick a glass bridge four thousand feet over the fucking Grand Canyon, didn't you?" Justin complained, shooting an apologetic look at an elderly couple standing nearby. "Sorry, I don't like heights."

"No apology needed, son," the older man said, his expression entirely sympathetic. He glanced down at the silver-haired lady standing next to him, snaking an arm around her waist, then looked back at Justin and winked. "We do what we have to do for the women we love."

"Yeah, we do." Justin sneaked a glance at the glass floor under his feet and shuddered. Taking a deep breath, he turned and faced Sarina, moving to close the gap between them even more. He stopped when he was within arm's length of her. "I'm here to do what I need to do for the woman I love."

"Justin." She shook her head, refusing to let the hesitant bubble of elation in her belly cut loose. She'd been here before and nothing like this had ever worked for her. Sarina had opened herself up and hoped to be loved but it never worked out for her. She'd been that kid who'd allowed herself to hope that the next place she was sent would be the place where she was loved. But too many rejections in too many foster homes and the failure of her adoption had taught her that this wasn't for her. Not everyone got their happiness and that would have to be okay. So she couldn't let Justin's arrival raise her hopes again. She couldn't fall for it now. "What are you doing here? Didn't Adam give you the papers?"

Justin nodded, reaching into his back pocket and pulling out the mangled and folded envelope. He waved it in her face, his grin breaking through his panic over being on the Skywalk. "Got them."

"So what are you doing here? File them. Be done with it." Sarina shook her head, getting a little pissed off that they were even having this conversation. What had they been doing all these weeks if he was just going to walk around with the damn divorce papers in his pocket? "Justin, I don't know what's going on."

"I'm here to do this," he said, extracting the papers from the envelope and ripping them in half, and then in half again. He waved them at her and smiled. "I don't want a divorce."

Sarina shook her head, letting her anger break the surface and coat her words with the hurt and betrayal she'd carried with her since walking away from Justin at the winery.

"Well, I remember you saying something very different at the party. In fact, I think I remember you calling us *'a mistake.'*" She leveled a gaze at him intended to make sure that he would think twice about coming any closer. Tugging on Wilma's leash, she turned away from him and moved to exit the Skywalk. "This is your mistake walking away. Don't follow me. Don't contact me. Find a way to file those papers. Let me know when I'm cut loose from your ass. Have a nice life."

"Sarina, wait."

She kept walking. There was nothing Justin had to say to her that she wanted to hear.

"Sarina," Justin shouted, causing people to stop and turn to see the real-life drama playing out before them. Forget the Kardashians. The Redhawks and Lings were giving everybody a free show. "Sarina Redhawk, I want you to marry me."

Justin's voice carried, amplified by the slight echo created by the canyon. If anyone hadn't noticed their little scene yet, they were all riveted now. Conversations around them had dwindled down to murmured directions to be quiet and shushing sounds. She didn't want to marry him but she wanted to strangle him. Was that an option?

Sarina turned to face down her husband, who now stood only two feet away from her.

"What the hell are you talking about, Justin? Thanks to you ripping up the divorce papers, *we are still married.*"

"I know. I know," Justin said in a calming voice, his hand extended in a gesture calculated to soothe but producing the opposite result. She was so tired of the games and drama.

"No, you don't know anything," she said through gritted teeth. "We made a mistake and now we can fix it. You don't want me, you just don't like losing. You don't like the fact that your family was right about us. Let it go, Justin. Let me go." She swallowed hard, stifling the emotions that pressed against her chest bone and shot pain up and down her body. "I need to go. I stayed too long."

"No. Sarina. You need to stay. With me." Justin reduced the distance between them a little more; now he was close enough for her to see the deep brown of his eyes, smell the smoky citrus of his cologne. "I told my family everything. I told them that I don't want a divorce and that marrying you was the best thing I'd ever done in my life. I told them that I love you and that you are my life. They are warming up to the idea and they'll get there eventually. Or not." He shrugged. "But you have to know, Sarina, I would have walked away from all of them and straight to you if they had refused to accept us. I choose you. Every time."

"What about Aerospace Link and the tabloid story?"

"I told the Aerospace Link people everything. They are completely on board and they won't care about the story because they know the truth. But even if they didn't, it wouldn't matter. I choose you, Sarina. Every. Single. Time."

Oh damn. He was close enough for her to reach out to him. If she did that he'd pull her into his arms and kiss her and make her feel like she was finally in a place where she belonged. A place where she was wanted. A place where she was the chosen one.

If she kept listening, he'd convince her to stay.

But she couldn't stay. Staying meant giving other people the option to tell her she didn't belong or to move on without her. She needed to go. Now.

So why couldn't she move?

Justin took her hesitation as all the permission he needed to continue. "Sarina, baby, marry me. Again. For real this time. Marry me with our eyes wide open. Marry me knowing all of my faults. Marry me in spite of my fear of heights, my meddling grandmother and my love of poker." Justin took two steps forward, lifting his hand to cover his heart. "Marry me because you make me feel like I'm good enough for the first time in my life. Marry me because you make me want to be a better person. Marry me and let me love you. Marry me and be my family and I swear I will always be yours."

Sarina closed her eyes, trying to erase the echo of his words in her brain and the bubbling joy running though her veins. She just needed to go. She needed to grab Wilma and get on her bike and keep moving until she was free again.

"Justin," she said, opening her eyes and looking at him head-on. She cringed at the wobble in her voice, clearing her throat quickly in an attempt to cover up just how hard this was for her. She loved him. She just couldn't stay. "I have to go. You know that."

"You want to keep running, Sarina?" Justin asked, his eyes searching her face.

Okay. Truth time. "I don't know how to stop, Justin. If I stop…"

She searched for the words to explain the panic and fear that washed over her. Justin closed the distance between them completely, raising his hands to cup her face. His eyes were focused on hers and then he smiled. That ridiculously wolfish grin that lit up his whole face and made her feel like she was the center of his world. That grin promised excitement and joy and laughter and acceptance.

Justin saw her. Fears and all. Prickly defense mechanisms and all. Scars and all.

"Sarina, baby, I'm not asking you to stop running. I'm just asking that you run to me." He leaned in and brushed a kiss across her mouth. "I love you, Sarina. Run to me. I promise you I'll always be here."

Sarina reached for him, her arms wrapping around his waist as she leaned up into his kiss. Justin hesitated for the briefest moment and then he slanted his mouth over hers, deepening the kiss with a groan. His hands slid from her face into her hair and the tug to give him better access was possessive and hot. Justin tasted like sin and safety, danger and homecoming.

He was her home. She'd found it in his arms and she'd never let him go.

Justin broke off the kiss and smiled at her as he released her. She protested the separation but her frustration turned to confusion as he dug around in his pocket, withdrew a small box and then dropped to one knee at her feet. Around them the crowd stirred into a wave of murmurs and gasps of surprise, and more than one cell phone was lifted and pointed in their direction. Sarina didn't care; she was laser-focused on Justin.

And he was focused on her.

"We didn't get to do this the traditional way the first time. I won't say that we did it wrong because it brought us together. So it was perfect. But I want to leave no doubt in anyone's mind that you are the one that I choose and the one I love." Justin opened the box and removed the ring, a square-cut sapphire surrounded by diamonds, reached out and took her hand and placed it on her finger. It was heavy but in all the best ways possible. "Sarina Redhawk, will you marry me?"

She was scared, terrified. But for the first time in her life she was more afraid of letting someone go without a fight. One word was all that was needed to take the leap and have a shot at the dreams she'd given up on a long time ago. This man was worth the risk. His love was worth the risk.

"Yes."

"Thank you." Justin rose to his feet and pulled her back in his arms, the kiss passionate and filled with laughter. He nodded at the crowd surrounding them, waving to those who held their phones up to film the proposal. Wilma barked and jumped around at their feet, wagging her tail in excitement. "I love you, Sarina Redhawk."

"It's Sarina Redhawk *Ling*," she answered, pressing a kiss to his lips. "I love you, too."

"Let's go home," Justin said, holding her hand as they navigated the crowd on the Skywalk. It was slow going, with everyone congratulating them and bending over to pet Wilma. "Fair warning. Nana Orla wants a wedding. She said that we couldn't come home if we didn't agree to have another wedding."

Sarina laughed, looking forward to a life with Justin. It would never be boring. "I can do a wedding. But not in Vegas. This time we do it right."

Epilogue

One month later

He'd marry her a million times over. Anywhere she wanted.

Sarina had looked beyond stunning when she'd walked down the aisle toward him just a few hours earlier. Wearing a white jumpsuit with full legs, a halter-style top with a plunging neckline, and a transparent, filmy train attached to the waist, she was the most beautiful woman he'd ever seen. He couldn't say that she was breathtaking because his every inhale and exhale, every heartbeat—they were for Sarina. Hell, the reason he got up every morning and hurried home each night was because of her. His wife.

Nana Orla had taken over the planning of the wedding, running everyone and everything in her orbit with a precision that rivaled the military. Now Adam wanted to hire her to head up their project management division at Redhawk/Ling. Justin was all for it if it would stop her from making a plea for another great-grand-child at every opportunity. He wanted a family with Sarina, wanted to build with her a life where their children knew they were loved and were always enough. But they had time. A lifetime together to make those dreams come true.

And today they were surrounded by two hundred of their friends and family, on the grounds of his family home.

"Nana Orla sure knows how to throw a party. This is amazing," Adam said, easing up beside him and handing him a beer. It was pretty epic and the hottest invitation of the year. Justin's only requirement was that the wedding not be held in a stuffy hotel, so their two hundred guests were gathered under several tents, with the entire lawn and pool area covered in white roses and lilies. The best catering in Silicon Valley and a live band at the reception ensured that everybody on the guest list was having a good time. Socialites and business colleagues mixed and mingled with a few of the kids from the Rise Up Center and some of Sarina's army buddies. Even Wilma was dressed to the doggy nines in a Chihuahua-sized tux jacket and rhinestone collar.

Roan eased up next to the two of them, saluting them both with his drink. "I need to hire Nana Orla to handle my next gallery show. She's incredible."

"We couldn't have done this without her. And I was determined to make it official again with your sister as soon as I could." Justin turned and tapped his beer bottle against the one held by both his best friend and brother-in-law. They were family now. For real. "Thanks for pulling double duty today, brother."

"You bet," Adam laughed, wearing the light gray linen suit Justin had chosen for the wedding. "How many times has the best man also given away the bride?"

"It meant a lot to Sarina that you two were here to walk her down the aisle," Justin shared, knowing that it was a significant step for the Redhawk family to take together. Everything wasn't settled between them but they were all trying to replace the hard memories and the loss with new ones of love, and fun, and being together. Justin threw an arm around Adam's shoulders. "The next big event will be when your son makes an appearance. I can't believe you're going to be a daddy."

"I know, man. But I'm ready." Adam flashed the smile of a man who was happy and content as he looked over at where the bride stood with Tess. She was radiant in a gray silk dress, cut to highlight her pregnant belly. Sarina had been anxious to have Tess stand up with her at the wedding, given that there were just a few weeks left before her due date. All in all, it had been a family affair. "Are you two ready to be godfathers?"

Justin snorted out a laugh and shook his head, humbled by the request. "I hope you know that Sarina is the adult in this equation. I'm on tap to take him to get his first tattoo and pick up girls."

"Or boys," Roan added, winking at the two of them. "Why should he have to choose?"

"Truer words have never been spoken," Justin agreed, and Adam nodded his head in assent.

"I have to go to Washington, DC, next week but I'll be back in time to meet the newest Redhawk," Roan said, his smile definitely the one worn by the cat that ate the canary. "I've been summoned to the White House by President Irons to paint the official portrait of his daughter."

"Whoa. That's huge, little brother," Adam crowed, drawing the attention of several nearby guests. "How did you score that job?"

"How did you ever get cleared by the Secret Service?" Justin asked, acknowledging the raised middle finger of his brother-in-law with the salute of his beer bottle.

"President Irons is the first Native American president and he's determined to represent," Roan explained, flashing a shit-eating grin that made them all laugh. "*And* he picked the best of the bunch."

"And that's you?" Justin teased, unable to resist.

"Yeah, that's me," Roan answered, giving them both a big wink.

"Well done, Roan." Justin placed his beer bottle on a nearby table and patted both of the men on the back. "Gentlemen, I'm going to dance with my wife."

He waved off their teasing farewells, making a short detour to the band and putting in a request before sauntering over to where Sarina chatted with Nana Orla and Tess. He eased up behind her and looped his right arm around her waist, placing a kiss on the soft skin of her shoulder. She leaned back into him, her fingers linking with his as they molded their bodies together. It was like he could only take a full breath when he was with her, like he only stood as a complete man when she was by his side. How had he thought he was living all those years before Sarina?

"Nana Orla, can I steal my wife for a dance?" he

asked, smiling down at the woman who'd given a home to Sarina when she needed it the most. If he hadn't already loved his grandmother beyond reason, that would have sealed the deal.

Orla nodded, smiling at both of them as she reached up and placed a hand on his cheek. "Of course, my love. Go and dance with your best girl."

He shook his head. "Sarina and I agreed—she's the love of my life but *you'll* always be my best girl."

"Flatterer."

"It's not flattery if it's true." He pressed a kiss to her cheek and reached a hand out to his wife, still in awe that she was really his. "Sarina, dance with me?"

She smiled, an expression that lit up her entire face and made her dark eyes shine like onyx. Her raven-black hair was pulled back in a sleek ponytail, diamond earrings sparkling in her ears. A gift from his parents, they were a peace offering. It wasn't a perfect fix but it was a start.

"Forever," she murmured, stepping into his arms as the band started the slow-dance version of "Just One Look." The recognition of the song fueled joy on her face. They'd collaborated on a playlist but he'd secretly added all of her favorite Linda Ronstadt songs as a surprise. "Thank you for this."

"I wanted your mom—both of your parents—to be here with you today." Justin leaned in to press a kiss to the end of her nose, pretending not to see the sheen of tears in her eyes. "I know you wish they could be here."

"They're here, Justin," Sarina said, conviction in her voice. "I've felt them with me all day. How could they not be here when I'm so happy?"

"I promise you that I will spend the rest of my life

making sure you're this happy every day," Justin said, soaking in her smile. "I love you, Sarina."

"I love you too, Justin." Sarina kissed him, long and sweet, the smile on her mouth a promise of forever. "Thank you for loving me, for being my family."

* * * * *

TWICE THE
TEMPTATION

SILVER JAMES

Dedicated to the weathermen I watched on TV growing up—Jim and Gary—and to "Tornado" Payne and his weather crew at "Oklahoma's Own," and to all the storm chasers in central Oklahoma. Your efforts and expertise keep us safe, so here's a big shout-out and thank-you!

One

Cooper Tate was a man comfortable in his own skin. He might be the chief operating officer of a billion-dollar oil and gas company, but he was far more likely to be found in jeans and a T-shirt working alongside his crews in the oil patch than in the boardroom. He left the fancy duds to his cousin, Cord Barron, the CEO of Barron Explorations. To Coop's mind, the key word in his COO title was *Operations*. If he couldn't do all that stuff out in the field, he shouldn't be the one in charge.

Now, as the winds of a Category 4 hurricane roared around him, he might have to rethink that stance. Living in Oklahoma, he was used to the wind sweeping down the plains, but this? He'd take a tornado over a hurricane any time.

The huge crew-cab he drove shuddered under the wind's onslaught. The windshield wipers couldn't keep up with the downpour. Two more miles. He only had two more miles before reaching the Beaumont field office of BarEx. He'd be safe from the storm there. He hoped.

After what seemed like a century, but in reality was only about twenty minutes, Coop pulled into the parking lot. The building was the only one with lights, which meant the emergency generator had kicked on when the area lost power. After a series of strong hurricanes, Cord had rebuilt the field offices all along the Gulf Coast. All of them were supposed to stand up to a Category 5 hurricane. All of them had emergency generators that ran on natural gas straight from the company's own pipelines. He'd tried to convince the skeleton crew that stuck around to help him shut down the rigs to stay at the office but they'd all gone to their own homes, wanting to protect their families and property.

He caught a break in the rainbands and used it to lock up his truck and dash around the building. All the hurricane shutters were secure. The roof looked intact, and all the outbuildings appeared to be holding their own. He was as secure as he could be until Lolita decided she'd had enough of south Texas and moved on. Locking and bolting the main door, he settled in for a long, lonely wait. Yeah, he was a wuss. Storms weren't his thing. Never had been, not since he was caught out in a severe thunderstorm that turned tornadic when he was a kid.

Pushing that memory to the back of his mind, Coop checked the interior. Supplies lined the walls of the workshop, all up on stacked pallets just in case floodwaters breached the outer doors. The refrigerator hummed along nicely, and all the lights worked, along with the microwave, industrial-size coffeemaker, and the small gas range in the kitchenette adjacent to the break room. He started a pot of coffee and snagged a cold bottle of water from the fridge. Dropping onto a couch, he clicked on the big-screen TV mounted to the wall.

All the local and cable news channels were running wall-to-wall storm coverage. He considered shoving a DVD into the player or checking one of the cable movie channels but stopped when one of the reports focused on Beaumont.

"Water continues to rise—" Wind whipped the reporter's words away as he leaned into the gale. "Expecting hundreds of rescues—" The picture froze, then pixelated before the telecast returned to the in-studio hosts. "We've lost our feed…"

Hundreds of rescues? That would depend on a lot of factors. Would levees hold? Had people evacuated? He doubted many of them had. Lolita's path had wobbled and then made a hard right, heading straight for Beaumont, instead of farther down the coast around Houston. Houston had been ready, mandatory evacuations in force for days. Beaumont? Not so much. Most people were probably sheltering in place. Some might have made it to one of the approved shelters. He hoped there weren't many who'd been caught in the inevitable traffic jams headed out of town. With only one interstate, and that one running basically east and west, there weren't many ways out. Plus, a lot of the evacuees from Houston had come to Beaumont.

The wind screamed around the building, raising goose bumps on his skin. "Not a tornado," he reminded himself. Uneasy, despite his attempts to reassure himself, he paced the room, continuously clicking through channels. The electronic alert from the weather radio on a nearby table made his heart race. The computerized voice advised everyone to shelter in place, reminded them that when the eye hit, to stay put, and that the storm swell would send Lake Sabine and connecting bayous to 500-year-flood levels. Beaumont was about twenty miles from the Gulf Coast, but lakes and bayous peppered the area.

Rain beat on the roof like rolling thunder and the wind continued to howl. He grabbed a cup of coffee, hoping the caffeine would steady his nerves. Weather was so not his thing. "Not afraid," he muttered. "Just cautious. There's a difference." Except his brothers still teased him. Well, that was their problem, right? They hadn't been out on horseback that day. They hadn't had to hunker down in the caved-in root cellar of an abandoned cabin. And they hadn't lost their favorite horse during the tornado.

Morose now, he clicked through the movie channels until he found one with car chases and explosions. Cooper turned up the volume in a vain attempt to drown out the storm.

"This is Britt Owens, reporting live from Beaumont, Texas, for KOCX, Oklahoma's Original." Britt signed off from the live telecast then reached to turn off the camera. Her cameraman and chase assistant, Leo, was in the hospital, having been beaned by a flying trash can earlier that day. That the former football lineman could be leveled so easily was a shock. She'd wanted to call off the live updates but the station back in Oklahoma City had overruled her.

She broke down the camera and tripod, stuffing them into her storm chaser's truck. She hadn't planned on growing up to be an adrenaline junkie but after surviving an Oklahoma tornado as a kid, she'd set her sights on becoming a meteorologist. Her original goal had been to work in the lab with computers. Her bank account and student loans had other ideas. Which was why she was currently in this predicament.

Britt hadn't volunteered for hurricane duty. Yes, they were amazing weather phenomena, but tornadoes were what got her pulse racing. And even though hurricanes spawned tornadoes on the leading edge, she was stuck covering the eye of the storm since the station paid the bills. Secretly, she wanted to be the one naming storms, not that she held a grudge and would use the names of people she didn't get along with for inspiration.

The wind blasted around the corner, sending her slamming into the side of her truck. *Ouch*. That would leave a bruise.

The intensifying storm had jumped from a Category 3 to Category 4 in an hour and the rainbands now swept in faster and faster. Time to take shelter. As soon as she edged her truck out into the main force of the wind, the big vehicle shuddered. She glanced at the weather instruments panel. As winds currently topped out at 137 miles per hour, shelter had become a necessity. Between rain and darkness, she could barely see the road. Debris passed on both sides. The truck, set up for storm chasing, had all sorts of computronics and instruments. It was big, with shatterproof glass and run-flat tires—all important for getting her through this in one piece.

She should have stayed at the hospital after dropping off Leo. Too bad her curiosity and the urging of the senior meteorologist back home overrode her logical brain, feeding into her inner adrenaline junkie. The wheel jerked in her hands and the truck hydroplaned. She fought for control, and managed to keep the vehicle on the road, pointed in the right direction. No way would she make it to the hotel. Or the emergency operations center in the basement of city hall.

A light gleamed through the sheets of water pounding her windshield. Someone had power? Maybe it was a fire station. She headed for the light, suppressing the spasm threatening to lock her muscles. A huge black blob appeared in her peripheral vision. She slammed on the brakes; the truck fishtailed and finally stopped. Once the world quit spinning, she discovered she could still breathe, once she remembered how.

Britt was *not* going to die. Not tonight.

A steady *thump thump thump*, sounding like his heartbeat echoing in Cooper's ears, was a bass drum to the wailing wind. The sound came again. He hoped none of the shutters had come loose. Then he froze. Was that a voice? He held his breath, listening hard after clicking mute on the TV.

Thump thump thump. "Is anybody here? Let me in!"

He set the coffee cup down so hard it sloshed and then he was sprinting for the front door. He didn't hesitate to unlock and yank off the brace bar to wrestle the door open. A woman stumbled into him, and he automatically wrapped his arms around her to steady her. He had to lean into her, fighting the wind to get the door closed and secured again. Once that was done, he discovered he'd pressed her back against the door.

He held his breath, aware that his body liked her—rain-soaked clothes and all—pressing against him. Yeah, parts of him seemed a little *too* happy about their position. He loosened his arms, but she didn't move. Her arms remained wrapped around his waist. He cleared his throat. She still didn't move.

"Ah, miss?"

She raised her head, clocking him on the chin.

"Ow!"

"Oh! Sorry!" She let go but couldn't back up due to the door behind her.

Cooper stepped away, rubbing his chin. "No problem but, darlin', I gotta ask, what the devil are you doin' out in this?"

The woman scrubbed at her face. "My job." Oddly, her statement sounded more like a question.

"Bad night for it."

"Definitely." She glanced at a reception area. "I'm... confused. You aren't trying to stay open or something, are you?"

"Nope. Temporary shelter. This place can withstand a Category 5 and has a generator. I'm hunkered down here for the duration."

She inhaled, waiting a long moment before exhaling. "Well, I'm glad you are. I wouldn't have lasted out there much longer." She stuck out her hand. "Britt Owens."

"Cooper Tate." He wrapped his hand around hers, very aware how his rough callouses scraped against the soft skin of her palm. Then he realized she was shivering. "Let me get you some dry clothes. And food. Coffee. Or hot tea. Got both."

He ushered her to the break room where he dug out a pair of sweats and a T-shirt from his duffel bag. Pointing toward the bathroom, he said, "You can change in there."

When Britt came out, Cooper pretended he didn't appreciate the way she looked in his clothes, nor did he acknowledge the buzz of possessiveness that filled him. Nope. Not at all. Something crashed outside and they both jumped, which jerked him back to reality in a heartbeat.

They ate sandwiches mostly in silence, though she explained she was in Beaumont to cover the storm for a TV station. When she yawned, Coop suggested they try to sleep. "There's an air mattress in the office down the hall. You can sleep there. I'll bunk on the couch."

Britt eyed the couch, gave him a once-over and rolled her eyes. "Yeah, like you'll fit."

"Not gonna argue, darlin'. My momma raised me to be a gentleman."

Elbow planted on the table, she leaned into her palm. Her eyes were brown, he realized as he got a good look at her. And they were flecked with a shade of gold close to the color of her hair. Her face, an almost perfect oval, was pale and drawn, dark circles marring her skin. Her full lips, even as they drooped with exhaustion, ignited an urge to kiss them. He resisted because she looked worn out. He brushed a tendril of hair off her face and whispered, "C'mon, weather girl. Let's get you to bed."

She followed him to the office he used when in town.

A thick air mattress, almost the height of an actual bed, sprawled in the open space between door and desk. It even had sheets and pillows. He grabbed a pillow and turned to leave. Britt blocked the door. Coop arched a brow, confused.

"Stay." She sounded insistent.

"Not a good idea—" he began before she cut him off with a breathy, "With me."

Oh, yeah. He wanted to do that. Which made it a really bad idea. "Look, Britt…"

She fumbled with the hem of the T-shirt she wore, twisting it in her fingers before she huffed out a breath, as if she'd made up her mind. She met his gaze. "I don't want to sleep alone. Okay?"

She was adamant, despite the nervous movement of her fingers, and she sounded almost angry. Honestly? Coop didn't want to sleep alone either. Which made him feel like a big ol' wuss but those were the breaks. Curious about her reasons, he asked. "Why?"

"Why what?"

"Why do you want to sleep with me?"

She blinked at him several times before a speculative look slid across her features. "Why not? You're a good-lookin' guy. I'm not exactly coyote ugly—"

That startled a burst of laughter from him. She was definitely not ugly. Her face suffused with color as her eyes narrowed and her lips thinned out. "Go ahead and laugh but…dang it!" She threw her hands up, beginning to pace the narrow confines of the office. "I watched my cameraman get slammed by flying debris today. He's in the hospital. He could have died. I've reported the death toll and that number is only going to rise before this witch of a storm goes away. People have lost everything. Eve…ry…thing."

She stopped right in front of him. "People have died." Her voice fell to a husky whisper, the edges still sharp-ened by anger. And fear. "There's so much bad out there tonight. Is it wrong that I want something good? That I want to feel strong arms around me? To be kissed? To…" Her voice trailed off, her cheeks no longer pink as reality seeped back into her.

"I'm…scared, okay?"

His hand caught the back of her neck and tugged her against him. "I'm scared too, Britt." Coop wasn't sure why he could admit that to a stranger—no, not a stranger. To her. To Britt. She rested her forehead against his chest and her arms circled his waist.

"I'm not crazy. I'm not a… I don't go pick up random men and proposition them."

"Shh. Didn't think you did."

"Just so you know." She was nothing if not persistent. Cooper smiled into her hair. Strands of the blond silk caught in his scruff as she tilted her head back to look up at him. "I just want to feel something…real. Something life-affirming."

Cooper didn't answer—not with words, anyway. He lowered his head, capturing her mouth. She tasted of grape jelly and peanut butter, and he swore that would be his favorite flavor from now on.

Britt leaned against him, her mouth and body softening. He deepened the kiss, taking her mouth with an urgency that swelled up from deep inside. Keeping one hand on her nape to guide the kiss, he skimmed the other over her back before cupping her rounded curves. He pressed her against his erection and she purred.

"Yes."

"Are you sure?"

"I want this. Want you."

That's all the permission he needed. He walked her to the bed and eased her down before joining her. He used both hands to touch her, slipping them under the T-shirt—

his shirt—to trace her smooth skin before divesting her clothes. As his hands roamed, hers weren't idle, stripping off the shirt he wore before working on his belt and zipper. He pushed her hands away, and sat up to kick off his boots and jeans. He stretched out beside her, and her hands traced his abs before seeking out more private parts. Tentative fingers gripped him, and he sucked in air.

"Britt." He needed to slow down, keep his wits.

"Please?" Her whisper teased his skin. "I want this. You want it. We're alive. Let's celebrate."

The wind screamed around the building and the roof rattled, adding an exclamation—and urgency—to her words. The small part of his brain that could still think admitted she could be right. He caressed her breast as she squeezed him. His hips pumped into her hands.

"Britt." Her name was now a plea. As his free hand sought her core, finding her hot and wet, his conscience jabbed him. Condom. Swiftly, he rolled them over and he fumbled along the floor searching for his jeans and the wallet in his back pocket. He found it and the foil packet tucked inside. She arched against him and his body went on autopilot, reacting to her desire. She moaned, hips pumping against his groin. She was hot and ready for him. Condom on, her body open to him, he slid inside her, catching her soft gasp with a kiss.

Something crashed and the building shook. Britt's nails dug into his shoulders. "Hurry," she demanded, as if the end of the world was imminent. Maybe it was, if the racket outside was any indication.

Adrenaline demanded he take this woman hard and fast. The urgent noises she made indicated she wanted the same, but something coiled inside him, holding him back, something that turned the hunger for frenetic sex into a craving to make love. If there was no tomorrow, he wanted to go out surrounded by the sweetness that was Britt Owens.

As if attuned to his thoughts, she gentled beneath him, met his slow thrusts with a whispered, "Yes."

He touched her, exploring curves and skin, hair and mouth, all while he continued rocking into her, rousing them both to higher levels of passion until they both crested and tumbled into the exhaustion that lurked in the dark.

Cooper pulled Britt into his arms, and they drifted off to sleep, the sound of the howling wind a terrible lullaby.

Two

Coop rolled over expecting a warm body but found only cold sheets. Sitting up, he scrubbed the heels of his hands over his face, thinking hard. The eye of the storm had hit about 3:00 a.m., followed by more rainbands. He vaguely remembered Britt getting up…when? Around dawn, maybe? He fumbled for his phone, read the digital numbers. Seven eleven. Too bad he wasn't in Vegas on the floor of Barron Crown Casino.

He pushed off the air mattress, found his feet and went in search of his guest. She was gone, but Gilbert Guidry, the senior toolpusher for BarEx's south Texas operations and Cajun to the soles of his boots, occupied a seat at the table, a cup of hot coffee in front of him.

"You lookin' for that pretty little *fille*?"

Cooper nodded.

"She let me in, told me to tell you she had to go be on television, and thanks." Gil pushed back from the table, fetched a cup of coffee and pressed it into Cooper's hands. "You look like you need some of this. Drink up."

Following orders, Coop did just that, wondering why it bothered him so much that Britt bailed on him. It wasn't like they had a relationship. Or anything. But still.

"You gonna put some clothes on, boss? The boat's on my truck and we're gonna be needed to help with the rescues."

True that.

A brutal eighteen hours later, Coop and Gil were headed back to the rescue command post set up for this part of town. Exhausted, hungry and desperately craving dry clothes, Coop was lost in his thoughts.

"Hello?"

Was that a voice? He cut the engine and let the boat drift.

"Somebody out there?" Gil called.

"Help! Over here." A husky—and vaguely familiar— female voice that held only a hint of panic called out.

As the boat floated toward the sound, Coop saw a light waving frantically. "We be comin', *cher*!" the toolpusher yelled.

Coop started the engine, easing the throttle. In the dark, they couldn't see what lay hidden beneath the murky water. He steered gingerly around a corner, hoping there wasn't a submerged street sign that would take out the propeller, and discovered an extended cab pickup with only six inches of window and roof showing above the rising water. Three women, two children, two dogs and a drenched cat huddled on top.

The woman with the flashlight—and familiar shape— shouted instructions. "My truck is in the middle of the street. To my right, there's a compact car submerged. My left should have a space clear enough to bring your boat alongside."

All traces of panic fled as Britt took charge. Coop

pressed his lips together to hide his grin. She wore a yellow slicker with reflective tape and as she turned, he caught the emblem and writing on the back. His storm chaser worked for his cousin's TV station. Her wet hair was pulled back in a ponytail but long tendrils had worked free to plaster against her cheeks. He recognized the jut of her chin, the rounded cheeks and the determined set of her shoulders. He liked women with attitude and Britt had it in spades.

Britt handed her flashlight to a boy of about twelve and dropped to one knee to help guide the boat. Gil helped the children and dogs into the boat, then the women. Only the cat refused to move. While Gil handed out blankets, Coop considered the situation. He was not a cat guy but even he couldn't leave it to drown. The creature was big, black, with glowing yellow eyes, and it looked like it could take on a gator. He glared at the cat. It glared back.

"I can leave you for gator bait, or you can get in the boat," he said, challenging the cat. "Your choice."

His storm chaser snorted. "You really think talking like that to a cat is going to work?"

"You're more than welcome to reach over and grab the thing, weather girl," he shot back. "Last chance, cat." He waited a few seconds then placed his hand on the truck's roof and pushed off. Before he could react, the cat was climbing his arm like it was a tree, then scurrying down his back to settle in the space beneath his seat at the back of the boat.

"Huh," Britt said. "I'm impressed."

So was he, even more than the previous night when she'd fallen asleep in his arms.

After several live broadcasts, Britt jumped in to help with rescuing people and now had resigned herself to spending the night huddled atop her truck with the family she'd rescued. The roof didn't offer much room for humans or furry critters and it would have been miserable out there. Then she'd heard the growly putt-putt of a small outboard engine. Thank the weather gods for a hot guy who could out-attitude a cat. The cat hadn't been part of the original rescue. It swam over and climbed aboard after the wall of water washed down the street taking Britt by surprise and they'd all climbed to the roof. It had ignored the fat Corgi and the gentle Lab mix sharing the roof with it.

She didn't want to consider the thoughts a very hot and sexy Cooper put into her head. His looks hadn't changed since the last time she'd seen him, asleep on that air mattress barely covered by a rumpled sheet. He was in his mid-thirties, at least six feet tall, hair almost too long hidden beneath a baseball cap, broad shoulders and chest and those long, competent fingers on the boat's tiller—fingers that had done all sorts of delicious things to her body the previous night. Top it all off with blue eyes, high cheekbones, strong jaw and full lips that showed he laughed. A lot. She liked a man who laughed.

One of the kids started to fuss and Britt reached for the little girl reflexively. Her hand collided with a brawny arm. Cooper scooped up the child and settled her on one thigh. "Can you help me steer, darlin'?"

It was like he'd thrown a switch. The toddler snuggled in, tears and fussing over, as a shy smile wreathed her cherubic face.

"There anybody left back in that neighborhood?" The man who'd introduced himself as Gilbert when she'd let him into the offices that morning gestured behind the boat.

Britt lifted a shoulder in an I'm-not-sure gesture. "I heard a call go out on the scanner about a family of three who were trapped by the rising water. They didn't have a car. I wasn't far away and my truck is—" She glanced back over her shoulder. "My truck *was* four-wheel drive and customized to work in storm areas. I loaded up Becca, the kids and their dog. On the way out, we saw Mrs. Gonzales. I grabbed her and George—" She pointed to the Corgi. "We got about three blocks. I knew the water was rising but I still had clearance and then four feet of water rolled down the street."

"Yeah, that's when the levee got breached. Gotta say, *cher*, didn't expect to meet you again so soon."

"Have storm, will travel," she quipped. "Thanks for the rescue."

"You're welcome." It was Cooper who replied, and he sounded just a bit…miffed. Maybe she should have woken him up to say goodbye but hey…she wasn't good at those awkward morning afters, especially since she'd been the one to throw herself at the guy.

What had she been thinking? Oh, right. She hadn't been thinking at all, running strictly on adrenaline and the very real fear that she might not see another day. That was her story and she'd stick to it. No need to mention she was also a little embarrassed by her actions but wow. What a man to fall into bed with, regardless of the circumstances!

The puttering engine filled the silence, but Gilbert was all about asking questions. In the space of the short boat ride, she learned that Becca's husband was in the National Guard and he'd been activated, thinking they'd be safe. Mrs. Gonzales was a widow, living alone with her chubby Corgi for companionship, her kids spread across Texas. Britt hoped at least a couple of those adult children would come help their mother.

Now that they were almost safe, Britt itched to get to a computer so she could study the storm models and radar. This hurricane was a thousand-year storm. She'd saved her laptop from the flood, but it wasn't up to the task.

It wasn't long before they floated around a corner and the water glistened with lights. First responder vehicles, red-and-blue LED lights flickering, the white glare of search-

lights, and the sweeping beams of high-powered flashlights
lit up the night, reminding her a bit of the Las Vegas Strip.
Their appearance was met with cheers.

Cooper cut the boat's motor as men in chest waders
guided them in until the bottom of the boat scraped against
the street pavement. Firefighters and EMTs swarmed, picking up the kids and assisting the women. One burly cop
scooped up George and followed behind Mrs. Gonzales,
assuring her that her dog was fine as the larger Lab waded
to higher ground unaided. A game warden offered his hand
to help Britt steady herself as she stepped out of the boat.

She scooted out of the way as Gil clambered out and
headed toward a big white truck with a boat trailer. Cooper
stayed in the boat, conversing with the man Britt guessed
was the incident commander.

"No," she heard Coop say. "Gil and I didn't find anyone so I doubt anyone is left. Ms. Owens had this group in
her truck and got caught in the backwash from the levee
break." He removed his ball cap and scrubbed one hand
over his face. His dark stubble glinted with a hint of au-
burn. He looked tired and she wondered how many rescues
he and Gil had made.

The truck backed the trailer into the water and with expertise, Cooper guided the boat onto it. He climbed out,
securing boat to trailer, and then walked beside it as Gil
pulled away. A frenetic yowl caught everyone's attention.
Malevolent yellow eyes glowered from an ink-black face.
Cooper's gaze fell on her and she held her hands out in a
no-clue gesture.

"The thing swam up and climbed on the roof of my
truck," she explained.

Someone growled and she wasn't sure if it was cat or
man. The two ended up in a stare-down. The cat blinked
first. Britt was totally impressed. He continued to stare
down the cat. "You gonna ride in the dang boat all night?"

She fought a laugh as the cat sprang from the boat, landed on Cooper's shoulder and hissed at anyone who came close. She knew just how the cat felt. She was even jealous of the darn thing because it was touching him. And yes, she was totally whacked. "Sleep deprivation," she muttered under her breath. As the men turned to walk away, she called, "Can I hitch a ride?"

Cooper glanced back at her and she had to suppress a shiver that had nothing to do with being wet or cold. *Nope.* The expression in his eyes warmed her from the inside out and she couldn't help but remember why she hadn't slept much the previous night.

"You want a ride?" His voice was like gravel rattling around in a velvet bag and his gaze was so intense she wondered if he had X-ray vision and could see that she'd gone commando that morning. She had to clear her throat before she could reply.

"Uh, yeah. That's why I asked. My truck's out of commission." She gave him a hopeful look. "I can still help. Besides, I don't have any place to go."

He'd rescued her more than once, and she felt as much a stray as the cat. Was he willing to offer her shelter again? She caught herself leaning toward him and straightened, which took far more effort than it should have.

"So," he drawled. "You want to help out?"

Yes, she wanted to help him out—help him out of those wet jeans that molded to his muscular thighs. Memories of their night together flooded her and she wet her lips without considering the consequences—like his gaze turning molten as his eyes fixed on her mouth. A crooked grin quirked the corner of his mouth, right before he deflated her hopes.

"Fine. You can cat sit." He reached up, peeled the angry feline off his shoulder and placed it in her arms. He strode off, leaving her scrambling to catch up. Gil had the back door of the extended cab F-250 Ford open and he offered her a hand. Even with her long legs, it was a big step up into the back seat.

The cat scrambled out of her arms and settled next to the far door. It then began to thoroughly lick itself, ignoring the humans. Cooper climbed into the driver's seat, Gil in the passenger's. "Where're we goin' to, boss?"

"Your house."

The drive didn't take too long despite detours for flooded streets. Cooper kept glancing at Britt through the rearview mirror and smiled when she fell asleep. When they arrived at Gil's house, he slipped out of the truck with Coop's whispered instructions. "Get some sleep, Gil."

The man tossed him a roguish grin. "I be tellin' you the same thing, boss." He glanced into the back seat where Britt slept soundly. "You take that little gal home and you go to bed." Then Gil laughed softly, the sound slightly bawdy like he knew what Coop was thinking. Then he winked and stalked toward his wife, who was waiting for him on the porch.

Coop considered waking Britt enough to move her to the front seat then left her alone. They were both running on fumes and he'd learned that you grabbed sleep whenever and wherever you could in an emergency. Luckily, Gil didn't live far from Barron Exploration Beaumont. When he pulled up to park at the field office, he was happy to see the large RV parked in the lot. Cord had come through for him by getting the RV delivered. It was far more comfortable than the air mattress in the break room. He climbed out and nudged Britt.

"Let's go, Girl Wonder."

Piercing yellow eyes glowered at him from the floorboards. Coop peered at the cat. The animal bared his fangs. "Got the feeling you're a devil cat. Guess I should call you

Lucifer." The darn thing purred at him, the rumble so deep it sounded like a diesel engine. He laughed, which startled Britt awake.

She stared up at him with bleary eyes. "What's so funny?"

"Lucifer."

Her forehead crinkled and she looked so cutely confused, Coop was tempted to drop a kiss between her eyebrows. "Who?"

"The cat."

"Oh. What happens if it turns out to be a Lucy instead?"

He laughed again. "I wouldn't be surprised, with all that attitude. Serious diva territory."

Britt stirred, pushing stray strands of hair off her face, blinking the sleep from her fuzzy expression. "Where are we?"

"Home, sweet home. At least for the duration."

Britt gave him the fisheye and he fought not to laugh. "I have a hotel room calling my name."

"One without electricity. My RV has lights, air conditioning and indoor plumbing."

"You have a point." She gripped his proffered hand to climb out. "Whoa!" She jerked and all but fell into his arms as the cat bolted across her shoulders and leapt to the ground.

Coop couldn't help the smile tugging the corners of his mouth upward. She was an armful and he liked the feel of her next to him. Liked it a whole lot. She rubbed her eyes and gazed around. "What's that?"

"My RV."

She gave an appreciative whistle. "That's not just an RV. That's the Plaza Hotel of RVs."

Coop led her over and opened the motor home's door, standing back so she could enter first. She stopped dead. He looked over her shoulder, wondering why she wasn't moving. He propelled her forward. "Showers. We need them. Then sleep, yeah?"

"Shower?" Britt's eyes drooped and she looked completely exhausted.

"Right," Coop muttered. He nudged her to the bathroom—and its full-sized shower. "You should grab the first shower and then hit the sack."

"Uh-huh."

"Britt?"

She shook herself and glanced up at him. "Right. Shower." Glancing around, her gaze met his. They were both exhausted—and stank of bayou. Shower. Sleep. And tomorrow? Yeah, he'd do all the things he'd planned to do with her the previous morning, only to discover she'd skipped out on him.

"Do you need help?"

"Maybe." She sighed. "Okay, probably."

He stripped them both down, with far less attention to detail than he would have liked. He turned on the water and ushered her into the shower.

Britt was so tired she barely acknowledge the hands soaping her body. This could have been a lot of fun if she'd been alert and less exhausted because really? Cooper was a dream man.

She swayed a little on her feet. The next thing she knew, she was wrapped in a towel and on the bed. Cooper stood, a towel riding low on his hips, with his back to her. *Oh, boy.* Too bad she couldn't keep her eyes open.

"Big bed," she hinted, then yawned hugely.

"It is," he agreed. He pulled the covers over her and she thought the gesture was sweet. He slipped in beside her and she stiffened. With Cooper's very hard body next to her, she couldn't fall asleep. Then he snored softly. Britt relaxed, right into a deep sleep.

When Britt woke up, she kept her eyes closed. Controlling her breathing, she listened. She didn't remember where she was. Stiff, sore, still tired, with a headache nudging at the edge of her consciousness, she assessed her situation. Soft bed. Light filtering in through blinds. Warm body at her back. Muscular arm draped over her.

"Mornin', Girl Wonder."

Cooper. His voice sleep-roughened and as sexy as that hard length pressing against her butt. She was in so much trouble now, thanks to the happy dance her libido was doing. Clearing her throat, she mumbled, "Still sleeping."

His body shook from laughter. Which translated into her body feeling things that made her want to turn, cup the man's face and kiss him. With tongue. Despite morning mouth. What was wrong with her?

But the scent of this man and the warmth of his chest pressing against her back, the weight of his arm over her waist? Her mind was going there for sure. Then his lips nuzzled the back of her neck and she surrendered. Sort of. She had one tiny bit of fight left. "Are you trying to seduce me?"

His lips brushed across the shell of her ear. "Trying? No. I *am* seducing you. Is it working?"

Cocky man. She squirmed a little and his arm loosened just enough that the hand cupping her hip could propel her over onto her back. She gazed up at him, with his amazing blue eyes and a few days' worth of stubble roughening his face. His lips were perfect—like an artist drew them. His brown hair showed hints of red where the sun caught it.

His fingertips stroked across her cheekbone before tracing her jaw. His gaze was focused on her mouth. "Yeah," he breathed. "Definitely working." Then he kissed her. Like he meant it. Lips and teeth and tongue. Searching, nipping, thrusting. Her heart rate kicked up and she melted against his bare chest.

Cooper chuckled against her mouth and she got a wild mental picture of his lips kissing another part of her body and what his laughter would feel like there. Need and desire welled up inside her. The leash she normally kept on her control snapped. She hooked one leg over his thighs and pulled, making space for his hips between her legs. She rubbed against the hard length of his erection and threw caution to the wind. She'd seen so much destruction, the devastation created by both hurricane and flooding leaving people in desperate straits. She wanted another reminder that there was life and laughter and love. Right now, she just wanted to be a woman. Not a storm chaser. Not a weather reporter. Just a woman in the arms of a sexy man.

"Are we doin' this, Girl Wonder?" Cooper stared down at her, his body relaxed, his expression curiously hopeful.

"What happens if I say no?"

"I take a shower that will leave plenty of hot water for you. And if the cold shower doesn't work, I'll take care of business while I'm in there."

"Business?" she mused. "Do you consider this business?"

"No, ma'am. This…" He waved a hand between the two of them. "Is strictly pleasure. If *I* take care of things, then it becomes business."

"Ah." She strained to reach his mouth. He obliged by meeting her halfway. "Yeah," she whispered. "We're doin' this, Hero Boy."

"I'm not a boy." His hand cupped her beneath the sheet.

"And I'm not—" Her breath rushed out as he tweaked her nipple. "A girl."

He pushed the sheet down and a slow grin curled the corners of his perfect mouth as his eyes crinkled. "I can see that."

A moment later, he was all over her—touching, cupping, teasing, kissing. His hands were work-roughened but not abrasive. A man with a manicure had never been her catnip. Cooper worked with his hands and she was definitely enjoying the way they worked her. Blunt fingers teased between her thighs, finding her already slick and ready. *This guy is not for you*, a little voice insisted. *It's bad for business. You need to get your tail in gear and get gone.* As his fingers teased her, she tuned out the voice. She wanted this. Him. For now, anyway. She pushed her hand between their bodies and latched onto his erection. He groaned into her mouth as his hand patted the small table next to the bed.

"Dammit, I know there's one in here somewhere," he muttered. "Gotta be."

Britt wondered what he was looking for when he let out a growl of triumph and she heard the sound of foil tearing. *Condom.* Good to know one of them was thinking.

When Coop rolled over to get the condom on, she noticed a deep scar running across his right thigh. Precaution in place, he started up where he left off—one hand stroking between her legs and his mouth taking her breast like he was starving and she was his favorite meal. He pulled away and looked into her eyes.

"Are you sure, Britt?"

No teasing now, because this much pleasure was serious business. "Yes."

She spread her knees as he rolled on top of her, bracing his upper body on his elbows and forearms. "Never thought I'd pull something so perfect from the flood," he murmured, dipping to kiss her again as he pushed inside.

Britt drew in a shuddering breath. Cooper did the same, then buried his face against her neck and exhaled. The previous night, they'd gone at it hot and heavy, but this? This was so much better. She clamped down on him as he thrust and withdrew, the friction of skin against skin igniting an astonishing awareness. Desire washed through her, seeking out every nerve and every cell of her body until she thought she would burn up.

Her thoughts scattered as sensation took over. Too difficult to think, or do anything but feel the hard length of him filling her. It was all so intense she couldn't form words, only make tiny noises as she spiraled up and up, reaching for something so profound, so all-consuming that she wanted to scream.

Braced on one arm, Cooper found the one spot that would release her frenzy with his fingertips. Moments later, her whole body arched off the bed and he caught her scream in his mouth as he kissed her with the same intensity. She held him tightly, fingers clutching, holding on. He thrust again and again, and then he groaned his own release and she felt him throb inside her.

He lay on top of her, spent, for several long minutes. Britt didn't care because breathing didn't seem all that important. The heat and feel of this man? Yeah, now that seemed crucial to her current well-being.

When he eventually rolled away, after a long and thorough kiss, she turned onto her side, hand tucked under her cheek. Eyelids heavy, she closed them until the bed shifted. With a yawn, she opened her eyes to focus on a very fine butt headed to the bathroom. A moment later, the shower kicked on. She found her watch and squawked. It was way past time to skedaddle. But she didn't have a vehicle and would have to wait on Cooper. Or find someone else to drive her back to the hotel.

Throwing on her clothes, she headed outside and found a small miracle—another storm team from Channel 2.

She plastered on a big smile and breezed toward where they stood talking to Gil. "Hi, guys. Time to go."

Three

Three months. He'd nursed his resentment for three months and there, standing across the ballroom, was the whole reason he refused to let bygones be bygones. Cooper hadn't wanted to come to this cocktail schmooze-fest billed as a fund-raiser for the University of Oklahoma School of Meteorology mobile tornado lab in the first place. Now, he wanted nothing more than to get out of the tuxedo and black tie his mother had forced him to wear. He and his six brothers might all be grown—well, except maybe Dillon, the baby of the family—but when Katherine Barron Tate arched a brow, her boys came to heel without a bark.

So here he stood, a watered-down whiskey in his hand, smiling politely at a weather geek waxing poetic about the revised Fujita scale and the need for more funding for research. Inside, Cooper was glowering at the beautiful blonde dressed in a sexy blue gown and surrounded by a herd of adoring sycophants. Yeah, so what if that was the word of the day on his secretary's desk calendar. It fit perfectly. Dragging his gaze away from the woman who'd starred in far more dreams than he cared to admit, he scanned the crowd for his mother. Locating her, he extricated himself from the one-sided conversation with the weather expert.

"Wow, that's awesome and all, but if you'll excuse me…" He didn't give the guy a chance to keep talking, ducking through the crowd toward Katherine. A man stopped him before he reached her.

"Well, if it isn't Cooper Tate. What are you doing here?"

Coop recognized an old fraternity brother. "Hey, Mark."

The man squinted at him as they shook hands. "I figured I was seeing things. A big oil tycoon like you mixing in with the science nerds?"

Coop glanced around to make sure his mother wasn't paying attention, then rolled his eyes. "It's Mom. This is her charity *du jour*. She was on the OU board of regents when the National Weather Service built their Severe Storms Lab down in Norman." He nodded toward a handsome man surrounded by a small crowd. "And I think she has a bit of a crush on Dave Edmonds from Channel Two. You?"

Mark made a face and said, "Somebody had to represent my law firm. I drew the short straw." He switched his expression to a smile as Katherine sailed up.

"Hello, Mark. How are your parents? Did they enjoy their cruise?"

How did his mother know all this stuff? It's like she kept a dossier on every person her sons had ever met. Or maybe she had his little brother Bridger on retainer, since Bridge worked for Barron Security Services.

"Mom's ready to sail around the world. Dad's still grousing about all the golf balls he launched into the ocean. He much prefers his eighteen holes on solid ground."

Mark and his mom continued to chat. Coop tuned them out. He'd never been one for small talk, especially not when it came to golf—Mark was bragging about being a scratch golfer, whatever that meant. Katherine appeared to hang on every word. Looking for a way to extract both of them, he touched his mom's arm. "I hate to interrupt but you'd mentioned something in the silent auction you wanted to bid on?"

She hadn't but if they were walking the long tables circling the room, they could pretend to be engrossed and he could avoid further conversation.

"So nice to see you again, Mark. Tell your parents I said hello."

Cooper nodded at the other man and steered his mother away.

"That was rude."

"You were as bored as me."

"One should always be polite in social situations, Cooper."

"Yes, ma'am." Agreeing with her was always easiest. "Oh, look!" He pointed out one of the items—a weekend at the Broadmoor Hotel in Colorado Springs. Katherine didn't stop so Coop trailed after her. When she did peruse an item, he pulled out his engraved Mont Blanc pen and added a bid to the sign-up sheet once she moved on. Then his mother stopped dead still and eagerly read an item's description. He came up behind her and read over her shoulder.

!!GO TORNADO CHASING!!

Why did graphics people put exclamation points in front of a header? More to the point, why was his mother so intrigued? He read the description. The high bidder would get to spend a day with a storm chaser from a local television station—one conveniently owned by his cousin Chase's company, Barron Entertainment. Who had time for that nonsense? Anyone who went looking for tornadoes was just plain loco in his book. Ever since his own up-close-and-personal experience with a twister when he was a kid, Coop was more than happy to give those suckers a wide berth.

Katherine raised her hand shoulder high and palm up. "Pen."

Cooper obliged. She accepted the pen and bent over the sheet, signed and added a ridiculously high bid. *Ouch.* He'd make sure his mother did *not* have the winning bid on this package, though he'd have to twist someone's arm to outbid her. Bridger was wandering around somewhere and he was an adrenaline junkie. Maybe he could talk his little brother into bidding. There was no way in hell he'd let his mom go.

He looked up and saw the picture attached to the description and read the caption beneath the woman's very attractive face: DANCE THE TORNADO TWO-STEP WITH BRITT OWENS. His mouth went dry. Britt Owens. Of course it would be her. Sexy-gorgeous even soaking wet and waiting for rescue from the top of her storm-chaser truck. Britt Owens, who sneaked away after incredible sex without a please, thank you or goodbye. Twice!

What was it about this woman? She obviously wanted nothing to do with him and yet he was drawn to her like iron to a magnet. So much for putting their encounter behind him because he was just wasting his time mooning after her, as his family reminded him often. He still wanted to kick himself for telling his brother, Bridger. The big blabbermouth. He was still staring at the picture when his mother elbowed him in the ribs. "Didn't I teach you not to drool?"

He blinked and by reflex, reached up to swipe at his chin—which was dry. "Dang, Mom. Seriously?"

She laughed, but he only managed to scowl before a local weatherman tapped the microphone on the stage, which caused ear-wincing feedback.

"Sorry about that," the man said with a laugh. "Those in

charge informed me dinner will get underway just as soon as we all get seated. Once everyone is served, the entertainment portion of our evening will start. Trust me, this is a show you don't want to miss."

Without looking at how she'd signed the bid, Cooper offered his mother his arm and guided her to their table near the front. He seated her then sat on her left so they were both facing the stage but he could keep his eye on the rest of the room. He didn't like a bunch of strangers at his back. He wanted to see who was coming, but he also wanted to see the annual video they always aired. Maybe there'd be footage of Britt. Not that he cared.

Bridger slid into the chair beside him, a cocky grin on his face. "You still pouting over that little storm chaser?"

He glared at his younger brother. "I don't pout."

Okay, his mother *and* brother laughing at him? That hurt. And no way was his mother winning Britt's package. Nope. He was wise to Katherine Tate's ways.

Britt couldn't help herself. She sneaked by her package on the silent auction table to check the bidding. The last bid on the list was offered in a flowing, flowery script. Great. Just…great. One of the society ladies so prevalent in the room had decided to sign up for an adrenaline rush. She hated the whole idea of this package. Civilians didn't belong on the chase. They just got in the way and created problems.

Leaning over to study the page, Britt almost choked when she translated the signature into a name—and saw the four-figure bid amount next to it. Cooper Tate? *No. Just… no.* With furtive glances, she searched the room. What was he doing here? She knew he was a Tate, cousin to the Barrons who owned the TV station, but that didn't explain his presence at the gala.

Breathing through the semi-panic attack, she fought

for composure. She'd made a crazy mistake last August down in Beaumont. Her face flamed with the memory and she quickly moved away from the auction table, worried about standing out. With luck, no one had noticed her agitation. As people found their seats, Britt headed toward the table sponsored by her television channel. She would not freak out. She couldn't afford to lose it, not with the station's chief meteorologist beaming at her. *Gah.* This whole fiasco had been his idea. The channel paid her more than her salary as an adjunct professor, so she needed to suck it up, buttercup.

She glanced at her watch as she arrived at the table. Three more hours. If push came to shove, she could always go hide in the ladies' room. The weeknight news anchor stood and held her chair. Britt sank into it and did her best not to fidget. The lights would dim after their food was served and with luck, she'd remain incognito. Salad plates filled with spring greens, tiny mandarin oranges and walnuts drizzled with balsamic vinaigrette waited at each place setting. Britt ate and listened as the station manager, the chief meteorologist and the anchor bantered back and forth. She didn't aspire to a career in TV. Nope. She wanted to finish her PhD then go into pure research. Though storm chasing and getting paid for it? Bonus!

Waitstaff in white shirts, their sleeves bunched with black garters, and wearing long black aprons, swirled through the tables deftly delivering artfully arranged plates. Once her table was served, conversation ceased and eating began. She cut into the pecan-crusted filet mignon, put the bite in her mouth and almost melted. The tender beef all but dissolved on her tongue. Herb-buttered new potatoes and steamed asparagus spears complemented the steak. Okay, the evening wasn't a total loss. She'd been expecting the usual rubber chicken so often served at events like this, even with a ticket price of a thousand dollars. The food she was enjoying with great relish was five-star all the way. Which was good, given her picky appetite these days.

The master of ceremonies took the stage and introduced the program—the history of storm chasing and the starring role Oklahoma, and the University of Oklahoma School Meteorology, played in the formation of tornado science. After inhaling the main course, Britt was unable to resist the chocolate mousse with raspberry dribble and a white chocolate tornado for garnish, spooning some into her mouth while her companions still finished their entrées.

She rolled her eyes at the good-natured ribbing as one of her segments splashed across the big screen behind the podium. A few of her graduate students wolf-whistled and she slouched in her chair as curious gazes focused on their table. Yes, indeed, the ladies' room was looking better and better. At the end of the video, the MC reminded people to bid and bid generously on the silent auction items. The lights came up and the cash bars reopened. A small musical combo began to play and people actually hit the dance floor.

When the anchor, a tall, broad-shouldered man, and his wife stood, Britt popped up beside them, and used them for cover, peeking around the barrier they formed to locate Cooper. No sign of him. That was bad. She needed to find him so she could avoid him at all costs.

The anchor glanced down at her and quirked a brow. "Problem?"

"Um...no." She twitched the flowing chiffon skirt of her royal blue formal gown, her gaze tracking across the room. She stiffened as she found the object of her search.

The anchor's wife laughed. "If I were single, he'd be the kind of problem I'd want."

Oh, yeah. The man was devastatingly lethal in that black, Western-cut tux. The lapels and vest had a touch of shine under the lights and he wore a bolo tie with silver tips and a concho clasp. The hatband of his black Stetson had conchos too. And yup, there were shiny black Western boots on his feet. Britt stifled the sigh welling in her chest.

Dr. Garcia, the head of the university's meteorology department, chose that moment to arrive at their table. With everyone distracted, Britt finally beat a hasty retreat to the ladies' room. Several overstuffed chairs and something that resembled an antique fainting couch were grouped in the anteroom. Poking her head into the inner room, she made sure she was the only occupant before sinking into a chair. She was more than prepared to wait out the rest of the event right there.

You're being ridiculous, you know, her inner voice pronounced. *He probably doesn't even remember you.*

"Shut up," she muttered. "You don't know anything."

"I beg your pardon?"

Britt jerked her head up and stared at the woman who'd just walked through the door. She wore a lace and satin evening suit in rich cranberry. Attractive silver strands threaded through her short dark hair. A pearl-and-diamond necklace graced her neckline.

Blushing, Britt offered a sheepish smile. "Sorry. Talking to myself."

"I see." The woman paused a beat before adding, "You're Britt Owens."

"Yes, ma'am."

"I'm Katherine Tate."

Her stomach sank all the way to the floor, leaving behind a hollow spot that quickly filled with lead. Cooper's mother. Britt pasted a smile on her face and swallowed the spit swimming in her mouth. "Nice to meet you." Good. Steady voice. No panic. Yet.

Mrs. Tate's lips twitched but her rather stern expression didn't change. "So you chase tornadoes for a living. Must be thrilling."

"It can be. Thrilling. Yes. Mostly just boring though."
Britt reeled off the statistical probabilities of a tornado
forming in any given thunderstorm. Mrs. Tate nodded and
looked moderately interested until Britt stopped babbling.
"I mostly do it for research. I'm working on my PhD, you
see."

"Fascinating," Mrs. Tate said as she looked Britt over
from the top of her head to the freshly pedicured and
red-painted toes peeking out from beneath her royal blue
gown.

Britt swallowed hard, again, unsure just what it was the
woman found fascinating—Britt's work or her as a person.
Most people thought storm chasing was glamorous and
exciting; surely that's what Mrs. Tate was referring to. So
why did this woman terrify her far more than all the massive tornadoes she'd encountered?

Pushing to her feet, Britt locked her wobbly knees. "So
nice to meet you, Mrs. Tate. I should be getting back—"
She gave a vague wave toward the door.

"Of course, dear. I'll see you again. Soon."

What did Mrs. Tate mean? There was something odd in
her tone, a weight to the words Britt didn't understand. She
pulled open the door and backed out, trying to decipher the
implications of Mrs. Tate's parting words. She continued
walking, all the while leaning to watch through the slowly
closing door. Britt turned around just in time to plow into
a hard body. Her forehead bounced off the muscled chest
as her nose was buried in a starched shirt. Her instinctive
inhale filled her lungs with the aromas of cardamom, ber-
gamot and... She sniffed again. Was that lavender? What
an intriguing mix of scents.

Strong hands gripped her biceps to keep her upright. She
raised her chin, tilting her head back to look up. Straight
into the frowning face of the last man on earth she ever
wanted to run into.

"Cooper Tate!" someone shouted from behind him.

Coop turned his head to face the man who'd yelled his name. He didn't have time to duck the fist swinging at his face.

"You got my little sister pregnant."

Four

The sucker punch caught Cooper on the jaw and he went down like he'd been poleaxed. He was still holding onto Britt, his legs tangled in her skirts. As he fell, she had to follow. Hitting the floor was going to hurt so she braced herself—only to land on something hard but giving. Surprised speechless, she stared at the man standing over them, fists ready for a fight. Then his words sank in. *You got my baby sister pregnant.*

Their meaning had barely registered before camera flashes blinded her. She glanced at Cooper and winced. His face was already swelling and his eyes were unfocused. Still, he'd been careful to hit the floor in just such a way that she ended up cradled in his lap. She fought the melting sensation in the pit of her stomach as she pressed up against him.

"Get up!" Cooper's assailant ordered. "Stop hiding behind that—" A broad-shouldered man with a determined look jerked the guy away before he could finish his name-calling. Even though he wore a tuxedo, the newcomer could handle the physical stuff. Suddenly, there were more men surrounding her and Cooper, and Mrs. Tate, blocking them from onlookers and the barrage of cell-phone paparazzi.

Great. Just...great. The scrum of hard bodies consisted of Barrons and Tates. The tabloid media had dubbed the cousins Red Dirt Royalty. And Cash Barron's company owned the television station she worked for. Her career could end up in the dumpster due to this craziness. Defaulting on student loans wasn't on her bucket list and losing this job meant she might end up doing so. She needed to get away. Pronto. Before she could scramble to her feet, two sets of strong hands lifted her, steadied her, and then Mrs. Tate was hustling her back into the ladies' room. That worked—except that now she was once again all alone with her.

The door swished shut, muting the din out in the hallway. Britt grabbed her phone, immediately searching for evidence on social media of the catastrophe that just occurred. So far, her name hadn't been linked to it, but oh, yes, indeed, there were photos of Cooper's mug hitting the sites and lots of speculation. In the one picture of her sitting on his lap, she could only be identified by her dress and hair color, her face mostly blurred. Didn't matter how much the gown cost, she was burning it as soon as she got home. Problem was, she needed to ditch the dress before people remembered her wearing it.

"Breathe, Miss Owens," Katherine Tate ordered.

She'd forgotten the older woman was in the room. And Britt *was* close to hyperventilating. Cooper had gotten someone else pregnant? No, no, no, *no!* This wasn't happening. Part of her wanted to scream. Part of her wanted to cry. Most of her just wanted to run very far and very fast and pretend that this night had never happened.

"My sons and nephews will deal with the situation."

Britt opened her mouth to say something—anything—
then snapped it shut. What exactly was there to say? Mrs.
Tate apparently didn't notice. She bustled about, glancing
at her phone when it pinged with incoming messages. The
woman finally smiled as the outer door opened and a guy
who looked a lot like Cooper, only a few years younger and
several inches wider, entered, supporting Cooper with one
of those broad shoulders braced under Coop's arm.

The man eased Cooper onto one of the overstuffed
couches in the anteroom and gave his report. "Chance and
Cash are dealing with the guy who cold-cocked Coop.
Chase is dealing with the media. Cord is standing guard
and diverting any of the ladies who might need the facilities. I think Jolie has gone in search of an ice pack. She'll
be in to check on Coop shortly." He paused, giving Britt
the once-over before returning his gaze to Mrs. Tate. "His
storm chaser?"

"I do believe so, yes."

Hello. She was standing right here, and it was time to
remind these people of that. She tried to speak for the second time just as the door popped open again. A beautiful
woman with chestnut hair and green eyes swept in, efficient and businesslike. She carried something bundled in
a cloth napkin in one hand.

"Hey, Miz Katherine," she greeted the matriarch. "I
brought ice. Move over, Bridger, so I can get a look at him."

The woman sat beside Cooper and Britt had to fight
a stab of jealousy. Instead of thinking about that pretty
woman's proximity to Coop, she attempted to figure out
all the players without a program. She was familiar with
the Barrons—Chase, Cash, Cord and Chance. There were
two more Barron brothers, Clay and Kade, but as far as she
knew, they weren't in attendance. Bridger had to be one of
the Tates. The woman might be Jolene Barron, who was
married to Cord. Wasn't she a nurse or something? Britt

couldn't remember, but she was far too relieved by the large diamond wedding set on the woman's left ring finger.

"Wow, he nailed you good, Coop. Can you move your jaw?"

Katherine slipped out of the ladies' room, leaving her son to the tender mercies of her nephew's wife, the pretty storm chaser, and his younger brother. The hallway was clear but for Cord leaning against the wall. He straightened immediately.

"Aunt Katherine?"

"Stay here, Cord. Jolie will be out shortly. I want to look into something."

She steamed off without a backward glance. Pausing at the nearest entrance to the ballroom, she surveyed the area. The musical combo was playing and the dance floor was full of couples. Others strolled along the perimeter of the room checking on their favorite silent auction items.

A tall, impeccably dressed man stood in front of the display advertising Britt's item. Katherine watched as he perused the sign-up sheet, which was all he did, making no move to add a bid. She filtered through the crowd, keeping her eye on him. She'd first noticed him during the altercation outside the ladies' room. He'd been standing back, watching things with an air of aloof satisfaction. He looked vaguely familiar but not in that *he's-a-friend-of-my-boys* way. She'd figure it out eventually.

The man moved away, stopping at another item and she gave him time to get much farther down the line before she paused to double-check Britt's sheet. Excellent. Katherine still held the high bid—but she'd left it in Cooper's name. Which he hadn't noticed. So far, so good. She was tired of her son moping around because he was too proud to go after the woman he wanted. He needed a proverbial kick in the pants and spending time stuck in close proximity with that woman was just the ticket, even if it cost four figures.

Her nephew Cash caught her attention from where he stood near the entrance. She nodded toward him then began a roundabout meander in his general direction. She was halfway there when she heard her name.

"Mrs. Tate?"

She turned. The man who'd been so interested in Britt's auction package stood a few feet away, smiling at her.

"Mrs. Katherine *Barron* Tate?"

Now wasn't that interesting, that emphasis he put on her maiden name. Her expression morphed into a very practiced and very polite smile. "Yes?"

"We've never met. I'm Alex Carrington."

Two things struck her. He emphasized his last name like she should recognize it and he watched her with an intensity that let her know he was extremely interested in her reaction to his surname. Her smile didn't change though she eventually quirked one brow. "Is there something I can do for you, Mr. Carrington?"

He dipped his chin and hesitated before speaking. "I only wanted to introduce myself so I could thank you for your patronage of the program."

Her cheeks plumped in a broader smile—one that did not reach her eyes. This man, who was older than he first appeared, was lying through his teeth. Without actually demanding his ID for verification, she'd estimate he was closest in age to Hunter, Boone or Cooper—her oldest three sons. And she *had* recognized his last name, though it was one she hadn't thought about in forty years. It was possible Alex was related to Colby. There were hints in the younger man's looks. Her one-time college beau had been handsome.

"Aunt Katherine?" Cash was at her side, his brother Chance coming up behind her as well. "Is there a problem here?"

She patted his arm, her smile now fond rather than chillingly polite. "None at all. Mr. Carrington was just thanking me for my sponsorship. Isn't that right, Mr. Carrington?"

The man eyed her nephews with disdain and she knew they didn't like his attitude from the way they stiffened, yet he answered with a very civilized, "Yes, ma'am. I won't keep you from the rest of your evening. Thank you again."

And with that, he was off, dodging through the crowd like he thought one of her nephews planned to follow and ambush him.

Cash took her elbow and steered her toward the nearest exit. "We need to talk."

"Of course we do, dear." She slipped one arm through Chance's and the other through Cash's. "And we have plans to make."

Cooper lay back on the couch, eyes closed, the ice pack firmly in place against his cheek and jaw. *His storm chaser.* That's what Bridger called Britt. And his mother knew. Of course she knew. Because Bridger had a big mouth. The conversation, what little there was, flowed over him. Until his brother nudged the armrest where his head lay.

"So, big bro. Baby daddy? Who's the lucky woman?"

He started to shake his head but stopped when stars danced on the backs of his eyelids and pain splintered his brain. *Ow. Reminder to self. Don't do that again.* "No clue," Coop muttered. "No clue who the dude is, or his sister."

"So who *have* you been seeing?"

Great. Bridger was in investigative mode. His brother would never shut up and go away now. "No one."

He caught the sound of someone snorting and cracked one eye open to see who. Britt. Yeah, he probably shouldn't have admitted that with her still in the room. She didn't need to know that he'd had no interest in any woman but her since coming home from Texas. And he wasn't about to tell her that he DVR'd the local news on the off chance she'd make an appearance. Pathetic. That's what he was. And the last thing he needed was for his brothers to find *that* out. They'd harass him unmercifully.

"The man who punched you seemed rather convinced." Britt managed to sound both annoyed and confident of the guy's right to throw a punch.

Cooper eyed his brother. "Maybe he confused me with one of you."

Rolling his eyes, Bridger laughed. "Hunter and Boone are in D.C. with Clay. Deacon and Tucker are both married. Dillon's been in Nashville. That leaves me, big bro, and don't even go there. I'm the stick-in-the-mud brother, remember?"

A second snort drew his attention to Jolie Barron, Cord's wife. "Pah-lease, Bridge. I'm wearing expensive heels and not a pair of hip boots in sight. You might be able to fool your mom and brothers but the rest of us?" She waggled an index finger at the younger man before blowing him a kiss.

The door opened and two giggling girls breezed in. They stopped dead, staring, gazes darting between the occupants. Coop groaned inwardly.

"I do believe that's our cue to skedaddle," Britt announced. "I'm not sure of the decorating scheme in the men's room, but surely there's a chair in there you can occupy while you sulk."

She was out the door before Cooper could say anything to stop her. The two girls parted like the Red Sea, though their gazes remained fixed on him and Bridge. Working his jaw gingerly, he sat up with only a little assistance from his brother.

"Don't mind us, ladies," Bridge announced as he hauled Coop to his feet.

Jolie insisted Coop keep the ice pack on his face and she pushed up under his shoulder. Still seeing more stars than he was comfortable with, he leaned on Bridger, too, as soon as they were out the door. Once his vision cleared, he searched the hallway for Britt. She'd disappeared. His brother and Jolie, followed by Cord, steered him toward a small sitting area in an alcove and settled him into one of the chairs.

"You were supposed to keep people out, Cord," Jolie scolded. "Especially people of the female variety."

"Like some random guy is going to push his way into the ladies' room?" Cord did an exaggerated eye roll. "My cousins being the exception to that rule. What went on in there and why are you not chasing the storm chaser? She's hot. Also, what the hell, cuz? You're having a baby?"

Jolie glared at Cord while speaking to Coop. "Keep the ice on your face, Cooper. I *will* be keeping track." She turned on her heel and crooked a finger at her husband. Cord followed willingly.

Bridger waited until the couple was out of earshot before dropping into the chair next to Cooper. "She's bad news, big bro."

"You don't even know her."

"Nope. Just what I've seen of her on TV. But I've got good instincts and my gut says she's going to bring you nothing but trouble."

Before he could argue, Bridge continued. "I know what went on down in Beaumont. I know what you've been like since you got home."

"You don't have a—"

"Dude, she left you. Twice."

Five

Cooper scowled at his brother's retreating back. Technically, Bridger was correct. Britt had ditched him without saying goodbye. Twice. After they'd made love. Well, maybe not…love. Wild monkey sex. Still, it was the best sex he'd ever had and there was something about the damn woman that aroused all sorts of deep-seated feelings inside him. She was bold and beautiful.

If his face didn't hurt so bad, he'd bang his forehead on the side table. Wasn't that the name of some soap opera his mom watched? He didn't have time for drama. He worked for a living. And Bridge was right. While he wasn't the ladies' man of the Barron-Tate clan, he didn't have to sit home twiddling his thumbs because the object of his affection chose to ignore him. There were plenty of fish in the sea. Only he didn't want tuna. He wanted filet mignon. His stomach chose that moment to growl. Not surprising since he'd been too busy watching Britt to eat much. He vaguely remembered beef. And potatoes. Yeah, he was hungry.

For Britt. The remembered taste of her settled on his tongue. What was it about her that heated his blood? Bold and beautiful, he reminded himself. There was something about her nerdy glasses, the scientific language. Who knew that a one-sided discussion of quasi linear convective systems made for good pillow talk?

And now this whole crazy allegation that he'd impregnated some girl. His accuser had been arrested and hauled off in handcuffs. What was Britt thinking? He wasn't reckless when it came to unprotected sex. Denver Tate had drilled that lesson into his sons' heads over and over. No condom, no sex. He didn't lose control and forget.

Britt probably thought he was a total bastard. Given the circumstances, he couldn't blame her. He closed his eyes and rubbed at his sore jaw. Then again, why would she care? She'd gotten out of his bed and walked away. Twice.

"Idiot," he muttered, before his thoughts were interrupted by a burst of applause. They were announcing the silent auction winners. Crap. He'd meant to fix his mother's bid. Too late now. He sighed, resigned to dealing with his mother when the time came to chase tornadoes with Britt. He considered slinking out of the museum and taking himself home. Bridger could give their mother a ride to her house when the event was over.

Reaching up, he tugged on his bolo tie and undid the collar button strangling him. He shifted the ice pack, not quite ready to abandon its cold comfort. Yeah. He'd go to his truck, text his brother and head home. That was a good plan. Right after he put Britt Owens out of his mind.

Coop heaved out of the chair and glanced around, furtive in his movements. If any of his family lurked about, his plan would fall apart. The coast was clear. He slipped outside into the cool autumn air and paused, inhaling deeply. Beyond the entrance portico, glittering stars scattered across the night sky. Something eased in his chest.

He was a country boy at heart. When it came to life in the big city with tall buildings, bright lights and traffic, sometimes it was hard to breathe but clear, crisp nights like this one helped him cope.

He headed across the parking lot toward his truck and stopped dead. Right in front of him, wrapped in decals touting KOCX TV's weather team, sat Britt's chase truck. Fate had to be working overtime. Or karma was about to rise up and bite him in the butt. He could just keep walking, get in his truck and drive away. Or, he could admit that Britt had gotten under his skin and he wanted her like he'd never wanted another woman.

His dad had taught his sons another important lesson. Don't be a quitter. Britt's actions had bruised his ego. He could admit that. But he wasn't a quitter. And he didn't run away. Time to make a stand.

Leaning against the push bars on the front bumper of Britt's chase vehicle, he settled in to wait. He was taking a big gamble but if things worked out, he'd reap a reward that would make everything worth it. There was just something about the woman that made him want to risk everything to keep her.

Unable to get her out of his head for the last three months, he'd been plotting ways to cross her path. In retrospect, the series of unfortunate events tonight leading up to him laid out in the women's lounge with Britt for company was a good thing. And yeah, he was probably a pathetic excuse for a single guy but he didn't care. The woman checked off every item on his list. Until he got her out of his system, he'd continue being in danger of losing his man card.

Better to confront the situation head-on. Even better would be getting his hands and mouth on her again. Things stirred inside him. This was nothing serious. Just chemistry. And just until he got bored with her. That was his story and he was sticking to it.

* * *

"Stupid shoes," Britt groused as she switched heels for the flip-flops she'd stashed in her evening bag. Her feet and ankles were swollen and sore. Holding her skirts off the floor, she headed for the exit with one thought in mind: get home. Her feet hurt. Her back hurt. And if she stopped to think about it, her heart hurt far more than it should. She knew what she had to do to be fair but after that scene tonight? How could she share her news with Cooper?

A few people spoke to her as she walked outside and she waved at them without speaking. No time for conversations. If she got detoured, Cooper might find her. Or not. Was he even looking for her? She didn't want to see him. Nope. Not at all. So why was she feeling depressed that he hadn't hunted her down?

"On the fence much?" she muttered to herself as she arrived at the asphalt parking lot. Some sixth sense had her raising her head to peer into the spotty shadows. A figure leaned against the front of her truck. A tall, lean figure, with booted feet crossed to match those arms across his muscled chest. Her idiotic heart fluttered with excitement. He *had* tracked her down. But she wasn't ready to talk to him. Not yet. Not until she found out more about that guy who'd ambushed Cooper. And the guy's pregnant sister. Because at the moment, no matter how much he set her heart on fire, if he was guilty as charged? No. She couldn't think about that other woman. She had to keep her wits about her to deal with him.

"Howdy, Girl Wonder." Why did his deep drawl have to sound so sexy? And why did it send shivers through all the feminine places in her body?

"Fancy meeting you here, Hero Boy." She wanted to kick herself for falling so effortlessly into their familiar flirting.

"I keep tellin' you, I'm not a boy."

She tilted her chin up and watched him through half-lowered lashes. "Coulda fooled me." She waited a beat then added, "Quite a scene tonight."

Did he blush? "I have no clue what that guy was talking about."

"Of course you don't." Sarcasm. Good. She could use sarcasm.

"You don't believe me." He gazed up at the stars. "Of course you don't."

Interesting. He could do sarcasm too. Good to know.

Cooper shoved his hands into his trouser pockets. "Look, this happens."

'What? You being accused of—'

"Yes." He cut her off. "People accuse my cousins and us of all sorts of things."

She knew that, yet she'd still been quick to judge.

"And due to those kinds of accusations, we are always extremely careful."

Not careful enough, she mused.

When he lifted his hand and cupped her cheek, she didn't back away. He stepped closer, lowered his head.

"I've missed you," he whispered against her lips.

She didn't fight him when he deepened the kiss. She should have, but truth be told, she'd missed him too. "What are you doing?" she murmured against his mouth. He didn't answer, not in words, but he pulled her closer, claiming her with the heat of his body and intensity of his kiss.

"Taking you home," he finally replied.

"This is my truck and I'm perfectly able to drive."

"Let me rephrase that. I'm taking you home with me."

Her brain processed his statement. Home with him? To his house? *Cooper* was trouble. She was walking and talking proof of that. And in all probability, he was somebody's baby daddy. *Somebody else's* baby daddy. And that thought hurt far more than it should, given the circumstances. She didn't know him. Didn't have a claim on him. Didn't want one. Nope.

Then he kissed her again. Every bit of good sense she possessed skipped out on her, like some carefree girl tromping through the tulips. She kissed him back, her arms snaking around his neck.

"Please," he murmured against her ear. "Come home with me."

They could talk there, with no one around to hear or see them. She wasn't ready. Not yet. Not with this other accusation hanging over his head but things still needed to be said.

Listening to her heart instead of her head, she agreed. Still, she was not going to be stuck without a ride. "Okay, but I'm driving."

"We'll take your truck but I'm driving. You don't know where I live." He held out his hand, palm up. "Keys?"

She dug in her clutch muttering about alpha males but she handed them over. He beeped the locks and helped her into the passenger seat. Before she could have second thoughts, the man who stole all her good intentions with a look was in the driver's seat. They didn't go far. Out of the parking lot, along 63rd Street, and a quick left onto a private drive with an electronic gate. The drive curved through trees and then opened up to a broad lawn. Perched atop a low hill, the house was a complete surprise with its buff-colored native stacked stone and metal roof gleaming beneath the moon.

Cooper parked, was out, and had the passenger door open. Too late to change her mind. The interior of his house was just as impressive as the exterior.

"You want a drink?"

"No, I'm good."

A grin that quirked one corner of his mouth. "As I recall, you're very good."

He walked into the kitchen and grabbed a frosty bottle

of water from the fridge. He took a moment to open it and
drink deeply.

"I know what you're thinking," he finally said.

Her hand convulsively curved around her stomach.
There was no possible way but she nodded.

"Look, Britt. I'm a Tate and two of my brothers are country music stars. I'm also a Barron on my mom's side. That
means money. A lot of it. False paternity suits are a thing."

"And I should believe you?"

"Yes." He looked so earnest. "My dad raised us to be
responsible. I haven't been—" He cut off whatever he was
about to say. "You'll just have to take my word for it."

Deep down, and for obvious reasons, she wanted to believe him. He slowly walked toward her, setting the bottle
down on the bar as he passed it.

"I've missed you, Girl Wonder."

Then his arms were around her and he was kissing her
again. She pushed against his chest and broke the kiss,
studying his face.

"I'm not the love 'em and leave 'em type, Britt."

He wasn't. She knew that on a level that scared her just
a bit.

"Will you stay with me tonight?"

How could she refuse? And why would she want to.
She kissed him, just a brush of her lips across his. "Okay."

He led her into a very masculine, very Cooper bedroom.
A wall of windows looked out over the lights of Oklahoma
City. The massive bed was dark wood with padded leather
head and footboards. She could get lost in that bed.

He was kissing her again, his hands caressing her sides
and back, her arms. She was suddenly too hot but goose
bumps prickled her skin. She pulled at his shirt but it barely
came untucked. He continued to kiss her while he stripped
out of his tux jacket and vest. Then she heard cloth ripping
and small pings. Had he ripped his shirt open?

Strong fingers found the zipper of her dress and in moments, it lay in a billowing pile around her feet. He picked her up and laid her down gently on the bed. Then Cooper was lying beside her, his hands and mouth roaming over her body.

Britt knew in her head that she should stop this but the chemistry between them short-circuited her logic, because her heart? Yeah, her heart wanted what was about to happen. So did her body. Surrendering to the inevitable, she turned into him and pushed the shirt off his shoulders before busying herself with his belt and trousers.

Just like the other times they'd been together, they were naked in no time at all. The man knew precisely how to tease her with his hands and his mouth; knew the exact places to touch and kiss and suck to send her flying hard and fast over the edge.

Now it was her turn. With a touch here, a kiss there, she had him flying. He groaned and before she could react, he'd flipped them so he was on top. He spread her legs and his sexy, half-lidded eyes drank her in. Then he was sliding inside her.

She shuddered around him, clutching at his shoulders as he pushed deep. "Yes," she murmured. "Oh, yes, please."

What seemed like hours later, groggy and sated, she snuggled in with her head and half her body draped across his muscular torso. Cooper had just enough hair on his chest to pet and her fingertips ruffled through the dark, copper-colored wisps. Her muscles felt like butter left in the sun and she could barely keep her eyes open. She wasn't spending the night. Doing so was dangerous. Tears prickled behind her lids and she cursed her volatile emotions. She had to get a grip. Her life was about to get even crazier. Coop deserved an explanation but she just wasn't ready especially in light of the things he'd said earlier. Despite her mixed feelings, his steady heartbeat beneath her ear and the rise and fall of his chest made her feel safe. *I'll rest for just a minute*, she decided. *Until I'm sure he's asleep. Then I'll go.*

Britt blinked awake. How long had she been asleep? Beyond the windows, night lightened to the dove gray of predawn. The man beside her snored softly. Good. He was still asleep. Time to go. Easing out of bed, she located her clothes—draped over a large leather armchair next to the bed. She didn't bother with anything but the dress. Undergarments could wait. She noticed one set of windows was actually a French door. She could slip outside and go directly to the driveway where her truck was parked.

Hesitating, she glanced back at the bed. The sleeping man lay on his back, one arm stretched to the side. The arm, she realized, that she'd been sleeping on. His hair was tousled and scruff shadowed his jaw and cheeks. He looked so handsome, so... No. Britt shook those thoughts right out of her head—literally. Cooper Tate was not hers. Not that she'd want him. She didn't need a man and while some female *might* try to trap a man, she wasn't *that* woman. Not after the accusations of the previous evening. Her heart believed his explanation. Her head? Nope. Her head was such a pessimist.

She now regretted shaking her head. She was already feeling too queasy for her peace of mind. She would not throw up here. It was time to make her escape. As she eased the door closed behind her, she couldn't resist taking one last look at the man who might have been hers. Under different circumstances, in a different time and place.

She'd have to talk to him eventually—tell him—but not today. Not after last night. Squaring her shoulders, she turned away, resolute. Time to go.

Cooper didn't move, didn't open his eyes, as he listened for the sound that had first awakened him. The weight on his chest moved. But it wasn't Britt, it was the damn cat.

The bed beside him was still warm. Maybe the noise was Britt in the bathroom. He waited for her to come back to bed. After a few minutes with no further sound, he glowered at Lucifer until the cat moved, then threw off the covers and stalked to the en suite bathroom. It was empty. Nothing had been touched. The sink was dry. Weird. He availed himself of the facilities before heading back to the bedroom. He rummaged in his dresser for a pair of boxers then looked around.

Her dress was gone, along with the frilly things she'd worn underneath. He stalked out, headed to the kitchen. It was too much to hope that she'd be there fixing coffee. The kitchen was pristine. His housekeeper had been there just yesterday and he'd come home from the office, showered, donned his tux, and headed to the Western Heritage Museum for the benefit. Which reminded him. He'd need to get dressed and hike over there to pick up his truck. Good thing he basically lived across the street from the museum.

Lucifer demanded breakfast so Coop poured out some kibble and added a couple spoonfuls of wet food. He set the cat's bowl on the floor and then got to the important stuff. Coffee. He poured a pot of water into his coffeemaker and snagged a mug while it brewed. Then he got the bright idea to check his security system. Not that he'd taken the time to arm the house last night. He'd barely had the presence of mind to disarm it, and that only because he didn't want to be interrupted by phone calls or knocks on the door. Barron Security was nothing if not thorough. And knowing his little brother, had the alarm gone off, Bridger would have been the one showing up and standing there in the doorway with a cocky grin on his face.

He swiped the electronic tablet on the breakfast bar that separated the kitchen from a large family room as he settled on one of the bar stools. Running the video feedback, he watched as they arrived the previous night. The feed followed him through the house, carrying Britt, but cut off at his bedroom. The next motion-activated camera clicked on at 6:26 a.m. The sky outside was still dark but traces of gray showed on the eastern horizon. Outside lights, triggered by Britt's movements, clicked on and he followed her around the corner to the driveway. She climbed into that monster truck of hers, started it and got it turned around so she could head down the drive. The cameras mounted on the gateposts at the street showed the metal gate sliding open at the approach of her truck, closing once she was clear. The last look he got was the rear of her truck as she pulled out onto 63rd Street and drove off.

"Note to self," he muttered. "Kill the pressure plate in the drive and put in a code pad." If he'd had that, she wouldn't have been able to get away. Again. He had to be the world's biggest glutton for punishment. Except the heat between them was enough to scorch the eyebrows off anyone standing too close.

Three times. They'd been together three times and he'd given her multiple orgasms. So why did she keep skipping out on him? His morning breath couldn't be that bad.

How many times would he watch her sneak away before he got smart? He was known to be stubborn but this whole deal had finally reached a level of absurdity even for him. He should cut his losses.

"Third time's the charm," he groused. His brother was right. He was cursed. And he was done. Britt Owens was not the only smart, sexy and totally fascinating woman in the world. Too bad she was the only one who kicked up a storm in his heart.

Six

Lost in his thoughts, Cooper was paying no attention that Monday morning when the Barron Tower elevator doors slid open and he took one step into a wall of muscle. His boss, Cord Barron, stiff-armed him back into the elevator car. Cord's brother Chance and Bridger joined them as the doors whispered shut. Bridger stabbed the button for the thirty-fourth floor, where Barron Security had offices.

"Somebody wanna fill me in on what's going on?"

The other three men simply stared at him. The car stopped, the doors opened, and two secretaries got on. Cord and Chance were both married but that didn't stop the women from checking them out before their gazes came to rest on Cooper and Bridger. That's when the flirting started. Bridge indulged. Cooper didn't. He was still steamed over Britt's disappearing act Saturday morning. As a result, he was annoyed with the entire female half of the population.

Thankfully, the women were headed to a different floor and stayed on when the elevator got to thirty-four and the men exited. He pretended not to hear the sighs and titters as the doors closed. Coop hunched his shoulders and followed the others through the impressive reception area of Barron Security.

"Still wanna know why I'm here," he muttered.

"You'll find out as soon as Mom gets here."

He furrowed his brows, staring at his younger brother. "Why is Mom coming into town?"

"Because this is her deal, according to Cash."

"Then why are Cord and Chance here?"

"Because Mom's involved." Bridger's tone implied that Coop was a simpleton. He didn't add the implied *well, duh*.

A low hum of activity followed them down the hallway to the executive offices. Cheri, Cash's personal assistant, handed everyone a cup of coffee as they passed the side bar on the way to Cash's office. A huge black dog lunged off the leather couch, barking happily as his tail cut through the air like an old-fashioned fan. The Newfoundland, belonging to Cash's wife, Roxie, greeted everyone before returning to his spot on the couch.

"Take your dog to work day?" Chance asked, smirking.

Cash rolled his eyes. "You try telling Harley he can't go for a ride."

As the men settled in the sitting area with their mugs, Coop remained standing. He wasn't out of the loop very often and the fact he was this time irritated him to no end. Considering everything that had happened Friday night, he'd been expecting his family to get all up in his business. They didn't. Which was unusual. So maybe they'd just been biding their time, gathering the facts, and were now ready to ambush him. Yeah, that's probably what this was.

His fingers brushed over the bruise on his face, compliments of the crazy dude who'd accused Coop of getting his sister pregnant. Except Coop hadn't been with anyone. Well, he'd been with *someone*…

Coop wanted to kick his own ass. He had to stop thinking about Britt. She was old news. They'd had an unfortunate series of one-night stands. They didn't have a relationship and since she ditched him after each encounter, they didn't have a future. It didn't matter that her sexy scientist vibe turned him on. He shifted uncomfortably, his body reacting to the memory of making love to her.

His mother chose that moment to breeze through the door. She made the rounds, doling out cheek kisses to all, sons and nephews alike. She held up a finger, freezing Harley as he sat up in preparation for an exuberant greeting but ruffled the dog's ears to show him he was still loved. Then she sank into a deep leather armchair, reigning like a queen.

Her gaze pinned first Bridger, who was bringing her a cup of coffee, and then Cash. "So," she said, accepting the cup. She sipped, swallowed. "Did you find out anything?"

Cash deferred to Bridger, who gave a brief rundown. "Alex Carrington, full name Alexander Adam Carrington, is from Hartford, Connecticut. He graduated from Harvard with a BS in business. He's a vice president of CCI, Ltd. As near as we can figure, CCI is some sort of holding company. His father is Colby Carrington the third."

"Trey."

Bridger continued to drone on about parentage, stepmothers and siblings, and Coop figured he was the only one who caught the breathy word his mother uttered. This whole conversation caught him off guard. He'd figured this was an ambush about the alleged pregnancy and/or Britt. But there was way more going on.

He watched his mother, noticing the hard glitter in her eyes. She was edging toward angry. It took her a long time to blow her stack but when she lost her temper, people ran for cover.

"He bought his ticket to the fund-raiser six weeks ago,

when it was announced," Bridger continued. "We don't know why he is here or why he would approach—"

"I know," Katherine announced. "I want to know about the other things I asked you to look into."

This time, Cash deferred to Chance, the senior partner of the Barron law firm. "The guy who attacked Cooper—and nice shiner you got there, bud—has no criminal record. He was arrested and released on his own recognizance." He looked back at Cooper. "You know a guy named Steve Maddox?"

Coop shook his head. "No clue who the dude is."

"How about Susan or Susie Maddox?"

"Nope."

"That's his sister and she's claiming that you're the father of her unborn child."

Hands fisted, Coop came off the wall where he'd been leaning and made it two steps before Chance stopped him. "I've confirmed she is pregnant."

"I didn't—"

"Of course you didn't, Cooper," his mother interrupted. "Your father and I taught you boys better. Hear your cousin out."

Chance nodded to Katherine before focusing once more on Coop. "I've also confirmed that she had a live-in boyfriend and that he moved out when she told him she was pregnant. Apparently, she's filing a paternity suit naming you. As soon as she does, I'll be filing papers with the court demanding a prenatal paternity test, along with costs and damages when her claim is proved false."

He walked a file over to Coop and handed it to him, a photo on top. "Be positive you don't know her, Coop."

Britt huddled into a chair at a table in the corner of the bright room. Every kind of soda pop bottle imaginable lined the walls of Pops 66. People at the other tables were enjoying all manner of roadside diner food and soda pop. Why she'd thought this was a good place to meet Ria Simms, the morning on-air meteorologist at Channel 2 and the closest thing to a best friend she had, escaped her at the moment. The food aromas made her stomach queasy and the ginger ale she'd ordered wasn't helping. The other woman breezed up and slid into the chair opposite her.

"You look like crap," Ria announced with a big smile. Her sunny disposition was perfect for the early newscast. Britt was not a morning person and perky just didn't help her mood, all things considered.

"Can you tone down the cheerful?"

"No. Besides, that's why you called me. You always call me when you're feeling down."

A waitress arrived, took Ria's order, and disappeared.

"How can you eat a double bacon cheeseburger at ten in the morning?" Britt's stomach lurched at the thought.

"I've been at work since four a.m. This is like noon to me. Don't worry. I'll share my fries."

Britt held up a hand, feeling more than a little green. "No. Don't do me any favors."

Dropping her voice, Ria turned serious. "So it's like that, huh? I remember those days. How far along?"

She held up three fingers and then wiggled a fourth. She could all but see the wheels turn in Ria's head and quickly preempted the other woman's question. "Don't ask how it happened."

"Fine. Then who's the father?"

"Don't ask."

"So I can't ask how and I can't ask who. Guess it's a good thing I do the weather instead of hard news." Ria paused while her drink was delivered. When the waitress was out of earshot, she said, "Well, whoever he is, have you told him yet?"

Britt didn't answer, suddenly fascinated by the bubbles in her glass of ginger ale.

"If you know who—"

"Of course I know who!" Britt was furious that Ria would even consider she didn't.

The other woman held up both hands to temper Britt's anger. "Down, girl. Wasn't insinuating you didn't. I was simply predicating my question. Since you know who, why haven't you told him?" Her eyes widened. "Oh, no. Please don't tell me it's someone at the station."

"It's not." Just a relative of the owner. Britt felt even more nauseous.

"Whew!" Ria swiped the back of her hand across her forehead to emphasize her relief at that news. "So what's the problem?" She blinked. "Oh, goodness. He's not married, is he?"

That earned her a growl from Britt. "Who do you think I am, Ria?"

"Well, I didn't figure you for someone who would get involved with a married man, but some of the men I know can be both slick and sneaky about stuff like that. I've had friends get caught in their traps."

While Ria ate her burger, Britt found herself inexplicably telling the whole story. Of the life-altering events in Beaumont, the need—and hunger—for a human connection. Of the off-the-charts chemistry between her and Coop, without naming him. And the fact that she'd been with him three times and had taken off without saying anything much less goodbye all three times. She let slip about the incident at the benefit and covered her mouth in shock as Ria did the same.

"Dudette! Do not tell me that you were in the middle of that…" Ria blinked rapidly. She grabbed her smartphone, did a search and scrolled through the pictures that popped up. "You *were*. I recognize your dress now. How you managed to keep your face out of those pictures…" She glanced up, stared. "It's a freaking miracle you weren't identified."

"Yeah, I know. Totally lucky. But here's my dilemma. I know I have to tell him. Well, I don't really have to—" She held up her hand to stave off Ria's argument. "I *don't have* to tell him. Not too ethical on my part if I don't. But at the same time, here's this bimbo who's also having his baby. I mean, it's not like I want to marry him or anything."

Except she had daydreamed what that would be like on more than one occasion. And now that she'd seen where he lived? *Wowser.* His house was perfect. She didn't think she could sit down and plan a house that fit her any better than his, at least from the parts of it she'd seen. And there was that zing of electricity that ignited whenever they touched.

But chemistry didn't equal love. And given the current situation, he might think she was just another gold digger.

"So you're worried that he'll think you did this on purpose to get his money?"

She tuned back into the thread of conversation, shocked Ria's thoughts paralleled her own. "What?"

"Britt, Cooper Tate is rich. I mean, serious money. His mom is a Barron, and half the Tate boys work for the Barron brothers. Then there's Deacon, who's a megastar in Nashville. I know for a fact that all of the Barron brothers have had at least one paternity suit filed against them." Ria tilted her head. "Except they were all proved false. Well, except for Cord. That whole story never made it into public domain, but there's no doubt that Jolene Davis's little boy is his. All you have to do is look at the two of them side-by-side. That kid is his dad's mini-me. Anyway, people are always trying to get their hooks into the Barrons and the Tates to get at their money."

"I don't want his money."

"I know that. But, hon, it takes two to make a baby and having a village to help raise it is a big help."

"He used condoms." Well, he had until last night. Of course, the horse was already out of the barn by then.

"And condoms break." Ria laughed, the sound as bright and breezy as her personality. "That's how Tick and I ended up with our first." She reached across and patted Britt's arm. "Honey, I know this is hard, but there's a couple of things you need to consider. One, as the biological dad, he has a right to know, and to take part in any discussions pertaining to—"

"No. I've already decided to keep the baby."

"Okay, okay. I figured, considering you're coming out of your first trimester. But have you considered the monetary side of things? Yes, we have good insurance at the station, and liberal maternity leave, but it's expensive to have a kid. As the biological father, he should be responsible and help pay medical costs and child support."

Ria was right. Britt knew that deep in her heart, but honestly, she was terrified of Cooper's reaction, especially coming on the heels of Friday night. That guy hitting him and claiming Coop had gotten his sister pregnant? *Crazy sauce.* And now for her to drop her little bombshell into the conversation, considering how many times she'd taken the chicken's way out and bailed on him? He was going to hate her. And she *could* raise this child alone. Her dad had done it with her and her little brother, after her mother took off. She could, too, because she really didn't want to be tied down to a man like Cooper Tate.

"You need to talk to him, Britt."

Squinting her eyes shut, she exhaled. "Yeah, I know."

"And the sooner the better."

Yeah, she'd get right on that. Not.

Seven

Fed up with civilization and the machinations of the female half of the human race, Cooper was relieved to have business that took him out of Oklahoma City. BarEx was drilling a new well down in the Anadarko Basin. Thanksgiving at his mom's had been a full-court press from his family. He hated being the center of attention, but at least everyone was on the same page. That whole deal at the gala had been a setup.

Before leaving the office, he'd changed into old jeans and a ratty T-shirt, though he also pulled on a polo shirt bearing the company logo—the clothes he usually wore when working in the oil patch. He planned on spending the rest of the day playing roughneck, getting his hands dirty. He had hopes the hard work would drive the thoughts of both the woman trying to trap him with her false claims and the woman he wanted to entice back into his bed out of his brain.

Music from his brothers' latest album filled the cab of

his pickup truck. Deacon and Dillon had gotten all the musical talent in the family. He couldn't carry a tune in a bucket and he'd driven the piano teacher his mother hired to teach him the basics to the nearest liquor store for a bottle of wine. But he could play ball—football *and* baseball, though not well enough for a D-1 school, much less the pros. Nope, he was just happy hunting, fishing and working on the ranch in his spare time.

Growing up on the ranch, he paid attention to the weather and its effects on operations. Last spring, they'd had record rains, followed by one of the driest summers and falls on the record books. Rain in the spring meant lots of green growing things. Summer and fall droughts meant dead things in the fields just ripe for catching fire. Driving along, he noticed all the red cedars and acres of dried grass filling the fields and pastures stretching along the section line road he followed to get to the well site. An early hard frost, especially after a summer and fall with little rainfall, made for a prime fire season. Except it was late November—an unseasonably hot and dry November.

Drilling an oil well was dangerous business under the best of circumstances. The scars on his legs were a testament to that. He and Cord had both been injured on a rig. Cord had almost died. Coop would have but for Cord's intervention. Since coming out of the hospital and off physical therapy, he'd made it his mission to make sure every well site and field office was as safe as possible. Given his childhood brush with a tornado, that included contingencies based on whatever the local weather could throw at them.

The site appeared on his right and he slowed to turn onto the access road they'd cut into the rancher's field. His truck rattled over the cattle guard and he eyed the site. The immediate area had been cleared and graveled. A retention pond held water and an overflow pond was lined and ready for drilling mud once they got to that point. The rig was in place, as were the propane and diesel tanks for fuel. A familiar figure stepped out of the doghouse—the control center for the rig.

Deja vu, Coop thought. Tom Bradley had been the toolpusher on the rig where he and Cord had been hurt. He'd worked with the man several times over the ensuing years and seldom thought back to that incident. Why, on this day, his head was tripping down memory lane, he couldn't say.

"Hey, boss," Tom called as Coop stepped down from his truck.

They spent the next fifteen minutes touring the area while Coop made note of what had been accomplished and what still needed to be done to get the site up to BarEx, and Oklahoma Corporation Commission standards. A breeze kicked up and a hint of smoke piggybacked on it. November was not the time to burn the alfalfa fields—not that any farmer or rancher would this year, due to the arid conditions. He slowly turned in a circle but didn't see any obvious smoke in the area. He noted both the tractor and the bulldozer that had been used for site prep. He might just leave those in place, at least until the area got some rain. Heavy equipment always came in handy during fire season.

Another vehicle, also bearing the BarEx logo, pulled through the gate. Good. That would be the field geologist. They could get down to business and drill some core samples. Yessir, this was just what he needed—fresh air, a rig site and a job to do. No room for women in his head now. That was his plan, anyway.

Britt stared at the rack of maternity clothes, her mouth turned down in a frown. She was not ready to give up her jeans and Henleys, or her boots. At the same time, the idea of buying jeans two or three sizes larger than normal was so not registering on her cool meter. Eventually, she'd have to admit to her bosses that she wasn't putting on weight, she was pregnant. She hated to do that for myriad reasons, mainly that the powers that be might take her out of the field. Sure, she could relegate her research to the computer lab, relying on others to feed raw data to her to analyze, but that wasn't how she wanted to do things. The way she looked at it, as long as her ob-gyn cleared her for duty, she should be able to do what she loved—chase storms and other weather phenomena.

Before she could convince herself to try on a pair of mom jeans, her phone trilled with the station's alert. She opened her text program and read the information. A small fire had cropped up southwest of Oklahoma City. Winds were out of the south but a weather front caused by an area of high pressure was due to sweep through the state in a matter of hours, bringing with it high winds and low humidity. Given the overgrowth from the wet spring, any fire had the potential to escalate into a disaster.

She hung the jeans back on the rack, and with her phone to her ear, headed for the parking lot. "This is Britt," she said when her call was answered.

"National Weather Service just issued a red flag fire warning for western Oklahoma. I've got crews up near Woodward where a couple of fires are flaring. Can you cover the one southwest of us? It's nothing yet but the potential is there."

"Sure. Where's Leo?"

"He's here at the station. Swing by to pick him up then head toward Chickasha."

"I'll be there in twenty."

Thirty minutes later, she was headed southwest on the H. E. Bailey Turnpike. Leo, settled into the passenger seat, fiddled with the onboard cameras and instruments that would take weather measurements. Neither of them talked. Once Leo was satisfied with all the electronics, he tested communication channels with the station. They were a go if anything newsworthy broke. The horizon in front of them looked clear. The sky to the north showed a thin line of high cirrus clouds, the only sign the dry front was colliding with the hot, humid air. Thunderstorms would be preferable to low humidity even if it meant a chance of lightning.

She'd covered storms of every ilk, a few earthquakes, floods, but wildfires? Fires scared the bejeebers out of her. Once a fire got started, it could create its own weather system, if it was big enough. She'd seen "fire-nadoes" and other phenomena, including pyrocumulus clouds created when what were normally cute, puffy cumulus clouds turned into Hulk clouds generated by the hot air and smoke from wildfires. They formed when a wildfire burned so hot, it generated an updraft. There was nothing cute or puffy about those suckers. They could literally rain fire and lightning down.

Leo spotted the haze first—a line of dark smoke stretching across the top of a hill. She got off the turnpike at the first available exit and headed toward it.

"You know what they say, where there's smoke—"

She took her eyes off the road just long enough to shoot him a withering glare. "Don't even," she threatened.

"Ah, c'mon, Britt. You know it begs to be said. In fact, I'll buy you a steak dinner at Cattleman's if you say it on air."

"No."

"Chicken."

"Poultry has nothing to do with it. I like my job and prefer to keep it."

"You're totally gonna say it."

"No, I'm not."

"Totally are." He snickered. "And if you don't, you know Dave will."

"Dave's the head meteorologist. He can say whatever he wants."

"Don't you want to move up the food chain?"

She pressed the brake to slow the truck for a stop sign and turned to stare at her partner as they rolled to a stop. "Are you kidding me? Why in the world would you think I'd want to be stuck in the newsroom?"

"Um…because it's a real job?"

"I have a real job."

"Storm chasing is not a real job. Not unless you do it for the Weather Channel. Or one of the universities. Or the government."

She rolled her eyes and moved through the intersection. "I'm also an adjunct professor."

"Oh, and *that's* a real job? No tenure, lower division classes, no teaching assistant."

The road dipped toward a creek bed and they rattled over a one-lane wooden bridge. Topping out on the next hill, Britt hit the brakes. The truck slid to a grinding halt on the red dirt road. Pastures dotted with cedar trees spread out before them. Dry cedar went up like Roman candles when fire hit. To see so many trees scattered across the prairie was a scary sight. Cattle grazed restlessly in a field. Beyond them, to the east, she could just make out the top of a drilling rig—the only part not hidden by another hill. To the west, the voracious fire marched northward, gobbling up the prairie, leaving mounds of smoldering buffalo grass and flaming cedar trees in its wake.

Britt threw the truck into Park, opened her laptop, and started calibrating instruments and analyzing data, all while keeping one eye on the clouds scudding inexorably their way. She grabbed her cell phone and called into the station. The news was not good—not for the rancher who owned that herd of cattle, and not for the crew on the oil rig. She used the running board of her truck as a lookout post, scanning the area for a house. The nearest place that looked inhabited was at least five miles away. In this part of Oklahoma, that wasn't unusual. This was farm and ranch country. If push came to shove—

The scanner and her and Leo's phones all went off. She answered the call while listening to the scanner—a radio call dispatching several fire departments to the grass fire.

"You got Britt," she said into her cell.

"And you got Ria. Dave's coming in and will be looking for live updates. Your GPS puts you near the Grady County fire. Have you got a shot? We'll take you first."

"I can be set up in a few. Will you keep me posted on the front's ETA?"

"For my BFF? Of course I will." Britt could hear the laughter in Ria's voice.

"Whatever. I've got cattle and a drilling rig that might be in the path if the fire changes directions."

"Got ya covered, babe. I'll put you on the Gentner when Dave's ready to go live."

Continuing to call the COMEX communications system a Gentner, the name for an outdated setup, was a station-wide inside joke from the old days.

"I'll go find us a vantage point so the viewers have something to look at."

Ten minutes and a change of position later, she was on-air reporting on the growing grass fire that Leo filmed. The fire was headed away from the cattle and the rig. There were no structures in its immediate path. So long as the strong winds remained blowing from the south, the rancher would lose grazing land but that was all. Sure beat the alternative.

Then Britt sensed the wind shift from south to west. This was bad. A straight front causing a quick directional change wouldn't be a big deal, simply pushing the flames back on the area that had already been burned. But this slow transition was bad. Very bad. The outer edge of the fire had fresh fuel as the wind shifted, spreading it even wider and in a new direction. She leaned across the seat toward the passenger window. "Leo!"

The door opened and the big man climbed in. "Go!"

She didn't wait for him to buckle up. She gunned the truck's engine and they took off down the bumpy road at a speed that wasn't safe under the conditions. She braked, skidding as she jerked the steering wheel to guide the vehicle past the gate leading to the drilling rig. A variety of work trucks and equipment was parked in a graveled area adjoining the rig. She recognized the large white pickup with the now-familiar Barron Exploration logo on the doors. She and Leo jumped out of her vehicle. The tall figure jogging down the metal steps from the drilling rig floor came as no surprise, but his appearance held a heaping helping of annoyance.

"Why me!"

Eight

As Britt tumbled out of her vehicle, Cooper caught what she said. The inflection in her voice indicated both a question and an exclamation, which pretty much summed up the way he felt. He glanced at the large Black man who clambered out of the passenger side. Part of his brain recognized the former football player, but the majority of his focus was on the little spitfire lifting her chin in an attempt to face him down.

"Wha—" The man clipped off what he was about to say as Cooper strode up, stopping in front of Britt.

Hands fisted on his hips, he let his eyes slide up and down her body. She was every bit as sexy as he'd tried to forget. The darn woman haunted his dreams. "Private property, Girl Wonder."

"Won't be any property at all in about ten minutes unless the wind changes." She jabbed a thumb over her shoulder.

He squinted into the sun and realized what had been

smudges of smoke on the horizon were now a solid line of roiling black.

"The wind shifted but not all the way. That fire is headed here. You need to evacuate."

Evacuate? He glanced around. The rig was brand-new, a ten-million-dollar investment. He wouldn't lose it without a fight. "We're set up for fire suppression."

"Don't be stupid, Cooper," she argued.

"I'm not stupid, Britt. Get the hell out while you can. We both know what can happen. We have a fire break and the retention pond is full. I have pumps and hoses and a bulldozer to clear more brush if necessary."

That's when he heard the lowing of the cattle. A small herd was bunching up against the metal fence they'd used to supplement the barbed wire fencing used by the rancher whose land they'd leased for the well. He turned on his heel and took off for the rig where the crew had gathered. He issued orders. A few who claimed prior experience with cattle ran for the fence. The rest split up, some going to move vehicles, the rest to set up the pumps and roll out fire hoses. Cooper headed to the bulldozer.

He climbed into the cab and fired up the diesel engine. Black smoke sputtered from the vertical exhaust pipe as the motor coughed several times before it caught and ran smoothly. As he drove the rumbling machine past Britt's vehicle, he yelled, "Get out, Britt."

The fool woman didn't. She gave her cameraman a shooing motion with one hand while she jumped into the driver's seat and moved her truck to set up in a slightly safer spot. Idiot woman. Bad enough he had to keep the crew safe but now Britt and... Leo. Leo Blevins. He finally put a name to the face.

He shoved them out of his mind and concentrated on doing what he could to keep them all alive. Chances of a rural fire district crew getting to them were between slim

and none. It was up to him, and once they were all safe? He
and the Girl Wonder were going to have a serious knock-
down drag-out about her tendency to risk her life. The
old joke "we have to stop meeting like this" wasn't funny
anymore.

Britt watched the big yellow bulldozer knock down a
section of the metal rail fence. The cattle weren't fright-
ened at all by the yellow monster belching black smoke.
They poured through the gap like some scene from an old
Western movie. Four men from the derrick crew waved
their arms and more or less herded the cattle toward the
large artificial pond. It was filled to the brim with water
and she suddenly figured out what the men were doing. If
the fire came through the site, they'd drive the cattle into
the pond and then jump in themselves. Not ideal but that
plan definitely beat the alternative.

Coop was through the gap in the fence now and using
the dozer's bucket to scrape up the prairie grass and other
vegetation in swaths the length of the site. Back and forth
he went as the flames licked ever closer. Leo filmed everything as Britt spoke to Dave, who had their scene live
on air. The smoke was getting thicker, and she fought the
urge to cough with every inhalation. For a quick moment,
she worried about any health affects the bad air might have
on her baby, but she had a job to do.

A wall of flames roared no more than ten feet away from
the dozer when Cooper turned the machine and headed
back through the fence gap. He drove straight to her truck,
killed the engine and jumped down. Without so much as a
word, he grabbed her around the waist, hoisted her up and
ran to the pond, Leo keeping pace.

The crew gathered at the edge of the pond. The cattle
had already been herded into the water and the humans
were just waiting to see what happened next. There was

a lot of dirt and gravel between them and the fire and the hose crews had wet down all the vehicles, the fuel tanks and the rig itself.

"Why didn't you get out of here?" Cooper growled. He actually growled at her, his voice low and rough, and the tone sent a frisson of sexual heat through her. She really needed to have a heart-to-heart with her libido and adrenal gland. Getting turned on in the face of danger was so not cool on so many levels she couldn't count them.

"My job," she managed to answer.

His eyes narrowed on her as his lip curled and he looked away to mouth something probably profane without speaking it out loud. His hand squeezed her hip, and that's when she realized he hadn't turned her loose, only set her on her feet.

Heat and smoke blasted them as a gust of wind hit. The fire was now large enough to generate its own mini-weather front. A fire tornado danced along the leading edge as they were seared again by hot air. The men all had their T-shirts pulled up over their noses and faces. Britt used her arm to cover hers. *Note to self*, she thought. *Start wearing a T-shirt.* Leo had his own T-shirt pulled up over his mouth but his eye remained glued to the eye-piece of his camera.

Her phone kept ringing but she was too mesmerized by the fire coming inexorably closer to answer it. She jumped when water hit them. Two guys remained on one of the fire hoses hooked up to a pump in the pond. They were spraying down people as well as vehicles now. It hurt to breathe, even using her arm as a filter against the smoke. The air was hot and she felt like a steak on a grill, despite the impromptu shower. Another blast of scorching heat hit them. A couple of the crew hit the pond. Almost ready to join them, she didn't get the chance to make the decision on her own.

* * *

Cooper reacted out of instinct. He pushed Britt into the water at the same time he ordered the crew in. He was about to shove Leo in, camera and all, when the big man set the camera down, lens still facing the fire, and then took a running leap into the water, hitting the surface with a belly flop. Coop was right behind him. Britt had just struggled to her feet and was as spitting mad as a wet cat. He didn't give her a chance to chew him out. He grabbed her and took her down with him. He'd heard her gasp as they went under and he really hoped she'd taken a deep breath before they did. Of course, he could always give her mouth-to-mouth. He smiled and wanted to laugh despite the gravity of their situation. For a man who was not an adrenaline junkie, hanging around with Britt was becoming not only hazardous to his health and welfare but somewhat addictive too.

When she thrashed against him, he loosened his hold just enough so their faces could surface. Then he raised his head and looked around. Everyone else slowly surfaced as well. The wind had shifted to the north at the very last minute. They were safe.

The cattle headed to shore, as did the crew. Leo grabbed his camera, checked it and grinned. "That was too freaking close, boys and girl."

"You can say that again," one of the crew muttered.

Leo opened his mouth and Britt cut him off. "Don't be that guy," she cautioned. She pulled her phone out of her hip pocket and grimaced. "Maybe a blow dryer and a week in a bag of rice will revive it. If not, I'll just mortgage my life savings to buy a waterproof phone."

Cooper pulled his waterproof phone from his pocket and handed it to her. "Here, feel free to use mine." She was reaching for it when her phone actually rang.

"It's a miracle," she breathed and answered, "We're still breathing, Ria."

The men wandered off to check the rig and their vehicles.
The cattle stood bunched together, a little shell-shocked,
which was precisely how Coop felt. They eventually wandered off to the side where there'd been no fire and nibbled
any grass they could reach through the fence.

A few of the trucks and the bulldozer had spots where
the paint had bubbled from the heat. The rig itself was fine,
as were the fuel tanks. He checked Britt's truck while she
talked to the TV station. It had been parked closest to the
retention pond and appeared to be fine. Sirens sounded in
the distance and within minutes, a line of fire engines and
brush pumpers passed by on the road, lights and sirens
going. Several vehicles pulled in, including a chief.

Coop walked over to talk to the man in charge of the
fire team.

"Y'all got lucky," the man called as he approached.

"For sure."

The firefighter driving the chief looked around. "Saved
the cattle too."

"Yup."

"Got enough water in the pond that we can use some to
fill our tankers?"

"Absolutely."

"And the bulldozer?"

"You got that too if needed. Whatever we can do to
help."

"Appreciate it. Sorry we didn't get here in time to keep
you from getting all wet."

Coop twisted the hem of his polo to wring out the excess
water. "Warm day. Cold water. Nice break."

The chief laughed. "Y'all take any damage?"

"Not to speak of. I make safety a priority."

"Smart man."

"I try to be."

The older man nodded. "I roger that. Appreciate the assistance. And if you don't mind, I'd like to set up my command post and R and R area here. The Red Cross isn't too far behind us."

"No problem. Feel free to draft my crew to help you set up."

Cooper's phone rang and he checked the caller ID. His office. "I need to take this, Chief." The man waved him off, speaking into a radio as Coop turned his back and answered just as Britt had. "We're still breathing."

"Good to know." Cord's voice sounded amused. "But we can see that. Y'all are live on the TV. Wanna explain why Britt's there and you're soaking wet?"

"We decided to have a pool party."

Cord was laughing out loud now. "No skinny-dipping?"

"Dude, the only female here is Britt and I'd hate to have to shoot our crew because they saw her naked. They're a good crew and I don't want to train another."

Still chuckling, Cord asked if Cooper needed anything. "Nope. We're good to go. Fire chief wants to use the site as his command post. Red Cross is gonna set up an R and R area. I've loaned them the crew to help set up."

"What are you gonna do?"

"Drive the bulldozer if they need it."

"Sounds like fun. Stay safe out there, cuz."

"Absolutely, boss."

"And, Cooper? All kidding aside, I'm glad you're okay and thanks for making me see the point of all the extra work. They're a good crew and I damn sure didn't want to tell their families that they weren't coming home."

"Just doin' my job, Cord."

"Well, nobody does it better."

They cleared the call simultaneously, Cooper feeling a little embarrassed. Ever since their accident, Cord had been as safety conscious as Coop. Still, it felt good to know his persnickety tendencies were appreciated. He tucked his phone away and headed toward the knot of official vehicles.

Two of the firefighters leaned against their brush pumper, watching Britt. He didn't like the glint in their eyes, or the speculative looks on their faces. As he got closer, he heard one say, "Pretty little storm chaser is all wet."

"Indeed she is," the second one agreed.

Cooper was not at all pleased they were discussing her. Britt was going to be his. Sooner or later. He glanced over at her. She wore a dark shirt so even though it was plastered to her body, it didn't reveal much. Except it was plastered to her body and Coop had been fantasizing about her body for months now and he darn sure didn't remember her breasts being that large nor the roundness of her belly. He blinked. And everything inside him went cold.

Nine

Britt continued to give spot reports until one of the regular reporters showed up to take over. In between conversations with the station and on-air time, she watched Cooper. The few times she caught him looking at her, she couldn't decipher his expression. He looked angry but confused, with a side of narrow-eyed speculation, almost like she was some sort of criminal. What had she done wrong? Her brain jumped on its hamster wheel and she caught a glimpse of her reflection in the tinted window of her truck.

Her clothes were wet, though drying. Except her cotton Henley was plastered to her body. *Really* plastered. Her added curves were visible to anyone who looked. And Cooper had been looking. A lot. She reminded her lungs to work. This was bad. If he guessed before she told him… Or maybe he'd just think that she was seeing someone else. Yes. That was the ticket. If he thought she had a boyfriend, then he would never think he was the father and she wouldn't have to tell him, except…she'd be lying.

And while she might be a lot of things, a liar was not one of them. She had to tell him. But not here and definitely not now.

A gust of wind blew through and it chilled her. Goose bumps rose on her arms and she shivered. She searched the back seat of her truck and found the go bag she'd stuffed in there earlier in the fall. Digging through it, she found dry jeans, a shirt and more important, underwear. All she had to do now was find a place to change. Straightening, she surveyed the rig site. A metal building that looked like some sort of office sat next to the rig. If she was lucky, it might have indoor plumbing too.

Cooper was the last person she wanted to talk to so she watched to see which of the BarEx crew she should ask. An older man seemed to be giving instructions so she waited to approach him until Cooper was busy with the fire chief.

"Um, hi," she said to the man's back. He turned around and smiled.

"What can I do you for, darlin'?"

"Is that building like an office or something?"

"Or something. Whatcha need?"

"A place to change clothes and maybe use the…uh…facilities?"

He managed not to smile but she caught the twinkle in his eyes. "Door's open, and there's a lock on it. Help yourself."

She flashed him a smile of thanks and jogged over. She checked Cooper's location to make sure he wasn't looking at her. He was still busy with the chief so she ducked inside and locked the door.

Britt ran into a problem when she tried to button and zip up the jeans. She muttered several four-letter words before stretching out with her back on the desk and just managed to get the darn things fastened. She had to roll off the desk because she couldn't sit up while breathing and at that point in time, breathing was of utmost importance. The jeans were uncomfortable and she considered popping both the button and the zipper and just keeping her shirttails out to cover up. Except as sure as she did that, someone would notice. Like Cooper. That man didn't miss a trick.

After a few moments, she got her breath back and decided she'd be fine so long as she didn't have to sit down. Sitting and breathing would be completely incompatible. She shouldn't have put off her shopping trip. And it was time to address the proverbial elephant in the room. She had to tell Cooper, the sooner the better.

Cooper covertly watched Britt. He didn't want to think what he was thinking. The odds were hardly favorable but given the file on Chance's desk concerning Susan Maddox's paternity accusation and the court-ordered DNA tests, he couldn't keep his thoughts from going there. Maybe she'd just put on weight. That was entirely possible. It wasn't like she was a true on-air personality who had some sort of contract clause that decreed she wear a size five or something. And she definitely hadn't been built like a runway model last August. But now? Not that he didn't appreciate the curves. He definitely did, yet something was different about her.

It took some maneuvering before he stood next to Leo. He opened the conversation with what he considered safe territory. "Tackle, right?"

"Nope. Tackle, left."

He laughed. "Good one. I thought I recognized you."

"Not many do anymore."

"How long have you been on TV?"

It was the cameraman's turn to laugh. "Not exactly *on* the tube. I was a communications major. Thought I'd do sportscasting if I couldn't go pro. Then I heard my voice."

He let out a booming laugh. "Yeah...no. Not to mention I hate wearing a tie. So I grabbed a camera."

"You been with Britt long?"

A bushy black eyebrow rose. "A while."

Cooper considered his next question carefully but Leo beat him to it. "If you're interested, I can save you the trouble. She'll shut you down like she does every other guy. That little gal hasn't gone on a date in the two years I've known her."

Which was a good news/bad news situation as far as Coop was concerned. Because she'd been with him. Several times. Two and two kept coming up four and he got a sinking feeling in the pit of his stomach. "Yeah...well. I'll just have to change her mind about that."

Britt stared out the windshield. This was so not a good idea. Why she'd ever agreed to meet Cooper for a late dinner was beyond her. She was tired and her hair still smelled faintly of smoke. Today's fire had been exhausting to cover.

"You're going to regret this," she muttered. She did not want to confide in him. Not that she wouldn't. The man had a right to know. She didn't see his truck in the Mexican restaurant's parking lot. Wondering why he'd suggested this place, she continued to just sit there. She'd wanted to eat here for ages but never had. Now, her stomach was turning somersaults and she wasn't sure she'd be able to sample the food.

She'd dreaded this moment from the instant that stupid pregnancy test showed a plus sign. Britt didn't have to wonder who the father was. There'd been only one. She snorted and rolled her eyes at her reflection in the rearview mirror. Wasn't that the tag line to some old TV show about immortal highlanders?

Someone tapped on her window. Britt squealed and recoiled. Then she recognized Cooper's face peering in at her.

"You okay, Girl Wonder?"

"I'm fine." Okay, that came out snippier than it should have, but he had startled her. "Just waiting on you to get here."

"I've been here."

She looked around the parking lot again. "Where's your truck?"

"At home. I brought my Expedition."

Well, crud. Of course he'd have more than one vehicle. "If you have an Expedition, why did you drive your truck to the gala?"

"Company branding."

"What?"

"Are you getting out or what? We can talk inside. I have a cold drink and hot queso in there waiting."

"Or what," she muttered under her breath, reluctant to open the door and get out. Still, it was time.

Inside the restaurant, he held her chair. She sank into it, gave her drink order to the waitress, and eyed the basket of tortilla chips, salsa, queso and relish. Her stomach rumbled. Good to know that she could eat. She reached for the chips and when the waitress returned with her iced tea, Britt ordered hot tortillas—a mix of corn and flour.

As she plowed through the chips, then the tortillas, she framed what she was going to say in her mind. Cooper sat across from her, watching with an amused look and occasionally getting brave enough to snatch a chip. Once their food arrived, she debated whether to wait until after dinner. Okay, until after she had a sopapilla. Those little pillows of fried bread drenched in honey were a favorite dessert. Too bad Cooper beat her to the punch.

"When are you due?"

She choked on the bite of enchilada she'd just put in her mouth, barely managing to chew, swallow and grab a gulp of tea before staring at him, eyes wide. She stalled, hoping she'd heard wrong. "Beg pardon?"

"When's your due date?"

Yeah. She'd heard him correctly. She took another sip then dabbed at her lips with her napkin before meeting his gaze. "First week in June." She watched him make the calculations in his head and decided to distract him. "How did you know I'm pregnant?"

Okay, it was fairly obvious—loose clothing, noticeable baby bump that was more like a small hill than a bump. He studied her, all traces of amusement gone.

"Who's the father?"

She glanced around the restaurant. No one was seated nearby to overhear her. That excuse to avoid the topic wasn't available. She lifted a shoulder in a negligent shrug as she lifted her chin in stubborn pride. "You."

"What do you want?"

Now that surprised her. No argument. No denial. No pleading. Just direct and to the point. Maybe this wouldn't be so bad after all. "Nothing."

That made him blink. He leaned his elbows on the table, framing his plate of beef fajitas. "Nothing?"

"You got it. I don't want your money or anything else from you." She leaned forward and dropped her voice conspiratorially. "I'm guessing the condom broke or something. Since you're the one who can't keep your little cowboy wrangled in your jeans, you should check the best-if-used-by dates on those things."

Britt hoped that by going on the offensive, she'd put Cooper off. She couldn't decipher his expression, and deep down, she wanted to poke at him to get a response. Some other woman might be having his baby. She definitely was. And his lack of reaction bothered her. A lot. He continued to watch her and she made a mental note never to play strip poker with the guy.

"I'm a big girl. I knew what I was doing and accept the responsibility." She put down her fork and leaned back. "I'm not trying to trap you, Cooper. We had fun together. We got caught. I'm dealing with it."

He continued to stare and she wondered what was going through his head.

"Sounds like you have it all figured out." His voice sounded flat. "And since you have, I'm curious as to why you decided to involve me at all."

Did he really just say that to her? "Because you're the father! You have a right to know." She rubbed at her forehead, hoping to stave off the headache forming behind her eyes. "Look. Bad timing, given that other situation."

"That *other* situation? You mean the woman trying to scam me out of child support for a baby that isn't mine?"

"So *you* say."

"I do say. And the DNA test will prove it. In the meantime, I have a solution to *this* situation."

The next words out of his mouth sent her into a tailspin.

"We'll get married."

She almost choked again. "No!" Now she leaned on the table and they were almost nose-to-nose. "You want to pay child support? Awesome. But I am not marrying you just because I'm pregnant."

"Why not?"

"What do you mean why not? Because…just…no. I don't love you." *But you could.* She shushed that voice in her head, all the while wondering why that was her first argument. "I barely know you. Granted, the sex is off the charts but that is not a good basis for a marriage."

He broke first—sort of. He didn't lose her gaze as he seemed to relax, leaning back into his chair. He raised a rolled tortilla filled with fajita meat and grilled onions and peppers to his mouth. Biting it, he continued to hold her eyes as he chewed, then swallowed. "Why didn't you do something about it when you found out?"

It was her turn to blink, surprised. Several things came to mind but it was the truth that tumbled out, much to her chagrin. "Because it's your baby too." She closed her eyes and rubbed her temple. "What I mean is, I wouldn't have done something like that without contacting you first. Granted most men would totally agree to the procedure—"

"I wouldn't have."

She slowly closed her mouth. He kept talking.

"I still want to marry you."

"I'm still confused. That accuser at the gala—"

"Is lying through his teeth. I'd never seen his sister before she arrived at my cousin's office with her brother and their attorney. Do you have any idea how many paternity suits my family gets hit with?"

"How do you know I'm not lying?"

"Because I know. I was there. I'm the one who discovered that the condom broke but by the time I got out of the bathroom, you'd already disappeared. Again. I assumed you were on some form of birth control. Guess you weren't."

She blushed, and slid her gaze away from his for a long moment. "I was busy and I forgot when I was due for my shot. I wasn't dating anyone so it wasn't a big deal. You used condoms. And then…" She made an exploding gesture with her fingers. "My world sort of blew up. By the time I remembered about the Depo shot, it was too late. I was throwing up and buying a pregnancy test."

"Were you ever going to tell me?" He sounded…hurt. That surprised her.

"Yeah. Eventually. I don't want you to feel obligated, Cooper."

"Yeah, you don't get it. I *am* obligated. You say you want to take responsibility. Well, guess what, Girl Wonder. It took both of us to make that baby." His lips curved up into a smile that would melt the panties off any woman who saw it. "As you say, the chemistry between us is exceptional. So, we'll get married and I'll take care of you and the baby."

"No."

"Why are you being so stubborn about this? Any other woman would be jumping at the chance."

"I'm not any other woman. I'm me."

Now it was his turn to sigh, close his eyes and rub his temple. When he looked at her again, his expression caused her heart to skip a beat. "If you won't marry me, I want joint custody."

Ten

Cooper didn't smirk at the look of surprised confusion on Britt's face. He'd remained very calm. He had to, given the evidence. The timing was right. The condom had broken. And, at least according to Leo, Britt didn't date or fool around. Except she had with him. He thought back to that night. She'd come on hot and heavy. The sex had been her idea. But then she'd disappeared the next morning. He didn't get the sense she was scamming him, though a guy could never be too careful.

"Are you kidding me?" she finally asked.

"Nope." He wasn't kidding. If the DNA test proved the kid was his, he'd support the child monetarily, but also emotionally. No way he'd go for anything besides joint custody. Of course, that would give him lots of reasons to hang around Britt. He wouldn't have been at all unhappy if she'd agreed to marry him. He was already half in love with her, crazy as that seemed. He wasn't the only brother who'd been hit by the Curse of the Tate Men. He always capitalized the phrase like it was a title or was important. Denver, his dad, sat each of his brothers down in their early teens for the birds and the bees talk, and he finished with two admonitions—always wear a condom and beware of the Curse of the Tate Men.

"Tate men," Denver Tate had said in that booming voice of his, "are cursed to love only one woman and to love her hard and forever. You'll know when the right one comes along. Don't be settlin' for less, boy. You hear me?"

As sure as his mother wore pearls, he'd been cursed.

And frankly, it didn't feel too bad. Britt was funny, intelligent, gorgeous, stubborn. Well, okay. Maybe that last one should go in the negative column but at least things would never get boring. She reminded him of his mother just a little bit, not that he would ever mention that to either woman. He might be dumb but he wasn't stupid.

"Why in the world would a man like you want to share joint custody of a child?"

"A man like me?" He didn't mean for his voice to sound quite as threatening as it came out but his tone sure made Britt sit up and take notice. Wide-eyed and pressed back in her chair, she stared at him. "What's that supposed to mean?"

She swallowed hard and he watched her throat work, which stirred up things inside him. Nope, chemistry was never a problem between them. When she just continued to stare, he cocked a brow—a dare he knew she couldn't resist.

"Well, you know."

"No, I don't know. That's why I asked."

"You're rich."

"I also work for a living."

"You're single."

"I offered to marry you."

"What do you know about kids?"

"I have nieces and nephews." Well, *a* niece and *a* nephew

that were Tates. There were more if he included the Barron cousins.

"Why would you want to tie yourself down?"

"Why would you?"

Her mouth opened. Closed. Opened. Closed. Forehead furrowed, she studied him. "Why would you even ask that?"

He held up his right index finger. "You work for a living—two jobs. One of which has crazy hours." He added his middle finger. "You're single." He ticked up a third finger. "What do you know about kids?"

Britt did the whole fish out of water imitation again before clamping her mouth shut. "Point to you," she finally admitted. "But you're a guy."

"Glad you noticed."

"Gah." She rolled her eyes. "You know what I mean. I figured a man like you would be glad to be absolved of responsibility."

"Well, I'm not. In fact, I'm kinda offended you'd think that."

That got a reaction. She rocked back, tucking her chin as she frowned. "I don't know what to say to that."

"Considering that you keep insulting me, maybe you should only open your mouth to eat." He didn't hide the smile sliding across his face as he considered other things he'd like her mouth to do. He focused on his own meal while watching her out of his peripheral vision. He'd call Chance once he and Britt were finished to fill him in on current events and to get some safeguards set up, just in case Britt continued to balk.

And didn't that make him all cool, calm and collected. He should be angry at the most, dubious and suspicious at the least. Except she hadn't shown up on his doorstep demanding things. In fact, Britt had done her best to avoid him. Then she refused his offer of marriage. He still wanted a DNA test but he knew with a certainty that surprised him the child was his.

"When's your next doctor's appointment?"

She very carefully chewed and swallowed the bite she'd just forked into her mouth before responding. "Why?"

"Because I'm going with you."

"Oh no you—"

"Yes. I need to speak to his—"

"Her. My OB is female."

"Good to know. I need to give her staff my insurance and contact information. I should help cover medical expenses. Besides, I want to be there."

Taken aback, she considered his offer. "It's an ultrasound."

"Good."

"Do you even know what that is?"

He leveled her with a cool-eyed look. "Yes. When are you scheduled?"

"Right before Christmas."

"Give me the date, time and place. I'll be there."

Cooper faced the room full of men. Their expressions matched the roles they were there to play. He was not looking forward to breaking the news to his family. They'd be concerned. He also wondered if he should warn Britt. His relatives, especially the Barron wives—or Bee Dubyas for short—could get overwhelming in a hurry.

He needed a cup of coffee before the dam broke. Nikki, ever her omniscient and efficient self, bumped through his office door bearing a tray full of mugs and a large thermal carafe of coffee. She flashed a cheeky grin and in a loud stage whisper said, "My birthday is next month and there's a pair of diamond earrings I've had my eye on. I'll put them on the company card in lieu of a bonus for my years of selfless service."

She deposited the tray on his desk and gave a perky wiggle of her fingers as she exited. Cord watched her leave before he turned to Coop. "She has a company card?"

Cooper stared at him. "Well…yeah. Doesn't Maureen?"

"Well…yeah, but that's different."

He rolled his eyes at his cousin and boss. "Sure it is."

Glancing toward the door, Cord muttered something about the accountants and discussing with his administrative assistant how she used the credit card. Coop laughed. "If Nikki actually followed through every time she threatened to buy diamonds with that card, we'd own stock in Tiffany's."

"Now that joke time is over," Chance interrupted, his lawyer face firmly in place, "we need to talk about this situation with Britt Owens."

"Not a situation, Chance, and *we* aren't doing a thing."

"Cooper," Bridger started.

"Look, I called y'all last night after I forced the issue with Britt. Paternity is not confirmed but it will be. What I need from you, Chance—"

Cash jumped into the conversation. "Chance is right, Cooper. We need to step back and assess things. We've all been here."

"Except me," Bridger said. "I'm the good son."

Cooper nailed him in the head with a wadded-up ball of paper. "You better knock wood, Bridge. I was with Britt. In Beaumont. The times line up." His pronouncement dropped into a well of silence. "I'm pretty sure I'm the father of her baby."

"Dad taught us better, Coop."

"I wore a condom, Bridger. Both times."

"Wait," Cord interrupted. "*Britt* was the one who disappeared on you down there? The one you've been mooning over since you got home in September."

Bridger nodded sagely. "Yup. She would be the one.

Mom had it figured out before any of the rest of us but, man…" He shook his head now, looking dubious. "The timing on her little announcement is all kinds of wrong."

"I've never been with that Susie…" Coop snapped his fingers a couple of times trying to recall her name. "Maddox. Have no clue who she is. And the DNA test will prove I'm not the father of her baby. I'm not in the habit of discussing my sex life with anyone much less you miscreants yet I've admitted that Britt and I were together."

Cord leaned back in his chair. "So if you wore a condom, how can you be so sure the baby is yours?"

"Because the damn thing broke."

Chance put down his coffee mug. "I want you to think very carefully about how you answer this, Cooper." His gaze was so intent, Coop had to clear his throat. Then he nodded, waiting for what Chance would say next. "What exactly do you mean by the condom broke?"

Coop could almost see the air quotes around those last four words. "Because when I took it off, the top had partially separated from the sides. It broke, Chance."

"She could have messed with it. Did she have the chance to get at your wallet?" his ever-helpful boss asked.

"Yeah…about that. I used the one in my wallet the night before."

"So she gave you the condom?" Chance pushed. "She could have poked a hole in the package."

"No!" Coop glared at his cousin. "She didn't touch the thing. I dug it out of the drawer on the bedside table of the company's RV." He felt sheepish and probably looked like it if the expressions on his brothers' and cousins' faces were any indication. "Who knew those things come with an expiration date. It had been in the drawer for…a really long time."

The others exchanged looks and Coop felt like he was

fourteen again, getting The Lecture from his dad—the one about girls and condoms and the Curse of the Tate Men.

Coop could still hear his dad's voice, a rich baritone with an edge, a gruff gravelly tone like he smoked two packs a day, though the man had only smoked seven cigars in his entire life. One for each of his sons. He missed his dad so much. A big man who worked with his hands, an old-school rancher who'd given his sons all the right advice. Then he'd died. Sudden cardiac death, the doctor said. He and Tucker had found him in the barn, sitting on a bale of hay, looking like he was taking a nap.

He'd watched Deke fall in love and then Tucker. And told both of them that they weren't being smart to fall so hard and fast. Quin and Noelle completed Deke, just as Zoe and Nash did the same for Tuck. Neither child was a Tate by blood, but they sure were by love. Deke and Quin had adopted Noelle and Tuck had adopted Zoe's little boy. Britt's baby was his. Did he love Britt? He wasn't sure. Was he falling in love with her? Oh, yeah. She wasn't anything he'd ever wanted in a woman but he'd discovered she was everything he wanted.

His phone pinged a reminder and he breathed a little easier. Inquisition over. "Britt's having an ultrasound this morning. I'm not missing it because y'all are doing this intervention thing. I plan to marry her, but just in case, I want papers…" He met Chance's concerned gaze. "Joint custody. If she won't marry me, I want joint custody. Make it happen."

Time to make his exit before his brother and cousins pounced. "I know y'all planned an intervention. I don't need one."

He exited to the sound of stunned silence.

Sitting in the break room at the TV station killing time before her appointment, Britt couldn't quite meet Ria's gaze. She sipped her orange juice, wondering why no one had figured out how to caffeinate juice. Oh, wait. That would be soda pop. But as far as coffee was concerned, her doctor insisted she cut back on the only substance guaranteed to get her through the day.

"Girl, you make me crazy." Ria *tsked*, shaking her head, an indulgent expression on her face. "At least he's stepping up and taking responsibility just on your say-so. That's got to be a first in that family."

She snorted. "Oh, he demanded a DNA test, but he's also convinced that he's the father."

"Which he is. You're my best friend. I can count the number of men you've slept with on one hand. And none of them in at least the last year. Of course he's the father."

Coughing to hide her mutter, Britt said, "Two years."

She'd been such an idiot that first time with Cooper. Seeing Leo—a huge man full of muscles and swagger—felled by a stupid trash can lid had done something to her. Watching the water rise, the wind rip buildings apart, knowing that people were going to die? All of that settled deep in her soul, making her understand how fragile life truly was. And how alone she was. When Cooper opened the door to the BarEx offices, all she'd wanted to do was burrow into his arms and hide. To do something spontaneous and outrageous and not like her. So she had. She'd grabbed life with both hands and propositioned him.

That night had been totally worth it. And then when he'd rescued her and the others that next night? And the morning that followed? Heck yeah, she'd cut and run both times out of fear and a sense of self-preservation. The man was a potent combination of funny and handsome, of brains and muscles, and all the things that made the alarm on her biological clock ring. And when that condom broke? Her sadly neglected ovaries must have gone into overdrive.

"I'm an idiot," she muttered.

"Yes and no. I think you're being smart to take things slow." Ria reached across the table and squeezed her hand. "He's taking care of the bills. That's only right. And he's interested. Good grief, the chemistry between you two is off the charts. Get to know him." She held up her free hand, cutting off Britt's intended retort. "I'm aware he asked you to marry him, and you think it's out of some antiquated sense of duty. Maybe it is but let me tell you, Miz Britt, men like that are few and far between. Date. Let him take care of things. Get. To. Know. Him. Who knows? That chemistry might just turn into the real deal."

And that was precisely what scared her the most.

Eleven

Britt walked into her doctor's office and halted midstep. Cooper stood at the check-in window, one elbow braced casually on the tall counter as he spoke to the receptionist. The woman stared at him raptly, like he was some Olympic god come to earth or something. Okay, he did look utterly awesome in those pressed jeans, boots, a shirt as blue as his eyes, and the leather jacket.

Everything went into slow motion as he turned his head to look at Britt, a smile teasing those so-kissable lips of his, the fluorescent lights catching in his eyes so that they twinkled. He checked her out, from head to toe, and heat washed over her.

Then she saw red as the totally skinny and primped woman behind the counter slid a card toward Coop and Britt read her lips. "Here's my number. Call me anytime."

Cooper ignored the woman and her card. Instead, he stalked across the office toward Britt. She forced air into her lungs. Who knew breathing was so hard to do? The red faded from her vision, but she noticed the gaze of every female in the place, from sixteen to sixty, was trained on him. The testosterone haze he exuded was so potent, she was pretty sure he could get a girl pregnant just by looking at her. Of course, she knew all about that, didn't she?

"Howdy, Girl Wonder."

No, her panties were *not* going to disappear just from the sound of his voice or the heat in his eyes. *Nope. Not happening.* Nor would she swoon because if she did, he'd catch her, and she'd be a goner if he touched her.

"Fancy meeting you here, Hero Boy."

"I keep tellin' you—"

"Yeah, yeah. You're not a boy. And I'm not a girl. I need to get checked in."

After she signed in, he led her to a couch set back in the far corner of the waiting room. They didn't have time to sit before her name was called.

Britt turned to go, stopping when Coop touched her arm. "I'd really…" He cleared his throat and she saw raw emotion shine through his eyes for a moment. "If you don't mind, I'd like to go back with you."

Her first instinct was to say, "No way." But she couldn't resist the plea in his eyes. "Okay."

The sonographer was all smiles as she walked them back to a fairly large room with an exam table, a couch and a comfy chair. A utilitarian cart filled with all sorts of electronic gear was parked next to the exam table. A giant-screen TV was mounted to the opposite wall.

"You can pull the chair over close to our little momma, if you want, Dad."

Britt gritted her teeth. Why did so many health care workers get all honey-sweet and cutesy? Their demeanor irritated the snot out of her on a good day and today? Today was so not a good day. She woke up with indigestion, a frantic need to pee and a headache. Then she'd had to cover a class for another adjunct professor who'd decided to take off for Christmas early, which meant an unplanned trip to the campus in Norman. And her truck was sitting on empty so she had to stop and get gas. The automatic shutoff on the hose didn't click off when her tank was full, gasoline spilled on her shoes and she'd gotten into a shouting match with the convenience store clerk over the mess.

And Cooper had been waiting for her all spit and polished and handsome, getting flirted with by a woman who looked perfect and—

"Shhh, darlin'."

She blinked at him. "What?"

"You're growling. Here. I'll help you up."

The next thing she knew, his hands were on her sides and he lifted her easily to sit on the table. While the tech got her prepped, Coop dragged the chair over, sat down and took her hand. Then the tech squirted cold, gushy gel on her bared belly. The sonographer pressed the wand against her skin then made some adjustments to the machine. Moments later, a picture popped up on the big screen.

For several minutes, the tech moved the wand, keeping up a running commentary. The baby was on track for its age. And it had a cute butt, which was the only recognizable body part she could see.

"Your little one is being shy. Let me move over here to see if we can get a look at its face."

The image on the screen blinked off and when it came back on, the silence in the room was as thick as red clay. Two heads. Were those arms? Britt quickly counted. Four. And four legs. The sonographer squealed like a cheerleader.

"Twins!"

Britt glanced at the walking definition of testosterone and had one thought. Of course, he'd produce twins. Heck, it wouldn't matter if the condom didn't break or if she'd been current on her Depo shot. Her eggs never had a chance against his champion swimmers. She stared at him while his eyes remained glued to the TV.

She heard some clicks and the wand moved again, followed by more clicks. "I'll print out two copies of all the pictures," the sonographer said. "They look so cute. Too bad we can't tell their sex."

She did *not* want to think about sex of any sort. That's what got her into this in the first place.

Thirty minutes later, the goop had been cleaned off her belly, they each had a set of the ultrasound pictures, and she was sitting in Coop's truck, too stunned to argue when he guided her to it in the parking lot. He settled into the driver's seat, started the truck and punched the buttons for the heater. That's when she realized she was shivering.

"I'm not cold."

"I know."

"Twins."

"Yeah, I know."

Did he sound gleeful? She turned to look at him. He was staring straight ahead but the grin on his face crinkled his cheeks and eyes—at least the ones on the right side. He shifted in the seat so he could look at her.

"Marry me, Britt."

"No."

"Why not?"

"For all the same reasons I've given you before."

"Then move in with me?"

"Wha—? Why?"

"So I can take care of you."

"I don't need anyone to take care of me."

"Darlin', we all need someone to take care of us."

She refused to acknowledge that bit of logic. He remained silent for a few minutes and the shivers stopped as the truck warmed.

"Then spend Christmas with me."

"No." Okay, that was a knee-jerk reaction but she didn't want anything to do with him at the moment, especially Christmas, because she couldn't trust herself.

"Why not?"

"I have plans." She didn't, but she'd make some. Today. And he didn't need to know.

"I want to introduce you to my family."

"No."

"Britt." He was wheedling. And it was working. She didn't have family. Not anymore.

"New Year's then."

"I have plans."

Cooper went stiff, his voice barely above a growl when he asked, "Do you have a date?"

Was he jealous? Britt mentally rolled her eyes. What did he have to be jealous of? Not that she *did* have a date.

Before she could confirm or deny, he added, "I'm sure I don't need to remind you that you're having my babies."

Jerk. She swiveled to face him. "Like I could forget? You're not the one with the swollen feet and ankles, the acid reflux, and the obsessive need to know the location of every public restroom between here and there. Why do you even care, Cooper? I've given you the perfect escape. Most men would thank me and disappear so fast they'd leave skid marks. But you? Noooo. Not you. You have to stick your nose in with your demands and your sense of duty and honor and responsibility. Why can't you just be a big ol' weenie like most—"

Before she could finish her rant, she was in his arms and he was kissing her. *Really* kissing her. Like he was dying of thirst and her mouth was the sweetest water in the world. She knew the feeling and wow, was she thirsty for him too.

She was in so much trouble. She pushed away from him and seeing the satisfied smirk on his face, she wanted to clobber him with a two-by-four. Since she didn't have one handy, she scrambled back into her seat, reaching for the door handle. "Go away, Cooper Tate. Go far, far away. I don't want to marry you. I'm not moving in with you. In fact, I pretty much hate you at the moment."

She clambered out and clung to the door until she got her balance. Cooper made no move to get out. She glowered up at him. "I don't need a husband *or* a boyfriend. Just stay away from me."

"I'll pick you up for dinner."

She slammed the door so hard the whole truck rocked. She could still hear his laughter as she climbed into her own vehicle. She managed to get it started, in gear and backed out of the parking space. The rest of her drive home was a blur until she realized she was parked outside her condo. Then she thunked her head on the steering wheel and ignored the tears.

"Twins." What was she supposed to do now?

Britt stared at the bouquet of flowers—a beautiful Christmas arrangement in a crystal vase. From the weight of it, the thing was real cut glass. She almost hadn't opened the door and was now wishing she hadn't. The delivery driver thrust the flowers into her hands and boogied back down the sidewalk before she could react. She cautiously set the vase on her kitchen counter. A card was tucked into the extravagant green and red plaid bow.

Her fingers shook slightly as she freed the envelope, opened it, and withdrew the card. The handwriting was bold. Firm. And she recognized the signature. *Merry Christmas. I'll pick you up at 7:00 for dinner. Dress casual. Cooper.* Her heart did a little giddy-up and she swallowed around the lump of anticipation in her throat. No. Just... no. He was wearing her down. Flowers. Lunches delivered from her favorite restaurants. And flowers. Not every day. But often enough. And deep down, what woman didn't appreciate flowers? Food and flowers were one path to her heart. His calls and concern and always asking if there was something he could do to help derailed her resolve.

The man was nothing if not persistent.

She'd go to dinner. And she'd tell him again, when he asked, that she would not marry him. Except more and more often, daydreams crept in. She'd be staring at a screen shot of a radar presentation looking for data and zap! Just like that, a thought of what it would be like to be sitting in her own space at his house would hit her. Surely there was room in that place for an office all her own, a spot where she could hang maps and whiteboards on the walls. With a worktable holding printouts and photos. A desk with her computer and a printer. A place that could stay messy— well, it would seem messy to anyone but her. She'd know where everything was. *Her* office where she could decorate it any way she wanted, where she could shut the door and walk away from her research, knowing it would all be in the exact same place the next time she entered. She really didn't want much.

And then there were those daydreams of sleeping in his arms, of the kissing and touching and making love that went with sharing the same bed. Since the night of the November gala, she'd found lots of excuses to take weird detours when she drove to the TV station, all of them designed to keep her away from Cooper's house, but she still ended up driving past it, and straining to catch a glimpse of it. Or the man.

And there she went again, lost in thoughts of the man who'd become the bane of her existence. But if he stopped calling, texting, dropping by—and sending her flowers— she'd miss him.

Cooper leaned back in his chair and pretended his fingers didn't itch to touch Britt. Since they'd first gotten the news she was having twins, he'd managed to con her into going out with him several times. The Christmas arrangement he'd had delivered that day also worked. After picking her up, they'd driven to Othello's in Norman, the iconic Italian restaurant on Campus Corner. Ensconced at a table in a dark corner, he watched her eat, plotting how best to get his way. He wanted to spend Christmas with her. And he wanted her to move in with him. Better if she married him, but just having her under his roof would go a long way in his plan to seduce her into accepting his proposal.

"Stop staring."

"I can't help it."

She blinked up at him, slowly chewing the bite of chicken parmigiana she'd just taken. He tracked the muscles in her throat as she swallowed. "What do you mean? Staring at people while they eat is just plain rude."

"You're beautiful."

She rolled her eyes in an exaggerated manner. "Don't change the subject. And don't you dare say I'm glowing."

He flashed her a half smile at that declaration. "Well, you might be glowing just a little. And you are beautiful. You also look tired. I don't like seeing the dark circles under your eyes." He reached across the table and took her free hand in his. "I want to take care of you, Britt."

She bristled, as he knew she would. "I can take care of myself."

"Of course you can. But you don't have to."

"Why won't you just go away?"

No way would he answer that question truthfully. This was a familiar dodge on her part and he suspected she mostly said it by rote. Besides, she probably wasn't quite ready to hear that he was falling in love with her, that he hoped she'd love him back. And it had nothing to do with the fact she was having his babies. He'd been mooning over her long before he discovered her bombshell. "Because I'm here to stay."

"Gah. Don't make rhymes." She paused to twirl spaghetti around her fork, then ate it. "What about your other baby mama?"

"She's not my baby mama. I'll remind you that the prenatal DNA test cleared me completely. As soon as Chance threatened to countersue, she agreed to the test and then dropped her suit."

She shook her hand loose and concentrated on eating. He let a few minutes of silence pass before speaking again. "Spend the holidays with me."

"I can't." Did she sound disappointed?

"Why not?"

"I told you before, I have plans."

"Change them."

"I can't."

"Can't or won't?"

"Both." She set down her fork and now she studied him.

"Why not?"

"We're too different."

"How so?"

"You're…old-fashioned."

"That's a bad thing?"

"You drive me crazy."

"You'll never be bored and since you're something of an adrenaline junky…" He deliberately let his voice trail off. That was a very touchy subject for them both.

"Face it, Coop. Things will never work between us. You have to know that."

"I know nothing of the sort."

Twelve

I know nothing of the sort.

Cooper's assertion had been ricocheting around in Britt's head for two weeks now—two weeks that she'd managed to avoid his calls and texts. She'd steered clear of his big family Christmas. She used the time to herself to work on her dissertation and avoid temptation. With classes at the university on winter break and storm chasing on hold because of the mild weather, she'd finished the first draft. She missed the thrill of the chase and so long as she had no complications, her doctor said she could continue.

She'd also learned that the documentary she and Leo had put together was up for a regional Emmy. With the awards gala a week away, she'd broken down and gone shopping. Her blue formal from November no longer fit and while she didn't believe she had a snowball's chance in hell to win, she wanted to look…pretty.

Not that anyone would notice. Sure, Leo and she were going together. So was his wife. She didn't have a plus-one on standby. Other than Cooper. And no way was she going to involve him any deeper in her life. Coming to depend on him wasn't a good idea. She was an independent woman and she would do this on her own terms.

Britt rubbed at her temple with the fingers of her left hand while she stroked the side of her belly with her right. The twins were more active and it seemed her stomach had ballooned almost overnight. She hadn't felt pretty at all in any of the dresses she tried on. So now she was taking a break at Cadie B's Southern Kitchen in Bricktown. She sat at a table near the windows overlooking the canal patio.

"Mind if I join you?"

Startled, Britt jerked her head around. Katherine Tate was already pulling out the chair across from her and settling into it. "Um…" She blinked several times, gathering her thoughts. "I guess not since you're already sitting, Mrs. Tate."

The older woman's frosty smile would have unnerved Britt but for the momentary twinkle in Mrs. Tate's eyes.

A waitress approached with a menu but Mrs. Tate waved it away. "You've already ordered?" Britt nodded mutely. Mrs. Tate smiled at the waitress. "I want today's special, water with lemon, and coffee."

Silence stretched between them until the water and coffee had been served. Britt, her nerves stretched tight, opened her mouth but snapped it shut when Katherine spoke.

"Please call me Katherine. You are, after all, carrying my grandbabies."

Shocked speechless, Britt stared at Cooper's mother. Her head tilted, almost of its own accord, and her lips pursed. All sorts of thoughts raced between her brain and her mouth while she attempted to form a complete sentence that would sound coherent.

"Something you will learn about me, Britt. I don't play

around. I speak my mind and I appreciate others who do the same."

"Okay." Britt stretched out the word, scrambling for something even semi-intelligent to say. If Mrs. Tate could be blunt, so could she. "You've surprised me. I'd think that you would at least question my veracity and motives."

"I know my son moped around for months and suddenly, he sees you at the fund-raiser and perks right up. I also know that his brothers and cousins remain…skeptical."

"But you aren't?"

"No. When that man accused Cooper and his sister filed that lawsuit, my son vehemently denied even knowing the woman. You?" Katherine inclined her head slightly in Britt's direction. "You he pursues with a single-minded intensity that reminds me of his father. It's like that with the Tate men. When they fall, they fall hard. And they fall only once."

Britt eyed the older woman, bewildered by Mrs. Tate's demeanor and the entire gist of this conversation. Her brain scrambled for an excuse she could use to extricate herself. No subterfuge came to mind so she chose bluntness.

"Why are you telling me this?"

Katherine fingered the pearls around her neck but didn't speak. Britt attempted to wait out the other woman, but impatience got the best of her. "Look, I don't like to play games either. I don't want your son. And I don't need him."

"Would you have told him if he hadn't discovered your condition on his own?"

"On his own? I told him." Even if she hadn't wanted to.

"After he found out you were pregnant and put two and two together."

"Fine. I had my doubts, especially after that scene at the museum during the gala. I figured if I told him, he'd want nothing to do with me. And that works just fine and dandy for me because…" She leaned forward, her gaze holding the other woman's while she very carefully enunciated each word. "I don't want anything from him."

"You don't?"

"No."

"Are you sure?"

She gaped. "Am I sure? Of course I'm sure. The only reason I waited to tell Cooper in the first place—"

"Is because he pinned you down."

"No, I would have told him." She blew out a breath and barely resisted rolling her eyes. "Fine. Still, I would have told him eventually because he had a right to know. You can tell your bullheaded son that getting married just because I'm pregnant is a stupid idea." She held up a finger to stall the retort hovering on Katherine's lips because she had a full head of steam up. "Tell Hero Boy that I don't need or want him. The babies are half his so he can damn well pay his share of support but me? I'm off-limits."

Katherine's smile was smug. "You'll do, my girl. You'll do quite well indeed."

Britt leaned back in her chair, thankful the waitress appeared with their food. She'd do? What did that even mean? She took a bite, keeping a narrow-eyed gaze on Katherine. What was it about this family that they totally ignored anything they didn't want to hear.

Like mother, like son.

Cooper sat on the couch in Cash's office, his cousin's huge Newfoundland dog sprawled across his lap. He loved the big goof despite the drool and shedding hair but Lucifer would demand his pound of flesh—literally—for Coop's species betrayal. His mother and brother sat in two armchairs while Cash propped a hip against the back of the couch. They were there to discuss his latest intel on the Carringtons.

"We have more information about Alex and Colby," Cash began.

"Tell me what you've found out about Trey," Katherine said.

"Trey?" Cooper repeated.

"Colby. That was our nickname for him in college. I haven't seen him since then."

Cooper and Bridger both leaned toward their mother. "Mom? You knew him in college? You wanna explain?"

"No, Bridger, I do not."

"Aunt Kath—"

"No, Cash. I will not regale you boys with tales of my misspent youth. I will tell you this much. Trey was a young man far more interested in me than I was in him. I was at Radcliffe at the time. He was a Harvard student." She looked at Cash. "Your father stepped in when Trey wouldn't take the hint that I was not interested. Cyrus and I may not have seen eye-to-eye on much, but I did appreciate his intervention." She smiled fondly at her boys. "He especially didn't appreciate that I appeared to jump out of the frying pan and into the fire when I met your father. Denver—" Her eyes grew misty and her smile was both sad and fond. "Your father was my world."

The relationship between his mom's brother and patriarch of the Barron family, Cyrus Barron, and his dad had never been what anyone would call cordial. Cooper glanced up at his cousin. "So why do you think Alex was at the gala, and why did he approach Mom?"

"I don't know. He's still in town, though. Nosing around several of the Barron companies." Cash studied Katherine. "Colby Carrington is the CEO of CCI, Ltd. As near as Chase and I can figure out, it's a family-held conglomerate. His net worth is in the high seven figures. He inherited his money and the company. Alex is his middle son, with an

MBA from Harvard Business School and a reputation as a corporate raider."

Cooper exchanged a long look with his brother before they both looked at their mother. Coop expressed what they were both thinking. "It could be a coincidence, but I don't like that he's poking around in our business."

"Neither do I." Cash was always blunt. "I plan to do a deeper dig on the whole family and their company." He studied the others before continuing. "CCI is headquartered in Hartford, Connecticut. I don't buy the fact that either Carrington is interested in investing here." His expression turned grim. "Aunt Katherine, what exactly did my father do to the senior Carrington?"

She sighed, her hand going to the strand of pearls around her neck, a gesture so familiar to Cooper that it was almost as comforting to him as it obviously was to her.

"Mom? We aren't dredging up the past for grins and giggles. There had to be a reason for his son to approach you the way he did. You said yourself that he introduced himself like you should know his name and pedigree. You obviously did, and I think it's smart you played reticent, but we need to figure out what's going on."

"I left Radcliffe after two years. Partly because I met your father and partly because the situation with Trey had become untenable. When I didn't return to school, Trey came out here looking for me. Cyrus had a rather stern talk with him and sent him back to Boston. It didn't last. He continued to write and to call me. And that spring break, he came back. Cyrus caught him. I don't know precisely what happened but—" She glanced up at Cash. "Your father's hands were bruised and battered. I suspect he gave Trey a serious beating, along with the threat that if he ever contacted me again, the authorities would never find his body."

Cooper was both shocked and impressed that his uncle

had that in him. The guy had been ruthless as all get-out and didn't care who he cut off at the knees—including his own sons—but as far as Cooper knew, he'd never gotten his hands dirty like that.

"Wonder if the old guy has a screw loose?" Bridge added.

"Something to consider," Cash agreed. "You have your assignment, Bridge. Work with Chase and Tucker. He has contacts he can tap into. And get our IT folks on this."

"Roger that, boss."

"In other news…" Cash turned his attention to Cooper.

"In other news," Katherine interjected. "What are you doing about Britt Owens?"

Cooper stared at his mom. "Excuse me?"

"Britt and your babies. What are you doing about them?"

"I asked her to marry me." He ignored the shocked intakes of breath coming from his brother and cousin.

"She's not very happy with you."

Cooper had a very bad feeling about that statement. He eyed his mother warily. "How would you know?"

"I bought her lunch today. Did you know she likes to eat at Cadie B's?"

Snapping his mouth shut once he realized it was hanging open, Cooper couldn't find words. Instead, he rubbed his forehead and squinted against the headache that was building. "Mom…" His tone was a warning.

"I just happened to be there and saw her eating alone. I wanted to get to know my future daughter-in-law. Independent little thing, isn't she."

That wasn't a question and he wasn't about to answer. He had the right to remain silent and with Katherine Tate for a mother, silence was always the best option.

She arched a brow at him. "I'm aware that she said no. You need to woo her, Cooper."

"Woo her?" Bridger stage-whispered before snickering. He sobered immediately when his mother turned to stare at him.

"It is unfortunate that she witnessed that little scene at the museum. You have your work cut out for you. Why didn't you invite her for Christmas?"

Cooper unconsciously rubbed his jaw where he'd been coldcocked at the gala then dropped his hand when he realized he was doing so. "I did."

"Why didn't she accept?"

"Why do you think?"

"She had other plans, even if those were sitting alone in her apartment." His mother pushed out of the chair and headed toward the door, apparently done with them all. She paused and looked back. "Fix this, Cooper."

Thirteen

Chase stared at him. "You can't be serious, Coop. This is kind of a big deal—at least to those who are up for the awards. I can get you in. That's easy, even with short notice, since the event is being held at the Crown Barron."

Well aware that the ceremony to present regional Emmys was being held in Oklahoma City at the family-owned hotel, Coop shrugged. "That'd be no fun."

"And crashing her party will be?"

His cousin had a point and he would need assistance to be seated at Channel 2's table, but he wanted Britt to be surprised and off balance—especially since she hadn't mentioned she'd been nominated and had been doing her best to avoid him. She and Leo had put together a thirty-minute documentary on storm chasers that showed how what they did as reporters was far more than just going after tornadoes. In fact, Cooper was featured in some of the footage from that November wildfire. He'd been down in the Gulf dealing with a new rig when it had aired. His mother DVR'd it for him to watch.

Britt's voice-overs and her eye for picking the most dramatic footage were amazing. He just didn't understand why she fought going in front of the camera as an in-studio personality. He wasn't an adrenaline junkie, but he got the appeal of her work. Except she was pregnant. The argument over storm chasing in her condition was ongoing.

"Just get me in, Chase. Without Britt finding out I'm going to be there."

"Black tie, dude. Just sayin'. I know how much you *love* dressing up."

For Britt? He'd wear anything. Heck, he'd walk around the bases at the Bricktown Ballpark buck naked in front of a sellout crowd if she asked. "My tux is cleaned and pressed."

"Whatever."

Savannah, Chase's wife, made a *tsking* sound. "You realize that we have to vet her, don't you? Make sure she's good enough for you?" She flashed both men a cheeky grin. "And personally? I think you surprising her is awesome. Ooh…" Her twinkling eyes landed on her husband. "If we knew for sure that she's the winner, you could arrange to have Cooper present it to her. How awesome would that be?"

Cooper choked and turned a wide-eyed stare on her. "Don't. Just…no, Savvie. If the Bee Dubyas get anywhere near her, I swear to heaven I will come hunting all of you and you won't like the consequences. I'm having enough trouble wrangling her without y'all's interference."

"We don't interfere—"

"The hell you don't," Chase muttered under his breath. Louder, he added, "Darlin', just stay out of this one. It's way more complicated than y'all think."

"Well, duh, Chase." Savvie rolled her eyes this time. "We *are* aware that she's carrying his twins. What we want to know is why she thinks she's too good for him."

Groaning, Cooper dropped his head into the palm of his hand. "Please, Savannah. If you love Chase, stay out of my life. And keep your sisters-in-law away too."

"Hey, we help!"

"No!" Cooper and Chase exclaimed at the same time.

She huffed and crinkled her nose. "Fine. You'll be sorry, and when you come crawling back asking us to get involved to save your sorry tail, we'll just laugh at you."

Unsure whether he should be relieved or apprehensive, Cooper dipped his chin in acknowledgment. "Thank you."

His phone pinged and after reading the message, he headed toward the door of Chase's office. "Thanks, cuz."

"Don't thank me, Coop. *I* think this is a dumb idea and the fact that my wife thinks it's a good one? Yeah, I'd be running fast and far if I were you, bud."

Britt stepped out of the limo provided by KOCX with help from Leo. Her truck was so much easier to get in and out of, even with the extra frontal protrusion. She patted her belly to remind the babies that she loved them despite her often snarky thoughts concerning them. Looking up, she realized there was a red carpet. A *real* red carpet with red velvet ropes keeping the photographers and fans away. Granted, it was nothing like Hollywood, but a little zing ran up her spine. She was glad the temperatures had turned mild for January so she didn't need a coat.

The doors to the historic Barron Crown Hotel swung wide. She, Leo and his wife walked through them. People milled about the lobby, following the trail of the red carpet. Deeper inside, a backdrop had been erected and everyone paused to have their photographs taken. She stood there a little dumbfounded and slightly starstruck. Someone touched the small of her back and urged her forward.

"This way, Ms. Owens."

Heat licked at her skin. She knew that touch *and* the

voice. Cooper! What was he doing here? She marched forward, quickening her step to draw away from the weight of his hand.

"Easy, Girl Wonder. You're wearing heels. Wouldn't want you to get tripped up."

His voice, like smooth caramel, poured over her. She'd managed to avoid him—mostly—for almost a month. It hadn't been easy. But she should have realized he'd try to pull a stunt like this. He just wasn't giving up. She almost had to give the guy props for his stubbornness, and deep down, it made her feel all mushy.

Cooper's arm slid around her waist, pulling her up short, dead center of the backdrop. He leaned over to whisper into her ear. "Smile for the camera, darlin'."

"Don't *darlin'* me," she snarled, right as the flash went off, blinding her for a moment. She closed her eyes to clear the sparkles.

"You are sooo gonna pay for this," she hissed under her breath. So much for those mushy feelings.

"I can think of all sorts of ways I can do that," he teased. Her skin flushed, the chemistry between them flaring white-hot. Her memory was far too good, and now that he'd put the thought in her head, her imagination was far too vivid.

She clamped her mouth shut, refusing to give him any more ammunition. Ever since he'd confirmed that she was pregnant, he'd been tracking her like a bloodhound. No. Bloodhounds were cute and cuddly. Cooper Tate was a wolf, pure and simple. A big, bad wolf. Who would use his big teeth and big paws and big everything else on her. She shivered and Cooper put his arm around her shoulders. Like it was the most natural thing in the world, she leaned into his warmth as he led her toward the ballroom where the gala was happening.

"Cold?"

"No."

She caught his knowing smile from the corner of her eye and let out a silent *argh*. Why had she ever told him that she was pregnant? And why couldn't he just be a jerk, offer her child support and stay far away? No, he had to be all gentlemanly and insist on marrying her. He didn't love her, and they mixed together like baking soda and vinegar with explosive results. They'd be divorced within a year and then where would the babies be?

Babies. Twins. Britt was still getting used to that idea. They didn't run in her family so it was all Cooper's fault. And she'd told him that on numerous occasions. The big jerk just puffed out his chest and claimed it was that potent Barron and Tate blood running in his veins.

Still, he was so dang handsome as he stood there beside her in his formal attire. His white tux coat was longer than other men's, with short lapels, three buttons, and a squared-off lower hem that hit him about midthigh on his black pants. She figured there was some fancy name for the style but she had no clue what it was. She did know that the style fit his broad shoulders and chest, and narrower waist and hips, to perfection. His vest was a slate gray and his tie was metallic silver. The black Stetson with the silver hatband sat atop his head like it had been created just for him. For all she knew, it had. Oil tycoon, she reminded herself. The whole outfit had probably been tailor-made.

They entered the ballroom and she stopped for a moment. The room looked like a set straight out of the glamorous early days of Hollywood—all white and silver art deco decorations and satin tablecloths and chair covers with big bows. Silver stars glittered behind billowing silk suspended along the arched ceiling, lit by gorgeous crystal chandeliers. Each round table held place settings of heavy silver flatware with snowy napkins folded into fantastical shapes with shiny silver chargers. Long stems of creamy calla lilies graced tall clear crystal vases, held by silver stones in the bottom. And it struck her that Cooper fit in perfectly while she felt like a whale out of water.

"Wow," she breathed.

Wow indeed, Coop thought. When she'd first stepped out of the limo, his chest ached at the sight of her. First he caught sight of a strappy, high-heeled silver shoe, then a skirt made from something sheer and billowy in a color that rivaled expensive champagne. The long-sleeved top of the dress was covered in silver sequins, and a man's eyes traveled to the lovely woman wearing it, not her obvious rounded belly. He knew very little about women's fashions but Britt looked like a dream. She'd pulled her hair back, leaving a few strands loose to curl around her face.

He'd had to grit his teeth as Leo helped her out. Leo was a good guy and Coop had recruited the other man to help out in his pursuit of Britt. He'd waited just inside the door and claimed her as soon as she entered.

Now they were in the ballroom and stars gleamed in her blue eyes. She'd tucked her glasses into the small purse she carried and, after looking around surreptitiously, she fished them out. Settling them on her face, she surveyed the area a second time. Her lips formed a perfect O as she inhaled deeply and let out her breath before surreptitiously stuffing her glasses back in her purse.

"Pretty swanky, huh?"

"Amazing."

A waiter with a tray of champagne flutes approached. Coop grabbed a glass with one hand while leaning close to whisper in the waiter's ear and slipping a folded bill into the man's pocket. The waiter promptly disappeared but returned moments later with a refilled tray and one flute in his hand.

"For the lady," he said holding out the flute. It contained a liquid that was a slightly different color than the champagne in the rest of the glasses.

"Ginger ale," Coop explained. Britt happily accepted the drink. He nodded toward a table near the small stage set at the far end of the room. "Do you need to sit or would you like to wander around and schmooze."

She laughed softly. "That's a word I never thought to hear coming from your mouth."

He shrugged. "I have rich cousins and a socially conscious mother. I get dragged to a lot of events. I also work for one of the biggest family-held energy companies in the US. Schmoozing was a required class in my family education."

Britt curled her lips to keep from laughing again. Cooper wanted to kiss her. Well, he really wanted to do all sorts of things to her. She looked different without her glasses and with her hair so prim and styled. He wanted to pull the pins out of the bun and bury his fingers in her blond curls while he kissed her until neither of them could breathe. Britt always turned him on, usually at the most inopportune times. Like now. With people milling about and a lot of his family present. The public would frown on him going all caveman by scooping her up into his arms and making off with her. But the Barrons had a suite in the hotel and he had the security code to get into it. One elevator ride and they'd be on their way to a really good night.

He gazed down at her, the brim of his hat putting both of their faces into deeper shadows. Cooper wanted more than just a few nights with her. He'd known it all along. This was the woman for him. Now and always. All he had to do was convince her.

"Big night for you."

Britt inhaled deeply. "We won't win. I've been working on my happy face so I can congratulate the winner."

"I've got faith in you."

She blinked up at him, her expression softening. "Really?"

"Truly." He brushed his fingertips across her cheek and smiled when she leaned into the caress. In a very soft voice, he asked, "When are you going to marry me, Girl Wonder?"

Fourteen

Britt forced air into her constricted lungs. She hadn't expected him to bring up the subject again, especially not in this setting. Between the man and her hormones, her emotions were all over the map. When things were good between them, they were very, very good. Too good. Her fingers curled with the urge to touch him and the lips she bit tingled at the thought of kissing him. He was handsome enough to be a Hollywood star. And rich. With a perfect house and a perfect life. Just like their sexual chemistry was too good, he was too perfect. And she wasn't.

"Never. And you need to get over your hero complex. I don't need rescuing."

His expression hardened just enough that she noticed the tightening around his eyes and the slight downturn of his mouth. This was not a man to cross. He might appear easygoing but she'd caught the fierce determination he harbored on more than one occasion.

Before things got more uncomfortable, a man who

looked very much like Cooper walked up with a dark-haired woman. Their identities clicked in her memory: Tucker Tate and his wife, country singer Zoe Parker. Zoe, evidently, was one to get directly to the point.

"When ya due, sweetie? And if it's not in a month or two, I hope there's not more than two buns in your oven."

She'd hoped that this dress, designed for a maternity collection and with its empire waist and flowing tulle skirt, would have partially disguised her condition. Obviously not. She pasted a fake smile on her face. Technically, Tucker was her great-granddaddy boss or something. He was the chief operations officer of Barron Entertainment, which owned KOCX. Even so, she couldn't keep a hint of sarcasm out of her voice when she responded. "How *sweet* of you to notice, *hon*. The twins are due in early June."

As if they didn't already know this. She doubted her involvement with Cooper was any great secret in the Tate family. Or among the Barrons, for that matter. She had the distinct impression that there were no secrets in that family.

Britt was surprised when Zoe didn't take offense at her sarcasm. "If those babies are anything like my Nash, you have all my sympathy, sugar." The woman glanced up at Tucker, eyes dancing with mischief. "And I just wanted to tell you that I've seen your documentary. We don't get quite so much wild weather in Tennessee so I surely do admire the work you do, Britt. Crossin' m'fingers that you win tonight." She slipped her hand through her husband's arm.

Something inside Britt twisted just a little at the look on Tucker's face as he gazed down at his wife, his expression both amused and indulgent. "What Zoe is too reticent—"

"Honey, there's not a reticent bone in my body, and you know it. What I'm leadin' up to is I would dearly love to ride along with you when you go storm chasin'. I know Mama Katherine, using Coop's name, won your silent auction prize at the benefit last November. I asked him to let me do it and he flat out said no. So…" Zoe batted long lashes at Britt, who had to suppress a laugh.

Zoe was not at all what she'd expected. She truly was a country sweetheart and while Britt suspected the other woman could hold a mean grudge, there appeared to be nothing two-faced about her. This was someone—despite Zoe's fame and fortune—whom Britt could be friends with. She pretended to consider the idea, one arm resting on her belly, hand cupping the opposite elbow, while tapping her cheek with one finger in the classic I'm-thinking-about-it gesture.

Britt had all but forgotten about that stupid silent auction. Cooper hadn't pressed things and she now wondered if he was keeping it as a backup plan or something. That would be just like him, to use the ride-along to get close to her. Still, taking a singing star on a chase would bring lots of publicity and she had a secret fan-girl crush on Zoe. She'd downloaded the singer's album the first day it was available. And what a way to derail any nefarious plans Cooper might have regarding their ride-along.

"Well…if you promise to sing to me, *and* give me an autograph, I bet we can work something out."

Zoe squealed and bounced up and down on her toes like a bobber on a cane fishing pole. That's when Britt realized the woman wore cowboy boots with her obviously expensive designer gown. Zoe looked like the girl next door with her long brown hair and big brown eyes. The dress? It was pure red carpet—flounced in front, long in back, some décolletage showing beneath the coppery sheer fabric. Pair that with fabulous boots as shiny as brand-new copper pennies, and she looked like she was ready to accept an award at the CMAs. The thought hit her that if she married Cooper, Zoe would be her sister-in-law. And Deacon Tate, the country music megastar, would be her brother-in-law. She started to hyperventilate. These people were so out of her league.

She had student loans out the wazoo, for Pete's sake. And just who was Pete, she wondered, the distraction helping to bring her breathing back under control. She licked her lips nervously as the three people surrounding her watched, worry evident in their expressions.

"Don't mind me." She waved one hand. "Nerves. I'm just a little anxious about the awards tonight." A good enough alibi, she hoped.

The overhead lights flashed, like in a theater lobby, to remind the patrons to return to their seats after intermission. Tucker and Zoe led the way. Britt followed with Cooper beside her, his warm hand resting against the small of her back. Heat spread through her and she fought against the magnetic pull of him—physically *and* emotionally. Cooper's breathing hitched, almost as if he felt the small tremors his touch evoked in her. Did he feel the same things she did? Was it possible that she was fighting her feelings for no reason?

As he held a chair for her and she sank onto it, she pushed those thoughts away. Deep down, she knew Cooper had the power to destroy her. He could take her job and attempt to take her babies. She could find another job but her children? She'd fight tooth and nail for them. But as she stroked her hand over her rounded belly, she knew Cooper would never do that to her. She glanced up and saw yearning in his gaze as he watched her touch her tummy.

He leaned in and whispered in her ear. "Everything okay? They giving you trouble tonight?"

"Not really." She studied him for a moment, made up her mind. "Want to touch?"

He dropped into the chair beside her and she guided his hand to her side. One of the babies chose that moment to kick hard. Cooper's eyes widened and a look of such wonder crossed his face that Zoe completely second-guessed her decisions. He was the father of the twins. He'd stepped up as soon as he became aware of that fact. And watching his reaction now? She knew deep in her heart that he truly wanted the babies. And maybe, he wanted her too.

Cooper remembered to breathe. He'd seen the twins moving on the sonograms but he'd never actually touched Britt's belly after he was aware of them being inside her. He'd felt that kick through her hand. Strong, powerful. And alive. It really hit him in that moment. Oh, he'd had a bit of a revelation when he'd seen them on that big screen at the doctor's office, but this? This contact, knowing his babies were in there growing and thriving, was amazing. Two little people that were half Britt and half him. He hoped they got her brains. Her stubbornness? Not so much. And if they were girls, he wanted them to look just like their mother. He was also guy enough to hope that they took after him if they were boys. Except he still wanted them to have Britt's intelligence.

"Wow," he finally said, moving his gaze from their hands to her face. Then he blinked and almost choked. "Does that hurt?" He'd never considered that it might and he never wanted to see Britt in pain.

She rolled her eyes at him but for the first time in ages, her expression was soft as she regarded him. "No, it doesn't hurt. Not exactly. It feels sort of like this." She punched him in the ribs, none too gently.

He grinned at her, but the wonder remained. He was going to be a dad. Before he could say anything else, the room darkened and the emcee began the ceremony. Cooper remained lost in a fog of happiness until he felt Britt stiffen beside him. He tuned back into his surroundings and noticed that everyone at their table sat up straight, anticipatory tension in their postures, as Britt's category was announced.

"*Chasing Down the Wind*, KOCX TV, Britt Owens and Leo Blevins."

The presenters went on to the other nominees but Cooper wasn't paying any attention. Not when Britt's hand had a death grip on his thigh. He carefully loosened her hold, substituting his hand. At long last, the woman at the microphone said, "And the winner is…"

The male emcee tore open the envelope he held, pulled out the embossed card, and smiling, leaned toward the microphone and announced, "Chasing Down the Wind." He went on to read all the names involved.

Britt squealed as Leo let out a whoop. He kissed his wife and before Cooper knew it, Britt was kissing him. After a long moment, she pulled away, looking surprised with herself.

"Congratulations, Girl Wonder. Proud of you." And he wasn't lying. He *was* proud of her. He just didn't want her putting herself in danger.

He pushed out of his chair and helped her stand. Everyone at the table stood with him, all of them clapping and whistling as Britt and Leo headed to the small platform, followed by a producer and Dave Edmonds, the station's head meteorologist.

Everyone gave a quick acceptance speech, passing the golden Emmy statuette around as each one spoke. Then the group was ushered off to the side where they posed for photographs as the next award was announced. Within a few minutes, they'd returned to the table for another round of congratulations. The rest of the ceremony went by in a blur.

Once things wrapped up, Cooper put his plan into action—mainly getting rid of his brother and sister-in-law, sending Leo and his wife home in the limo, and bustling Britt into his brand-new Lincoln Navigator. The only delay was a game of rock-paper-scissors between Britt and Leo to determine who got to take the Emmy home for the night. Lucky—or intelligently conniving—as always, Britt won.

Inside the Navigator, with the heat blasting, he glanced at her, and was surprised to find her studying him. "Penny for your thoughts…"

"It's a dollar now. Inflation and all that." She smiled when he pulled out a dollar bill. "Funny."

"Britt…"

"Cooper…"

His turn to smile now. "Will you come home with me?" He glanced away from her to focus on driving. "We'll put that shiny statuette on the mantel, build a fire in the fireplace, snuggle in on the couch and admire it."

"Sure we will." Britt touched his arm and he looked at her. She winked at him and he breathed. "Yes, I'll go home with you."

When Britt opened her eyes, gray winter sunlight drifted through the filmy drapes curtaining the French doors and casting a golden glow on the statuette prominently displayed on Cooper's bedside table. She'd won a freaking Emmy! And…she'd slept with Cooper. Again. Despite her best intentions, she couldn't stay away from him.

Her dilemma currently snored softly at her back, one arm draped over her and a warm hand cupping her belly.

She shivered when lips nuzzled the nape of her neck. "You like my house," Cooper murmured against her skin.

"Maybe a little." She could admit that much but wasn't about to tell him she thought his house was perfect.

"I like having you here." His hand caressed her side. "You could live here…"

"I don't think so."

"Why not?"

"You know all the reasons, Cooper."

Their cell phones both beeped alerts. Since his arms were around her, Britt reached for hers. The banner text made her sit up, swing her legs out of bed and head for the windows. A winter not-so-wonderland stretched out before her.

"What the—" There hadn't been an ice storm in the forecast. A cold front had been predicted for the start of the week but not overnight. This was why weather fascinated her.

Cooper joined her at the window. He offered her a long-sleeved T-shirt, even though the air in the room was warm. He helped her into it and she smiled at the sweet gesture. The shirt swallowed her, the sleeves trailing way over her hands and the bottom hem falling to midthigh. When he kissed her temple, she didn't shy away.

"I'm going to grab a quick shower then I'll start coffee and breakfast. Take your time. I've got some calls to make."

She tilted her head to look up at him. "It's Sunday morning."

"And we woke up to an ice storm. Half the state is shut down and I have active rigs in the alert area. I need to make sure my crews are okay."

Britt had never considered exactly what Cooper did. In the back of her mind, he was just some rich oil executive with a corner office in Barron Tower. Except he traveled to hurricane zones and volunteered with the Cajun Navy. He drove bulldozers and rescued trapped cows—cattle, she amended. He *did* things. Physical things that got his hands dirty. Literally. He rescued her and he lived in a perfect house on a perfect acreage and he cradled her while she slept.

And her resistance was beginning to crumble.

Fifteen

After two months, Cooper should have been used to this. He was waiting in the kitchen when she walked in just past five o'clock. "You snuck out again this morning." He kept his voice level, not that he was really upset. Okay, maybe just a little. She made a habit of sneaking out and he always woke up disgruntled when he found her side of the bed empty. After the three-day ice storm back in January, most of her clothes had slowly migrated from her apartment to his closet, along with some personal items over that time. She was all but living with him but she would not, despite all his best efforts, admit that she was.

"I had to be at work at eight." She bristled, arms folded across the large swell of her belly.

He raised a brow. Britt raised her chin. He had to be a truly sick puppy to enjoy her stubborn temper as much as he did. "So?"

She gave him the stink eye, arms crossed, feet splayed for balance as she leaned toward him.

"I didn't want to be late."

"How long would it take to wake me with a kiss and tell me goodbye?"

Color rose up her neck to eventually stain her cheeks. He liked that he had that effect on her.

"You don't do '*goodbye*' kisses." Her hands came up to make air quotes.

"I don't?"

She waggled a finger. "No, you don't. You start with a kiss and then you get all grabby hands and…and… I'm suddenly naked and late. I'm not a big boss like you. I'm a lowly adjunct professor, and part-time at that. I can't afford to be late and it's a longer drive from your house."

Britt was gearing up for a tirade and whatever happened next was sure to be entertaining. He added fuel to the fire. "I'm sure the powers that be at the station would hire you full time for in-studio stuff. That pays more than being an adjunct professor and you wouldn't have to drive all the way to Norman."

"I *like* teaching. And I'm not the anchor type."

"Working at the TV station means no rush hour traffic."

"I hate it when you're logical," she groused.

"Then I'll be illogical. Marry me and quit."

"Don't even go there. Just because I'm pregnant—"

"I love you."

Her eyes softened and he had hope until she spoke.

"I don't love you, Cooper."

"You will."

"Don't be so sure."

He used his boyish grin, the one that hinted at a dimple he didn't really have but always drove the girls crazy. "I'll wear you down eventually."

That got him an exaggerated eye roll. Part of him knew better than to push her but he was getting tired of the long game. As much as Britt frustrated him, he also adored her. Of course he was in love with her. How could he not be?

"Are you hungry?"

Britt looked confused for a minute. "What?"

"Dinner. I can cook or we can go out."

"I think I just got whiplash from the change in subject. And I can cook."

"You look tired. Why don't you put your feet up and I'll fix something."

"You're changing the subject because you were losing the argument."

"I was winning but you do look tired."

"You're coddling me again, thinking it'll help your cause."

"Yes, yes I am. Is it working?"

"No." She huffed out a breath. "Maybe."

He'd take that.

Britt settled on a bale of hay in Cooper's horse barn. March had roared in like a lion but was currently playing the lamb. Bored, she'd trailed after Cooper when he headed outside with a casual, "Got chores to do," called over his shoulder.

She wasn't much of a country girl but hey, hay was hay, right? Horse and cow food and a place to sit while she watched Cooper brush a big gray horse. Yes, that summed up hay nicely. And was about as deep as her thoughts could get at the moment. Cooper wore a heather-gray T-shirt that molded to his body. Faded jeans hugged his butt and every time he bent over, she had to swallow the saliva pooling in her mouth. Why was he so sexy? And such a nice guy. She really needed him to be a big ol' jerk because her heart was at stake, which it shouldn't be. They shouldn't hook up just because they were going to be parents.

Granted, they'd had a series of one-night stands, which

stretched into a series of one-week stands and now it was almost April. She had no excuse for her actions. They had nothing in common. He was rich. *Really* rich. He belonged to a powerful family. He looked as good in old jeans and a T-shirt as he did in a designer suit and that, she decided, was a tough act to follow. He tripped her feminine switches with his rugged, outdoorsy good looks. He always had. She'd all but thrown herself at him—okay, she *had* thrown herself at him like five minutes after she first saw him.

He should be a jerk, she reminded herself. But he wasn't. She watched the muscles of his arm bunch and relax as he brushed the horse, concentrating on that rather than his broad back. Little shivers teased through her body. Why had he turned out to be a really good guy? The good ones were supposed to be as rare as unicorns.

"What's her name?" Britt had to focus on something besides the man.

"His. This is Tramp. He's a gelding."

"Okay…"

Cooper glanced over at her. "Three kinds of horses, Girl Wonder." He held up an index finger. "Mares. Those are the female horses."

"I knew that," she muttered.

"Stallions," he said, holding up a second finger.

"Know that, too."

"And geldings. Who used to be stallions."

"That's weird. When dogs are neutered, they're still just dogs."

"It's the same with cattle. A bull that's been cut is a steer."

"Cut?"

"That's the cowboy term for neutering a horse or cow."

"I thought a cow was female. So you spay cows?"

"Cow is the singular term for any bovine. It is also a female cow, as opposed to a bull or steer."

"Stop. You're going to make my head explode."

He moved around the horse to brush the other side, watching her over the big animal's back. "Okay. I won't explain about calves and heifers or colts and fillies then."

She glowered and moved her curled hands up to both sides of her head and expanded them with sound effects to indicate that her head had, indeed, exploded, at least figuratively.

"And then there's—"

"Shut up, Coop. Just…shut it."

The grin he flashed was full of wicked intent. "Make me."

"I can do that," she said, her own expression just as wicked.

A few days later, Britt stood in the archway separating the dining room and kitchen. Cooper sat at the high counter dividing the kitchen from the family room spooning something into his mouth. Her eyes narrowed as she recognized the fragrance that had enticed her.

"Did you leave any for me?"

Cooper's head jerked up, his expression bathed in guilt. Britt managed a poker face though it was hard to resist curling her lips between her teeth to keep from smiling. The empty dish spoke volumes—as did the empty container proclaiming it had once held vanilla bean ice cream. He slid off the stool and padded over to the refrigerator. His faded jeans rode low on his hips, his back flaring into broad shoulders. *Nope.* She wouldn't be distracted by his obvious charms. She was not going there. Especially since he'd eaten her peach cobbler.

His head and shoulders disappeared into the fridge and he withdrew something. Then the freezer drawer opened, closed. He kept his back to her but said, "Have a seat, Girl Wonder. You need real food."

Britt *humphed* but settled on the stool he'd vacated. She glanced at the bowl he'd been eating from. A pool of melted ice cream and a smear of gooey sauce left from the cobbler was all that remained of the treat his mother had dropped by. For her. Not Cooper. For Britt. She knew that because Katherine had called her to say she was dropping off a peach cobbler just for her because it was her favorite. She absently rubbed the side of her rounded belly. One of the twins was using her rib cage for a jungle gym.

A chef's salad appeared in front of her. "Eat all of that and you get dessert."

Coop held another cobbler and carton of ice cream.

"Tease," she groused.

"Absolutely."

She poured blue cheese dressing over the salad, impressed that he'd cut the hard-boiled eggs into precise slices. Even the fresh ham and turkey had been julienned. And there wasn't a tomato in sight. She had nothing against tomatoes. They were perfectly nice as long as they involved ketchup, spaghetti sauce or BBQ. For a man who seemed mostly clueless, Cooper sure did pay attention when it came to her likes and dislikes. She stabbed at some leafy greens and swirled them through the dressing. She was chewing when Coop set down a napkin-covered basket. Hot breadsticks hid beneath the cloth. Who used cloth napkins? Well, what bachelor used them? Besides Cooper Tate, obviously.

Of course, she'd met—and been vetted—by Katherine Tate. The woman wore pearls, for gosh sakes. *Of course* there would be no paper napkins on her table. Britt preferred paper towels herself. Then again, she hadn't exactly eaten at home. She dined a la carte—from Taco Bell, Sonic, KFC, Arby's. Fast food was definitely her cuisine of choice. Since all but moving in with Cooper, though, they often ate at home, usually with him cooking. Living here was easy to get used to. And she shouldn't. A part of her kept wait-

ing for that proverbial other shoe—or in this case, boot—
to drop.

A dark shadow appeared on the opposite wall and she
watched as Lucifer slunk toward her. The cat was a sneaky
devil and he loved ice cream. She wondered if he liked
cobbler. She shoveled salad into her mouth. A strip of ham
fell off her fork and didn't make it to the floor. Luci caught
it midair and scarfed it down. Then he sat back on his
haunches gazing at her with a baleful expression, demanding she drop more meat.

"Don't feed the cat. He has his own bowl."

She glanced up, her guilt apparently obvious on her face,
based on Cooper's grin.

"Whatever," she muttered. But there was warm peach
cobbler and ice cream to distract her from the sexy man.

Cooper had hung the swing from the big tree near the
fire pit on a whim. With his cousins' children coming for
the occasional visit, it seemed like a good idea at the time.
Now? Now, he decided the idea had been utterly brilliant.
Britt, wearing a loose dress covered with flowers painted
in outrageous hues, pushed off in the swing. Her rounded
belly peeked from behind the riotous colors as she pumped
her legs and leaned back to swing higher.

For all intents and purposes, they were living together.
He liked having her under his roof and in his life. A rough
meow drew his attention to his feet. Lucifer sat beside his
scuffed boots, eyes fixed on the colorful display. Britt continued to swing gently, her barefoot toes reaching for the
sky on the upswing, in dappled shade for a moment before
they disappeared in the long skirt as she folded them beneath the swing on her way back down.

He moved closer, standing by just in case. He would
give her a push whenever she asked, whenever she hollered,
"Higher!" She didn't ask so he remained on the sidelines

with Lucifer. "We need to figure out a way to make her stay," he muttered to the cat. He glanced down. Luci stared up at him, his gaze malevolent. "You know you want her to stay just as much as I do."

In a display of feline disgust, Luci appeared to roll his eyes as he shook his head, flipped his tail and sauntered back toward the main house. The cat couldn't fool him. He'd caught the darn thing curled up next to Britt, snore-purring while she petted him, more than once.

Cooper settled into a lounge chair and watched the woman he hungered for. The sun disappeared as gray clouds collided overhead. The wind changed, bringing the scent of rain and ozone. Britt slowed the swing, dragging her feet in the grass until it stopped. She hopped out and strode toward him, calling "Where's my phone?"

He pulled it out of his hip pocket and handed it to her. As she checked for messages, the first fat raindrops fell. Coop grabbed her hand and pulled her toward the house. They were drenched by the time they reached the French door opening into the master bedroom. Laughing like kids, they surged into the house and headed to the bath. He grabbed a thick towel and wrapped it around her before snagging a second one he used to dry her long hair.

"What about you?" Britt asked, eyeing the way his shirt molded to his chest.

"I'm not so sweet that I'll melt because I got wet. You? You might."

Cooper didn't smile at first when he saw her expression go soft. But looking into brown eyes the color of melted chocolate, he felt his own expression soften.

"You shouldn't say things like that," Britt murmured.

"Why not?"

"Because you'll make me like you and I don't want to like you."

"You're carrying my babies, Britt. You should like me."

"No, I shouldn't," she insisted as she face-planted against his wet shirt. "You're a serial impregnator."

"I don't think that's a word."

"It should be."

He gently gripped her biceps and leaned away from her while keeping her in place. He met her gaze dead on. "I've never gotten anyone but you pregnant, Britt. And if I'd been thinking with the correct head, I would have realized the stupid condom was old."

"But that other woman is stuck in my head..."

"Shh." He released her arms, his hands moving to cup her face. He bent and brushed his lips across hers. "I'll show you the DNA test if that will help. I promise, Britt. You are the only one carrying my children."

She rocked back and while he let her go, he didn't break eye contact. She studied him, her gaze flicking over his face, his body, then the area around them.

"You have a swing in your yard," she whispered.

"Yeah."

"I love swings." The soft expression on her face was replaced by one filled with worry. "Do you really want the twins?"

She sounded so fragile, not brash and sure like his Girl Wonder at all. "C'mere, sweetheart." He wrapped Britt in his arms, but he didn't answer her. Instead, he eased off her wet clothes and dried the damp left behind from the rain. Then he dressed her in one of his T-shirts and set her on the counter while he stripped and dried off before pulling on a pair a loose cotton gym shorts. Lifting her into his arms, he carried her to the bed.

They lay together, listening to the heavy patter of the rain, lightning occasionally flashing through the windows, followed by thunder. He stroked her lightly, and simply enjoyed holding her as they lay together.

Eventually, he spoke. "I have six cousins, all brothers

by three different women. I have six brothers. Same mom
and dad. Family is kind of a big deal around here. I was
with Cord right after he learned about CJ. He was devas-
tated that he'd missed so much of his son's life because
Jolie didn't tell him. And Deacon? He didn't give a damn
whether Noelle was his by blood or not. He became that
little girl's dad the moment he picked her up. The same
with Tucker. He didn't care that Zoe was having another
guy's baby. He loves Zoe, and Nash is his. End of story.
How could I not want our babies?"

"Your family is a little weird."

Laughter burst out before he could stop it, the explo-
sion ruffling Britt's hair. "A little weird? Darlin', you don't
know us at all. My mother wears pearls to ride horseback.
My oldest brother is a super ninja dude, my baby brother
is a musical genius, and the rest of us just hang on for the
ride. Well, I just hold on for the ride because I'm the only
normal and sane one in the bunch."

Britt giggled. "Deacon seems pretty squared away."

"Deacon is married to a former highway patrol trooper."

"So?"

"Who do you think keeps him squared away? I mean,
dude. He's a Nashville country music superstar."

"You guys are all overachievers."

"I blame it on sibling rivalry."

"So what's your superpower?"

"Saving pretty storm chasers."

"I don't need saving."

Did her voice sound a little wistful? There beneath the
indignation? Yeah, Cooper decided. He'd heard it. He settled her with her head on his shoulder so they could both
watch the rain out the window. A comfortable silence
stretched between them. After a while, the rain petered
off. The delicate, sweet fragrance of honeysuckle washed in
through the open windows on the fresh breeze. The storm

rumbled in the distance as rain changed to drizzle. Though the storm had come to an end, neither of them moved. Daylight faded to dusk, but he didn't turn on a light.

"I love that scent," Britt finally said. "Rain and honeysuckle. It reminds me of spring."

He kissed the top of her head. "Rain and honeysuckle will always remind me of you."

"Stop saying stuff like that." She raised her head and twisted her neck to look at him. "Just stop being sweet."

"Ha," he teased. "You do like me."

Sixteen

There was always calm before the storm. They'd been getting along so well, but then again, they'd had a mild spring, Until now. Severe weather was out there waiting and Cooper realized he'd probably just stepped in a big ol' pile of cow patties when he decreed that she was not going to be chasing tornadoes this year.

"You have no right to tell me what I can and cannot do, Cooper Tate." Britt was spitting mad. "It's spring. Storm season. My job is to be out there—" She swept her arm in a wide arc indicating...the world. "This is what I do."

"You're pregnant."

She cupped her palms on both sides of her belly. "Gee. Brilliant deduction. What was your first clue, Sherlock?"

"Britt—"

"Do not go there, Cooper. Don't get all conciliatory and condescending. I'm perfectly healthy and thus capable of doing my job. My doctor has cleared me to work. The station has cleared me."

He inhaled to argue again but she cut him off. "I sit in my truck. I drive my truck. I look at instrument readings. I'd say I take pictures but that's what Leo is for. He'll be with me. He's perfectly capable of driving too. It's just that trying to work the cameras and the communications equipment is better done when not driving. I'm not due until June. This is April. Heck, the doctor said I could work right up to the point my water breaks."

Coop resisted the urge to stick his fingers in his ears and sing la-la-la-la like a six-year-old who didn't want to hear his parents. He'd undergone a crash course on pregnancy and childbirth with his cousin Kaden. Despite being squeamish, he was looking forward to the birth of his children. The little duo hadn't yet revealed their genders, and they were on the small side for how far along they were in the gestation period. He knew this because, yeah, he'd taken a *second* crash course because these were *his* babies. And he was ready for them. Sort of. Mostly. As ready as any man could be.

He swallowed his anger and tried logic instead. "You're having twins, Britt." He ignored the look she leveled on him. "The doctor said there is a chance you could go into premature labor. What happens if you are out in the middle of nowhere?"

"Every town and city has a hospital. And doctors."

"But not *your* doctor."

She huffed out a breath. "I don't want to fight with you, Cooper, but let's get something straight since you still haven't gotten it through your thick skull. You are not the boss of me. You can't tell me what to do, especially when it comes to my job. Or my body." She added that last under her breath but he heard it all the same.

"They're my babies too, Britt. Why is it so terrible that I want to keep you and them safe?" He caught her face in his hands, and she met his gaze. "I love you. The idea of you being out there somewhere I can't get to you, of you getting hurt—or worse? It makes me crazy."

Her expression softened only a tiny bit, her insistent anger still riding just beneath the surface of her emotions.

"You make *me* crazy, Coop." Her hands circled his wrists, and she pulled his hands away. "Just because I'm carrying babies and my body is a hormonal stew doesn't make me less than what I've always been."

"I never said that, Britt," he answered hotly. "Not once. It has nothing to do with your abilities or your intelligence. But it's not just about you anymore. There are two other lives depending on you. Three, if you include me. I want to marry you. I want you to be my wife. I want to raise our babies together and have more of them whenever you're ready. Why does that make me the villain in all this?"

"This isn't about you or what you want," she spat out, her anger in full bloom now.

His phone chose that inopportune time to ring. Fishing it out of his hip pocket, he answered. Several four-letter words knocked around on his tongue, wanting to be let loose as he listened to the caller. He swallowed the curses, but when he spoke, his voice also held a bit of anger.

"Someone else can deal with this." He listened again, noting Britt's retreat. She curled her upper lip in a snarl and mouthed, "We're done." Then she turned on her heel and marched in the direction of the master bedroom. If he was lucky, she'd lay down with her feet propped up. If he wasn't, he'd find her packing all the clothing that had migrated into his closet.

Cooper went looking for her after he finished the call. He found her in the shower. He hoped that boded well for him and his side of the argument. He tapped on the bathroom door and raised his voice to be heard over the running water. "I have to go deal with a situation on one of the rigs. I'll be gone a couple of hours."

Time enough for her to think things through and maybe see his side of the situation. He got no response. "Will you…" He stopped, biting back what he wanted to say—*will you be here when I get home?* His next thought wasn't much better but he asked anyway. "Will you be okay while I'm gone?"

A strangled noise erupted from the shower stall. It sort of sounded like *argh*, but far more growly. He backed out of the room, realizing he'd pushed his luck way too far. He'd give her time and space, though not too much of either. He wanted to marry her before their babies made their way into the world. He was old-fashioned that way. His parents had been married when his oldest brother Hunter was born. No one believed the family story that Katherine Tate got pregnant on her honeymoon with Denver and that Hunter was born prematurely. It had been the '70s. And condoms did break. He had personal experience with that particular mishap.

When he first found out Britt was pregnant and he was probably the father, he'd been royally pissed off. That Susie Maddox was alleging the same thing when he knew damn well it wasn't true, just made matters worse. Still, something inside him just…*knew*. Britt was the one he wanted. Stupid Tate curse.

Now, as Cooper drove down the long drive and waited for the electric gate to open, he glanced in the rearview mirror and wondered if Britt would be waiting when he returned.

Britt considered staying in the shower until the hot water ran out. Then she remembered the house had a tankless water heater. She could be in there all day. Glancing at her Swiss Army watch, she figured twenty minutes was long enough. That call had sounded urgent. For Cooper to back out of an argument, it had to be. She turned off the water and listened intently. Silence. Snaking out a hand, she clutched the huge cotton bath sheet hanging next to the shower and wrapped up in it.

She stood alone in the bathroom. So far, so good. On tiptoes, she headed to the bedroom and peeked around the doorjamb. No Cooper. Letting out a relieved sigh, she dried off, brushed her wet hair into a ponytail and dressed. These days, her outfits mostly consisted of stretchy yoga pants and an oversized T-shirt. In the closet, Britt had a large roller bag open and partially packed before she realized that not only did the T-shirt she wore but over half of those she'd packed belonged to Cooper. If she could have bent over, she would have banged her forehead on the top of the built-in dresser.

"Tough," she muttered. She liked his T-shirts. That's why they'd migrated from his drawers into hers. She wouldn't think about the possessive—and totally disarming—grin Cooper wore whenever he caught her wearing his clothes.

She called him a few names in her head. Definitely time for her to get out of here and reclaim her life. Bossy man. Trying to tell her what to do, and when and how she could do it.

Pregnancy did not affect her ability to work. Everyone comprehended that except Cooper. Old-fashioned jerk. Speaking of which, they didn't have to be married to parent the twins. That was the other thing they argued about. A lot. She could manage as a single mother. Even with twins. He'd pay her child support. Heck, he'd already put her on his insurance, much to the happiness of Channel 2's human resources lady. He'd also paid all her deductibles and out-of-pocket expenses. He'd pay for day care, whether he liked it or not. He was such a chauvinist that he probably expected her to stay home and take care of his house and kids.

That thought brought her up short. No, she had to be honest. He had never once said that. He also didn't oppose her working as long as it was at the station. Indoors. Where it was safe. And he'd never said anything about her stopping storm chasing after the twins arrived and her maternity leave was over.

She rubbed her eyes with the heels of her hands because they were stinging all of a sudden. Cooper didn't object to her storm chasing. He just didn't want her to do it while she was pregnant. They'd never discussed her staying home or going back to work after the twins were born. He'd suggested she take some time to finish her doctoral dissertation, submit it, and finally get her PhD. She realized in that moment that, in his way, he supported what she did. And she did want those initials before and after her name. Dr. Brittney Owens, PhD, Meteorology.

Something soft brushed against her calf and she jumped. "Dang, Lucifer," she growled. "Don't do that."

The scruffy cat stared up at her, his gaze reproving. Why couldn't Cooper be a dog person? Something big and goofy. A Bloodhound maybe. Or a Newfoundland like Harley. Harley was a cool dog. Lucifer? He just had a bad attitude, sharp teeth and claws, and didn't like anybody but Cooper. And she wasn't totally sure the cat actually liked Cooper.

Conceding the staring contest to the cat, she glanced around the closet. How had so many of her clothes ended up here? It wasn't like she'd officially moved in with him or anything. Was she the only one denying that's what it really was?

He'd tried to convince her. And it was easy to let the charm of the place win her over. Though the house was surrounded by city—the view of downtown Oklahoma City was spectacular at night as they sat on the covered deck—the place was insulated by several acres of pasture and trees. A historic home, the inside was updated and while mostly masculine, it felt homey and comfortable.

Too comfortable. Yes, definitely time to go home. To stay. She'd make arrangements to get the rest of her clothes later.

She hoisted the suitcase onto the floor and froze as her lower back twinged. Lucifer's expression implied a very feline, "I told you so." She curled her lip in an answering snarl. "I'm fine." But she did make a note to self to not lift the suitcase. Which meant getting it into and out of her truck would be problematic.

The cat trailed her to the front door. Britt set the alarm, let herself out, and locked the door using the electronic keypad. In the short time she'd been with Cooper—

"No!" she corrected herself. "We aren't together. Not *together*. Just…together. I'm not living here." Except she'd left a boatload of clothes behind. She'd come back to get them later. Because she was so done with this. He didn't trust her to be smart when it came to the twins and there was no way she could be with a man who dismissed her like that.

"We aren't a couple," she reminded herself. "We aren't even friends."

Nope, definitely not friends. They fought too much, but there were amazing benefits. The sexual chemistry between them was freaking amazing. And he didn't mind that she basically had a beach ball strapped to her middle. Cooper found inventive ways to get both of them off.

Nope, definitely couldn't think about that. If Cooper got his way, he'd walk all over her. She had a life to live and she was better off without him. That was her story and she was sticking to it.

Seventeen

Two weeks. It had been two weeks since Britt had left. She wouldn't accept his calls. Blocked his texts. Stubborn woman. Half her clothes remained in his closet. He had been petty enough to have Bridger set up codes in the alarm system so he'd get an alert if she sneaked into the house to retrieve the rest of her stuff. He could be just as stubborn as her.

He was almost desperate enough to do something drastic—like have Chance file the court papers to ensure he got joint custody when the twins arrived. And he was doing everything he could to keep his temper in check.

But this morning, when Bridger walked through his office door, his brother's announcement blew the lid off.

"We need to talk about Britt, Coop."

His fist slammed the wall two inches from Bridger's face. "I'm not falling into that trap."

"Dude, you aren't falling, you're running full steam

opped ringing, the intercom on his desk buzzed. He ig-
ored it too. Two minutes later, Nikki knocked twice and
uck her head through the door before he could tell her
go away.

"You need to answer your phone, boss. Your little
other is slightly hysterical."

Coop exchanged a look with Bridger. "Little brother?
Which one?"

"Tucker. Something to do with Zoe and Britt."

His cell rang again and he snagged it. "Tuck?"

"What the hell, Coop? Your idiot girlfriend has dragged
oe out in that monster truck of hers."

"Wait. What?"

"Storm chasing, Cooper. I got home and found a note
om Zoe. She's with Britt and they've gone storm chasing!"

Britt pulled off to the side of the road to check her com-
uter. Zoe was wide-eyed and all but bouncing up and down
the back seat. Leo rolled his eyes though Britt figured
e was a little awed by their VIP passenger. The big teddy
ear was a fan. She looked out through the windshield. A
assive shelf cloud swirled around the bottom of a classic
nvil formation. It was just a matter of time before a su-
ercell storm formed.

Leo was on the phone with the station. Dave was peri-
dically going live with updates and the station would be
king her shot soon. Everything was ready.

Zoe leaned up between the bucket seats. "I promise to
e quiet when you go on the air. I'm just so excited that you
alled me and that Tucker and I were in town so I could
ome out and play with you. I've been tellin' everyone in
ashville that I was gonna get to go storm chasin' with
ou. They're all jealous."

Laughing, Britt said, "If this storm turns into a supercell, and it's showing every indication that it will, you' definitely have something to talk about."

The next few hours were a whirlwind of driving, heav rain, gusty winds, back roads and that big storm buildir to gigantic proportions. The Gentner crackled with com munications among the various chase teams. Britt and Le were both on their cell phones and Zoe was taking picture with her smartphone and posting them on Instagram. Bri watched the storm front; Leo watched the GPS mappin system installed in the truck.

"Britt, we're getting into ranch country. That mear closed sections and maybe running out of road."

"We'll be fine. I have a feeling this sucker is going drop a big one, Leo. We need to be right there when it does

Something *pinged* on the roof of the truck. More ping Britt kept driving while talking to Dave on the air.

"There's a massive hail core with this storm, Britt," Dav said. "And it looks like you are right on the edge of it."

"We are, Dave. It started off with pea-sized hail and nov we're experiencing quarter size. No, wait. Do you hav Leo's shot up? That's golf-ball size and it's really pounc ing the truck."

A voice buzzed in her ear. Ria. "Britt, there's some ser ous rotation cranking up to your southwest. Can you mov that way? It will get you out of the hail core and radar showing winds gusting up to sixty in the area of rotatior If there's an updraft—"

Britt cut her off. "We're on it."

She didn't bother trying to turn around. They were th only vehicle on this section line road so she just threw th transmission into Reverse and backed up until they hit th next crossroad. Turning around, she headed south unt they could get a road headed to the west. That's when sh got her first good look at the storm's presentation. A mas sive supercell complex of clouds looking for all the worl like a gigantic spaceship hovered over the plains of western Oklahoma. The entire base was rotating and rain fell in cascades at its center. The inflow and updraft were apparent.

"Holy cow, Leo. Please tell me this is streaming live."

Dave's voice came over the Gentner. "You're live on the station's app as well as live here in the studio, Britt. This storm is every bit as dangerous as both the EF-4 and EF-5 Moore tornadoes. People need to take their tornado precautions immediately. Get underground. If you live in—" Dave named off all the towns in the storm's path, but Britt was too busy to pay attention. She had radar up on her laptop, with one eye on the screen and the other on the storm. She'd studied the long-track storms that often hit Oklahoma and this monster looked just like them.

Excitement built, fueled by adrenaline. She'd stopped on a hill and could see all the way from the Wichita Mountains down by Lawton to almost the Oklahoma City metro area. There was a lot of territory to cover before this storm hit the city but she'd bet money that it would track close.

A wind gust rocked the truck and she checked her instruments. "Ria," she said into the Bluetooth receiver pinned to her shirt. "We just got hit with eighty-mile-per-hour outflow. I can feel it. This supercell is going to start dropping tornadoes any minute now." And then Zoe was squealing, Leo adjusting the cameras, and Britt was yelling into the microphone. "Tornadoes on the ground, Dave. We have multiple tornadoes on the ground."

Eighteen

Cooper stood on the brakes and his big truck skidded to a stop in the travel center's parking lot. His heart pounded in his chest like a jackhammer and he could barely breathe. It took effort to peel his fingers off the steering wheel. Tucker was already out of the passenger door and sprinting toward Britt's chase vehicle. When he jumped down, he slammed the door so hard the truck rocked.

By the time he arrived, Britt and Zoe were chattering excitedly. His brother glared at Britt while his hands checked his wife. Tuck visibly relaxed as Zoe's words penetrated.

"Lordy be! That was the most excitement I've had in ages. I mean, I haven't been in a car goin' that fast since that time in Knoxville when the Smithees came after us." Zoe turned her face to her husband, eyes dancing and face beaming. "You remember that time, darlin', right? I almost ran you down in the Volunteermobile."

Coop had heard that story and it had nothing to do with now. Britt looked every bit as excited as Zoe. Emotions so intense he could neither name them nor have any chance of controlling them surged up. Before he could stop to think, he grabbed Britt's shoulder and spun her around. His hands reached for her and he gripped her biceps. As much as he wanted to shake her, he held her carefully. Too bad he couldn't control his voice with the same care. His question came out as a shout. "What is wrong with you?"

She flinched and he clamped an iron fist on his roiling anger. No, not anger. At least not completely. No. This was beyond anger. Fear. It was unadulterated terror that took his heart and lungs captive so that he couldn't breathe, could barely think. He had his hands on her, could see she was alive and standing here, acting for all the world like she'd been on some wildly fun carnival ride. He didn't know whether to kiss her or kill her, because she'd come far too close to death as it was.

"Look at me," he yelled when she wouldn't meet his glare. "What were you thinking?" He bent closer to her so they stood eye-to-eye. "Oh, wait. You weren't thinking."

She pulled against his hold, her anger splashing her cheeks with bright pink. "I was doing my job."

"Your job? Where in your bloody job description does it say you have to be so damn close to a storm that you have to run for your life when it drops a tornado on top of you?"

"I'm fine." Britt spat the words from between gritted teeth.

"You could have died." The words tore out of him, wrenched from the very depths of everything he felt for this woman, for who and what she was to him.

She rolled her eyes and huffed out an aggrieved sigh. "But I didn't."

"No, by the grace of God you didn't. Did you stop to think what would happen if Zoe got hurt by your stupidity?"

"My what?" She arched up like an angry cat and all but

spit at him. "I'm not stupid, Cooper. I was paying attention. But sometimes, spin-ups like that happen in places where they shouldn't. It happens all the time."

"Spin-ups? That wasn't a spin-up, Britt. That was a freaking F-3 tornado. And it chased you. For miles. I watched. Because you were live streaming the whole damn thing. Was getting views and likes more important than your safety? Than Zoe's?"

"Of course not. We're fine, Cooper. Zoe has an awesome story to tell when she's interviewed. Leo got amazing footage."

"Nope." The normally affable cameraman held up his hands and backed away from the little group. "You leave me out of this because you know what? I happen to agree with Cooper, Britt. Given those roads and the way that storm was spinning, the gust front that built up? I may not be a degreed meteorologist like you, girl, but I've done my share of watching from the co-pilot's seat. We should not have been that close."

Britt's lip curled up in a snarl and her nose crinkled. Once upon a time, Cooper might have thought her expression cute. Now? Now it just caused his anger to boil over. Before he could speak, she turned on Leo.

"Thanks a lot, Leo. I thought you were a team player. Good to know that you believe I can't do my job. I'll let the station know you won't be riding with me anymore. In fact, you better just call them right now to get a ride because I'm done with you. I know what I'm doing. I'm good at what I do. Stuff happens. It happened today. But I got us away. Because. I. Know. My. Job."

She stepped back from Tucker and jerked hard. He let her go because to hang on would mean tightening his grip and he didn't want to hurt her. He was so mad he wanted to hit something, but it wouldn't be Britt. Cooper glanced around. Tucker had Zoe snuggled up close to his side and

Coop recognized the dawning realization in her expression. Leo just looked disgusted with the whole thing.

"I'm fine. We're all fine. Whether anyone wants to admit that or not. You know what. I'm done with this. That storm is still out there. My truck is running fine and I'm going back out." She jabbed a finger at Leo. "With or without you." Then she whirled to Cooper. "And you don't have a say in this. We're done."

Britt stood there breathing fire like she had a reason to be angry at him. She might be done, but he wasn't. "We aren't done, Britt. I have every right to—"

"You have no rights, Cooper." She threw up her hands. "I'm so outta here."

He clenched his fists to keep from reaching for her. "You're having my babies, Britt."

She grimaced, eyes narrowed, cheeks flushed, hands on her hips. She had to loosen her jaw to speak. "Trust me, I'm totally freaking aware of that."

He pointed to her truck. The back seat window on the driver's side was cracked. The hood was peppered with dents from the hailstorm they'd been caught in. The tailgate had a huge gouge where a piece of debris, driven by tornado-force winds, had slammed into it. "You. Could. Have. Died. And killed my children. *Our* babies." His voice dropped and he leaned toward her again. "Zoe was in that vehicle with you. My sister-in-law. The love of my brother's life, the mother of his little boy. And Leo. Your friend and colleague. He has a family too. But even if they weren't there, even if it was just you in that truck, you. Could. Have. Died. You, Britt."

Britt inhaled and he braced for another one of her tirades—about how it was her job, about how she was perfectly capable, about all the total bullshit she'd spouted at him for the past six months. But he beat her to the punch.

"I sat there, watching that damn tornado running up

your tailpipe, Britt. Praying you got away. Knowing there was no way in hell you could. And I knew." He thumped a fist against his chest over his heart. "I knew right here that I was going to lose it all. You. Our babies." The breath he sucked in sent shudders through his body. "You wanna know what was going through my head?"

She blinked up at him, wide-eyed, the rosy color draining from her face. "What?" she whispered.

"Picking out your coffin. Buying a burial plot. Music. Flowers. All the stuff that goes with planning a funeral instead of a wedding and a honeymoon." He had to stop, to blink the sting from his eyes because he wanted to see her face, wanted to see her expression. "I faced my worst nightmare, Britt. I sat there thinking that I would have to bury you and our babies before I ever got the chance to meet them. To love them. To love you. Except I already do."

Someone sniffled but it wasn't Britt. Probably Zoe. And knowing Zoe, the woman would most likely turn this whole fiasco into a song. He stared at Britt. She stared back. Her blank expression shouldn't have surprised him. She was so determined to prove that she was always right, that she could do everything all on her own. What she didn't understand was that he admired her. He thought she was a little crazy, but he respected her intelligence and her drive. But she was having *his* babies and being reckless was no longer an option. When she gave him no response, he turned to walk away but paused for one last comment.

"Losing you? Losing them? I'm not sure I could survive that."

Britt stood there in shocked silence, her anger melting away into…something she didn't quite recognize. Remorse? Maybe. She was a woman in a man's field and she constantly fought for every scrap, standing up for herself, asserting her independence and abilities. And then she'd gotten pregnant. By a man with old-fashioned values. A man who understood responsibility and was willing to step up and accept his. He was also overbearing and irritating and pushy and if she wasn't careful, she'd hand him her heart and he could crush it so easily. Just like she'd crushed his.

I sat there thinking that I would have to bury you and our babies before I ever got the chance to meet them. To love them. To love you. Except I already do.

Those words had seared her ears and burned their way into her brain. *To love them. To love you.* Did he mean that? He'd told her that more than once and she just blew him off for trying to manipulate her. She closed her eyes, fought the urge to rub them because she knew she was perilously close to crying. *Except I already do.* What did he mean by that? That he loved the twins? That he loved...*her*? That couldn't be. He didn't know her. Not really. Oh sure, they'd shared a bed, lived in the same house. Had sexual chemistry hot enough to set off a four-alarm fire. But how could he love her?

Losing you? Losing them? I'm not sure I could survive that. She'd started to scoff but then the force of his emotions slammed her like hundred-mile-an-hour straight winds. He meant every word. He loved her. Loved their babies. And losing them? That would be the end of his world. And she knew that feeling so freaking well because their babies meant everything to her too.

She opened her eyes to realize that Cooper was walking away. Leo stood near her truck looking aggravated and disgusted. Tucker and Zoe stood in a tight embrace, their faces hidden. Her vision blurred as understanding washed over her.

"You're right. I'm sorry."

She saw that her soft admission shocked Cooper when

he turned around, brows raised, mouth slightly opening as his jaw dropped.

"What did you say?" His voice was whisper quiet but held a hard edge, like he didn't quite believe her.

"I said that you're right and that I'm sorry."

Cooper pushed a booted foot forward as if he was stepping toward her but then halted, frozen in place. His arms hung limp at his sides and his expression held both confusion and despair. And yeah, he was still angry. She supposed he had a right to hang onto some of his mad. Most of all, though, she could see the fear and hopelessness. She remembered that look on her father's face when her little brother had been hit by a car. He was in a coma for three days and her dad kept a constant vigil before Bruce came out of it. Her mother had been long gone by then.

Britt had adored her dad and appreciated everything he'd given up to raise her and her brother. He'd never remarried after the divorce and died while she was in college. She and her brother drifted apart and she was a bit jealous of the close family ties Cooper had. Still, if a single man could raise two kids, she could raise the twins. She wasn't going to be like her mother. No way.

But what if her mother had taken her away when she abandoned the family? It would have killed her dad. And seeing that same look on Cooper's face now? Yeah, she had to fix this.

If Cooper wasn't going to come to her, she'd have to go to him. She supposed it was about time because truthfully? He'd always been the one to reach out to her and she'd swatted him away each time. No wonder he was a little gun-shy.

She took the first step toward him. Then the second. Slow. Easy. Like she was approaching a scared dog. She almost smiled as she thought the words, "Easy, boy." But she didn't. Cooper wouldn't understand a smile at this point. She stopped in front of him. Slowly, she raised her hand and brushed her fingers along his jawline, her eyes glued to his. Deep blue, his eyes. All the Tate brothers had blue eyes but Cooper's were a blue that reminded her of the twilight sky.

"I'm sorry, Cooper. I'm sorry I yelled. I'm sorry I took chances. I'm sorry I scared you."

His hand captured hers so fast she gasped. He raised her fingertips to his mouth and he kissed each one before lowering their hands to his chest. He pressed her palm over his heart. The thump-thump-thump beat against her hand, slightly erratic like he'd been running, but strong and true. Just like the man.

"Feel that, Girl Wonder?"

She nodded.

"That's what you do to me."

A surprised smile tugged at one corner of her mouth and she felt her expression soften with no effort on her part. "Good to know," she murmured, looking away.

His arm curled around her back and she looked up at him. Now it was her heart's turn to beat erratically. This man…he undid her. She wanted to kiss his full lips, to lean into his warmth and find shelter there. And then he spoke.

"Marry me."

Again, it came down to the line she couldn't cross, the leap she couldn't take. She'd caught a brief glimpse of his fear, his vulnerability, maybe even his love for her. But were they really any closer to seeing eye-to-eye, or would they go back to bickering once the crisis blew over?

"I'm sorry, Coop." She backed away from him and all but ran to her truck. She leaned on the hood and called, "I just can't."

Nineteen

Coop stared out the window of his office and considered his options. He had to admit that maybe he shouldn't have mentioned marriage right when Britt was admitting she'd messed up, one, by taking Zoe storm chasing, and two, by getting too close to that supercell. She'd stormed off, pun totally intended, because all he had left was a warped sense of humor.

Someone cleared their throat and he glanced at the reflection of his office in the glass, surprised to find his boss's wife there. "Jolie?"

"Cooper."

He turned to face her and discovered compassion rather than censure in her expression. "Let's hope you haven't totally mucked this up."

"I probably have."

"You know what Cord and I went through. I left town without telling him I was pregnant. I even managed to get through nursing clinicals while I was pregnant. I also raised CJ as a single mom until he was four." She flashed him a wry smile. "Not the brightest thing I ever did, but I managed. What I've seen of Britt, she can pretty much do whatever she wants. You need to remember that. Pregnancy isn't a handicap."

He turned back to the view outside his window and leaned his forehead against the glass. He knew that. But Britt's job—what she did when storm watches were issued—could be dangerous. And she was carrying twins. *His* twins. He loved her and wanted her safe. Wanted their babies safe. No one would believe him if he admitted that he awoke in the middle of the night, heart pounding, breath caught in his chest. His nightmare? That Britt was out in the middle of nowhere, a tornado bearing down on her while she was in labor and he couldn't get to her. Just like two weeks ago.

"She scares me," he admitted, his voice hoarse.

"No. What she *does* scares you. Y'all need to work through this, Coop." Jolie came up behind him and slipped her arms around his waist for a loose hug. "I've got faith in you. If the Bee Dubyas can help, all you gotta do is holler."

He patted her hands where they rested on his abdomen. "I know. And it's appreciated."

Jolie slipped out of his office as quietly as she'd come in, leaving him alone with plenty of time to think. As long as Britt was at his house, he knew where she was. As long as she was at the station, he knew where she was. As long as she was with him, he knew where she was. His brothers said he was crazy. Except maybe for Tucker and Deacon. They had wives and kids. They'd get it.

It had been two weeks. Britt had reverted to refusing his calls and texts so he'd stopped after the first couple of days. And she'd been storm chasing. He almost couldn't watch Channel 2 when the weather turned bad. Which was turning out to be almost every day. Thunderstorms with torrential rains leading to flooding. Thunderstorms with hail ranging from quarter-to baseball-sized. Thunderstorms with high winds and tornadoes. And Britt was out there, confronting the storms and relaying information back to the station.

She was out there. Day and night. Dark circles were constantly present beneath her eyes when he caught her on-screen. It was like Britt had to prove herself, over and over. Which wasn't true. Cooper discussed things with Tucker. Both the station manager and head meteorologist would happily make a spot for her on air in the studio but she was such an adrenaline junkie she refused every offer.

His cell phone pinged from where it sat on his desk. He glanced over. A weather alert. Great. He debated deleting the app, knew he wouldn't. Ever. Because Britt would always be out there in it, facing danger. Picking up the phone, he read through the warning. Severe storms, yada yada. He flipped to the radar portion of the app and hit his intercom.

"Nikki, you watchin' the weather?"

"Yessir. I have radar up on my computer. I'm in the process of calling our people now."

Coop let out a half laugh. "Why do I even bother?"

"Well, in that case, how about a raise?"

"Don't push your luck, Nickelodeon."

"Can't blame a girl for trying, bossman." She chuckled and muttered, "There's always diamonds."

He clicked off and returned to the windows, circling around for a different view. From this angle, he could see the front moving in from the southwest. Something twisted in his gut. This was going to be a bad one and Britt would be right in the middle of the storm. There was no way he could sit still. He grabbed his phone and headed out.

"I'm going to check on the rigs. Send the staff home early."

"But—"

"Tell Cord to check radar. This storm is shaping up just

like those monster Moore tornadoes. Nobody needs to be
caught out on the highway."

"Says the man who's going toward the storm."

He ignored her and headed toward the elevator.

Britt awoke that morning feeling out of sorts. So what
else was new? Even Ria was put out with her. Leo refused
to get in the truck with her until she got her temper under
control. She'd argued that she didn't have a temper, while
promptly losing it. Men! They were good for opening pickle
jars, reaching stuff on the top shelf and zipping up dresses.
Nothing else.

She stayed in the shower for longer than normal. Her
back ached—so what else was new with two potential soccer stars in her womb. She was angry. Two weeks. And he
hadn't come after her. But he totally loved her and the babies. *Right.*

Okay, to be honest, she *had* walked out on him without
a word. He'd tried to talk to her but she hadn't responded.
Nor had she accepted his calls. And she wasn't one of those
women who played games. Yet here she was doing just that.
What was wrong with her? She rubbed the side of her belly
where one of the terrible twosome had just hit her with a
roundhouse kick. "Swear to God I'm gonna name you guys
Chuck and Norris."

The babies settled a bit. Distraction over, her thoughts
returned to her very complicated relationship with Cooper. She truly hadn't left with the intent of him following
to beg her to stay. But he'd been so persistent in his pursuit.
Why would he suddenly stop? Had he found someone else?
Someone skinny and beautiful? Or sweet? All three of those
criteria could be met by ninety-nine percent of the female
population of Oklahoma City and surrounding environs.

Coming out of the shower, she'd found her phone blown
up with texts, missed calls and several voice mails. She lis-

tened to those while reading her messages. Great. A big
storm front with all the signs of producing multiple supercell thunderstorms was amassed in the southwestern part
of the state, moving northeast toward the metro area. The
skin on the back of her neck prickled as goose bumps rose
on her skin. She didn't believe in psychic stuff but she had
a bad feeling about this storm.

Mind made up, she loaded up her truck to head toward
the station. If Leo wouldn't ride with her, she'd coerce one
of the other photojournalists.

Driving northbound on the interstate, she still had a
funny feeling in her stomach, sort of a cross between butterflies and a stomachache from too much sweet stuff. And
she was still angry at Cooper. She really needed to get over
that. But the farther north she drove, the madder she got.
If she took the back way to the station, she could drive by
Cooper's house. If he was there, she could stop and give
him a piece of her mind.

The longer she thought about it, the more it seemed
like an excellent idea. She could tell him what she really
thought about him.

A sharp pain stabbed her in the lower back and she felt
a gush between her legs. She managed to steer the truck
to the side of the highway. A growing red splotch stained
the hem of the light blue maternity T-shirt she wore. Nau-
sea racked her body and she managed to find a plastic bag.
Light-headed, sick and in pain, she groped blindly for her
phone and hit the first number on her favorites list.

Three rings. Four. "Pickuppickuppickup," she chanted,
terrified she'd pass out—or worse.

"What?"

"Something's wrong."

Every nightmare he'd ever had about Britt and her pregnancy froze Cooper in place as he stepped off the eleva-

tor in the parking garage and heard her voice. "Where are you?"

"I... I'm..." Her voice faded and he was terrified that she was out in the middle of nowhere, that she might lose cell phone reception. "I-35. Um..."

"Baby, you gotta talk to me."

"Northbound. South of I-40."

He ran toward his truck. "Have you passed the Shields Boulevard exit?"

"I... I don't know."

"Britt, talk to me. What's happening?"

"I... I'm not sure. There's... I hurt. And I can't think. There's blood." Her voice caught then she sobbed out, "There's blood, Cooper. I'm scared."

He didn't stop to think. He just jumped in his truck and tore out of the Barron Tower's parking garage. He had enough presence of mind to put the phone on Bluetooth so he could drive with both hands. "I'm comin' that way, sweet girl. Just hang on. Keep talking to me."

"Coop..."

"I'm here, darlin'. I'm here."

"Something's wrong with the babies. I... This morning... I was all... I don't know. Feeling weird. And my back hurt. Down low. I took a hot shower. I was so mad at you."

"Mad at me?" He tried to keep his voice light and teasing. "What'd I do now?"

"You weren't here. And you don't believe in me."

He laughed but it sounded bitter, because he was. "I believe in you, Britt. I just want you and our babies safe. Is that so terrible?"

His damn pride—and fear. If not for that, he would have been with her when this happened. He wouldn't be driving like a maniac trying to locate her.

"No. But you could have talked to me instead of getting all bossy." Her voice sounded very small and unsure and that was not Britt. She was a confident woman full of life and energy. Salt and vinegar, his mother called it.

"Yeah, Girl Wonder, I could have. Wanna know a secret? I've been miserable without you."

"Good."

He had to smile at her snippy voice. That was so much better than before. She'd sounded so…lost.

"I'm comin' now, Britt. And I won't ever let you walk away again."

"Promise?" She sounded lost again and his heart broke a little bit more.

"Cross my heart."

Navigating downtown streets, road construction, and the weird loop to get on I-40 and southbound on I-35 took all his concentration. He didn't talk. Neither did Britt. He listened to her breathing, noting each change, and fought the panic welling deep inside him. With the impending storm, traffic was thick but police were scarce. He drove his truck like it was an Indy race car while scanning the northbound shoulder for any sign of Britt's storm chaser vehicle. It would be easy to spot.

He found her just north of Northeast 27th Street in Moore. He used the exits and on-ramps to execute a U-turn. He pulled up behind her, jumped out and ran to the driver's side door, jerking it open. Britt all but fell into his arms, sobbing. Blood pooled in the seat beneath her.

"Are you having contractions?"

"No."

He should call 9-1-1. He didn't. He grabbed her backpack and locked her vehicle. Cradling her in his arms, he loped back to his truck, strapped Britt into the passenger seat, and jumped in behind the wheel. They were less than three miles away from a satellite hospital with a Level II trauma center. He called Britt's doctor first. Then he called his mother. He briefed her quickly, his attention ping-ponging from their conversation, to Britt, to traffic, to the dark line of clouds he could see out the windshield.

Cooper finished up. "Gotta go. We're here. Stay at the ranch, Mom. Weather's getting worse. I'll keep you posted."

He stomped the brake pedal and the truck skidded to a stop next to the emergency room entrance. He was out and easing Britt into his arms when a security guard appeared.

"Never mind. Move the truck later," the man directed as soon as he assessed the situation.

A nurse met them in the reception area, leading them straight back, chattering instructions as they went. Most of the information went straight over Cooper's head. Passing through an interior waiting area, Coop glanced at the TV mounted to the wall. Dave Edmonds was on-screen, pointing to huge splotches of brilliant red on the radar image behind him. The sound was turned up.

"Ria," Dave was saying. "Where's Britt? Is she on the Gentner yet?"

He'd have to call the station. Someone would notice Britt's empty truck sooner or later. He laid her on an exam table and stepped back, but not out of the room, as the nurse shooed him away. More calls—one to Channel 2, and one to Bridger to deal with Britt's vehicle—all the while also listening to the nurse and then the doctor—ER, not OBGYN—who came jogging in.

Ten minutes later, following an exam and ultrasound, they were watching a live stream of KOCX's weather on Coop's phone because Britt wouldn't settle and all the medical personnel kept fussing at her to relax to bring her blood pressure down. Coop sat on a rolling stool, arm propped on the exam table, holding the phone so they both could watch.

The live footage was terrifying, invoking memories of the historic F-5 tornadoes on May 3, 1999 and May 20, 2013. A massive funnel churned across the landscape de-

vouring everything in its path. Dr. Morgan, Britt's OB, arrived and paused to watch. Then she turned to Britt.

"Decision time. The good news is, the twins should be
fine, we've got equipment here and a pediatrician is on-call,
just in case. Bad news is, we need to get them born ASAP."
She rolled right over Cooper's question and Britt's denial.
"The choice you need to make, young lady, is whether to
induce labor or go with a C-section. If we induce, we might
still have to do the C-section if they go into worse distress."

Her eyes found his and he knew what his decision would
be. The C-section. Get them out and to medical help immediately. But it was her body. He shrugged. "Up to you,
Britt."

One of her hands stroked the mound of her belly. The
other squeezed his arm. "How soon can you do the C-section if nature doesn't work?"

"We can prep you now and do it as soon as the pediatrician gets here. Anesthesiologist is in the building. OR
nurses are prepping the room. You've begun to dilate, and
we've started the Pitocin drip. We'll know shortly if that
works."

Britt inhaled and held it as she watched the news feed
for several moments, reading the radar. Then she exhaled.
"That's what we'll do then. Tell the baby doctor to get here
fast. We need to get this show on the road."

Twenty

The drugs kicked in before they got Britt moved to the operating room. Cooper had no idea she could heap so many curses upon him, the doctors and nurses, and the world in general. The doctor just chuckled and muttered that Pitocin hit some women like a race car going from zero to 100 in 3.2 seconds. Britt went from barely dilated and no contractions to having hard contractions two minutes apart. Too late for Lamaze classes so he was winging it, and trying to keep her occupied by watching the live footage of the impending storm.

Britt snatched his phone and stared at the radar presentation. "No-no-no," she murmured.

"I need current data." She glanced up at him and, as another contraction hit, gritted out, "I need a TV. I need the live feed."

The nurse gave her an odd look so Cooper explained. "She's a meteorologist at KOCX."

The nurse's eyes widened in surprise. "That's why you look so familiar! You're one of the storm chasers."

Five minutes later, a maintenance man rolled in a cart with a TV. He fiddled with cords and cables and then the screen flared to life. "What channel?" he asked.

"Two," everyone in the room chorused.

As soon as the channel changed, Britt let out a stream of muttered words that Cooper had no hope of translating. Then he realized she was doing some sort of calculations in her head. She turned to the nurse.

"How many people are here?"

"I'm… I have no idea."

"What's your emergency protocol?"

"For storms?"

"Yes."

"Move everyone to the basement," the nurse replied.

"Then you need to do that. Now." Britt doubled up as another contraction hit, but her words had been forcefully calm.

Cooper squeezed her hand. "Britt?"

"It's on the ground, just like the monsters that hit this area before. Same track, Cooper. People need to be underground. Like…now."

A woman in a business suit appeared in the doorway. "I'm the hospital administrator One of the nurses said there was a situation."

"You need to implement your emergency protocols." Britt cut her off, pointing to the TV. "Unless that sucker decides to collapse, the tornado is going to tear through here."

Edmonds's voice droned in the background. "Radar indicates wind speeds well into the EF4 range. I can't stress enough that any of our viewers in the path of this storm need to get off the roads and get underground. Now."

Britt shuddered through another contraction. "You heard the man. Now."

Controlled chaos ensued. One nurse stayed with Britt while the rest of the staff worked to move patients and visitors into the basement storage area. This meant moving monitoring equipment, IVs, beds. Britt squeezed Cooper's hand. "You need to help."

"No. I need to be here with you."

"Running out of options, Hero Boy. Time to put on your cape."

He didn't want to leave her but he could hear rising voices outside. People were starting to panic. He kissed her, saying, "Don't have those babies until I get back."

Britt rolled her eyes and snorted. "They'll get here when they get here."

Stepping outside the operating room, Coop waded into the pandemonium. Glancing out a window, he understood why. Straight winds of at least eighty miles per hour pushed debris across the parking lot, rocking cars and uprooting trees planted in medians. The wind was so strong, the torrential rain was driven horizontally. He borrowed a few of Britt's more colorful curses to mutter under his breath as he grabbed a hospital bed and helped the nurse guide it into the elevator.

Ten minutes later, he and the ER doctor cleared the second then the first floors of the hospital. Everyone had been evacuated to the basement. Everyone but Britt, Dr. Morgan and a nurse who volunteered to stay in the OR. The twins were premature. Moving Britt into an unsterile area like the basement for their birth was out of the question. The weather conditions outside continued to deteriorate and Cooper and the ER doc headed across the lobby, one of the front windows blew out. He pushed the doctor through the interior doors, slammed them shut and dragged furniture in front of them before jogging to the operating room. As they entered, Cooper realized that Dr. Morgan was at

the foot of the operating table, and the only word she sai‹
that he understood was, "Push."

"I *am* pushing," Britt yelled.

The lights flickered as Cooper shut the door behind hin

"Don't worry," the nurse called. "We have a backu
generator."

Cooper *was* worried. He'd caught the latest radar righ
before the window shattered. They were in the direct pat
of the tornado. He shuffled to the head of the bed an‹
grabbed one of Britt's hands as she flailed them. Goo‹
thing his ego wasn't fragile. She yelled all sorts of thing
about him. All of a sudden, she curled up toward her kne‹
and bore down. He slipped an arm around her back to su‹
port her.

Two things happened simultaneously—the lights we
out and a baby cried louder than the roar of the freight tra
bearing down on them.

Bridger stared at the ruins of the hospital. One lone fi
truck was there, along with a police car. The tornado h‹
scoured a long path through the southern edge of Oklahon
City and smack dab through the middle of Moore. The
weren't enough first responders and too many civilians wl
didn't know what they were doing or were too shell-shock‹
to help were clogging the parking lot. Cell phone servi
was dead—too many cell towers damaged or destroyed a
too many people trying to make calls tying up the towe
still working. Good thing he had a two-way radio in l
SUV. All Barron Security officers and agents had then

"We're watching the footage," Cash said seconds af
Bridge called in. "What do you need?"

"Wreckers, pole trucks, anything that can lift debris
shift rubble. Coop let me know that everyone in the ho
pital had evacuated to the basement. Except him, a cou‹
of doctors and Britt. She was in active labor."

"The basement isn't the only safe room in that hospital, Bridge."

"I know but the top floor is just…gone. And what's left of the first floor is buried. I can see the full extent of the damage, Cash. Both directions. There's…this…it's bad. It's so much worse than what it looks like on TV. I can smell gas and there are fires. So many people hurt. Gonna be some casualties. I figure other cities are mobilizing to send help, that whole Oklahoma Standard thing that happened after the Oklahoma City bombing, but Cash…" His voice cracked and he swallowed around the lump in his throat. "Cooper's in there with Britt and maybe his babies. We gotta get them out."

"We will, Bridge. That's a promise. We're working on this end. Cord is here. He's rounding up heavy equipment and crews. They'll be there as soon as they can. The roads…some are blocked. Near as we can tell, I-35 is still open. Do what you can until we get there."

Three black SUVs arrived. Cash, Cord and Chance were the first ones out, followed by employees from BarEx, Barron Security and Chance's law firm. A few minutes later, a semi-truck hauling a flatbed trailer pulled in. The oil field crews from BarEx abandoned what they'd been doing—shifting rubble by hand—to unload a front-end loader and bulldozer.

"Crane's stuck in traffic but will be here soon," the semi driver yelled over the noise. "Two pole trucks are on their way."

Over the next hour, more people and equipment arrived, along with a news crew from Channel 2. Bridger worked tirelessly. He wasn't surprised when Tucker, Deacon and Dillon arrived, not only ready to work but with messages from their brothers, Boone and Hunter, who were in Washington, DC, with their cousin, Senator Clay Barron. Kade Waite, the Barrons' half-brother, arrived with power tools from the Barron Ranch. Deacon's tour bus arrived, driven by Chase Barron. The Bee Dubyas were all onboard, along with Katherine Tate. The wives immediately set about distributing food and drink while Chase pulled on work gloves and asked where he was needed.

Bridger stopped dragging a chunk of concrete when his mother touched his back. He straightened and almost refused the bottle of water she held out. He didn't want to stop. Stopping meant time to think, time to worry about his brother. Their last conversation about Britt hadn't been comfortable but he'd been worried about Cooper and wasn't sure about Britt. But hearing Cooper's voice? The worry in it? Cooper loved Britt and that was the bottom line. He loved his brother and he'd do whatever he could to help him win the woman he loved. All he had to do was rescue them alive and in one piece.

"Drink, son. You have to stay hydrated. You get sick you can't help your brother or any of the others."

"They're in there, Mom." He just managed to keep his voice level.

"I know. And they'll be fine. Cooper always comes through a scrape unscathed."

"This isn't a scrape—"

"He's lucky, Bridger. And this isn't his first tornado. He's fine." She studied the path the rescue workers had carved toward the front entrance. "And probably sitting in there grousing about how long we're taking to get them out."

"I hope you're right, Mom."

She patted his arm. "I'm always right when it comes to you boys."

Britt's phone battery had died, along with those belonging to the medical personnel. Cooper was hoarding his remaining charge like a prepper facing Armageddon. The OR was basically intact, though the false ceiling had com-

own, bringing with it some of the medical equipment from
he floor above. No injuries. Britt was resting, his daughter
nd son, both healthy, lay swaddled in blankets in her arms.
Ie'd managed to get the door to the OR open and to shift
ome of the debris blocking the hallway, but there was no
vay to get Britt and the babies out. They'd just have to wait.

Cooper *knew* his family was outside doing their best to
escue him and the others. That's the way the Tates worked.
And his Barron cousins would be there. At the moment,
hough, Britt and the babies consumed his thoughts. His
ttention focused on them as the nurse's voice ghosted
hrough the darkness.

"What are their names?"

"Not sure," Britt murmured. "I'm thinking something
iterary."

"Oh? Like what?"

"Archie and Veronica."

He choked. She couldn't be serious. "No way—" The
grumble of a diesel engine and the scrape of a metal blade
on concrete cut off the rest of his protest.

Lights appeared and he snagged his cell phone, clicking
on the flashlight app. "In here!" he yelled over the noise.
The motor immediately cut off.

"Cooper?"

"We're in here, Bridger!"

"Are you okay?"

"We're good. All good."

His brother's head poked through the door. "Britt and
he babies?"

"All good. I'm a dad," he said, his voice full of wonder.
'A girl and a boy."

The message was passed back to the crowd outside and
cheering ensued. Thirty minutes later, Britt and the twins
were carried out in a Stokes basket as roughnecks, firefighters and a column of Tate and Barron brothers passed

them over the debris. His mom, sisters-in-law and the Be
Dubyas clustered around the open doors of an ambulance

Coop was torn. He should stay and help the rescuer
get to the basement stairwell but the woman and babies h
loved with all his heart were about to be shuttled off to an
other hospital. His mom gave him a quick hug.

"Get in the ambulance, son. There's plenty of help here
Your new family needs you more."

And they did.

Epilogue

Cooper glared at Britt. "We are not naming them after comic book characters."

She offered up a cheeky grin. "We aren't. *I* am."

"Britt."

"Cooper."

The reverend looked from one to the other, her expression noncommittal though Coop caught the twitch of the woman's lips. His entire family was gathered around the baptismal font of St. Paul's Cathedral, the historic Episcopal Church in downtown Oklahoma City. Tucker and Zoe stood as godparents. He turned to his brother for backup.

Tucker raised his hands. "I'm not getting in the middle of this."

Zoe laughed. "Me neither. I'm the last one to throw stones about baby names."

Cooper snapped his mouth shut. This was true. She'd named her son Nashville Vanderbilt Parker, which was then legally changed to Nash Parker Tate when Tucker formally adopted the little boy.

The reverend cleared her throat. "Can we proceed?" She continued with the ceremony after Cooper huffed out an aggrieved sigh. When she reached the part in the baptismal sacrament when she announced the babies' names, Cooper sucked in a breath.

"Daniella Katherine Tate and Denver Owens Tate."

"Daniella Katherine for my dad and your mom and Denver Owens for your dad and my family name." Britt's eyes glistened with tears.

Cooper bent and kissed them off her cheeks. "I love you, Girl Wonder."

"Good, because I love you too."

He opened his mouth, then closed it. He didn't want to fight. Not today of all days. Then the woman he adored beyond all reason surprised him.

"Aren't you going to ask?"

"Ask what?"

"Huh. Seriously?"

Then it dawned on him. Except he wouldn't ask her again.

She arched a brow, looking imperious. "You'll never know if you don't ask."

"I've already asked."

"So. Ask again."

"Fine. Marry me."

"That's not a question."

"Okay. Will you—"

"Down on one knee, Hero Boy."

He glanced around. His entire family grinned at him. He dropped to one knee, but Tucker tapped him on the shoulder before he could continue.

"You're gonna need this, big brother."

Bridger, having stopped by Cooper's house, placed the

ring box Cooper had hidden in his sock drawer all these months in his hand. He popped the lid and in a voice that sounded a tad hesitant, he asked, "Britt Owens, will you marry me?"

"Yes."

He managed to scramble to his feet and jam the ring on her finger before she changed her mind. His family cheered. The woman he loved had agreed—finally—to be his wife and their baby daughter and son were healthy and very much loved. Cooper Tate truly was comfortable in his own skin, and in his new, and wonderful life.

* * * * *

COMING SOON!

We really hope you enjoyed reading this book. If you're looking for more romance, be sure to head to the shops when new books are available on

Thursday 4th February

LET'S TALK
Romance

For exclusive extracts, competitions
and special offers, find us online:

- f facebook.com/millsandboon
- 🐦 @MillsandBoon
- 📷 @MillsandBoonUK

Get in touch on 01413 063232

For all the latest titles coming soon, visit
millsandboon.co.uk/nextmonth

MILLS & BOON

THE HEART OF ROMANCE

A ROMANCE FOR EVERY KIND OF READER

MODERN

Prepare to be swept off your feet by sophisticated, sexy and seductive heroes, in some of the world's most glamourous and romantic locations, where power and passion collide.
8 stories per month.

HISTORICAL

Escape with historical heroes from time gone by. Whether your passion is for wicked Regency Rakes, muscled Vikings or rugged Highlanders, awaken the romance of the past.
6 stories per month.

MEDICAL

Set your pulse racing with dedicated, delectable doctors in the high-pressure world of medicine, where emotions run high and passion, comfort and love are the best medicine.
6 stories per month.

True Love

Celebrate true love with tender stories of heartfelt romance, from the rush of falling in love to the joy a new baby can bring, and a focus on the emotional heart of a relationship.
8 stories per month.

Desire

Indulge in secrets and scandal, intense drama and plenty of sizzlir hot action with powerful and passionate heroes who have it all: wealth, status, good looks…everything but the right woman.
6 stories per month.

HEROES

Experience all the excitement of a gripping thriller, with an intens romance at its heart. Resourceful, true-to-life women and strong, fearless men face danger and desire - a killer combination!
8 stories per month.

DARE

Sensual love stories featuring smart, sassy heroines you'd want as best friend, and compelling intense heroes who are worthy of the
4 stories per month.

To see which titles are coming soon, please visit

millsandboon.co.uk/nextmonth

JOIN US ON SOCIAL MEDIA!

Stay up to date with our latest releases, author news and gossip, special offers and discounts, and all the behind-the-scenes action from Mills & Boon...

 millsandboon

 millsandboonuk

 millsandboon

It might just be true love...

MILLS & BOON

MODERN

Power and Passion

Prepare to be swept off your feet by sophisticated, sexy and seductive heroes, in some of the world's most glamourous and romantic locations, where power and passion collide.

Eight Modern stories published every month, find them all at:

millsandboon.co.uk/Modern